dARKNESS GAINS

CONQUERORS OF K'TARA
BOOK 3

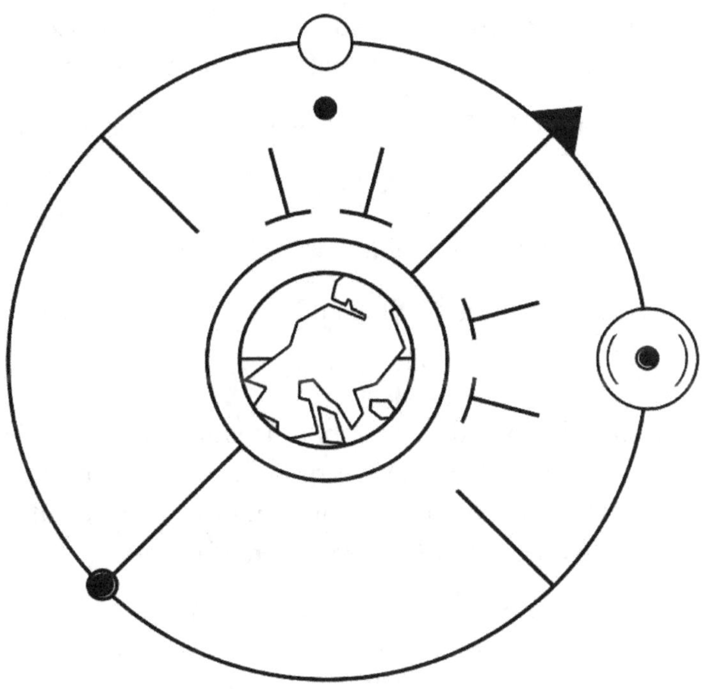

L.A. DI PAOLO

ACKNOWLEDGEMENTS

My acknowledgments, this time, will be even shorter. To begin, I'd like to thank Mark T. Anderson, who took over from Michele (Mikehleh) Parisi as my illustrator. I was worried another artist might not be able to render new scenes with illustrations developed by someone else. But I believe you will agree that Mark has done a fantastic job creating the cover for this book on the basis of the drawings Michele had done of the Serpent.

My thanks also go to Deborah Murrell for her editorial work as well as for her advice, which I was most glad to receive and consider as it often helped to make the text clearer.

Finally, I would like to give a special thanks to those who have continued to encourage me, and to my good friend and writer Jim Chrichton without whose input the story would not have been as well tied together.

L.A. Di Paolo

Contents

1. A NEW ATTACK BY THE SERPENT

I. Alert

The soldiers approached the woman's house, with their younger recruit following apprehensively.

Areto, a lanky, pale-skinned type with red hair, asked, "Are you sure no one will know what we are doing here?"

One of the older soldiers said, too loudly for the bashful recruit, "Really, Areto. Are you a man or a tree? Soothing yourself will no cause you to break your oath."

"But what will the commander do if he finds out?"

"As we've already explained, Areto, he won't do nothing. He's aware that the men come here. In fact, the entire command of the king's armies encourages it to ensure no one starts getting any funny ideas and soothes himself by forcing himself on someone during drawn out campaigns; it's a practice that's been around for ages."

Shocked, Areto said, "I thought they were able to prevent anyone with violent sexual tendencies to join."

"It works during peacetime, but not during times of conscription."

The young guardian pulled his head back in surprise. "Okay, all right. But what if I develop a—"

The veteran replied with a scoffing laugh: "A dependence? Seriously?"

Areto nodded uncertainly.

The tall and imposing Hanne replied this time. "Have you ever heard of anyone developing a dependence to imagined things?"

Areto shrugged his shoulders, but he still hesitated and asked, "Will she be watching?"

With a long, patient sigh Hanne said, "Her eyes will be closed as she'll need to enter the Bind to connect to your mind and do what she does. So, you don't need to worry about her seeing that tiny bulge of yours."

The company laughed raucously. Areto flushed, ground his teeth, and balled his fists. But soldiers did get a charge out of taunting each other, he knew it, and his curiosity—as well as his adolescent urges—got the upper hand of him. He blurted a simple "Whatever!"

One of the other two veterans accompanying Areto to visit the elicitors—women who had Sensing abilities but were not members of the Sisterhood and used their skills to provide personal services to men—said, "So are you going or not? We don't have all day."

And, after one more nervous look around, Areto went in.

***

Lina Lux Baiula had been listening for alarms for several hours now and she rubbed her head with exhausted motions. Just as she was about to disconnect to go rest for a while, she received an alert from one of the Sisters in Upper Alvinor; the woman had just sighted the Serpent, and it did not appear to be out for a leisurely flight—if she was interpreting the signs properly. Lina Lux Baiula released a long, loud groan then sent a question to her colleague, *"Do you know where the Serpent is headed, Alna?"*

"It is crossing the Peaks and if it maintains its course, it will end up at Capua, a small town on your side of the mountains."

Lina felt her pulse accelerate despite her fatigue. She cursed and thanked her Sister then disconnected from the Bind. She shot up from the floor of her apartment almost too quickly, and swayed a moment. She steadied herself with another curse and ran to the First Barrier's offices with all the speed she could muster, caring not a whit how she must look to the men who saw her sprinting in her Yellow Sash's robe.

The woman irrupted into Laiella's chambers and said, "First Barrier! The Serpent! It has returned."

First Barrier Laiella Lux Baiula—now a *prima* in the Prince's Guard—had been reading a document with her back to the door. Upon hearing Lina's unexpected and urgent voice, she spun and shouted: "What did you say?"

"The Serpent, it is making its way toward Capua. We need to send a defensive team there at once!"

"And who communicated this to you?"

"Alna; she's stationed in Kipoth, a town along the western edge of the Furan Peaks."

"Is she *certain* it is going to Capua?"

The woman nodded hesitantly and said, "Based on its direction and on the elevations in that area, its most likely exit *will be* at Capua."

"Damned! Then, raise the alarm!"

Lina Lux Baiula wasted no time and rang the bell from where she stood using a sonactic Binding. But, having spent the night listening for alerts, her energy stores were low, and she had to try twice to send the sonactic vibration toward the bell in the middle of the fortress before she hit it. Muscles seized throughout the stronghold upon hearing the gong's urgent clang. Soon, though, the guardians' training took over, and officers and soldiers began assembling in the plaza. In the village, hearts stopped too, though the villagers knew, from the pattern of the alert, that Horn's Pass was not in danger—this time—and everyone returned to what they had been doing, though a few did pray that the danger stayed away.

Presently, the lord commander rushed into his first officer's chambers.

"Laiella, did *you* sound the alarm?"

The clamor of soldiers assembling in the fortress added to the urgency of Laiella's reply, which she gave as she moved toward the prince and the door: "Lina did. The Serpent has been sighted moving eastward. It is expected to come out at Capua. We need to go there now. I hope the quintanals[1] are ready."

Toras felt his muscles tense up. "They are."

Laiella did not reply, but simply nodded and waited for her commander to turn around and exit.

Once in the plaza, Laiella approached one of the two secundi whose men would be the first to be put to the test as members of a quintanal and said with clear irritation, "It seems you are short a few men, Secundus Yuuto. Where are they?"

Yuuto cursed while explaining that the men had gone into the village to...he did not finish his sentence. Annoyed, he shook his head. His long, wobbling Pargahni nose would have made his expression comical if not for the seriousness of the situation. Fortunately for Yuuto and the guardians in question, the missing soldiers had just crossed the fortress's portico atop their vorans and were galloping toward the stables to exchange the animals for their furans, almost hitting a few of their comrades along the way.

Laiella spat a "Men," followed by a "See to it they are ready with the others within twenty minutes."

Yuuto saw to it, and when the prima reappeared with her own furan, all fifty furanteams were assembled and waiting to depart, soldiers and their furans standing side-by-side.

Toras sat nervously atop Scorch, next to Laiella, who sat astride Root. She looked hard as stone as she scanned the company to verify their readiness. To her right was Xena Lux Baiula atop a tall, grayish furan; one of the oldest in the pack. Despite its age, the animal was still reliable, but it was also an

---

[1] Quintanal: A unit of fifty furanteams developed to fight the Serpent.

easier mount for an unseasoned furanrider, though, from the looks of her, she was as ready and willing as anyone else.

This coming encounter with the Serpent would be Laiella's first, but Xena's second and Toras's third. The former hoped the men were ready, while the latter two *prayed* they were. Indeed, they knew the horror these men had faced and understood the toll it exacted from many.

But one thing gave Toras hope: the reorganization of the Black Guard into quintanals, the specially trained companies of fifty furanteams each. These men and their furans had been trained more thoroughly and intensely than any other company ever before. Toras was certain they were ready, though he knew Laiella still had her doubts regarding the use of the simulacre and of the projection as training methods.

Just now, Laiella set her eyes on Toras, as if expecting something.

"What?"

"Will you speak to them, or will I?"

"I hate speeches. I prefer to just give orders."

Laiella rolled her eyes as she looked away from the prince and toward the men in front of them, while another nine hundred and fifty other pairs of eyes watched from around the plaza or the fortress's ramparts.

"Men! Your chance to prove yourselves has come. It has been a while since you faced the Serpent, but we will see if the grueling hours spent training against Master Neros's *beast-on-a-swing* will have produced the result…the lord commander and I expected." Laiella turned to look at Toras, to make certain he realized that she had just included herself in the responsible party.

"The Serpent is making its way to Capua or thereabout. We are going to fly there and intercept it to prevent it from destroying another village."

The men stomped the ground.

"Are you ready?!"

The men responded with more stomping and challenging shouts.

Toras thanked Laiella then added, "Guardians, this is going to be a difficult flight because we need to get to Capua within a couple of hours, where it would normally take us two to three. So, set up your watering gear, mount up and let's go!"

The flight toward Capua was as demanding as Toras had intimated. The suns were no trouble given that the Blue sun was now hidden behind its red twin, but the winds were fierce and blowing from the south. The company pushed the furans as much as possible without exhausting them before the clash with the Serpent, which was sure to happen—it *must* happen. Turning the valve on Scorch's watering gear for the second time now, Toras was glad he had ordered everyone to bring the pouches. Normally, the practice was only used for long flights during the warmer months given that the bags weighed the furans down a little.

The quintanal was now some ten kilometers from Capua. The town, a fairly well-to-do municipality at the foot of the Furan Peaks responsible for much of the wood and wood products sold across the kingdom, was visible in the distance. The teams covered this final stretch of sky with nervous trepidation, a nervousness which did not spare Laiella and Xena who started eyeing each other and praying that their skill with the nebula would prove sufficient. Indeed, they had practiced daily generating it, and they were now able to create it more or less at will. However, the radius of their nebulae was smaller than that achieved by Elyana, and they had had no way to test their effectiveness, at whatever distance.

If only they could have gone back to Urbs Lucis for a fourth; Laiella had been told that her second in command was replicating the Serpent's mental attacks to train Sisters of every Sash. Well, Laiella and Xena would know whether their nebulae worked when the Serpent tried to fry their brains.

When they reached to within two kilometers of Capua, near Eight after Highsun, Toras raised a hand and everyone slowed their furans until they came to a complete standstill, hovering in mid-air. Toras examined his men and their furans; they appeared to be well despite the intense flight.

Toras then scanned the area for their foe—nothing. The Serpent might still be there, though, hiding behind the red angry cloud of smoke billowing over the village. The smoke writhed with ire under the Red sun's light as a screech pierced it and reached for them, sending shivers down their spines.

Laiella raised her voice to overcome the wind, and said, "Commander, do you see it?"

Toras started shaking his head just as the Serpent, surrounded by too many rokons to count, appeared from behind the death-bearing haze. Toras looked at the Lux Baiulae, who were flying on either side of him, with questions and incomprehension marring his face. This moment did not last long, however, and Toras's heart shouted for action. But what *were* the rokons doing with the Serpent? Or *were* they rokons? *Shit!* Shit indeed. And what did it matter what those things were?

Toras shouted, "Prima, we need to attack. Now!"

Laiella, though she had been as surprised as Toras, had processed what data her vision presented and calculated the risk; she blew her horn to order the men to detach the water pouches and to form ten pentagons. She also sent a thoughtcall to Xena, and as soon as the nebulae were formed, the quintanal resumed its flight. If not for the wind, the officers would have heard the prayers that arose from every single member of the company as well as the curses of those who had difficulty unlatching the water pouches. But soon, a strange rain filled that area of the sky.

As they approached, the number of rokons became a little clearer through the smoke; there were perhaps two tens. Laiella thought: *Let's hope they don't have the same abilities as the Serpent.* Laiella enhanced her voice this time to shout, "Everyone ready yourselves." As furans and Humans steeled their nerves and narrowed their eyes, and as the Humans checked their weapons, the rokons split up into two groups, a dozen following the Serpent, who was turning south, and the rest—another dozen it seemed—heading for them.

Toras kicked Scorch's left flank to move him toward Laiella. "Prima, take half of the quintanal as well as Xena and intercept the Serpent; I will stay here with the rest and take care of the rokons. We will follow as soon as we are done and have checked on Capua."

Laiella shook her head.

"What are you objecting to?!"

Laiella would have kicked Toras for that, but she said, "We do not know whether the smaller ones are natural rokons or capable of the DEBSA like the Serpent. You should keep Xena."

With the rokons approaching rapidly, Toras did not argue but grumbled and replied, "It goes. Now go! Don't lose that monster."

Laiella acquiesced and left at once with her twenty-five to catch up with the Serpent and stop it before it destroyed its next target.

Toras thought he should wish the pursuers—wish Laiella—good luck, but he did not want to shout it, so he cursed himself instead. He looked at his soldiers and wondered how many he'd lose this time. They all knew how to chase away or bring down rokons, but they had always done that from the ground. Now, they were fighting on the enemy's ground, so to speak. And what if these rokons were capable of generating the DEBSA? *I pray Aiala that Laiella is wrong about this.*

The prince also prayed that the training they had done against the Serpent's replica and its projection would help the men and furans keep their fear in check and their wits in place. Toras called Marius, a Lucian-trained medic who had recently been assigned to the Black Guard and sent him down to wait with the pack furans. He then turned toward Xena, and after receiving a nod of readiness from the Red Sash, they flew to meet the creatures.

Uncertain what they would find, Toras ordered his men to fly in as tight a formation as possible so that Xena might cover them all. This caused a few injuries as wings smacked other wings but there was nothing to do about it for now, and Toras's unit continued toward its target—or its assailants—which was now but two hundred meters or so ahead of them.

Soon, arrows were nocked and released with prayers to the gods or to K'Tara or to Mother Luck. But, with the wind blowing against them, only a few hit the targets, and they did so without any effect. In fact, the winds started coming in fierce intermittent gusts, making their crossbows quite useless. So, soldiers put their bows away and took their swords out.

The clash was brutal. The rokons certainly looked like normal ones, but they were much fiercer—as if driven to madness by some external compulsion—and their fierceness was frightening some of the men as well as some of the furans. Indeed, the steeds were slightly smaller than their reptilian opponents and, with Humans on their backs, they had some difficulty swerving and avoiding their attackers, especially while remaining in a tight formation.

Still, twenty-six furanteams should have done some damage to the fewer rokons, but the lizards were crazed, and their interminable screeches deafened everyone at close distance.

As the air battle progressed, Toras noticed that a few furanteams were most definitely outside the range of Xena's nebula. And yet, they were unharmed. Toras ordered Scorch around to approach Xena. The woman's face looked harder than usual, perhaps because she had almost gotten disconnected from Switch—her furan. Toras shouted and told her about the men beyond the nebula. The Lux Baiula understood immediately and a smile of relief appeared on her stone face.

A moment later, the first firebolt hit a rokon and dropped it to the ground to the cheers of the men. The death of one of theirs seemed to frighten the remaining rokons into greater fury. As one, they began to speed toward the furanteams with the wicked spiraling motions which they were known for and which they used to shred and tenderize their victims' flesh. These motions also rendered the swords utterly useless and Toras ordered the men to grab their lances instead. Meanwhile, Xena launched another firebolt and brought down another rokon. This redoubled the remaining rokons' fury.

Toras realized the furanteams would be cut to strips if they stayed in formation any longer, so—with a loud yell and urgent hand signals—he ordered them to spread. But no one had heard him, and no one had thus looked his way to notice his flagging arms—the rokons' screeches swallowed his shouts, and their unnatural motions mesmerized his men.

Toras raged, but moments did not pass before a thought presented itself to him. He leaned down on his furan, and yelled, "Scorch, I need you to tell the other furans to break formation, now!"

A few breaths later, and just before the crazed rokons speared through them and shredded them to pieces, furans dove in a dozen different directions, jerking their surprised riders. Xena cursed at her own mount, who went down and left, nearly spraining her neck.

Scorch chose a sudden dive to evade the oncoming lizards, and Toras felt his guts reach toward his throat. As he recovered, he looked behind and noticed the creatures were getting ready for a second pass. He needed to give his men another order, so he asked Scorch to call the other furans' attention. The furans turned their way, and the men did not resist their movements this time. Xena, however, refused to let her furan take control and pulled on the reins. Toras noticed and waved his arms furiously. After a moment that felt too long to Toras, the woman noticed and allowed her furan to turn toward him.

Toras used hand signals to accompany his shouts. He ordered the soldiers to attack as pairs, to check their front and back straps, and to strap their legs onto their furans so they could rise from their saddles and have a longer reach.

Toras paired up with the young recruit named Areto, who rode a small but sturdy furan. The man gave him an apprehensive look. Toras shouted, "We will get a rokon to pass between us. Make sure your straps are hooked properly and hold on to your lance!"

When the rokons charged again, Xena resumed her Bindings and everyone else waited for the lord commander's signal.

"Charge!"

At once, the eleven pairs and one triad attacked, while Xena moved her furan, Switch, to the side of the airfield, so that she might be able to strike the oncoming creatures without the risk of hitting her own people.

Xena chose to form smaller projectiles and sent each toward a different rokon. That slowed a few of them but did not stop them. She decided to form a firewhorl instead and succeeded in engulfing one rokon in flames.

Having selected his target, Toras gave his partner a shout and the two adjusted their furans' flight to place themselves on either side of the oncoming rokon. They were immediately mimicked by the other teams.

"Three, two, on—"

The impact of the rokon against their lances would have pulled both Toras and Areto off their furans if they had not been tied to them. The furans themselves were nearly jerked off-course. But the tactic had worked and the rokon gave an agonizing scream when two deep cuts, corkscrewing around its flanks and wings, lacerated it.

Toras was about to shout in joy when he noticed two furanteams and one man fall to their deaths. The man's furan had turned to try and catch his rider before he crashed on the ground, but a rokon rammed him and sent him tumbling through the air while his rider hit the rock, cracked his skull and joined the Black Skies along with the other two furans and their respective rider.

"Founders! I told them to check their straps."

Toras hardened his heart to assess the situation. *Five rokons left against twenty-three teams, not counting Xena and her furan. This is good.* There was also a now-riderless, vengeful, and furious furan. *I can't do anything about him. So long as he doesn't get in the way.* Toras asked Scorch to signal the others to turn in his direction again, and he instructed them to charge the remaining rokons in paired teams once more.

Xena dispatched another rokon all on her own, while two lizards were butchered by the paired lances that sliced through their flesh when they were caught between two furanteams; the last two lizards soon fell too, although one brought with itself the lone furan who had plunged his beak into its neck and would not release it.

When the last rokon's frightened and angry shrieks ceased, the survivors of the airborne clash did not erupt in joy. Instead, the men shook their heads with dejected expressions and then gave in to a silent gloom, disturbed only by the sound of the furans' wings which beat the air with exhausted motions.

Toras broke the mourning to call Xena and Secundus Yuuto to himself, "Xena, please send a message to Lina Lux Baiula and have her dispatch a recovery team to bury the furans and bring back the bodies of our fallen."

The Red Sash responded with a quiet hardness that made the religious Secundus Yuuto swallow and say, "How many more unnatural things are we going to be battling, Commander? Surely Aiala can't let the Dark One turn everything on K'Tara."

The only response the secundus received was a long, discomforting glare which only broke when a buffeting gust pushed Scorch back. When the furan returned to his initial position, Toras said, "We need to check on Capua. Call your men, Secundus. I'm descending." And with that, Scorch dropped and took the prince toward the remnants of what had been a proud town.

The scene in Capua was one of horror. The destruction was worse than it had been in Horn's Pass. People keeled over with terrified and frightening expressions on their faces; others lying on the ground, their flesh being slowly digested by the rokons' enzymes but left there to be devoured by scavengers; homes destroyed, and deathly silence all around. Not even the soldiers made a sound until their commander ordered everyone to split up in pairs and inspect the homes to look for survivors.

Toras went with Areto. The young man seemed to need someone to give him courage. *I guess it's a good thing, this rule against men serving in their native regions. Though they're probably all wondering if the same thing will happen to their hometowns. Founders!*

The prince and the guardian entered a home with a partially torn-off roof, but it was mostly intact inside. In the living room, they found the entire family—father, mother, children—all prostrate and with the most horrible, contorted grimaces on their faces. Dried-up, shriveled eyes dangled from their eye sockets. The youngest, a child of no more than a few months old, had blood all over, which seemed to have erupted from the pits on her twisted face. Areto emptied his stomach just then, though not before turning away from his commander.

The prince shook his head and heaved a burdened sigh. He scratched his brows a moment, unsure whether he should pretend to be occupied with something or try to console the man. In the end, he approached the red-haired soldier and patted him on the shoulder. "We will kill that thing. I promise."

When the man bobbed his head, Toras said, "We should keep looking. If someone has survived this, they will need our help. Ready?"

Areto nodded, got up, and followed his commander.

The two inspected another nine homes, finding their occupants as dead as those in the first one and looking like flesh-covered versions of the petrified victims of volcanic eruptions, their bodies frozen in horrifying terror. However, it was shrill, frightened screams that greeted them when they stepped into the main bedchamber of the eleventh house.

A mother and her daughter survived. They were clutching each other and their dead family members.

It took Toras a while to get the woman to let go of the bodies of her husband and her son, and though she did eventually stand up, her continued sobs made him wish Xena were here to take care of her. Her daughter, on the other hand, did not make a sound and stood rigidly behind her mother. Toras directed Areto to the girl with a nod, hoping that his young face would draw her mind from wherever it was locked.

The prince cleared his throat a few times then said, "Mistress, do you recognize me?"

The woman looked up for a briefest moment before returning her stricken gaze to her dead husband and son.

"I'm really sorry for what happened to them. If we could have gotten here earlier to stop the attack, we would have."

The woman broke into another sobbing fit.

Not knowing what to do, the prince asked the woman her name.

"Mistress Ita, I would like for you and your daughter to follow us."

"But...I can't...I won't..."

"We need to take care of you and your daughter first, Mistress Ita."

The mentioning of her offspring brought the woman back to the present. She turned toward her and saw that the girl had a hand in the young soldier's own hand. Mistress Ita reached out for her daughter then followed the prince while embracing her daughter as if she were afraid that the girl, too, might be taken without warning.

Toras took them toward the source of some commotion. His soldiers and Xena had assembled the few other survivors they had found. They were in what must have been the town green.

A few adults were crying and sobbing together, while one sat alone, catatonic, and two boys stood by themselves and apart. Marius, the medic—recognizable by the white flame on his arm—was attempting to get a response from the sitting man without success.

Toras called the medic and said quietly, "I don't think you will be able to help him, Marius. That man's not dead, but I can tell he suffered one of the Serpent's mental attacks."

The medic looked toward his patients then back at the prince and said, "I wish I had been at Horn's Pass when it first attacked you. I would be better prepared, now."

"Well, you would not have been prepared then, and you will be next time! As I said, that man is beyond your help."

The medic was about to object but thought better when the scar on the prince's face—the scar he had gotten that summer near Spiritii—flashed angrily.

When he saw that the soldier was ready to do as ordered, Toras pointed with his chin behind him and said, "Please take care of Mistress Ita and her daughter."

As the medic moved to tend to the women indicated by the prince, Toras added, "Areto can help you. I think the girl trusts him."

The young Areto stood frozen for a moment then nodded and moved to assist Marius.

Spinning around toward his officer, who stood a few steps away, Toras said, "Secundus, please have two men take the survivors to Horn's Pass to be sheltered there…for as long as necessary."

Mistress Ita, who had heard, cried out with alarm, "But my husband, and my child? Is priest Orvald even alive? I need him to perform the passing ritual. How will their bodies be taken by the gods on the Day of Union otherwise?"

Toras wanted to groan, but he kept his complaint to himself and asked Secundus Yuuto about the cleric. Yuuto shook his head.

"I'm sorry, Mistress. No one else survives."

The secundus cleared his throat and indicated that he could perform the ceremony himself—if Mistress Ita would accept it.

The woman, who was familiar with the deep religiosity of the Pargahni, accepted without hesitation.

While Yuuto took care of the ritual, Xena approached the prince and said, "Lord Commander, we need to go as soon as Yuuto is done. I have received a faint thoughtcall from Laiella and from the sound of it, they need our help."

The prince balled his fists anxiously and looked toward Yuuto and the Capuans with an impatient sigh.

II.   Neaj's Report

Just before dinner was meant to arrive, Neaj Trebloc asked for an audience with the prince. Master Rovali let him in with only the slightest annoyance.

"My prince, pardon me for disturbing you at this hour."

"Not at all, Master Trebloc. I know you are not the verbose kind, so please go on."

"You asked me to look into Kildare's acquaintance…a young man by the name of Luvius Arco." He waited for the prince's nod of recognition and continued, "I had to dig quite deeply to find out that our gentleman's fortune has been on the decline for a while. Indeed, his father, Linus Arco, still goes about presenting himself as a successful merchant, but the facts show quite the opposite." Now, Aithen cocked a very curious eyebrow and Neaj continued, "I tried to follow Luvius and his father's movements through their debit notes and other means and discovered that Luvius Arco was in Urbs Lucis before coming here. While there, he had a meeting with Master Lusk Methrim at one of the city's upscale restaurants. The restaurant note had been drafted in Master Arco's name but was then paid by Master Methrim."

Aithen snorted several times, each time his eyes narrowing further.

"Did you find anything else that might seem suspicious?"

"No, that is all."

"Thank you, Neaj. Very well done."

Trebloc replied with a thankful gesture, turned and left.

Aithen spent a few minutes mulling things over, muttering to himself and scratching his right thumb with his index and middle finger. There was nothing suspicious, really, about Methrim meeting with this Luvius, but it was just too coincidental. There were millions of Humans in Alvinoria, and three hundred thousand in the northern part of Upper Alvinor. It had to be more than chance that brought them together. *Unless the Arcos, being down on their luck, reached out to Lusk to gain access to his smuggler network. Perhaps. I hope that is what's making Kil uneasy when he speaks of this new acquaintance of his because I have bigger problems to take care of. Damned!*

III. Success and Murder in Urbs Lucis

Kelysia Lux Baiula had been listening to the device almost nonstop since Gina had installed their brick's counterpart in that tavern in Kartak. Initially, she had strained to decipher any of the words she heard through the reversing device which sensed the changes in the entangled brick sitting next to it and transformed them back into sounds. But slowly, her brain had gotten used to certain noises—those which were repeated every so often—and she began to recognize words among them. Despite it, she still could not piece sentences from the sounds; her brain expected certain words to be sequenced in a certain manner, but the sounds she heard did not fit the expected pattern. Kelysia was about to abandon her attempts and had just placed a Quieting Cloth on the reverser, when Gina arrived.

Gina rubbed her hands with excitement and said, "Sister! I imagined you would be exactly there, listening. How does it go?"

"Gina. I did not expect you back so soon. You must be an ace on a furan."

The woman did not know how to respond to the praise, so she said, "Well, the winds were good. So, have you heard anything yet?"

Kelysia said with a grunt, "Well, some things. I was able to decipher some of the sounds, but most of it is still unintelligible."

The younger woman replied defensively, "I'm certain I followed your instructions properly to install the device."

"Oh, I do not doubt it. Saara and I knew the device might still need improvements. But with the war at hand, we released it for use as it is. The sounds are still unclear, and although I've been able to isolate many into words, I cannot make sense of the conversations."

Gina said, "Well, in that case I am not surprised. The unclarity of the sounds, coupled with the fact that the people over there don't speak like you and I, would make it difficult."

Kelysia corrected her, "Like you and me."

"That's exactly what I'm saying."

When Kelysia blinked Gina added, "I mean, we need someone to listen that's familiar with the jargon spoken by those ruffians."

"And which Sister might this be?"

"Well, I don't speak the dialects used there or their dirty, foul, criminal jargon. But I did have a brother, before joining the Sisterhood, that had questionable tendencies and friends."

Kelysia frowned at the improper grammar but thought that perhaps Gina's experience was exactly what they needed. She said, "In that case, please give it a try, Gina."

The younger Sister sat down in front of the two bricks: the companion of the brick in Kartak—or receiver—and the reverser. "These bricks must be made by men to be so large and thick."

The older Yellow Sash blinked at the comment but made no reply.

Gina said, "If a Nonsensor saw us sit in front of these bricks with the wonder a child feels when sitting in front of an aquarium containing a fan-finned fish mesmerizing its prey, they would think us strange…perhaps even mad. But to me, the entangled brick, in particular, is more amazing than anything nature has ever created. This is *our* creation; a creation that's somehow able to replicate sounds received by its companion hundreds of kilometers away."

Kelysia smiled. She agreed with her colleague's sentiment.

Gina uncovered the reverser. Blaring sounds came through. "Someone must be yelling." Hearing the sounds of voices nowhere near her, hundreds of kilometers away, was the most thrilling thing Gina had experienced in a long time; even more thrilling than going on the mission to place the source brick in the tavern's wall.

Gina sat back with a childish grin on her face and listened, patiently, spending the first hour simply becoming familiar with the sounds and trying to isolate words from them. Her face began to twitch with excitement when she recognized the first words, and then more. Sometime during the second hour, she jumped and clapped her hands breathlessly, causing Kelysia—who was sitting at another desk deep in thought while reviewing her and Saara's notes on the development of the devices—to shake her head in disapproval of the childish reaction. "I just understood an entire sentence!"

"Huh. Well, what was it?"

"A man—probably the tavernist—was telling another one that his companions should arrive in about fifty minutes. And I think he said he would install sound dampening devices before the others arrive, so they may have some privacy."

That got Kelysia's attention. "Are you sure he said, 'sound dampening devices'?"

"I think so."

"Where would they have gotten them? We don't sell resonant minerals to anyone except to the Crown, the landholders, and other people we trust."

Gina shrugged her shoulders.

Kelysia muttered, "I hope they don't interfere with the entangled brick."

Gina said, "Me too. I have no wish to go back to Kartak to install a new brick in that tavern or anywhere else in that town." She then turned her attention back to the reverser and said, "They're not talking anymore. I think these horrible screeches are just the chatter of the other people in the tavern, away from the brick."

"All right, then we wait. If the patron wants privacy, it may mean he'll be discussing things of interest to us. And let's hope the dampening devices don't interfere. Founders! I may need to bring this to Bilena's attention later."

And so, the two Sisters waited. Gina set the alarm on the time disk and returned to her own seat to study her notes on the Kartaki language. Meanwhile, Kelysia looked for data that might indicate whether the brick was susceptible to the effects of the resonant minerals in the dampening device.

Sometime later Gina heard a sound through the reverser, a sound she was certain was a loud fart; she laughed and turned to ask Kelysia if she too had heard, but the woman was gone. "Ah yes, she said a minute ago she wanted something to drink. Oh well."

Gina jumped when the time disk rang, but she put her notebook down and returned to sit in front of the reverser with anxious anticipation. Not much time passed before she heard a man welcome his companions. Excited flutters stirred Gina's belly. Aloud, she said, "Kelysia!" But Kelysia had not yet returned. Gina blurted a small curse, shrugged her shoulders, and dismissed any further thought of her colleague.

For thirty minutes, the men exchanged only drivel. Gina was about to put the Quieting Cloth back on the reverser in frustration when she heard words that frightened her for the first time. These were being spoken by the man who was the apparent leader. He said, "The Umbra … sending … to Kynaria … Gr … Priestess and … our targets … must be swift. We will then contact … in Urbs …" Gina felt her pulse accelerate. She wished Kelysia were there to hear the transmission too, but alas. Another voice now said, "What is … name?"

Just as the leader started uttering the requested name, Gina heard footsteps grinding a grain of stone behind her. She turned urgently, with a finger on her mouth to tell Kelysia not to make noise. But she was surprised to find another of her Sisters there instead. Before Gina could say anything, the woman covered Gina's mouth, and Gina felt her brain explode as if it were being torn apart. And then no more; she was dead. The intruder released her, smoothed the Yellow Sash's face, and left.

IV. Serpent and Rokons

The flight toward Laiella and the rest of the company was one filled with anxiety for the prince, and the only thing that kept him from giving up hope was the fact that Xena confirmed, through her connection with the Barrier, that Laiella was alive. But the Lux Baiula's replies also left him worried because each time he asked for an update, she merely added a short and terse, "They need us." And each time, he inadvertently spurred Scorch, which caused the furan to become quite irritated and to respond with exaggerated upward motions of his wings, which struck Toras's flanks.

Some fifteen minutes later, Toras and his half-quintanal finally caught sight of the others. The unit looked severely diminished and embattled, surrounded by the rokons and the Serpent, as they were. Several furans flew riderless. Toras felt his gut tighten up.

Something gave him hope that his unit might be able to help extricate the others from the vise in which they found themselves. Indeed, neither the enemy nor Laiella's men seemed to have noticed them yet. Toras raised his arm and assembled the other teams around him to form a plan.

Toras yelled, but not too loud, to overcome the sound of the wind caused by all the furans and asked, "Xena, is the Serpent using its mental attack?"

Xena reached for the Bind then shook her head.

"Very well, then we can attack safely."

It took a couple of seemingly interminable, excruciating minutes for the unit to agree to use the tactic they had practiced against the Serpent's simulacre in Horn's Pass, with Toras shooting nervous glances toward the fighting every so often. "Everyone! Take your positions. Hopefully, Laiella's unit will follow our example and assemble into groups of five as well. Marius! See if you find anyone alive down there and pray no one else drops to the ground."

The furanteams assembled themselves in groups and Xena formed a nebula around them all in case the Serpent decided to use the DEBSA. Just then a guardian spied one of the embattled teams being struck by a rokon; he yelled to tell his commander who watched another man and his furan drop to the ground. Toras felt his ire bubble and burst, and he raised his arm to give the attack signal, but Xena shouted a "No!"

Toras looked back with daggers in his eyes. "What do you mean, 'No'?"

"The First Barrier just sent me a thoughtcall to instruct you to not attack now, Commander."

"What?! Why?"

"I do not know."

"Then ask her!"

Xena tried but could not reach Laiella.

Curses flew and the lord commander's patience vanished when he saw another one of Laiella's teams get hit by a rokon. Uncaring of Xena's renewed protests, he ordered the attack and spurred Scorch forward with all the urgency he could impart on him, and—this time—the furan did not complain.

The Serpent was the first to turn its head in their direction and it raised the alarm at once with an angry cry, sending five of its flesh-tearing cyclones toward them, cyclones which launched themselves forth with all the rage of the Nethers.

Toras prayed the tactic they had developed to use against the Serpent would work against its more natural cousins. He yelled, "Men! Remember to let your furans take control if they ask."

The Humans readied themselves, some with clenched jaws and white-knuckled holds on their mounts' reins and others with nervous twitches that agitated their furans.

Having selected their target, the prince extended his arm to point at it as he yelled to the members of his pentagon, "That one!" At once, Toras and the other four riders adjusted their furans' flight so that the rokon would be forced to pass between them.

The clash was terrible, but the tactic did allow three formations, including the commander's, to eviscerate a rokon each. Two lizards, however, spiraled their way toward the pentagons aiming for them at such furious speeds that their rotations knocked the lances out of the soldiers' hands and lacerated the flanks of furans and riders alike.

This first bout ended with cries of agony from left and right, and above and below, as six men and their furans dropped to the ground to go lie next to the bleeding reptilian corpses.

Before the rest of the rokons came about, Toras stole a glance toward Laiella and her teams. He shook his head and growled when he saw they were still trapped by the Serpent and its companions. He stole another glance toward his own teams and saw them reorganizing into new pentagons. A shout brought his attention back urgently.

"Commander, another rokon is charging us!"

"In formation!"

Toras became alarmed when the rokon aimed itself toward one of the furanteams on the ring instead of heading for the open center. He yelled, "We need to fly toward it to force it into our center! Now!"

As the men spurred their furans forward, Toras signaled Scorch to break formation and position himself in the center of what was now a quadrangle. The men yelled and cursed at him, but Toras raised his arm to quiet them.

The prince positioned Scorch a few meters behind the quadrangle, told him to hold the position, secured his grip on his lance, and then growled to goad the rokon toward him and Scorch. The lizard responded at once and flew toward them, hissing and screeching and spinning like some crazed tornado. Toras grinned, with the madness of exhaustion and frustration deafening him to his men's cries.

"Lances!"

The lances, which had been sharpened the day before until their edges were razor thin, drew blood as from a mooer's neck when the rokon finally passed through the center of the quadrangle. The rokon shrieked as the blades sliced its flesh. Warm liquid sprayed the creature's attackers. But wrapped as it was in its wings as it sped through the quadrangle, the lances had not cut the creature's body. The rokon was still fiercely and furiously alive when it slammed into Scorch.

Scorch screamed and reared up, his legs stretched out in a strange position three hundred meters in the air, his short claws extended on all four limbs.

When the rokon hit his furan, Toras felt his body separating from his mount, and his heart seized for a brief but frightening moment. Then his arms stretched out toward Scorch's neck reflexively. Toras's heart slowed when his fingers found the animal's fur and they grabbed onto it.

Scorch now struggled to get the rokon off him, while Toras tried in vain to assist his steed with his sword. Furan and rokon continued fighting this way several long minutes, with the former trying desperately to disengage himself, and the latter seeking feverishly to get its beak into Scorch's neck, while Toras got repeatedly smacked and bruised by either Scorch or the rokon as they beat their wings to remain aloft.

Toras had no hope to assist Scorch from his position and he cursed himself, the rokon, and the gods for his utter uselessness. And he cursed some more when he heard a low, pain-filled moan rise from Scorch at the same time as his muscles seized. Toras thought their end had come. But the rokon released an abrupt and awful cry and let Scorch go. As the creature tumbled away, Toras noticed an arrow in its back. Across from him, standing straight atop his own furan, Areto smiled widely, overcome by relief.

Toras nodded his thanks and turned his attention to Scorch. The furan had several lacerations on his belly and flanks, but fortunately for him and for Toras, those had been made by the rokon's claws rather than by the venomous teeth covering its belly and the outer surface of its wings. Toras took a hurried, but nevertheless soothing, breath before asking, "Are you okay to continue, Scorch?"

The furan bobbed his head, and the prince ordered his men into formation again. They swallowed the objections they were preparing when they saw him join them on the ring.

Toras took the briefest pause to assess the situation and choose their next target. "Seventeen teams on our side and," Toras swallowed as he counted what was left in the prima's half-quintanal, "eight on Laiella's." Toras's face twitched with worry and disgust. "And one, two, three…six rokons plus the Serpent left opposing us. That makes five pentagons to take seven of them, unless Xena and Laiella can bring down another two rokons with a Binding."

That hope was soon quashed given Xena had joined a pentagon and was no longer throwing any Bound projectiles at the creatures.

Toras looked toward Laiella again and saw a rokon heading straight for her. His heart clenched. He thought about helping her when the Serpent turned his way, locked eyes with him, and gave him a murderous hiss that crossed the distance as easily as if a god had spoken from the sky above. The shriek shook everyone's bones. Toras raged and ordered his unit toward the vile creature.

When they reached to within two hundred meters of the main battle, a terrible screech pierced the sky and Toras's teams—men and furans alike—began experiencing throbbing headaches.

Xena shouted the vilest profanities at the prince as she tried to establish a nebula. But the last few sweet salt candies she swallowed a few minutes earlier had been insufficient to replenish her energy stores, and all her efforts resulted in no more than a slight diminishment of the intensity of the Serpent's vibrations.

Now, the furans began flying with erratic, jerky motions and their riders' orders, insults, and pleas were all equally ignored by the hurting steeds.

Realizing that she would not be able to help with any Binding given her condition, Xena sent a thoughtcall to her Sister. She said, *"Laiella, do you hear me?*

It took a moment for the First Barrier to reply, *"I do."*

"What do we do? My nebula is too weak; I am too weak. This needs to end."

Laiella's reply came as an angry murmur, *"It does. Curse the prince! But I do not have any other options."*

"What do you—" Xena clasped her head when the Serpent's Bindings suddenly grew in intensity.

Laiella, drained as she was after two hours of fighting and resisting the Serpent and losing two-thirds of her unit despite it all, looked toward the prince with fury, anger, and desperation welling inside her. But this was not the time to let her emotions have the better of her, and she paused to consider her options. Fortunately for her, she did have enough energy left to shield herself and her furan from the Serpent's DEBSA. And yet, even this small nebula was beginning to weaken, and she could feel the debilitating vibrations seeping into her brain. Only one viable solution presented itself to her, the only one that might put an end to the Serpent though she might very well die trying.

Snorting dejectedly and turning away from the prince, she ordered Root into action. Root responded with as much momentum as he could muster to get beyond the reptile. As soon as Laiella saw the Serpent's back, she steeled her nerves, primed her metabolism to defend against the digestive enzymes, detached herself from her furan, and jumped.

Her landing on the Serpent's back was met with the pain of the laceration of her shins. Her hands, fortunately, were gloved and did not get cut, though she did feel the teeth pushing through the leather. The Serpent roared with rage at being physically assaulted by one of the puny Humans. The Barrier did not waste time and forced her thick-soled boots into the creature's dorsal teeth to secure her hold in case the creature started spinning. With one swift and determined motion, she then planted her glaive between its shoulders. She did not know whether the cut would debilitate the creature or not. But, the Serpent did respond.

Its cries and its voice, as it roared raging insults at her, were deafening, and Laiella was forced to use the Bind to block the sound before the intensity of it knocked her out or tore her eardrums.

The creature tried to reach her with its beak, but the movement brought it pain and it stopped. Instead, it started spinning, forcing Laiella to flatten herself onto its back, grabbing the dagger and pressing her feet and thighs against the creature. The Lux Baiula prayed that she'd have enough energy to keep her liver active and neutralizing the toxin that got in through the multiple cuts she was sustaining.

After two interminably long minutes passed, minutes during which the Serpent did its best to shake the Human off its back and Laiella did her best to hang on despite the continued incisions and the multiple, heart-stopping, moments when she thought she would fall, it was her turn to release a terrible cry; the Serpent had intensified its mental attack and was directing it straight at Laiella. Her nebula failed, and she now felt an excruciating pain seize her brain, as if a vise were being tightened around it.

The Serpent sent a merciless thought to the Barrier, *"You will know agony as no other Human ever has! You—"*

The Dark One's Wings did not finish its sentence; Laiella had used whatever strength she had left to thrust her glaive deeper into its back. An exploding cry erupted from the creature, and it shook itself so violently that the Lux Baiula lost her hold on it and was thrown off to fall toward the distant ground.

Her screams were picked up by Root, and the animal dove in without a moment's hesitation to intercept his rider. But he was stopped in his tracks by a rokon that rammed into him. Root sent an urgent chirp to his congeners before losing consciousness. Scorch, who had recovered from the Serpent's earlier attacks—as had Toras—alerted his master, who turned to look in the direction indicated by Scorch. Toras's heart seized when he saw Laiella in free fall; he released a powerful shout to draw Xena's attention toward him. Not realizing that his yell had shaken her and her mount to their bones and caused Switch to jerk violently, he used hand signals to tell her to engage the Serpent even as she struggled to regain control of her furan and while he dove after Laiella. Xena sent a curse after the prince.

As they neared the Serpent again, Scorch was the first to feel the creature's mental attack, and he jerked. "Founders! Scorch, you need to make it!" Indeed, Laiella had perhaps ten seconds before hitting the rocky ground. Just now, Toras clutched his head too, and knew that he, Scorch, and Laiella were lost. And then the Serpent's attack ceased; it seemed the blade in its back had finally taken its toll. Scorch straightened his flight as best he could and when he felt his master lying down on his neck and putting his feet forward—the cue for him to dive—he dropped like an arrow shot from the sky. It took all of Toras's strength to not empty his bowels on his steed, so tightly his belly was being squeezed by the back strap pulling on his belt.

Approaching the unconscious woman, who was now only a few seconds from splattering on the ground, Toras's body stiffened, and his legs squeezed Scorch's flanks to prepare himself and Scorch to catch the Lux Baiula. A moment later, Toras pulled on the reins, Scorch swerved suddenly, and Laiella's limp and body slammed into them heavily. Scorch jerked, and Toras's eyes went wide when Laiella slipped from his hands. But he wasted no time thinking now; with the perfect, exact motions that only a life-or-death emergency can elicit, he pulled his prima back up onto his legs, removed his back strap and attached it to her before finally taking a breath and ordering Scorch to slow down.

As he surveyed the situation, the prince realized there was no strategy or tactic that would secure a victory now, and he said to Scorch, "We need to retreat." He reached for his horn, but the instrument was stuck beneath Laiella, so he ordered Scorch to call the other furans back.

Those who still had their rider on their back responded at once and turned to follow Scorch. The few solo animals, however—three of them—ignored the call completely and launched themselves at the Serpent in a final fit of rage against the unconquerable creature. One was caught by the Serpent's beak and sent a distress call with its last breath as its back was broken. Men clenched their teeth as their mounts sent mournful calls to each other and to the two furans who continued in their mad—and futile—attempts against the Serpent and the surviving rokons.

Fortunately for what remained of Toras's quintanal, the Serpent did not pursue, nor did it send the remaining rokons after them. Toras did not know if they owed their luck to the two furans who had decided to die trying, or to Laiella's blade. But he was glad they would get to live another day—and try again.

***

31

It was with sullen, gloomy motions and growls that Toras's company landed at the Mountain Lake outpost thirty minutes later. The soldiers, dazed as they were and with splitting headaches, dropped from their mounts with unusual sluggishness and clumsiness. As for the furans, they plopped themselves on the ground, uncaring of the saddles still on their backs, and they moaned low and long before closing their eyes to rest.

Sergeant Tamas was already there with his men to assist the combatants, Humans and animals alike. Tamas himself ran to the lord commander to help him; Toras was holding his unconscious prima in his arms.

As he moved to grab the prima's legs, the sergeant asked, "Lord Commander, what happened?"

Toras shook his head and said, "She needs medical attention, Sergeant. As for what happened, mind your business!"

Tamas started but quickly replaced his surprise with an empathetic expression.

Marius approached the prince and took the prima from his arms to carry her to the barracks. The middle-aged, clean-shaven man asked the sergeant, "Do you have an infirmary?"

"I do. Lento will take you there. He's our medic apprentice."

Marius nodded and followed the curly-haired healing apprentice, who had just arrived.

Toras now looked around and shook his head when he saw his men moaning and groaning just as badly as the furans. Scorch, himself, was silent, but he was nursing several injuries with tired motions.

The prince moaned in his turn, in response to a horrible headache. He rubbed his forehead then said to Tamas with a voice constricted by pain, "Sergeant, please have your men see to my soldiers and mounts."

"Of course, Lord Commander. But perhaps you should have someone probe you too."

"I'll be fine, Sergeant. Please do as I asked."

Tamas did not argue longer and moved to give orders. Following the man with his eyes, Toras realized that something was wrong with the outpost. He shouted, "Sergeant, what happened here? What is that hole in the roof of the furans' paddock? Did the Serpent and its rokons attack you too?"

The officer turned around and said, "No. We were attacked by gnarlers last night, and our mounts' only way out was through the roof; it was a lucky thing they were able to break through it, or they would all be dead now."

With alarm, Toras asked, "How many did you lose? Were any men—"

"We lost three furans, and a man."

"Damn the Founders! Damn them and the crazy shit they do for who knows what reasons!"

"So, you were attacked by that foul Serpent and...*rokons*? And they did this to you?"

"Yes! Crazy, *shitting* rokons directed by the Serpent, coming at us like they didn't care if they died so long as they brought us down!"

Tamas hesitated, but finally asked his question, "How many did you lose, Commander?"

"Too many! Half our quintanal..."

"A quinta what?"

Toras shook his head "They're the new companies of fifty we trained to fight the Serpent."

Tamas nodded. "And the Ser—?"

"The Serpent and the surviving rokons were continuing south. But I'm tired of being questioned, Sergeant. I'm going to go see La—"

The poor Tamas was going to apologize to his commander when a brooding Xena approached.

The Red Sash hesitated a moment, seemingly trying to decide how to address the prince while in prey to her own anger. Finally, with a fatigued but sharp, grating voice, she said, "Commander, First Barrier Laiella needs medical treatment that none of us here can provide. I have already sent a message to my White Sash Sisters in the region, and Mara Lux Baiula said she could have one of her colleagues from Spiritii reach us by tomorrow. Mara said the woman should be able to treat the mental injuries First Barrier Laiella has suffered as a result of those…*unfortunate* events."

Toras's face stiffened and his eyes filled with resentment. He said, "Why are you using that *tone*, Lux Baiula?"

"Your *prima told* you not to approach the battle, but you did anyway. And because of it, she is there in the throes of who knows what agony while you stand here unharmed."

Sergeant Tamas sensed that this conversation was going to degenerate, and he backed away and turned arresting looks to everyone else to order them to stay away as the prince started to fume with ire and disbelief at the woman's nerve.

"What did you say to me, woman?!"

"That this is all your fault, Commander."

"My fault?!" Toras snorted furiously, unable to believe the woman's nerve. "I am the commanding officer of this force. I have to make decisions based on facts."

"The First Barrier instructed me to tell you to hold back because she suspected that if the Serpent saw us—and you in particular—join the battle, it would start using the DEBSA again, and neither of us had enough energy left to form proper nebulae. As it turned out, the Serpent *did* use its mental attacks again, and you saw what happened. Most of us would be dead if not for the First Barrier's courage."

"And how was I supposed to know that, since you did not tell me?"

"If you had tempered your reaction, you would have known."

"I would have known?! You should have given me the information I needed from the start! That's what you should have done. But you didn't, and I made my decision. And now—aghrr!"

A sudden realization hit Toras just then, and his chest deflated as quickly as a popped balloon; he knew everyone was watching him, and he had enough experience to know that a public 'debate' was only going to make things worse. And because he needed Xena, though she sickened him now, he clenched his jaw and stormed off to go to the infirmary.

Xena felt the men's eyes on her just then and she did not know whether to stare back at them, challenge them, or simply walk away. In the end, she stiffened her expression and walked off toward the woods to find a spot where she could sit and meditate a while.

The lord commander found Marius tending to Laiella in the small room that served as the infirmary. Lento served as his nurse.

An angry scowl meant to conceal his guilt carved the prince's face when he saw the awful condition that the red-haired, green-skinned woman—soldier—was in. Her face, normally strong, firm, and vibrant, was now contorted with pain and flushed by the beginnings of a terrible fever. Chills were starting to shake her body.

Without turning his head to acknowledge the prince, the medic said a little brusquely, "I need some cool water."

Lento was obviously already annoyed with the man, but he left to go fetch a bucket of cold water, giving the lord commander a frustrated look as he passed him by.

The prince watched his prima with grinding teeth, sighing loudly, and combing his hair with his hand. Something irritated him and he said, "She needs to be covered," as he moved to get a thin blanket he had noticed in the corner of the room.

The medic had not heard the prince's comment, and when Toras approached to lay the cover on Laiella, his reaction finished angering the prince.

Marius stopped the prince with a blocking hand and said, "I am sorry, Lord Commander, but native Breminese have a slightly different physiology and should not be covered."

An exasperated growl started to rise from Toras. But he clenched his teeth instead, pulled the cover away, and made a few futile attempts at folding it.

Suddenly, the medic shouted, "Where's that Lento?! And why isn't there any fresh water in this room?"

Toras did not reply.

The medic stood, urged his commander to not touch the prima, and left to go fetch some water himself.

A moment later, Hanne entered the room. He had come to see the prima. When he noticed his commander's expression, he said, "I know you didn't mean to see the prima hurt, Commander because I know you care for your soldiers; I have seen you throw yourself in front of danger to keep us safe, though it annoys us."

Toras did not respond. Instead, he thought to himself: *If Kendor had been here, this wouldn't have happened. And yet...* When his eyes fell upon the shivering woman again, he shouted, "Damned Founders!"

Uncertain what to do, Hanne said, "You shouldn't be so hard on yourself, Commander. I knew you even before I came to Horn's Pass from this outpost, and I know—"

"I don't need you to cheer me up, Hanne. This shouldn't have happened, and now it might cost—"

The prince stopped himself when Lento and Marius returned with the water. "Thanks for your words, Hanne. Medic, please do everything you can for her."

Marius nodded and said, "I will do what I can for her body, Commander. But we will need a White Sash quickly, because I can't do much about the injuries to her mind."

Toras rubbed his forehead with remnants of guilt, gave the agonizing and moaning Laiella one last look, then addressed both medics without looking at them, "One will be here tomorrow. Just do the best you can until then and alert me if anything changes."

As he left, Toras thought: *I need to find Tamas; I treated him a little unfairly, earlier. And then I need to check on Scorch...and the men. Founders!*

V. In Zeblinia

With barely hidden scorn in her voice, a woman said to another, "*Eternal Advisor*, why would we not use the men? They no longer have any utility for us anyway; you said so yourself to our Greatness, Queen Zebula."

The two were quarreling in a large office filled with objects of all sorts on the walls and on the shelves lining them, the objects sequenced by type, color, and size, in six different permutations of their attributes. The display had always—for as long as the queen's Eternal Advisor could remember—appeared utterly strange to anyone who had ever stepped into her office, and it was no less incongruent to her current guest.

With a perfectly pitched voice made grave by time, though her appearance belied her age, the queen's Eternal Advisor said, "I *did* say so, General Marikai. But I fear that they might now turn on the army, or simply defect, if you brought them along. I would therefore urge you to bring a reduced number, if you must bring any."

"And where will we find space for the Alvinorian males we bring back if we keep our shutsha here?"

With a dismissive hand, the Eternal Advisor said, "There are other ways to remove the unwanted. I know why you wish to bring our males. But you do not need them; the Lux Baiulae are weaker than your Janarae. I have redone my calculations, and I can see this now; you will defeat them easily if you use proper military strategy."

It was all the general could do to keep herself from replying with shocked indignation. 'Proper military strategy?' Who was she to give her military advice? No one! As her name rightly proclaimed: *Nihildrina*. General Marikai looked down to take a deep, calming breath before speaking. Still, her tone was ice. "*Proper* military strategy requires that one use one's elite forces to deliver the fatal blow, not to soften the enemy's ranks. The males will cause no trouble—I assure you that—and I will bring the numbers I need to achieve our goals with minimal losses to my Janarae in this foolish war. Or do you believe shutsha to be more valuable than Janarae, *Eternal Advisor*?"

The general's accent grated on Nihildrina, emphasizing all the wrong syllables.

"General, you di—do realize that the queen has endorsed our course, and that it is therefore everyone's duty to ensure its success. This being so, one must believe in the mission. Doubting the righteousness of it is not acceptable as it puts the queen's decision in question and weakens the resolution of those charged with implementing her will." Nihildrina paused before locking gazes with the general to challenge her: "Do you believe in the mission?"

The general's face had been flippant and mocking before, but it hardened to the point of cracking now. General Marikai was glad she did not carry a blade, because she might have done something the queen would have made her regret.

Nihildrina recognized the woman's reaction for what it was: the reaction of a woman unused to being tested. Without softening her gaze, she said, "General, the question I asked is one we must all answer in our service to the queen. So, I ask again, do you believe in the mission?"

"I will carry out my orders successfully, Eternal Advisor."

Nihildrina studied the woman with eyes used to inspecting and analyzing every detail of someone's face, to know their motivations, their intent. And having known the general for two decades now, she knew her well; her reply was one the woman had given many times over the years. She justified it with the illogical, backwards equation between cause and effect, saying that if the effect of her actions was what the queen desired, then the cause must be her belief in the mission. Nihildrina had always doubted the logical link, but she had never been able to prove the general's disloyalty. Of course, she knew the general disagreed with invading Alvinoria—the most powerful kingdom in the Terrae Regis—simply to acquire males, especially to use them to rejuvenate their creatics. The idea revolted Zenara Marikai more than it did the queen.

"Very well. As usual, I accept your answer. If it is still your wish to use our men as infantry, I will advise the queen that bringing a portion of the force you had intended to take into Alvinoria should be acceptable."

The general's features did not soften, but she forced a smile and left the queen's advisor's office, snorting and shaking her head as her gaze caught the mad decoration on the walls.

When the door closed behind the general, Nihildrina walked to the covered porch at the back of her office. Her sanctuary—her home for the past four hundred years—was located on the outskirt of Zeblinia. Standing in front of the window, she looked at the grand but foreboding landscape. Zebulonia was a cold land for the greater part of the year. Its winds were fierce, and when they blew and turned up the slopes of the sky-touching Sagr, they dropped unending snows. The Zebulonian civilization could have let nature control it and focused its energies on keeping warm and fed, but it had not. Instead, it had developed—under Nihildrina's careful guidance—into a powerful society, engineered through and through: physiologically, socially, civically. The slopes facing Nihildrina's property glittered in their thick whiteness, but down here—within and around the capital, which Nihildrina could see toward the right—there was very little of the snows. Indeed, all major cities in Zebulonia kept their streets, plazas and surrounding areas clear with the use of enormous plows harnessed onto varagoths. Furthermore, the Bind was used to clear the roofs of a few buildings, which for one reason or another had to be flat; algal sprays, which turned the streets, roads, and courtyards into luminous canvases of red-orange streaks that always delighted the children—and sometimes, Nihildrina too—were used to prevent ice formation. And the majority of buildings were like gigantic cylinders sticking out of the ground at a forty-five-degree angle, with a giant piece of glass forming the northern face. Nihildrina sighed when her gaze returned to fix itself on the snow-capped mountains; Zebulonian snows were very different from the dust-filled, grayish ones Nihildrina remembered from another place, another time, and she often wondered whether those memories were even real.

Turning her head back toward the door, the Queen's Surgeon and Eternal Advisor said to herself, "This is not exactly what I wanted. It may leave Zenara with too great an Alterintrant force when she returns, and I do not like the thought of *this* general returning with a victorious army."

Nihildrina was not worried about being spied upon. She had warded her home against unwanted vibrations.

"I need to contact Lusk to get updates on the Alvinorian defensive plans. But first, I must see Zebula to remind her of my departure this afternoon. It will be pleasant to spend some time in warmer climates, though I don't know how much I will enjoy the rit—Aghrr! I cannot appear in front of Zebula still making these mistakes!"

VI. In the Magna Mater's Office

The atmosphere in the Magna Mater's office was tense, to say the least. Larca was reporting on the disappearance of a third Sister in the space of as many fourths—all women from her Sashate dispatched across the kingdom on scouting assignments.

Krystiana said, "And you have no idea what happened? Don't you require your scouts to be connected?"

The Praefecta milites gritted her teeth angrily. "Of course, we do, Mater. If they were killed or abducted, their murderers or captors knew what they were doing and made certain they took them by surprise with no time to react and send a message."

"Why do you assume they were captured or killed? Could they not have been turned and decided to disconnect so that they might join the enemy?"

Larca's fanned braid bristled. Bilena, who was moved by a need to bridge the decade-long cold between them, came to the general's rescue. She cleared her throat and said, "As you know, Mater, when a Sister willingly disconnects from another, we either receive a warning or nothing at all. In the case of these disappearances, their officer received a vibration which stung her telesensory cortex as if a rubber band had snapped in her brain. This leads me to believe the scouts did not disconnect voluntarily."

Krystiana bobbed her head, accepting the reasoning.

Bilena opened her mind for anything that might come from Larca and was happy to intercept a faint swooshing vibration—gratitude. She resisted the temptation to look over her long Pargahni nose to acknowledge the general's sending. Instead, she sent a similar vibration back then let the feeling of a possible success soothe her.

The exchange had not gone unnoticed by Krystiana, and she wasn't certain what to make of it yet, but she filed the fact away for later recall and said, "Let us assume they were captured or…killed, then. What will you do and how are you going to prevent further losses?"

"I have already sent teams to search the areas where they were last sensed. They have orders to return by fourth's end if they do not find anything and to wait for backup if they do find something. As for plans to prevent further disappearances, we are still considering them."

"It goes. Please keep me informed, General. This is very disturbing news although I am well aware of the risk involved in scouting."

Larca nodded and Krystiana sat back on her soft-cushioned Lacora Leaf chair, hands crossed, indices touching her lips, and her eyes shifting as she forced herself to put her worries aside and broach the next topic.

When her eyes set themselves on her praefectae again, she said, "So, what have we learned from the Zebulonian, Saara?"

The Praefecta medicas scratched her neck reflexively as she replied, "Well, we have probably learned all that we can learn from him, Mater. And it has not been easy."

Krystiana cocked her eyebrows.

"I am certain you've heard about this way he has, which turns most women into bleaters the moment he sets his eyes on them, whether they be commoners or Lux Baiulae. So, I've had to oversee most of the questioning sessions, which have…drained me, to say the least."

Krystiana said, "Yes, I've heard you're the only one who can withstand his charms. Are you certain he is not a danger to us? Are you certain that his irresistibility is not a sign of his being a…a Temptator?"

The praefectae became alarmed at the Magna Mater's supposition. Did she really think they would let one of the Dark One's minions have free rein within their Sanctum?

Bilena spoke up and said, "Mater, that has been a worry—a risk, in fact—we've been concerned about from the beginning. But we have no data to suggest he is anything other than what he says he is: a Healer."

Krystiana turned to Saara to ask for confirmation.

With a voice croakier than usual, Saara said, "I agree with Bilena, Magna Mater. I can only surmise that the strange, stupefying vibrations we get from him are due to his being a Zebulonian."

Krystiana said, "The girls are Zebulonian. Don't you get the same confusing vibrations from them?"

The women made uncertain gestures.

"How can you not know whether you receive similar vibrations from the girls?"

Bilena cleared her throat and said, "They are similar in many ways and dissimilar in others; it is possible that Zebulonian males have different vibrations than their female counterparts. We have, in fact, established that they harbor distinct microbial floras from each other as well as from us."

With a sigh, Krystiana said, "All right, so what *have* we learned from him that may be of any use?"

Saara scrunched her face, unsure where to begin. "A lot, and not so much. What I mean is, we have learned a lot about their physiology and about the ways in which they access and use the Bind; we have learned that they are almost impervious to disease unless their skin is broken, which seems to be the only way microbes or parasites can infect them. And we have confirmed that their Alterintrants harbor six-fold as many M. fulgur as we do. Hypothetically, this might make them much more powerful firebinders."

"Anything else?"

Saara and Bilena shook their heads.

Her tone frankly soured, the Magna Mater said, "In summary, then, we know the Janarae may be more powerful than we are and that their physiology may give them such endurance as to outlast us in a drawn-out battle." Krystiana's scowl almost pierced her praefectae's stolidness, and she continued, "On the other hand, we know we will need to break their skin to make them susceptible to vitacsis. Not very encouraging, I would say. In fact, quite disappointing."

The praefectae showed their deep discomfort with the motions of their lips, the turning of their heads and the unnecessary adjustments to their seating positions. But none spoke and Krystiana said, "Any suggestions as to how we can prepare ourselves given the disappointingly insufficient intelligence we have gained from our Zebulonian guest?"

Larca seized the opportunity to give her thoughts on the matter and said, "Do you know why we have not yet learned how to fight them, Magna Mater? I will tell you why. It is because we have not pitted our Sisters against any of them. Yet that is the only way to know how we stand against each other and to adjust and hone our skills."

"Are you proposing we attack them? Or perhaps proposing that we have our Sisters test their skills against Lusk Methrim—a Healer?"

"I am proposing we face the Janarae; face them in a controlled situation to give us a chance to learn what we need to know before engaging them in open war."

The other praefectae became alarmed, but the Magna Mater sat back and rubbed her hands, with her head tilted downward, as she considered the proposition.

"Please continue, General."

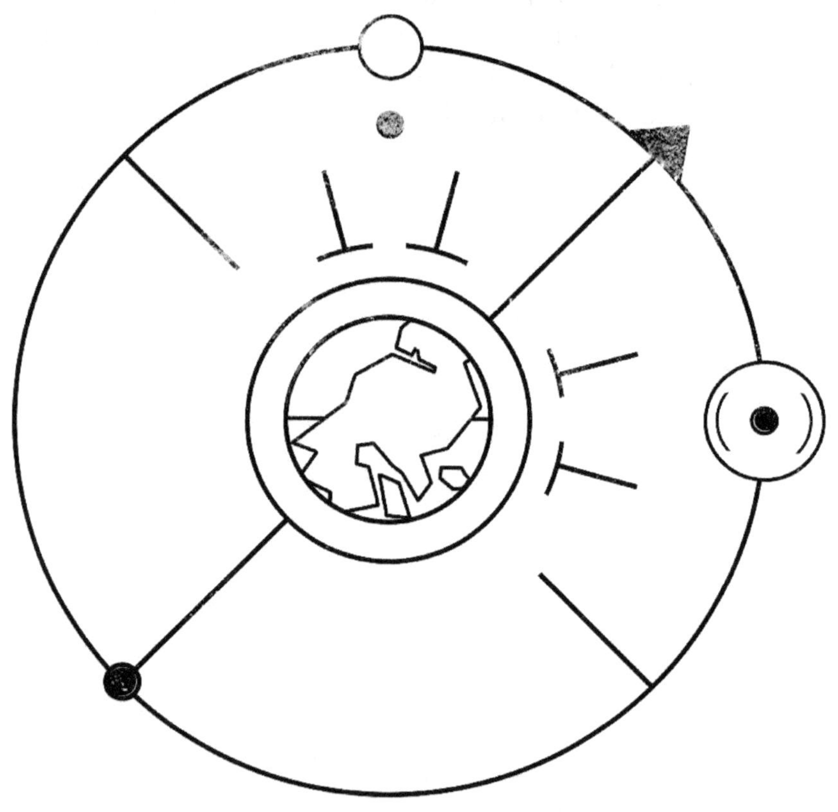

2. UNCERTAINTY

I. Accounting

Listening to the leader of her Assembly with somewhat less tension than she had expected when she had entered the woman's office but with tension nevertheless, Elyana did her best to parse the words and their meaning, to judge the severity of whatever punishment may come as a result of her actions when she stopped the assassin at the fair.

"The truth is, Elyana, that you cannot be faulted for having a skill, the teaching and the learning of which are prohibited. If you looked under our covers, I would not be surprised if you found that many of us have skills which are frowned upon. And as much as Larca would like to punish Sisters for having unsanctioned abilities, we can only rightly be punished for the uses we make of them, and your use of…of mind violation was in defense of someone, and not an unimportant someone."

Elyana's only reaction at her leader's hesitation was a slight movement of her lip.

Ramela, an outstanding Sensor herself, easily picked up on her acolyte's involuntary signal. She said, "My hesitation was not due to the offensive nature of what you did, but simply to the fact that the term we have for it implies a terrible, ugly deed." Again, Elyana's lip made a barely perceptible movement. "I, myself, do not consider it that, but your act was and is a forbidden act."

Elyana's sprouting hope quickly withered.

Ramela rubbed her right lobe a moment, considering her next words. Raising her head, she asked, "If you were in my place, Elyana, and I were the one coming to you having done what you have done, how would you counsel me? Do you have memories from others that would help inform such counsel?"

Her superior's aperture took Elyana by surprise. She made several aborted motions, while Ramela scrutinized her with a cool yet expectant gaze, before she replied with unusual anxiety, "I suppose I would heed Procta Lux Baiula's advice and tell you that you should acknowledge the illegality of your act and your willingness to accept its consequences, and yet demand that the law be revised given the changed circumstances so that if other Sisters should find themselves confronted with the need to use certain skills, they may do so…within the confines of a new law."

The Praefecta consuasores opened her eyes wide and then nodded to herself, having confirmed something she had suspected. "Procta Lux Baiula. I remember learning about her. She was involved in what became known as the 'Days of Necessary Expiry' during the Trionian War."

Elyana nodded.

"Did you, then, come back here ready to take this stand?"

After a brief hesitation, Elyana bobbed her head ambivalently.

"Yes and no?"

"I believe Procta is…was right—I apologize, I have never gotten used to talking about the women whose memories I carry—but I will not take this position without your support, as I would not wish to undermine your authority."

Ramela snorted softly as a small smile stretched her lips. She said, "That is not the counsel I would have given you, Elyana, though I can see its wisdom. I sometimes wonder whether my *una memoria* makes me less suited for my position. All the other praefectae have at least one Transferred Memory; I have none to draw upon to evaluate and resolve new problems."

Elyana pulled her head back in surprise.

"Regardless, I agree with Pro—with the advice." Ramela paused with a curious slant to her lips. "I see what you meant about the strangeness of referring to Transferred Memories."

Elyana nodded. "We rarely speak of them. At most, we speak of the memories."

"Well, as I started saying, I agree with the advice, and I will support you, if that is the position you wish to take, when you face the Light's Assembly."

Elyana closed her eyes and then, as she reopened them, a hopeful, thankful expression painted her face. "Thank you, Praefecta."

With a benevolent smile, Ramela said, "The fact is, you are one of the most respected persons in the Order, Elyana, and that should grant you the benefit of the doubt. But even we, Lux Baiulae, tend to let seemingly horrible or reprehensible acts cloud our judgment and cause us to *become* horrified. Once that happens, a person's reputation is all but forgotten. But I, for one, still know who you are, as does Krystiana. And I think that with the two of us vouching for you, the Assembly may decide in your favor."

Elyana acknowledged her leader's careful but encouraging words then put her hands together, their movement showing some discomfort. A crease appeared between Ramela's brows and Elyana asked, "Praefecta. The concern you expressed earlier…about your lead—"

A Barrier irrupted into the praefecta's office, her face hard and showing signs of great distress. With clenched teeth and a quick nod of respect for the leader of the Purple Sashate and a forced one for the woman's guest, she said, "Praefecta, Manu Dextra, you are required to attend the Magna Mater in the Auditory Laboratory at once."

Ramela asked, "Why? What is happening?"

"I am sorry, Praefecta, I cannot say. You must come at once."

Ramela turned to Elyana with a foreboding expression. She took a deep breath, stood, and followed the Barrier, with Elyana right behind her.

II. The Need for New Methods

A meek male voice posed a question to Ylana Marin Dar'Muntake, "Supreme Priestess, have you considered whether the coming conflicts will require more trained animals?"

Ylana, always cautious, said, "I have considered it, but I have not yet made a decision, Priest Trainer Morek. Where would we obtain all the additional animals?"

With obvious discomfort, the middle-aged Morek said, "We would need to obtain them from the wild, Supreme Priestess. And it will be a big effort, depending on how wide the conflict spreads. Just in terms of Trackers, we could need as many as a thousand or more specimens from different subspecies of lincots to be sure priestess trackers can always distinguish them from the local populations."

"Again, I am not certain I would support the expansion of such a system, Priest Trainer. What would we do with them afterward?"

Looking horribly uncomfortable with the idea of having to capture so many wild animals but seeing no other solution, Priest Trainer Morek said, "Well...I frankly do not know, Supreme Priestess. Unless you decided to leave Kynaria completely out of the war, this will be a price to pay."

Ylana snorted loudly and said, "Firstly, Priest Trainer, we cannot impose the *'price'* of Human conflicts on nature. And it will, indeed, not be possible to remain totally uninvolved; we will need to support Octavius, in some way. Providing trained animals is one such way. But I would rather that we find a way to connect directly with wild, native animals, and track *them*. In either case, I wish you to find a way to train more Lux Baiulae as you have Marena, so that we need not directly involve our clerics in their war." When Morek started to object, Ylana raised a hand and added, "I know it is not easy, and I remember what I said at the Ball, but it *is* possible. This must be our foremost contribution to the war."

The cleric shifted uneasily on his seat. "I understand, Supreme Priestess. But you must know we have been trying for years to find a way to connect to wild animals and track them directly without success. And it took years, as well, to train Marena. Moreover, I do not know how we would test the safety and effectiveness of a priest or priestess's connection to a wild animal if it's not contained in a small environment and visible at all times."

"Morek! Instead of giving me reasons for things being impossible, please return to your offices, and come back to me once you have a solution to both problems."

III. Potential Solution

"Aria, have you heard what the Supreme Priestess has asked Priest Trainer Morek to do?"

"I have."

"Aria, this method you developed, you need to tell them about it."

"What?!"

"It may be just what they need to solve the problem."

"You must be joking. Why would they listen to me, a senior neo? And my technique has not even been tested."

"I think they will listen, Aria. They will!"

"First you tell me that you don't want to learn it yourself because it is prohibited, and now you want me to go and tell them I developed a new technique outside of class?"

Carasina gestured affirmatively. "The situation is different now. A war is coming."

Aria wrung her fingers nervously.

"Aria, if you won't speak with the leaders yourself, maybe you can tell your aunt about it. She can speak for you, prepare them to hear you."

Aria looked uncertain and upset by her friend's insistence.

"Aria, you know your aunt will listen to you after she gets over the fact that, once again, you ignored the rules; she will."

The Halfblood replied with a sigh, "It goes. I'll tell her about the technique tonight. But I'd like you to be there."

"Why? How upset can she get?"

Aria raised her shoulders awkwardly.

"All right."

But Aria did not look thankful. Instead, her expression appeared even more troubled.

"What is it, Aria? What else is wrong?"

After a moment of hesitation, the princess said, "Well, my technique sometimes causes the animals pain."

Carasina's eyes opened wide with sudden understanding. "So, you're the reason Brutus has been having twitches?"

Aria nodded.

"Hmm, I'm sure there is a way to adjust your connection, so it doesn't cause them the pain. And perhaps it's just Brutus because we've been working with him so much."

"No, it's happened to the flyers that nest on the tree outside Disciples House too."

Carasina tried to encourage her friend with some hopeful remarks about perhaps simply needing to adjust the intensity of the connections, but Aria replied with a depressed 'perhaps'.

When, after a moment of silence, a knowing frown twisted the bright-eyed girl's face, Aria blurted, "What?"

"That is why we are not supposed to try things on our own."

Aria blinked, confused. "Weren't you just telling me that I might save the day thanks to these illicit skills I've been developing?"

"I was. I'm simply stating a fact. Anyway, I'll be there when you tell your aunt. You will tell her, right?"

Aria sighed and thanked her friend, though she doubted things would go as well as Carasina was imagining them going.

IV. Alarm

Elyana and Ramela found the other three praefectae as well as the Magna Mater, Kelysia, and the Second Barrier in the Auditory Laboratory.

Saara Lux Baiula was probing Gina's stiff body, grinding her teeth and snorting in disbelief. Larca and Bilena stood by Krystiana, looking at their dead Sister with absolute consternation, while Kelysia sat stricken with her face in her hands, and Second Barrier Sasha stood with a murderous glare on her face and searching eyes.

Bilena, with her pale Amalorian skin tone looking properly ghostly now, and a voice that almost betrayed her Lucian training, said, "Who would do this? And to *her*?"

The Magna Mater replied with as stolid a tone as she could manage, "I do not know, Bilena. But we need to perform the Memory Transfer without delay. If we are lucky, the Receiver will know who did this to her."

In her raspy voice made harsher because of the situation, the Praefecta medicas said, "I do not think we will learn anything from the Receiver, Mater. Because if the murderer is one of us, she will have erased those memories."

The Praefecta milites said, "It could be one of our guests! How can it be anyone else? We are all sworn to the Sisterhood's protection."

Elyana interjected carefully given that no one had noticed her and Ramela's entrance yet, "I do not believe it was one of our guests; I think it was one of us."

Bilena, Larca, and the Second Barrier turned around with either unwelcoming glares or decidedly icy stares for Elyana, and hesitant acknowledgments for Ramela.

Larca drew in an audible, irate breath and hissed her words as she exhaled, "Mater, I do not think Elyana should be here now."

"She is still the Manu Dextra, Larca, and while she is, she has a right to counsel me wherever I am."

Seeing that Larca was going to object, Saara intervened and said, "She does, Larca. And I happen to agree with Elyana."

The Praefecta milites gave a sardonic snort then turned toward Kelysia to interrogate her, obviously meaning to get the upper hand in the proceedings. She said, "What do you remember of last night, Kelysia? When did you leave Gina? Where did you go? Who did you meet there and to do what?"

Kelysia shook her head dejectedly, "I do not know, Praefecta. I have no memory of anything after leaving Gina."

"But you remember leaving; why did you leave her?"

"I…I do not remember. I think I…I do not remember."

"Why are you still alive when she is dead?"

Kelysia's long-trained, tempered composure dissolved completely under the cruel question and she broke, unable to keep a sob from spilling though her clenched throat.

Bilena, horrified by the scene, tried to defend her acolyte, but Larca dismissed her arguments.

Krystiana, who was doubly horrified, wondered if this new Dark Battle was going to destroy the Sisterhood. She felt an urgent need to go to the spinning spheres on her desk to consult the dead Magnae Matres. Perhaps later. Now, she rubbed her forehead in an expression of frustration, shot an angry stare at

Larca, and said to everyone, "Enough! This is undignified and unworthy of any of us."

That startled the women, and even more so Elyana, who had never heard Krystiana speak with such sternness.

Krystiana continued, "The murderer is here, and I believe she is indeed one of us. And since none of us would have done this in her right mind, whoever she is, she is a Convert or, at the very least, under the influence of a Temptator."

Expressions of horror marred all the Sisters' faces, and each reacted with her own idiosyncrasies at the thought that one of them might be the murderer.

Finally, Ramela said, "I hope not, Mater." Then, turning to Saara and Elyana, she asked, "Why do you think it was one of us?"

The older woman replied with a nod toward the workbench, "The device that should be next to the brick is missing, and no one outside the Sisterhood knew of its existence."

Elyana added, "And Gina was killed with the use of the Bind."

Second Barrier Sasha said, "Then it could be that male, Lusk Methrim. He is an Alterintrant, and he has been here long enough to know of the experiment."

Bilena said, "No, we have probed and tested him repeatedly since Elyana brought him here, and we have never found any vibration in him that indicates he is one of them. We probed him again just yesterday, in fact."

The Second Barrier muttered some unintelligible disagreement then spat, "Then, either you made a mistake, or it is, indeed, one of us." No one noticed Saara's discomfort.

Krystiana gave a reluctant nod and, turning to Bilena and Saara, said, "Praefectae, I know your methods are not yet where they need to be to properly detect a Temptator or one of the Turned or Converted—whatever you call them—but you must perform the test on us, here, now. First, you will perform it on each other." Turning to Sasha, she said, "Second Barrier! Please fetch Kita; she has just arrived from Pargah, so she is not the murderer; she can monitor the praefectae's vibrations for signs of violence done while they test each other. Once we know—as imperfect as our methods are—that you yourselves are in the clear, you will test the rest of us here."

Unsensing witnesses might have interpreted the women's stiffness, just then, as a sign of their cold, inhuman nature, but initiates would recognize the tangible signs of dismay and consternation freezing the women's lips and hands and every other muscle in their bodies.

Finally, unable to stand the silence anymore, Larca said with an indignant quiver in her voice, "You think one of us here may be the traitor?"

Krystiana exhaled softly and replied, "No, but a person turned is not necessarily aware of it, as Saara has explained several times already."

Larca objected, "Mater, I was with my officers last night. And others here may have been doing other things which would preclude them from being suspects. I do not wish to be subjected to an unproven method."

Saara replied for the Magna Mater, saying, "Larca, given that one who is turned may find it easy to lie and—if they are an Alterintrant—to stupefy those around them so that they have no recollection of certain events, I agree with Krystiana: we must be tested, all of us."

"You agree?! It seems all you can *do* is agree tonight!"

Krystiana leveled a warning stare at her general, and the woman turned away for a moment so that she might calm herself.

The Praefecta consuasores took advantage of the opportunity to ask, "Saara, Bilena, although I do not agree with the logic of Larca's objection, I do have concerns too, about the reliability of this experimental method."

Although Larca did not appreciate her colleague's comment, she did welcome her skepticism, and she nodded appreciatively, surprising Ramela.

It was with some hesitation that the Praefecta philosophas answered, "Those we have trained are able to identify turned individuals eighty percent of the time."

With some alarm, Larca asked, "Do you mean then that twenty percent of the time they incorrectly identify someone as being turned even if they are not, or that they do not identify individuals who are turned twenty percent of the time?"

"Fortunately, not the former. But we do have false negatives."

Ramela rushed to speak before Larca took control of the conversation again. "So, it is possible we won't find the murderer anyway."

Saara and Bilena gestured it was indeed the case, the former doing so more equanimously than the latter.

But Larca would not be quieted and just as her lips started to pull apart to speak, Krystiana said, "Given the nature of Turned people, we will begin here, Larca, as weak as the method is."

However, Ramela voiced another objection, "Mater, how could any of us five have been turned? We barely ever leave Urbs Lucis."

Saara said, "It actually happened to your predecessor, Ulota Lux Baiula, during the Dark Battle, Ramela. Of course, we do not know the exact circumstances of her turning, but it *can* happen." Saara turned a challenging glare at Larca before completing her thought. Understanding from the woman's posture that she was going to keep quiet for once, she said, "Krystiana is right to take this approach."

To Krystiana's relief, all finally nodded their assent, and she said, "Bilena, as soon as all of us here are cleared, you will perform the Memory Transfer. Who is next on the list of Receivers?"

Bilena blinked and said, "It is actually Kita, Mater."

"That is a surprising coincidence. Anyway, assuming we do not find the murderer among the eight of us, we will perform the Memory Transfer, and then..."

Krystiana paused before saying, "...then lockdown the Inner Sanctum. No one is to enter or leave until we have tested everyone, Sisters and guests alike. Sasha, if you are cleared," the words twisted the Barrier's face into an ugly, affronted frown, which the Magna Mater dismissed with a soft sigh, "you will personally lock all the doors, and guard them until other Barriers can take your place."

Saara shook her head, as if disagreeing. Krystiana said, "You object to my orders?"

"No. It is just that the testing will take forever, Mater. And if the murderer is not uncovered immediately, she may very well take some other action before we get to her."

Elyana interjected and said, looking at Krystiana to get her consent as she spoke, "We will sound the alarm and restrict everyone to their quarters. Every Sister we clear will be given orders to watch the others."

Larca shot daggers at the Purple Sash, then said, "Are you mad? Sound the alarm?"

Krystiana replied in Elyana's stead. "No, she is not mad, Larca. That is exactly what we will do."

"Now, Barrier, please fetch Kita and return with her at once." As Sasha was about to execute her orders, Krystiana held her hand up, and asked Elyana to join the Barrier, in case Sasha was their culprit, which brought another vexed huff from the woman.

As the others left, Bilena said, "Mater, you must know that this will rattle every one of us, to see suspicion cast on us all."

"Good, because if we cannot find the face of the murderer inside Gina's memories, perhaps we can uncover it the old way: by the suspicious look on her face, though a Lux Baiula she may be."

When Sasha and Elyana returned with Kita Lux Baiula, they found the others brooding or meditating, and all of them, except for Krystiana, showed their nervousness by the movements of their lips, eyes, or hands.

Krystiana, who had been studying her dead acolyte's face, turned around and said to the thin, blond, freckled and middle-aged Yellow Sash, "Kita, you are here because one of us has been murdered while another," and she looked toward Kelysia, "was rendered unconscious during the murder." Kita had to steady herself upon hearing the news. "I need you to monitor Praefectae Saara's and Bilena's vibrations for signs of violence or untruth while they test each other using the new… test for Turned people. If they are cleared, they will then test you—I know you have just arrived and cannot be a suspect, but anyone across the kingdom could have been turned. If you pass, you will receive Gina's memories. You will need to process them immediately; I know it is not the usual procedure, but we need to know whether the identity of her murderer is in there because our testing may well fail to uncover the assassin."

It was with a mixture of disbelief and near unwillingness that Kita Lux Baiula accepted her charge. Not only could she not believe any of them might be the murderer, but monitoring the praefectae's vibrations made her most uncomfortable; indeed, they were…praefectae! It was worse than putting a hand on a king or queen or other leader. The thought of receiving Gina's memories, on the other hand, saddened her deeply; indeed, Gina had always been a kind, respectful, joyous person. Why would anyone have killed her? And although she *did* want to know who had done it, she knew that the memory—if she found it—would be frightening and terrible.

It took ten minutes of intense, nerve-racking probing for Saara and Bilena to clear each other and for them to then clear Kita. It was with great relief that everyone released their breaths, except for Saara, Krystiana and Elyana, who were aware that this test proved nothing and was only *suggestive* of innocence. Larca noticed their reservations and complained, asking how they were supposed to trust each other if there remained any doubt.

"We will need to be vigilant, Larca. But we must remain rational even while watching each other for signs of turning, otherwise we will surely destroy ourselves. Rationality is what we are known for, after all."

When Larca was done cursing, Krystiana said, "You and Sasha are next, Larca. Then the others, and finally me."

After a long, tense half hour, all women in the Auditory Lab had been tentatively cleared of suspicion.

Krystiana turned to Sasha and repeated her instructions to her, after which the woman left to go sound the alarm and secure the Sanctum, followed by eight pairs of anxious eyes, though the causes of their anxiety differed.

Presently, Bilena called Kita over, then ordered her to disconnect from all external stimuli and enter the Bind. Bilena did the same and began the Memory Transfer.

Elyana turned to Krystiana and said, "Mater, I think it would be good to hide Kelysia and to not reveal we found her incapacitated."

"You think it might help unmask the killer?"

Elyana nodded.

"Very well. Kelysia, did you hear Elyana's suggestion?"

"I did, Mater."

"Wait here. I will send someone to take you to one of the chambers in the tunnels."

Without any more ado, and with a tense, unwilling step, Krystiana left with the others to go tell everyone what was happening.

The alarm sounded a minute later with a deafening, strident cry emitted by a Bound horn. The sound arrested every woman's and man's heart in the Inner Sanctum. Those teaching and those learning, those reading and those writing, those talking and those listening, as well as those treating wounded or ill people—all froze, except for the unconscious. The moment passed, some rushed to their windows, others left everything as it was and sped to the plaza, while others cursed and ignored the emergency to complete a healing or experimental procedure.

It was a fortunate thing that Lux Baiulae had such excellent control of their emotions and reactions or Tiana Lux Baiula might have caused a dangerous release of toxic substances from her patient's liver. However, there were some who had not yet learned the self-control so common to Lux Baiulae, and a junior, who was learning to conjure firewhorls, ignited the matter she had picked up to form the weapon right there in front of herself, singeing her own hair.

The faces of those assembled in the courtyard were painted with their questions. Some eyed each other, wondering whether one or the other knew anything. Others stood anxiously—mostly the non-initiates. The few men in the courtyard stood out like sticks on a mooer's cocoon, especially Lusk, who was surrounded by four juniors in their cream-colored garb. Barriers stood stiffly, surrounding the crowd, and adding to its restlessness, which was further compounded by the abrupt cessation of the chanting by the Voces Lucianis so that Krystiana could deliver her message.

The Magna Mater and her council watched those assembled from the top of the palace's front steps.

Krystiana flicked her finger to call Elyana's attention and sent her a thought, *"What if one of those Barriers is the murderer?"*

"I believe Larca has established a mind-tie with them; that way, if any of them is the killer and she intends to do harm again, Larca will know."

Krystiana made a small nod, which Larca noticed. The Praefecta milites suspected the Magna Mater was having a conversation with her Manu Dextra. It disturbed her, but what could she do? She turned and scanned the crowd instead, pausing on her Barriers with conflicted urges.

Krystiana said quietly to Larca, "You've sent Barriers to scout all the buildings? Especially the medical school, in case there are some who could not come into the plaza?"

With some ice in her response, the general said, "I have, Mater."

Krystiana took a deep, soothing breath, and readied herself to make her announcement as a Yellow Sash-bound junior placed a Wide Communicator in front of her, so that everyone might hear her, whether in the plaza or indoors.

Without preamble, Krystiana said, "The Inner Sanctum has been placed on alert because there was a murder last night."

Before the Magna Mater could add anything else, unending gasps and a wave of heads turning this way and that to seek confirmation of what they had heard overtook the courtyard. Inside the buildings, Krystiana's voice arrested everyone, even the medics, who cursed once more. Voices in the plaza demanded to know who had been murdered. The answer shocked them all; some women covered their faces, while others simply averted their eyes to hide their reactions.

When a measure of calm had returned, the Magna Mater swallowed before making her next statement. As she prepared to do so, she wondered whether any of her predecessors had ever had to do such a thing, and she was surprised to hear one of them speak to her to tell her to be careful. *Careful? Careful about wh—*

A hissing whisper interrupted Krystiana just then. Elyana said, "Mater, they are waiting for you."

The Magna Mater responded with an uncharacteristically angry moan, and the praefectae turned toward her worriedly.

After berating herself for her reaction, Krystiana approached the Wide Communicator and said what she had prepared to say: that the Inner Sanctum was on lockdown, and that everyone was to go to their apartments for the rest of the day until called to be probed.

The disquiet that rushed through the plaza, this time, was like the daily tidal bore that swelled the River Argon.

Elyana swallowed reflexively and wrung her hands; indeed, by telling everyone they would be probed, Krystiana had now warned the murderer, who might shield her thoughts—or *his* thoughts, though she hoped it was not Lusk because if it was, she would never forgive herself. And yet, too many things pointed at him, though an equal number of things said he was just what he claimed to be. She needed to find a way to pierce whatever veil covered him, if there was one—hiding something.

"Please go to your chambers now and wait to be called."

Turning to Larca, Krystiana said, "General, please have your acolytes tested first as I prefer not to have the murderer be among those guarding the Sanctum."

Larca's face started to twist itself into an indignant scowl, but the Magna Mater's stare boded ill for any challenger, and so, Larca nodded and left to carry out her orders.

Krystiana watched her general make her way through the crowd without much regard for who stood in her path. Without turning, she said to her Manu Dextra with a remnant of anger in her voice, "This is a dark day, Elyana. One the consequences of which I am unable to foresee."

Elyana did not reply but made uneasy motions.

From Krystiana's right, a scratching throat called the Magna Mater's attention. Krystiana turned and Saara said, "I would like to have my acolytes probed soon after the Red Sashes, Mater, so they may use this…opportunity to learn the difference between unaffected and affected persons—assuming we find her, of course."

Krystiana retorted, "Or him," eyeing Lusk who was giving parting words to Moradien and her group.

Elyana looked at her befuddled. "Mater, pardon my insistence, but as Bilena said earlier, he was probed just yesterday; it cannot be him. Clara Lux Baiula, one of our finest Sensors, works with him daily to train the Razebian girls, and she has never sensed anything wrong either."

Krystiana stiffened and said, "We will test him again, along with everyone else who was here last night. And you can have however many acolytes attend the probing once they are declared…once they are released."

Krystiana's insistent and unveiled uncertainty regarding their ability to declare a woman free from external influences crimped both Elyana's and Saara's faces.

However, something in Saara's bearing unsettled Elyana. *She is not tapping her fingers, but she is touching her thumb to her fourth finger, despite herself; she is hiding something.* A desire to question the old Sister followed by an urgent injunction against it curdled Elyana's frown; the warning had come from Procta Lux Baiula. Elyana thought: *You are beginning to annoy me, Sister.* The inner voice that spoke the ancient woman's thoughts, thoughts which were captive within the Transferred Memory and yet somehow aware and still learning, snorted. Elyana smoothed her face, excused herself, gave Saara a nod impressed with a hidden question, and returned to her offices.

As she spun, her eyes fell on Lusk Methrim. She halted her movement a moment and cursed silently as two conflicted thoughts surfaced: she did not wish him to be the murderer, and yet it would be better if he were and not one of her Sisters, though this would further damage her standing in the Order, given that she had insisted repeatedly on trusting him.

V. Surprise

The Serpent waited at the top of Green Peak on the Mountains of the Sagr. He waited for the Umbra, complaining to himself about having to fly the Founder's creature to Mo'Tarkoth, as if he were someone's mount.

I am the Alis Domini, and he will *show me respect…or I will drop him over the Sea of Tarkoth,* by all that created me, *I will!*

The Serpent shifted his body on the mossy ground to dislodge some bothersome stones, then let himself sag and exhaled a determined breath to mark his decision. As he did, he felt the dull pain of the stabbing wound between his shoulders flash from there all the way to his tail; for some unknown reason, it was healing unnaturally slowly. K'Tara had made a complete revolution on itself since that mad, miserable Human female had jumped on him and plunged her dagger into his back, and still the injury pulsed.

The Serpent repositioned himself until the pain lessened. While waiting, he watched the Red sun descend slowly, wondering what its blue twin might be doing. No answer came, and he berated himself for thinking such stupid questions when a warm breeze—unusual for this time of year in the south, especially over the Sagr—blew across the peak's crest. The Serpent dismissed his questions and let the gentle wind soothe his pain.

After some thirty minutes, a cloaked rider approached from below, atop a snowvoran. He was followed by a Great Howler pulling a cart with a saddle and two exceptionally large baskets.

The snowvoran was a beautiful beast, for sure, with its thick white coat and black mane. But although the Serpent liked the snowvoran's more muscular body compared to that of its Alvinorian counterpart, he still found the animal's call quite silly. He wondered whether the Humans had created trumpets to sound like vorans, or whether the vorans had been bred to sound like trumpets, for he knew that creatures could be shaped and transformed; his master had done exactly that to him. Noctiferus had created *him* from a simple rokon.

Presently, the voran dislodged some scree as it stepped onto the plateau, and the Serpent gave the Umbra an insincere welcoming growl.

The voran emitted its stupid call, and the Serpent roared in response, causing the voran to rear up. But the animal was quickly brought back down by its rider's soothing caress.

"You should be more careful with your snarls, Alis."

The Serpent lifted himself on his haunches and responded with a low rumble, followed by a louder and longer complaint.

The Umbra looked at him questioningly as he hopped off the snowvoran.

The Serpent spat his response. "We met the Humans from Horn's Pass on our way here."

The Umbra scanned the creature and said, "Is that why you asked me to bring a medical kit? Your skin looks freshly renewed; it seems you've met another Lux Baiula."

Hissing his reply, the Serpent said, "I did. She was part of a company of mounted furans—five tens of them. But my rokons routed them all, and I massacred the inhabitants of a village by the central northern mountains."

"Did you lose any rokons?"

"Four and ten."

"Cum eis confligere non debuisti! Rokones non iam parati sunt."[2]

"I disagree. They are under my complete control. They do as I ask and fight well, as simple-minded as they are."

"Then why did you lose so many?"

With another hiss, the Serpent said, "Because they are plenty."

The Umbra put his hands to his head. "That is a foolish strategy, one which will eventually leave you defenseless. You are no longer to engage Humans until I agree the rokons are ready."

The Serpent gave an angry growl, followed by a groan of pain.

"Will you still be able to carry me to our destination?"

The Serpent did not immediately respond. His expression alternated between resignation and defiance, but he eventually settled on the former. He said, "I can carry you, but I need you to heal my wound first."

The Umbra closed his eyes, annoyed by the Serpent's lack of respect. He then walked back to his voran, tapped its shoulder gently, and added a simple "Home" to send it back to his property on the northern side of Zeblinia.

The animal turned its head to look at its master, lowering it in acknowledgement and took off with another trumpet.

The Umbra now approached the howler to retrieve his medical case from one of the baskets on its back.

------

[2] You should not have engaged them! The rokons are not yet ready.

The Serpent asked, "Why do you care so much about the voran?"

"Snowvorans are rare beasts."

"I am rarer."

The Umbra took a deep breath, kept it a moment, exhaled and approached the Serpent without a word more. He removed his boots and socks, shaped his foot so that he might hold onto the incisor-like scales lining the reptile's skin, then climbed onto its back. He did not need to scan long before finding the stab wound between the wings.

"How did you let a Human jump onto you?"

"The prince—Toras—and his Guard, they have been training, and not just to protect against me, but to *fight* me. I do not know how they train. But it is making things more difficult than I can ever remember. It was a good thing I had the rokons with me."

While listening to the Serpent's account of the last attack, the Umbra took a sponge from the medical case, wet it with alcohol then disinfected the wound, which was covered by a scab, but still dirty and inflamed underneath. He took a scalpel and removed the scab and cleaned the wound again. He then took a small vial, opened it, swirled it and poured a drop of the reddish silvery liquid into the wound. The Serpent's flesh began to reknit itself immediately.

The Alis Domini gave a low, long, joyful groan after which he begrudgingly thanked the Umbra for the healing.

Meanwhile, the Umbra retrieved from the cart the saddle and the baskets, which should have needed two men to carry, and placed them on the ground next to the Great Howler.

The Umbra clicked to get the howler to lower itself so he could fasten straps around it, then attached the baskets, which would be hanging a meter beneath the animal once they got airborne. That done, he picked up the saddle and went to the Serpent.

The Serpent asked, "Do you remember where the saddle goes?"

The Umbra did not reply. He *did* remember, though it had been an age since the last time he had climbed onto the Serpent's back. The saddle, which he had had crafted back before the Dark Battle, had remained surprisingly supple.

After checking that all was secure, the Umbra said, "Let us go. And do not make me regret my patience. We have to be in the Yeltchek in four days."

The Umbra attached himself, and the creature took off. The wind caused by its wings bent the grass across the peak for tens of meters in every direction.

The Great Howler took off soon after. It groaned when the weight of the baskets pulled on the straps. But the wind gave it the uplift it needed, and its load did not feel so heavy anymore, and though it had to beat its wings twice as fast as the Serpent did to keep up, it had the endurance of a belwohr and would have no trouble following, so long as the winds remained true until they reached their destination across the ocean.

3. TRAINING AND ENCOUNTERS

I. Training

On Urbs Lucis's training grounds—a square kilometer expanse of targets of all sorts to capture, move, hold, maim, explode, or obliterate—three Red Sashes and a Yellow prepared to instruct their students, including novices, juniors, and Sisters from all Sashes, in the arts of defensive and offensive Bindings.

Given the previous day's events, some had asked whether the training should be postponed. But both Krystiana and Larca had agreed that it was unnecessary to do so. Everyone had been tested and the murderer had not been found. So, either they had left, or they could not be found by the means currently available to the Sisterhood. And given that they could not keep the entire Order on hold until new or better means of detection were developed, normal activities would be resumed, despite the risk. Notwithstanding this, measures would be taken to help protect everyone, such as increased vigilance and ordering everyone to remain in the company of another at all times until the threat passed.

However, a thornier decision had not been made yet. It was about whether to implant the Locari's Monitor into the minds of all the Sisters, as they had planned to do, or not. The women were discussing this very topic in the Magna Mater's office even while the students were assembling in the training yard.

Larca almost lost control again—a thing she had learned to temper since she was put in charge of the war preparations— when Saara suggested that the Monitor should be set in every Sister's mind.

The general yelled that it was preposterous to think to set the vibration in *any* Sister's mind, adding that it should perhaps even be removed from Elyana's mind—if it were possible. That received indignant glares from everyone.

But Larca continued, insistent, "Implanting the Monitor in everyone's mind, given the high likelihood that the murderer is still among us, would give our enemy an advantage they should *not* have."

Saara asked, "Then what do you propose, Larca?"

"That we only give it to a few we trust implicitly."

Krystiana interjected, "Can we trust *anyone* implicitly?"

Elyana and Saara groaned silently.

Ramela cleared her throat. When they turned to her, she said, "I think we *should* give it to everyone. That way, all of us will be better protected even if we happen to give some advantage to our enemies by so doing."

Larca growled and threw her hands up while the Magna Mater paced her office to consider their options.

Krystiana asked, "How do we decide between these two positions, Praefectae, Manu Dextra? They are both valid."

Hiding her lingering hesitation but readying herself for any challenge Larca might address to her when she spoke her opinion, Elyana said, "I do not think they are equal, Mater."

To Elyana's surprise, it was not the Praefecta milites who questioned her but Bilena, and with unusual asperity. "How not, Elyana?"

Elyana resisted the desire to look toward Krystiana for support and replied calmly, "If you only give it to a few among us and by misfortune one of them is the murderer, our enemy will have the advantage because they will not have any compunction about spreading the Monitor among their ranks. Therefore, it *is* best to give it to every one of us."

Unsurprisingly, Bilena objected to Elyana's position. The Praefecta philosophas said, "I disagree, Elyana. Statistically speaking, restricting it to the fewest numbers will greatly reduce the probability that the murderer will receive—"

Elyana interrupted her colleague with a sincerely apologetic but determined voice, "I am sorry, Bilena, but statistics are irrelevant here. Even though what you propose would reduce the probability that the enemy might be among those who would receive the ability, the consequences to us—if it should happen anyway—are so great that we cannot take the risk. We will be in a much better position if the entire Sisterhood has the skill, even if it means the enemy will too."

Assessing the Magna Mater's mood before saying anything and seeing that Krystiana had not yet reached the limits of her tolerance for disagreement, Larca cleared her throat loudly. "Elyana, you must know, having your ear on the Sisterhood's pulse, as Manu Dextra, that there are other objections to your plan, and one in particular, which has not yet been considered."

Elyana took a deep calming breath while Larca and Bilena exchanged looks of rare mutual support.

"There is a faction that has sprung up since your return opposing the idea of having a creature's Binding implanted in them, especially one that has not even been properly studied by the Yellow *or* the White Sashate yet. How can we be sure this…Monitor, as you call it, will not harm anyone?"

Ramela, always composed, dropped her head for a moment, then signaled Elyana to let her answer instead.

"Harm us, Larca? The prince and Elyana have had one implanted in them without any ill effect. I admit it is not a large sample to prove the Binding's safety, but they *are* both safe and in good health. Moreover, we have medics here, and I am sure Saara won't mind instructing them to monitor everyone for the next few days to be sure no one is harmed by it."

"That will not placate them, Ramela. Monitoring is no guarantee that no harm will come in the first place."

Ramela considered her colleague's argument for a moment and saw the logic of it. But she knew that Elyana was right about the need to place the Binding in everyone. She turned to Bilena, to ask what the experimental data said to date, hoping that the woman would not let her reservations twist whatever observations her acolytes had made about the safety of the device.

It was obvious, from the woman's motions, that she did not wish to answer the question. But a direct question had been asked, and she had to provide a reply. With much annoyance in her voice, she said, "We've only been studying the Monitor for a fourth now; please remember this. But based on what we've sensed from Elyana's temporal lobe, where the Binding is located, all appears normal. No other regions of her brain have been altered, and…Saara can confirm that no unusual changes in her health, her brain activity, her reasoning, or her impulses have been detected."

Larca turned to the old Lux Baiula hoping she would detect hesitation in her, while Ramela, Elyana, and Krystiana did so hoping for the opposite.

With her usual forthright attitude, Saara confirmed Bilena's statement. A frown of disgust passed on Larca's face while a resigned one covered Bilena's.

After a few more impatient paces and an aborted movement toward the spinning spheres on her desk, Krystiana faced her praefectae and declared, "The Manu Dextra is right, and the implant appears to be safe; we will give the skill to everyone."

Larca stood and left the Magna Mater's office as quickly as was appropriate without insulting Krystiana, whereas the others left with a paced movement but with darker or brighter—though not completely relieved—complexions on their faces, depending on their sentiments.

***

The training field was abuzz with activity and shouts when the Praefecta milites arrived, ruminating atop her roan voran. Instead of stopping the animal with the usual Binding—a signal sent to the voran by way of a vibration which pinched the upper neck, and which the voran had been trained to break by coming to a stop—Larca yanked its reins, causing it to hop in retaliation. The woman cursed, then checked herself before she made things worse; she was not a Beast Reader after all, and the only way to calm her mount was to calm herself, despite the contrary impulses she felt.

As soon as she got down, Larca handed her voran to a Barrier guarding the entrance, shook her head to try and forget about the Magna Mater's decision, then scanned the immense ground with a measuring gaze. There was a palpable tension in the air.

Noting the praefecta's expression, the Barrier—an old woman with a stance straighter than a junior's—said, "The students have been here since Seven Ahn[3] and they are anxious to get started, General. I do not recall ever participating in a training such as this. Do you think this will work? Training so many women in so short a time?"

"If K'Tara wills it, it will. And if she doesn't, we will make it work, Bietta, because if we fail here, we will fail later, on the battlefield."

The old Sister grunted, then saluted the praefecta as she moved away with the woman's voran to take it to a paddock nearby.

Larca walked over to a promontory with a table and chair from where she could watch the entire scene. A brief smile appeared on her face when she heard the voice of Sasha Lux Baiula.

---

[3] Ahn: After Highnight.

75

The Second Barrier stood like a pole, her left hand tucked into her belt as she yelled instructions to the students, telling them they would spend the morning practicing offensive and defensive Binding skills and the afternoon practicing hand-to-hand combat.

Larca barked a laugh when she heard Sasha order Iyawa—one of the instructors—to have her students ready to defend against the Quatiô[4] in ten minutes! The woman was certainly decisive and to the point.

As the instructors took their respective groups to one area or another, Larca followed Iyawa with a skeptical, troubled gaze. Indeed, Iyawa was the only non-Red Sash that Elyana had been able to successfully train to date in the formation of nebulae. This seriously concerned and frustrated Larca because it meant that many of her acolytes might still be forced to protect against the Serpent instead of using their skills to bring it down when they met it next.

One thing alone gave the praefecta and general supreme some hope, though she hated to admit the fact: Iyawa's notorious sensibility. That sensibility enabled her to feel and recognize the vibrations of any Binding and to replicate them precisely, accurately, and consistently. It also made her an outstanding instructor, being able to sense whether her students properly replicated the Bindings she taught them and help them make the necessary adjustments to quickly progress toward mastery of said Bindings—so long as mastery of a particular skill was in the realm of possibilities for them. Larca hoped that the woman had properly learned the nebula-forming skill, which she had obtained during a Mind Transfer, from Elyana. With a sigh, she

---

[4] Quatiô: Term coined by the Sisterhood during the Dark Battle to refer to the Serpent's mental attacks, known at the time of the current events as DEBSA (deep energy brain surge attacks).

thought: *I suppose we will find out soon enough whether we will be sending Sisters to their deaths or to victory.*

Presently, something else attracted Larca's attention, which brought a deeper frown to her face. Elyana had arrived and stopped to speak to Sasha, probably to inform her of the decision regarding the implantation of the Monitor. The Barrier did not look pleased. Of course, Sasha was among those who would protest the forced procedure. Moreover, the woman had not yet accepted Elyana's impunity in the matter of her usage of Mind Rape to stop the king's would-be murderer. *I don't blame her. But how many more times is the coming war going to be used as a reason to excuse the bending and breaking of our rules?*

Larca returned her attention to the two women below and her eyes and lips were pulled downward when Elyana looked her way for a very brief instant.

The next moment, Sasha laughed loudly, mockingly, then yelled a 'So be it' followed by an order, which she projected with enhanced voice to Bela, Iyawa, and Akula to send ten students each to Elyana.

Larca sighed and prayed to the Founders this was not a mistake. Or did she hope it might be? She wondered for a moment, then dismissed Elyana from her thoughts and walked toward the eastern end of the field, where Bela had taken her one hundred and thirty-two novices along with twenty-five White Sashes, who formed a perimeter around the recruits to teach them some simple sonactic and vitactic skills.

Bela was a permanently cranky woman. For a trainer of the Red Sash the attitude was not an issue, of course. Especially one assigned to teach recruits. On the other hand, her methods were a little unusual, and many disapproved of them, but not Larca. The woman got results.

Bela gave her leader a quick nod upon noticing her approach then turned toward the red shoots and, with a stern tone that belied the meekness of her name, said, "All right! Since you couldn't even coax a single fiber to burn last fourth, let's see if you've at least learned the rudiments of sonacsis and vitacsis. I will show you once more how to perform the push and the freezing and you will then pair up with a girl you hate. If you can't—"

Just then, a courageous brown-haired girl asked, "Pardon, Lux Baiula, but…why do we need to pair with someone we …hate? I mean, this assumes we—"

"Because for the first part of the exercise you need to try and harm your opponent; it will be easier to do against a girl you dislike. However, myself and ten of my Sisters will then attack each pair using the Bindings you will have practiced and the *only* way you will be able to resist our attacks will be to work *together* to defend against us. You will learn it on the field when you're surrounded by the enemy, if you don't learn it here, that being able to cooperate with your Sisters, regardless of whether you love them or hate them, is a sine qua non[5] condition to your survival and, more importantly, to winning a battle."

When a nod of understanding and confirmation passed between the general and the trainer, a nod noticed by many, the questioning girl excused herself, and Bela completed her instructions. "So, after I've demonstrated the skills for you, you will pair up and try and topple each other using sonacsis. You will then use vitacsis to try and cause each other's bones to chatter." Pointing at the medics, she added, "The White Sashes are here to be sure no one gets seriously injured."

With that, Bela proceeded to show her students how to correctly perform each Binding.

---

[5] Sine qua non: Latin locution meaning an essential condition; a thing that is absolutely necessary

Larca observed the trainees as they began to replicate—or tried to replicate—the Bindings with keen interest, trying to identify those who might progress to junior Sisters and those who would need to be sent back home after, at a minimum, learning to control their Bindings. She was glad to see that most were learning. Satisfied that Bela had things under control, Larca moved on to the next field, situated at the northern end of the training ground.

She found Akula instructing juniors bound for the Red Sash, as well as a few bound for other Sashes, in the creation of fireweapons. Most of these were in their twenties, though a few were in their fourth or fifth decade of life.

Larca respected Akula, a fair-skinned Jarahni, with short brown hair tied in a bun at the back, and dark eyes. It gave the woman a predatory look she liked. Akula was known as a master firebinder, though some questioned the notion, given that she had a tendency to use more energy than was necessary to achieve her Bindings. This propensity of hers had actually caused her to set her hair afire in her younger years, and the resulting scar had caused frustrated novices and juniors to call her 'scarhead'.

The women were each facing a puppet, composed of one material or another, which they were supposed to light using a firewhorl. When they succeeded, a target of a different composition would be placed in front of them.

Four Sisters of the Yellow Sash created a tunnel around each girl's lane to ensure that their shouts and strikes did not accidentally harm anyone else.

The general's scanning eyes stopped when they alighted on the Lady Moradina's daughter, Moradien—the troublemaker, who apparently decided to test for the Red Sash and spend a few years learning the warrior's way before testing for the Purple Sash—her ultimate goal. Many of her instructors wondered why.

Some said it was because of her secret admiration for Elyana, whose path she wanted to follow as a means to achieve greater power. Temporary stays of students in the Sashate, just to learn the skills, had always upset Larca. *Well, so long as she can learn our discipline and our Bindings and then help us repel our enemies, she'll be as welcome as all the others. Still, the Red Sashate is not a transition station.*

Larca watched Moradien inspect the surroundings between her position and the target. The girl appeared frustrated; a wavering resolve tensed then relaxed the lines on her face. Her previous attempts must have failed, judging by the unscorched puppet.

But soon, a barely audible hiss escaped the junior and twigs and leaves started floating in front of her. Her hands concentrated the vibrations emanating from her throat, moving as if around a clay pot she were forming. The flammable mass spun within, faster and faster, until she projected the entire thing toward the target—but it ignited midway there, and nothing was left to light the puppet. A curse, which must have been loud and forceful, but which was dampened by the force field around the lane, reached the praefecta, who shook her head. Inside the tunnel, the girl wobbled.

Akula signaled the tunnellers to drop the shield and then approached her student with an angry step, a White Sash rushing behind her and shaking her own head.

"Moradien! How many times have I told you that you must wait before igniting the matter? You must wait until the mass is ten meters from your target!"

As the girl prepared to hiss her response in embarrassment, the sound of someone clearing her throat came from behind the women.

Akula looked around and said, "Praefecta!"

Larca nodded but directed her words to the girl. "Moradien, is it?"

Moradien's angry posture did not relax to acknowledge the general's words.

Disliking the girl's unyielding stance, Larca said, "At ease, Junior. I have heard about you, both the good and the bad." Larca paused. *She is containing her anger and resentment. Good.* "Do you know why you failed? I will tell you why: you lost control. And if you had reacted the way you did in a battle situation, facing the enemy with your Sisters next to you, you could have disabled them too, if not worse." *Hmm, I see the twitch in her lips. At least she understands the truth of what I am saying.* "It does not matter so much that you lost control of the Binding. But it does matter that you did not use your anger to pick up new material, reform the firewhorl, and hit your target. That is what you must learn to do. It requires determination, not quitting, and continuing until you have *reached* your goal. I saw the hesitation on your face earlier; it will not do. You must use the same determination you put into defying conventions to the accomplishment of your tasks. If you do that, you will succeed and become *all* you can become, which I hope will include a permanence in the Red Sashate; if I am to believe your instructors, your skills and temper would be wasted elsewhere."

Moradien, who normally looked at her instructors with her head high whether insolently or pridefully, struggled to do the same now, until a thought or an impulse jerked her, and she said, "I must return to my exercises, Praefecta General."

Larca snorted quietly, sent a thought to Akula, and made her way to the western end of the training grounds. Her face scrunched itself when she shifted her gaze southward, toward the place where Elyana was implanting the Monitor. The line of women waiting for their turn had grown. It angered her to see so many Sisters willingly and unquestioningly accept the Binding that no one had yet had the time to properly study—a foreign Binding, an *animal* Binding.

The nebula-forming exercise was being held within an enormous, transparent Insulated Chamber that had been specially built for the purpose. Indeed, Elyana and Sasha quickly realized that the DEBSA, otherwise known as Quatiô, which Sasha was going to generate to attack her Sisters, could not be entirely contained and directed toward any particular target, and it was therefore necessary to conduct the training within an Insulated Chamber to ensure no one was accidentally harmed who might be in the vicinity, unprotected.

Larca took a seat on a bench set on the outside of the structure. Sasha waited impatiently as Iyawa finished getting her group of ten Sisters—a mixture of Blue, White and Yellow Sashes—to each establish a nebula around herself. Iyawa and the medic in attendance had already created a mind-tie between everyone so that they might keep track of the students' condition as the exercise proceeded.

Larca reflected about other things concerning her as Iyawa performed one final round of inspection.

The corner of Iyawa's lip pulled upward, creating a disappointed frown with her brow, when she came across three shields that weren't formed to her specifications. One of them was the nebula of a Sister of the Yellow Sash, expert in mind-tying, but today, learning to form the disruptive fields.

"Kelysia, your nebula, it is still uneven. I feel weaknesses all over it. You need to increase the intensity, to even out the field."

The woman sighed and bobbed her head, then did as instructed. Iyawa nodded in return and went to Sarrinia Lux Baiula, the White Sash responsible for the health of Sisters.

Iyawa could see Sarrinia's tight lips and intermittent twitches. She also sensed the extreme tension in the woman's nebula.

"Is the nebula still causing you pain, Sister?"

The woman grunted.

An impatient voice came from the side of the structure.

Iyawa sighed and asked Sasha for one more moment.

Iyawa closed her eyes, entered the Bind, and inspected the connection between Sarrinia, the ground, and the nebula. A moment later, she said to her student, "I am afraid you may never be able to do this properly, Sister—though none of us will know if we are doing it right until we face the creature—but I suggest you diminish the flow of energy from your S. tensio colony and increase that of M. fulgur instead."

Sarrinia knitted her brows questioningly.

"I know it seems counterintuitive, but it will help."

Sarrinia did as her instructor suggested, and a surprised smile flourished on her face as the pain faded and her nebula became more uniform. She gave the instructor a grateful smile.

Iyawa, a native of Pargah, had not really wanted to join the Sisterhood after they had given her the minimum of training required for all Alterintrants; she had felt out of place, with her dark skin and deeply religious beliefs, though her religion asserted the importance of one's connection with all living things and K'Tara itself, which was also one of the Sisterhood's central tenets. But after returning home and finding no path for herself, she realized that perhaps becoming a Lux Baiula was just what she needed, and that she could do good through it. So, here she was now, one of the most respected, if not one of the most powerful, Lux Baiulae.

Just then, an impatient shout came from Sasha, loud enough to have come through the communicator; it pulled Larca out of her cogitations.

The general watched Iyawa give one final glance at the ten Sisters and then establish her own nebula, which appeared around her as a distortion in the air that surrounded her and the medic. That done, she said something to Sasha, who nodded with relieved impatience.

This was, for Larca, the most important of all the trainings. If Iyawa failed, her own acolytes would be effectively manacled against the Serpent. Larca took a deep, hopeful but tense breath as she watched Sasha prepare her initial strike.

A span later, the woman attacked. The only initial indications of it were Sasha's open mouth and the intensity of her expression. Larca waited for the trainees' reaction, but except for a look of surprise on their faces, they showed no signs of pain at all. Had Sasha's Binding failed? Concern began twisting the lines on her face when she saw Iyawa's nod toward Sasha. Larca thought to herself: *Good, it seems they're only testing the trainees' focus.*

Sasha repeated her earlier performance and, a few moments later, three of the students wobbled. Larca sighed, relieved for a moment to know that Sasha's Binding worked, but caught herself and frowned instead, wondering if the students' nebulae were too weak or if the attack had been too strong to cause three women to be affected by it.

Iyawa signaled the medic, who scanned the trainees. When the woman nodded that all were well enough to continue the exercise, Iyawa gave them additional instructions, after which the Lux Baiulae rubbed their foreheads to dispel whatever pain they were feeling, and all readied themselves for the next attack.

This time, there were no signs that anyone had suffered, and Iyawa tipped her head again in Sasha's direction.

From this point on, however, each of the invisible attacks left one more woman showing signs of suffering. On the eighth attack, Iyawa, herself, reacted with pain. Her normally smooth features became tense, and she rubbed her temples with fierce motions. She halted the practice and took a few moments to consider things.

Fear gripped Larca when she noticed blood dripping down the Yellow Sash's lips. She was about to stand and go to the Communicator to ask for a report when she saw Iyawa shaking her head and walking over to Sasha after waving the medic away.

Larca did not hear what the two said, but Iyawa was obviously upset, while Sasha appeared to disagree with what the other said. Seeing that the women's gestures were becoming more and more intense, Larca stood and walked to the structure's door and asked to be let in.

As she approached the altercating pair, she heard her acolyte say, "Perhaps it didn't, but—"

Iyawa replied firmly, "It did not."

"Regardless. It is possible you are not forming the nebulae properly."

A small growl started to rise from the Yellow Sash when Larca reached them.

Sasha and Iyawa turned toward the praefecta, Iyawa holding herself back from lashing out and Sasha showing no desire to admit any wrongdoing.

To both Larca said, "What is happening here?" Then to Iyawa, "What happened that you are bleeding?"

"Sasha insists that her Binding is a perfect replica of what she learned from our books as well as from Elyana and that the problem must be with our nebulae. But I can assure you that, though the students' nebulae are weak, mine is a perfect replica of Elyana's. This should not be happening."

But the Barrier was adamant that she was right and said, "General, Iyawa must know that with each new intermediary between a language's native speaker and the learners, the quality of the instruction diminishes. The same thing is probably happening here. Elyana is not a primary holder of the nebula; she got it from Transferred Memory. She taught it to Iyawa, and she is now teaching it to others. That's three removed from the origin. I do not know why we cannot find the method for the generation of the nebula in our manuals, but the procedure for the Quatiô was preserved, and it is therefore likely that my Binding is more accurate than Iyawa's."

Iyawa's face darkened.

"You disagree?"

"I do, Second Barrier. My learning of the Binding to form the nebula was likely more accurate than your learning of the Binding to *generate* the DEBSA. Moreover, Elyana successfully protected herself and others using her nebula against the real thing. I should therefore be able to do the same against you. It makes me believe that your Binding is not a *DEBSA*, but something else."

Having heard enough, Larca intervened before Sasha could object again. She wished very much to support her acolyte, but she knew of Iyawa's reputation, and she knew the woman deserved it; Iyawa was unparalleled at learning even the most intricate and obscure Bindings, whereas Sasha was *only* a skilled and deadly warrior and officer.

The general said, "Sisters, I will tell you what you will do. You will let Alanna treat anyone who needs healing before continuing—that includes you, Iyawa, as we cannot afford to have you disabled. In the meantime," Larca paused a moment before naming a woman that seemed to be in the middle of everything they did, a woman she had once respected then had resented for leaving the Red Sashate, and whom she had finally come to distrust more than trust, "I will have someone fetch Elyana so she can come and observe your Bindings to be sure they are correct before you resume the exercises."

The women nodded, one reluctantly and the other with surprised satisfaction. With that, the praefecta left them to see to their affairs and slowly made her way back toward the entrance of the training grounds after sending an attendant to get Elyana.

Larca Lux Baiula, Praefecta of the Warrior's Assembly and now General Supreme of the Sisterhood, gazed at the various groups with a mixture of satisfaction and persistent worry. Finding new recruits, in particular for the Red Sashate, had not proven easy. Only one hundred and thirty-two women, ranging in ages from seventeen to forty-four, had been identified and brought to Urbs Lucis since the start of the effort, three months earlier—a woefully insufficient number to face Queen Zebula's army of Janarae. And the number of Alterintrants identified each fourth from the high king's lands was diminishing quickly, even with Marena's AAD—the Alterintrant detecting device she and her colleagues had developed a few months back. So, Larca had recently decided to send recruiters to the vassal kingdoms of Jarah, Pargah, and Yerlah, despite the skepticism of the Purple Sashate.

But what preoccupied Larca the most was the training of the non-Reds in the formation of nebulae; this was vital, perhaps even more so than increasing the number of Red Sashes, because if non-Reds did not develop the skill, her own acolytes would be effectively shackled. Hopefully, Elyana would be able to help Sasha and Iyawa adjust whatever needed fixing; she must.

As she came near the area where the Monitor was being implanted, Larca's face took on a dark hue. Soon, they would be coming for her, to do whatever they needed to do to insert that animal skill into *her* brain. Elyana was leaving instructions with Lupa before following the junior who had come to get her. The Manu Dextra noticed her and turned to gaze at her with what looked like…satisfaction.

The praefecta pulled her eyes away from the Purple Sash and looked at the women amassed in a small area to the right of Lupa's desk. They were chattering, chattering and blabbering, shifting between silence and more blathering. They appeared surprised, excited. Some of them appeared to be feeling dizzy and were being probed by one of the medics in attendance. But soon, even these moved on to return to their respective groups to continue their training. Many stopped every few steps, startled and thrilled at the same time, turning around to look for one woman or another with the purest delight on their faces. They were behaving like children! One of them even bumped into another. Larca shouted a question to Lupa, pointing toward the seemingly intoxicated women.

Lupa shouted back, "It's the Monitor. It is working, General. But it takes some getting used to. Elyana is planning to speak with the Light's Assembly tonight, after the implantations are complete, so that some rules can be established for the use of the skill. She will come see you later, when she returns, to discuss it."

Turning her attention back to the processed women, Lupa shouted, "Remember, you need to be in the presence of others to establish first contact. Once you've identified each other's signatures, you may make contact simply by thinking of each other."

Larca snorted, sputtered, and walked away to get the scene out of her sight. *This had better not be a mistake, or the Black Skies will rain on her!*

II. Announcement

Harlion, Kendor, Aithen, Mitsuko, and Irania sat in the king's Private Audience Chamber, eyeing him curiously as he paced slowly at his end of the room, stretching and testing his new vest.

Octavius had recovered from the latest attempt on his life, but now a new pain seized his muscles, a pain which Tania Lux Baiula had told him would probably never go away. Fortunately for him, Lacora Leaf chairs helped soothe the ache, as did the Lacora Leaf corset. This garment was perhaps the Clerics of Elande's greatest creation: it used the Lacora plant's response to pressure and heat to form a sustaining garment. This could be 'sewn' in order to gently massage the wearer, wherever that was necessary, by carefully positioning the contractile branches of the plant within the piece of clothing. The only disadvantage of this type of corset was that it must be worn alone, leaving immodest gaps that showed the wearer's skin. But for patients of means, which the high king certainly was, the clerics could create pieces that were both functional and slightly more modest in appearance.

Presently, Octavius swept his gaze toward Harlion and Kendor and asked how the defense against the Serpent was proceeding.

Taking their eyes away from the king's clothing, both officers made to answer, but Harlion sat back when he realized the question was not truly directed at him, given that he was no longer responsible for military matters. He looked at Kendor with a face that did not completely hide the resentment he felt toward this undesired change in his life.

Aithen noticed and clenched his jaw. He and Octavius had promoted Kendor to High Captain of the Royal Guard earlier that fourth, and elevated Harlion to Prefect Praetorian to oversee the king's Praetorian Guard and all intelligence activities. Secundus Telpornion had been promoted to Primus and now led the Mounted Assault battalion in Kendor's stead. They had hoped that Harlion would welcome the change. It was obvious, now, that the aging captain was taking the change rather sorely.

Kendor looked down uncomfortably before replying, "The use of Lux Baiulae as watchers is definitely helping, my king. And the training methods developed by Lord Commander Toras had almost given us the advantage, until the Serpent started bringing rokons along. So, we are back at square one. Things would be different if the Red Sashes could help strike at the Serpent, but they are still restricted to maintaining the nebulae."

Octavius ground his teeth and grunted, then said to Irania, "And how goes the training of your Sisters, Lux Baiula?"

"Slowly, Sire. But we should be able to pick up momentum soon."

Octavius raised a curious brow.

"Indeed, Elyana has finally been able to teach the formation of the nebula to Iyawa Lux Baiula, who is one of our most skilled Yellow Sashes and is able to perfectly reproduce any Binding, whether she sees it, reads it, or remembers it from Transferred Memory. She is now beginning to train others—mostly non-Reds—in the formation of nebulae."

Octavius reacted with surprise, saying, "That is certainly a remarkable ability, so long as the Bindings she replicates are good representations of the originals."

Irania replied with a slightly affronted, "Yes, of course, Sire, you are right; she can only be as good as the source she studies, which in this case is Elyana, who has effectively defended against the Serpent's DEBSA."

"Point well taken, Irania."

Turning to Aithen, Octavius now said, "What is your opinion on our defenses, son?"

"That the training of non-Red Sash Sisters in the generation of nebulae is urgent but that it is also urgent we update our aerial offensive and defensive methods if we want to be ready to fight the Serpent *and* the rokons when our forces meet them. Fortunately, the creature disappeared again following its encounter with Toras's quintanal. But I do not doubt it will return soon."

"Yes, most likely. Have you asked your brother to send one of his officers to train our men?"

Aithen nodded, but added, "One of the techniques he has developed also requires the assistance of a Lux Baiula. Irania is looking into this."

"I am looking forward to seeing these techniques Toras has developed."

Then, talking to himself, the king added, "And it pleases me to know he did so in collaboration with a Lux Baiula. It is encouraging."

"But, returning to our forces, Aithen, how goes the ground training of the men? Especially the new recruits?"

With an uncomfortable sigh, Aithen said, "It is going well enough. Our regulars are ready to meet whatever may come at them, but—"

Aithen stopped when he saw his father grimace in response to a new jolt of pain.

Annoyed by his son's reaction, Octavius growled, "You need not be concerned by my aches, Aithen. Just answer my question."

"Yes, I am sorry, my king. As I was saying, our regulars are ready, but the recruits *are* having some difficulty learning to defend against both the Nonsensing and the Sensing. What's more…they are not so attached to us yet and, because of it, their discipline is markedly lacking."

A hint of displeasure appeared on the king's face, but his expression also showed a lack of surprise, "Well, it is not unexpected, Aithen; recruiting men past a certain percentage of the population invariably leads to diminished quality. Moreover, even the finest men must be allowed to develop a sense of unity with their comrades and of trust toward their leaders before they will submit without question, neither of which we have the time for. All that remains is iron-fisted, rigorous discipline."

"I know your theories about war, Father. We all do. But I am not sure that even firm discipline will suffice to form them into a cohesive unit."

Hoping to avoid another rush of pain, Octavius returned to his seat and said, "Then they must be used to tire the enemy and exhaust their ammunitions."

Consternation painted Aithen's face. Harlion and Kendor had an expression that simply said that they did not look forward to doing what they knew must be done, and Irania remained unreadable, only glancing at the others to study *their* reactions.

"Father, you can't be serious!"

"I am. It is the only way. Every aspect of an army's logistics, and tactical and strategic operations is as important as the rest and cannot be entrusted to undisciplined men. The only place we can use them, then—for we do need them—is at the front, with the regulars behind them and to their sides, and the enemy before them."

When Aithen shook his head in alarm, Harlion made to reply but Kendor preempted him. Aithen spotted the older man's frustrated reaction, and the guilty turn of lips on Kendor as he replied, "The king is right, my prince." The newly appointed high captain looked toward his predecessor before adding, "I am certain Harlion knows it too; if the recruits cannot be trusted, the front is where they must be put, or we risk not only losing *them*, but also endangering the rest of the force."

Aithen's shoulders sagged, seeing that his old advisor made no objection. Finding no other arguments to challenge his father, the prince stepped back in a sign of acceptance, but not without glancing at his mentor with unsaid things.

The king was not blind to his son's obvious unease, but he had a goal for this meeting, and he would need to worry about

Aithen and Harlion later. He smacked his tongue and said, "Now that we are agreed on this, I would like to move onto another topic."

All imagined what the topic was, and they prepared for another unpleasant discussion.

"Prefect, how goes it with the assassins? Have you learned anything of import yet?"

Unused to being addressed by that title, it took Harlion a moment to respond. When he did, he did so with a sorry frown and a gloomy tone, a tone he had had since his heart seized while chasing a would-be assassin at the fair that summer. "We have, Sire. It has not been easy, but we have finally been able to draw some information from our prisoner: The assassins are directed from Kartak."

"Kartak. Of course! And who leads this band?"

Harlion gave an embarrassed shrug.

"Have you debriefed Toras about his scouting missions there? I asked him to surveil the area during his patrolling tours."

Harlion nodded and indicated that though the prince's information confirmed the presence of a nest of assassins in the town, it did not point to a leader.

"And I suppose there is still no way to send spies into the town?"

"No, Sire. Kartak is a dangerous place for the Unsensing. But perhaps the Sisterhood has found a solution using some…artificial means of spying on the vermin."

Octavius said, "*Artificial* means?"

Irania responded with surprising hesitancy, "Yes, Sire. Praefecta Saara, working with Kelysia Lux Baiula, has recently completed the development of a device which allows us to hear things from a distance without using the Bind. Two Sisters," Irania paused briefly, "two Sisters were sent to install the device in a tavern in Kartak."

Octavius's eyes initially widened with pleasure—scientific advances had always excited him—but he had detected the hesitation in his advisor's voice, and he asked the reason for it.

The delay in the Purple Sash's response filled the room with sudden tension and apprehension. Irania tried to avert Mitsuko's gaze as she answered, "One of the Sisters who installed the device was murdered yesterday."

The statement shocked and muted everyone. Mitsuko's normally smooth and equanimous expression took on a ghostly appearance. Kendor broke the deathly silence with a disbelieving curse, Harlion regarded the Lux Baiula with blinking eyes, and the prince and king looked at each other with sinking feelings.

Octavius said, "How is this possible, Irania? How did it happen? Who was murdered?"

"It was Gina Lux Baiula, a young Yellow Sash. She was listening to the spy device when she was killed. There were no witnesses. But the motive is obvious."

Octavius continued, as if speaking to himself, "I am sorry for your loss. But this is exactly what we suspected might happen; the enemy has begun infiltrating our institutions, and we are still fumbling for solutions."

No one offered a reply.

Octavius looked at the Lux Baiula, "Is the device still functional? If it is, when do you think we will start receiving information from it, Irania?"

Irania appreciated the return to business and said, "It appears it still is, Sire. Though there is the possibility that its twin in Kartak will be discovered soon, given…the murder."

Octavius made some inaudible imprecations then stood from his chair. The plant's leaves unclicked their hooks again, and the branches followed the heat of the body that had been sitting on it. The branches stopped moving when the plant no longer felt any heat above it, and the leaves reknit themselves to each other with more clicking sounds as the plant returned to its default position.

The king rubbed the contractile lead of his vest with a downward motion, to stop the massaging effect, then paced as his advisors watched anxiously. The king's face soon relaxed again, and Aithen sighed silently.

Octavius said, "Let us hope Urbs Lucis uncovers the traitor quickly, Irania. Now, on to something else. As you know, tonight, Mitsuko and I are going to enter the Bind to meet Marcus and…" the name of the former pariah still made the Sisters' skin crawl and Octavius noticed a barely perceptible turning of the lips on their faces which caused him to pause and stare at them, "…and the Zebulonian Lub Methor. The Magna Mater and Lusk Methrim will also join us. Given that both the Order and the Crown will be sending warriors to assist in the Zebulonian revolt, it is time Krystiana met with the rebels' representative. As for Master Methrim, it is time he met the other Zebulonian in this equation." When Mitsuko's nares flared as if she had smelled something unpleasant, Octavius said, "Do you disagree with this too, Mitsuko?"

"Pardon, Sire. But Master Methrim, I simply find him unsettling, always, and I am not certain I would trust him in your place."

"Well, that may be so, Lux Baiula, but he was released by your colleagues to practice as a medic for the Royal Guard as well as to serve me as an informer. And I, myself, have never been bothered by him. Perhaps, as Elyana has suggested many times, it is only his unusual vibrations which disturb many of you. And aren't there two other Zebulonian Alterintrants now in Urbs Lucis? Two women? I am certain you can compare his vibrations with theirs, and you might find that they are similar."

"I assume our Sisters in Urbs Lucis have done so, Sire. But I do not know. Perhaps Irania does."

The king's advisor shook her head.

"Then find out."

If the king's minder resented his curt attitude, she did not show it, but her words carried her feelings just the same, "It is also my duty to protect you, Sire. That is the reason for my warning."

"Yes…yes, it is everyone's duty to protect me. But the result is rather a feeling of imprisonment."

Aithen started to interject, his voice filled with unhidden indignation and annoyance, "Father—"

Octavius sighed loudly as he said, "Yes. I know what you are going to say, Aithen. And I understand the necessity of it all. It is just…I wish it were *not* necessary." When others started objecting, Octavius put his hands up and added, "Do not misunderstand me; I accept all the security measures. But the feeling of it all is nevertheless one of burden."

When Aithen stood back, having heard the resignation in the king's voice, Octavius finished what he had started to say, "Anyway, where was I? Ah, yes, Master Methor. He is likely to tell me that the guilds are ready for our…incursion into their nation. If he does, and given that Harlion's frumentarii have confirmed Zebula's intentions, we—that is a special contingent of our furanry and of the Sisterhood's Red Sashate—will soon be leaving for Zebulonia's capital."

III. A Zebulonian Meeting

Later that day, Mitsuko was sitting across from the king on the floor of his living room. The woman kept looking at him with a curious expression, surprised to see him sit on the floor. To his left sat Irania, who would keep a watch on him in case something happened, and Mitsuko needed her help. But Irania would not join them in the Bind; indeed, the king thought it might intimidate Lub Methor to find himself outnumbered by Lux Baiulae.

Mitsuko said, "Sire, we should connect now."

Octavius nodded.

Letting the sound of the rain carry him into trance, a rain which had just begun falling on the northern Alvinorian coast, Octavius counted down from ten to descend to a Level 2 state, while he listened for Mitsuko's heartbeat. He knew many people descended into trance without the counting—many even found it a silly practice—but the counting helped him focus, forget about the physical world, and so he continued to use the technique.

The continued beat of Mitsuko's heart helped Octavius find the woman at once. She greeted him with a welcoming, satisfied nod. He had learned to focus his senses while connecting with Darya, many decades ago, before custom had forced them to separate. Every day—and sometimes multiple times a day—they had practiced the connection. That had allowed Octavius to follow his progression into trance, from full consciousness to entry into the Bind, and to notice the slow disappearance of all stimuli, except for the sound of Darya's heartbeat—his beacon.

Presently, Mitsuko prepared to establish a mind-tie between the king and herself. Indeed, Octavius wished her to lead the search for the others in the Bind so as not to reveal his Sensing and Binding abilities. She had been pleased by his caution. Mitsuko took her time; it appeared she did not wish to lash him too aggressively with the typical, undulating ropes of light. The process *was,* nevertheless, violent.

Octavius wondered, for a moment, why a saner way to establish the tie had never been developed.

Once the king sent his final lash and Mitsuko knotted it to herself, she congratulated him and the two readied for the search.

They would meet with Krystiana and Lusk first, then seek out Marcus and his guest.

Just now, Mitsuko sent him a thought impregnated with a repugnance that made him want to sigh: *"The Magna Mater and Lusk Methrim should be here momentarily, Sire. I have called her."*

Octavius's form bobbed its head.

A time later—the king found it difficult to remain aware of the passage of time in the Bind—Krystiana and Lusk Methrim appeared in front of them.

Mitsuko's form shifted as if she wished to distance herself from the Healer. Octavius did not perceive Lusk's resentful stare, but he was becoming annoyed at seeing Mitsuko's form constantly switching position. Their mind-tie meant he could know her thoughts or feelings anytime, but he still preferred visual cues and, with her random dislocations, that would not prove easy.

Presently, Krystiana sent, *"Octavius, you are well-found."* When the king's minder reappeared next to him, Krystiana greeted her too.

The king replied similarly, but he thought he perceived preoccupation on the Magna Mater's visage. He kept the thought to himself.

Lusk now sent his own greetings to the king, *"Sire, I give you my thanks for allowing me to join you."*

"You are welcome, Master Methrim. You must realize that the reason I asked you to join us is that I will need you to go to Zebulonia with my army to act as our guide and intermediary. Be aware that the man we will be meeting with shortly, to discuss our incursion, is a member of the OLZM. His name is Lub Methor. Do you know him?"

Lusk Methrim worked hard to not roll his eyes apart in a sign of contempt, though no one understood his facial expression.

"I know him, Sire. He was a short man."

Octavius pulled his head back, unsure what the man might mean.

Krystiana intervened and said, *"He means your contact was a 'man of little importance', Sire."*

Octavius fought back a surge of annoyance. Were the day's negotiations going to be derailed already? He said, *"Things have obviously changed for him in the years since you left your country. But will you be able to work with him?"*

Fully aware of his ultimate mission, Lusk forced a nod.

But the king noticed the lack of commitment behind it and said, *"Why the hesitation, Master Methrim?"*

Lusk's form dissembled as he replied, *"Sire, I—I do not wish to return to Zebulonia."*

A sudden urge to accede to Lusk's request took the king, but he resisted the feeling, repressed it sharply and the urge vanished. However, once the feeling was gone, so was the memory of it. He was now only aware of Lusk's comment which angered him; if a man was going to ask him to make war upon someone else, he had better be ready to march with his army. Octavius said, *"It is unfortunately essential, Master Methrim. This is not negotiable. I understand your reticence, but you must understand that your own body must be put at risk here, alongside those of the Alvinorian men and women who will be engaging your former queen's forces. Still, you will be protected, and you will not be asked to sacrifice yourself for us."*

Lusk's form shifted away and back toward the group as he considered the king's words. When he finally came to a resolution, his form stabilized itself next to the others, and he said, *"Sire, I am here to serve."*

Octavius acknowledged the Zebulonian's confirmation with slanted lips then said, *"Let us join the rest of this committee then."*

Mitsuko now reached inside the king's memory to get a fix on Marcus's vibrations and took the lead in the search, to continue to mask the king's Sensing abilities.

As they moved across the spans of the ethereal place, colors bright and blinding lit the way. The group wound around one shape and then another—countless others. Each time Mitsuko perceived a vibration which seemed to match what she had sensed in the king's brain, Octavius processed it to either validate it or reject it, thereby continuously increasing Mitsuko's accuracy and speed. After the eleventh attempt, Mitsuko finally latched onto Marcu's vibrations, and after receiving the king's confirmation, she took the group toward two new forms.

One form—that of Marcus Vrol, tall and pale-skinned, dressed in his usual clothes though he could have imagined himself in fancier garments—said to Octavius, *"My king, it is good to hear you."*

Something fleeting made Octavius hesitate, but not knowing what had caused his pause, he sent, *"Likewise, Marcus."*

Lub Methor bowed to the king next and was welcomed too.

Pointing to his friend but looking at Krystiana with a measure of apprehension in his form's eyes, Octavius said, *"Magna Mater, you recognize Marcus Vrol, of course."*

The king studied Krystiana's face, her hands, her posture, for signs of acceptance or distrust. But he found these attributes more difficult to interpret in the Bind than in the Outer World. Indeed, though people's brains tended to create images of their bodies with expressions that were familiar to them, a person practiced with Roaming—such as the Magna Mater was—could shape and reshape her form at will and do so in ways Octavius was no longer familiar with and which he could no longer decipher as easily as he used to. Notwithstanding this inconvenience, he was able to pick up on some passing but likely meaningful changes in the Magna Mater's appearance. They said, *'I still resent this man's freedom though he was exonerated of the crime he was banished for all those decades ago.'* Octavius frowned inwardly and hoped Krystiana would not interfere with their task.

When Krystiana tipped her head in response to his statement, he continued his introductions. *"Master Methor, this is Magna Mater Krystiana, leader of the Order of the Sisters of the Light. Mater, this is Lub Methor, the Zebulonian thanks to whom we are all here."*

Octavius observed a welcoming smile on Krystiana's vaporous face, but it hid something. *Hmm, that smile seems to be covering a slight stretching of her lips, which, in the Outer World, would be the sign of a sarcastic sentiment. I suppose she still resents being forced into this agreement, being drawn into it without having participated in the initial negotiations.*

Lub Methor now bowed with marked diffidence. *That is not unexpected. Hopefully, Krystiana takes it for what it is: the natural aversion Zebulonian males have for female Alterintrants.*

Octavius introduced the rest of them to each other. Perhaps unsurprisingly, Master Methor eyed his compatriot with twitching lips. However, it surprised the king to see Marcus's benign appearance harden for a fleeting moment as he acknowledged Lusk. Octavius sighed inwardly again. *It will be a marvel if this meeting concludes successfully. And why does Marcus seem to resent Methrim's presence? He does not know the man.*

Shaking the questions out of his thoughts, Octavius said, *"Master Methor, you might remember Lusk Methrim, who I believe was a former member of your organization."*

"Yes, Sire, he wazze so."

"Master Methrim will accompany my army into Zebulonia, to act as an intermediary for us as we do not know your language, and I will therefore need you to work together to make this plan of ours succeed."

Lub Methor did not respond to Octavius's statement except with a stiffening of his face.

"I understand you may still resent him for leaving the OLZM some years ago, but I assure you he still has the same objectives as you: the toppling of Zebula and her Janarae."

It took several minutes of back and forth between the king and Methrim on the one hand and Marcus and Methor on the other before the latter agreed to let Lusk into their plans and to work with him as intermediary for the king's forces. Marcus had appeared to want to shrink every time he heard Lusk Methrim speak. Octavius felt overwhelmed by all the undercurrents he sensed and witnessed. But what could he do, here, now? He would have to get to the bottom of it all later.

When some sort of understanding was reached between the parties, Krystiana glanced at Octavius before saying to the Zebulonian: *"Master Methor, before Urbs Lucis sends its forces to assist your revolt, we will need to receive certain information from inside Zebula's palace."*

"I amma sorry…Magna, but—"

"You will not be asked to send anyone into the palace; as you know, we have sent two of our own people—two girls of Zebulonian descent—to obtain the information. But we would like your assistance to facilitate their entry into the queen's citadel. The king said you have contacts among her staff, and that they could hire the girls as…glass fillers?"

"Yes, that could be possible, and it is a good task for spying. But the girls, they speak fruitful Zebulonian? They are beautiful?"

Alarms chimed and sent shivers of horror through the Magna Mater's, the king's, and Mitsuko's forms.

Krystiana shouted, *"Why should they be beautiful? I will not send any girl to be violated or to be used as an object by anyone, Master Methor!"*

Methor's form vibrated and shrank from fear. He looked toward Marcus rather than toward his former countryman for an explanation of the Lux Baiula's reaction. *"Violated?"*

Marcus ground his teeth suddenly, nervously, also confused by what his guest might have meant. He did not answer Methor and instead told Krystiana that he did not understand the Zebulonian's question.

Before things worsened, Methrim put his hand up to quiet Methor and turned to Krystiana to explain for her and everyone else's benefit. He said, *"Magna Mater, do not be alarmed. The only motivation behind Master Methor's question is that the queen...prefers to be surrounded by beauty; she demands it in all her staff regardless of gender, though there are—or there had been—exceptions. Either way, the girls will not be violated, and they will they not be asked to perform or participate in any...debasing acts."*

While the tension vanished from the Alvinorians' forms, Lusk turned to his ex-compatriot to explain the misunderstanding. The man looked contrite and blushed, despite himself, for having unnerved everyone with his inexpert command of the Alvinorian language and cultural background.

Looking somewhat relieved, Krystiana said, *"I apologize for our misunderstanding, Master Methor. This simply confirms I made the right decision in sending women of Zebulonian descent on this mission and having had Master Methrim educate and prepare them for whatever identity they will need to assume once in Zebulonia. And, in answer to your questions: Master Methrim assures us that the girls have a sufficient command of High Zebulonian to not raise any suspicions. As for whether they have the proper looks, I could not say as I cannot judge what may please your queen—or what may please any Zebulonian for that matter. Perhaps Master Methrim can tell you. But I truly hope that will not be the determining factor in the success of their mission."*

Lub Methor turned to Lusk. When Methrim gave an upward nod with wide open eyes, Methor bobbed his head; it seemed to indicate relief though the manner in which he continued to eye Methrim pointed to lingering doubts toward a man who had perhaps left their organization on less than amicable terms.

Krystiana was nevertheless able to get them to cooperate and they spent a while discussing the particulars of her spies' entry into the kingdom, the capital, and finally into the palace.

Once *that* was agreed, the group discussed plans for the entry of the king's force into Zebulonia, a force which would be composed of the elite of both the Royal Guard and the Sisterhood.

Every so often, Octavius was distracted by Marcus's furtive glances toward Lusk Methrim. He let a mental sigh make its course through him, then his form zapped as a decision settled in his mind.

Noticing that the discussion was now ending, the king refocused and said, *"So, we are all agreed on the initiation of the revolt on the first of Primus."*

All nodded, Methor doing so with a wild eagerness the king had not seen in him before, while Krystiana bobbed her head resignedly.

Octavius put his hands together and nodded in his turn, but not without wishing he had brought Kendor to the meeting. In fact, he wondered why he had not asked him to come.

Swiveling toward his minder, whom he found standing far to the left, Octavius said, *"Very well, Mitsuko, I believe it is time for us to return to our bodies."* Then, privately to her, he sent, *"I will let everyone leave, but I will keep Marcus here. Pretend to leave and hide yourself when you return; I wish you to scan him. But be careful."*

Mitsuko did not make any motion indicating she and the king had exchanged thoughts just now, but something stirred in her. Her leader turned an eye in her direction, which Mitsuko did not return though she sent a thought to her to let her know all was fine. No one saw the widening and subsequent narrowing of Lusk's eyes in response to a sudden discovery.

Addressing the others, Octavius said, *"Krystiana, my thanks to you. Master Methor, we will speak again on fourteen tredecimus."*

"I am sorry, Sire, tredecimus?"

"In two months."

Methor confirmed his agreement and after the customary nods, bends, or bows, the group left the Bind, except for Marcus, whom the king retained.

Each guest's departure left behind a wind of pale yellow and green vibrations that distorted Octavius's and Marcus's forms.

When all became still again, except for the scarves of light undulating in the distance, the king said, *"Marcus, now that we are alone; will you tell me what has been bothering you?"*

Marcus blinked. *"Bothering me? No, Sire, nothing, though the culmination of all these months of work and the lifting of my banishment have left me overwhelmed, somehow."*

Octavius's form cocked an eye. Why did Marcus address him so formally, just now? *"Yes, I imagine it would. But I do sense something, and I can't—for the life of me—put my finger on it. And why were you constantly glancing at Lusk Methrim? Do you know him?"*

After a hesitation that lasted a moment or an eternity, a hesitation accented by the unexpected snapping of scarves of light in the vicinity, Marcus replied, *"You know how our senses can trick us, sometimes."* And with a forced laugh, he added, *"I think they are tricking you now…old friend."*

If Marcus's intention had been to assuage the king, his comment failed miserably. *"What are you saying, Marcus? That I am mistaken?!"*

"With respect to what you might have sensed from me during the meeting, all I can say is that you must have mistaken certain vibrations you no longer recognize for suspicious ones. I know you are a strong Sensor, Octavius, but you haven't practiced your Sensing skills in years. And as regards this Lusk Methrim, I do not know him, but I, too, was probably being misdirected by vibrations I did not recognize, though in his case, I assume they are the result of his being an Alterintrant of another race whose vibrations I never learned. He is an Alterintrant?"

Octavius nodded slowly then took a time to consider his friend's words, his own form shifting, dissolving, and reforming again. When he finally stilled himself, he said, *"I suppose you are right, Marcus. Thank you for indulging me. And I will need to resharpen my senses, as something tells me these meetings in the Bind are going to become a more frequent occurrence."*

Marcus bobbed his head, and a time passed in silence, both men looking at each other, considering.

Tired of trying to decipher other people's emotions through a body language—the language of immaterial forms—he no longer mastered, Octavius sent, *"What is it, Marcus? What is in your mind?"*

As his former officer's form started to speak, Octavius felt a wave of dizziness overtake him, and an urgent voice rang in his mind, startling him and dispelling the lightheadedness. When Mitsuko spoke in his mind again, he replied with a bark that he was fine and that he had not called her. The woman wanted to pull him out of the Bind, but he refused and ordered her to simply keep watching.

When Marcus's words seeped back into Octavius's consciousness, the man was in the middle of giving the king the answer to his question: *"...do urge you to be wary of the Order. Krystiana may be your ally, still, but she cannot vouch for all her Sisters."*

Octavius tried to force down an access of indignant anger followed by another of nausea. Both sentiments seemed to grow to disproportionate measures. He felt confused and put a vaporous hand to his forehead. Remembering, for a very brief moment, that he was connected with Mitsuko, he asked her if she was amplifying his emotions. He did not receive any answers, but the nausea had dissipated again, and when it did, he had forgotten feeling sick. He said to Marcus, without responding to his statement, *"Very well...I look forward to seeing you again soon, my friend. But I must return to my body now before a Lux Baiula comes back here to pull me out."*

"As do I, Octavius, before my guest becomes concerned. May Alba keep your path clear until we find each other again."

Octavius nodded, then his form trembled and winked out of the Bind, followed by Mitsuko's.

IV. Under the Cloak of Darkness

In a large, rock-hewn but surprisingly warm chamber at the bottom of the Temple of Aiala, Krptus listened to the scarred, wild-eyed cleric. The man was standing at the top of a high dais, looking down at his disciples, making wide gestures to accentuate his statements.

From the second to last row where he sat, Krptus could also observe the eclectic array of the city's plebe and patriciate mixed in rows regardless of rank or race. Krptus watched it all as well as the proceedings with hidden apprehension. He felt uncomfortable, and more than once he feared he might be recognized by someone who knew him to be a member of the Royal Guard. He had thought of covering his head with a cowl, but given that everyone else was bareheaded and barefaced, covering his head would probably have given them a reason to look his way, so he had decided against it. Hopefully, those seated around him—in the last rows—were all like him and would keep to themselves.

He had come here tonight at Senator Sur'Elando's invitation. The senator had heard about his spiritual conflict ahead of the attack by the Serpent on the capital, three months earlier, by way of the First Cleric. Krptus's decision to attend this meeting had not been an easy one given his position in the Guard and the respect he felt for his former commander, now Prefect Harlion, who had a deep dislike of the First Cleric. Perhaps, Harlion's reassignment had helped Krptus's decision, along with realizing that the Church of Elande, which had helped him integrate into the Furanite life, was not going to give him what he needed: a useful theology in the face of the coming troubles. The Church of Elande's prime belief was total resignation to all events and pains; but Krptus needed to believe things could be changed and harm prevented.

Moreover, the recent events combined with his repressed spirituality and his feelings of alienation which had really remained unchanged ever since he and his sister had been brought to Furan City, all this had stirred a deep desire in him to become involved in something meaningful. And it seemed the

Church of Aiala provided just that to its adherents: meaningfulness.

Presently, First Cleric Galadrin called on his expectant audience to stand. The man had understood long ago that to move a mass to action, they must hear the call from an erect position. Indeed, standing among a crowd of similarly predisposed individuals freed one's mind to express its intentions through the effects of motion on thought, which in turn reinforced one's purpose in a virtuous circle until one's mind and body were effectively one with each other and with all the members of the crowd, united in a feverish belief that could only find release through action.

Imposing and awe-inspiring in his red robe, the cleric said, "Our orb is under attack. The cause of it is clear, and I will make it known to you." Galadrin put his hand on the First's Skull which stood on a pedestal next to him. When he did, he closed his eyes and shuddered, while the skull glowed. The congregants stood in awe, awaiting they knew not what. He reopened his eyes and said, "What has angered the Founders is the lack of faith among their children, and especially among our leaders who, because of their own faithlessness, are driving people away from our creators. You know this to be true, even among your own families and circles."

"The Serpent and the awful creatures attacking our cities and villages are the direct result of this drifting. The high king and his wicked allies, the so-called Sisters of the Light who can never speak plainly because their darkness would reveal itself otherwise, as well as the Kynarians who prefer to commune with beasts rather than with their brothers and sisters, all of them have brought this strife upon us and only *we* can lift it from our shoulders, by taking action."

Galadrin paused, put his hands together and his head down, before raising it with a provocative look to say, "There are some who believe that all those who die in this war will be rewarded when the Day of Union comes, so long as they took care of their bodies and used them to do good. But tell me, will the bodies of those who fight *for* the heretics or of those who hide and let the heresy fester be worthy?"

"You know, because you are enlightened ones, that the spirit lives not only in our brains but in every particle of the body and for the body to be worthy it must be inhabited by a worthy spirit. That is the truest tenet of pansoma; a body worthy of Union is a body inhabited by a devout mind, a heretical mind can only taint the body in the eyes of the Founders, no matter its exploits."

Some in the audience shuffled uncomfortably, though the majority—to Galadrin's great satisfaction—turned to their priestly neighbors with indignant, entreating faces. The clerics set the example, beginning to intone, "Heretics and bystanders, bodies unworthy! Only the actors are worthy! Heretics and bystanders, bodies unworthy! Only the actors are worthy..." The common folk picked up the chant with tumultuous alacrity and it continued so for many long minutes.

Krptus watched and listened with guilty conscience, unable to pick up the chant though he saw the truth in it. When the First Cleric gestured for quiet to return, Krptus sat with the others, hoping that no one had noticed he had not participated.

But he was startled, and his heart lunged into a furious gallop when he heard the First Cleric's voice reach him directly: "Young man!" He looked toward the dais, then around himself as if feeling guilty for having attracted the First Cleric's attention. The Church's leader called him again, more insistently, "Young man, you seem to doubt." Krptus set his jaw, ready to fight, the soldier in him taking command.

Galadrin said, "Do not fear. You are welcome here, as all those who join us." Krptus's tension eased a bit. "I recognize you. I saw you the day of the attack by the Serpent; you were a bystander." Krptus's body tensed again. "But now you see the truth and wish to become an actor. I can see it in your eyes. Come."

Krptus turned his head left and right, looking for some indication of what was happening. Those who met his eyes simply urged him forward, motioning him to go toward the First Cleric.

So, he steeled his nerves, relaxed his hands the way one relaxes a hand around the pommel of a sword—ready to grasp and draw—, and walked down to the dais. As he descended, he felt a tingling. Something pulled his attention to the right of the chamber; it was Senator Sur'Elando. The man tipped his head encouragingly. Krptus nodded nervously.

The soldier stopped a few meters from the dais, still looking around anxiously. But why should he be so frightened? He was a soldier. And yet, he was terrified, as terrified by his inability to resist the cleric's call as by the throng which urged him on. And for what purpose?

With a benevolent wave, Galadrin invited Krptus to come stand next to him.

Krptus hesitated for as long as he could without embarrassing himself, then went. Galadrin waved him on until Krptus was but a meter from the man. The cleric reached forward and put his hand on his shoulder.

"Good man, welcome. Krptus Bentani, isn't it?"

The soldier nodded.

Hands clapped on legs to welcome him.

"Your attendance tonight is itself a true act of courage, and this alone makes you worthy of our Founders' gifts. But I can see that doubt still has a hold on you."

Krptus made no reply, but he stood by the cleric as rigidly as a man being asked to perform some vile public act.

Galadrin continued to smile benevolently as he bore into his eyes with an expression seemed to say 'This is how I will hook you'. Krptus made a weak attempt at stepping back and the First Cleric said, "I wish to give you a gift, one which is rarely given."

Krptus's eyes narrowed suspiciously.

Pointing to the First's Skull, and looking at the audience, Galadrin asked, "Do you know what this is?"

"I…I have heard of it."

"Indeed. It is the skull of the first Human put here by our great Originator herself, over twenty-four hundred years ago."

Krptus's face twitched as he wondered why the cleric was talking about the relic.

"The First's Skull is a direct link to our great Founders. It is through this that the Originator and others speak to me and to those deserving their counsel."

Again, Krptus made to recoil, but Galadrin said, "I wish you to hear her, so that you may know the truth, so that all here may know it."

The soldier's mind reeled with confusion. His face was a picture of incredulity. He turned toward the audience, hoping to find Sur'Elando, to get some confirmation that he was not being made a fool of. When he finally crossed eyes with the senator, the man nodded once, then nodded again for emphasis.

Krptus blinked, resolved himself to whatever madness he was being asked to partake in and looked back toward the cleric who motioned him to place his hand on the metallic skull.

"Krptus, hear the Originator."

And Krptus moved to do so.

Twice he slowed his hand as it neared the skull which did not look like a Human skull with its buffed metallic surface. Before he touched the glowing cranium, his eyes shut themselves instinctively while his head turned away as if fearing what might happen.

He was not smitten, nor did the crowd erupt in laughter; in fact, an eerie silence had befallen the cavernous hall. Krptus's mind was now wholly focused, and all fear seemed to have vanished. He let himself feel the smoothness of the object, smoother than any cranium he had ever touched before. He wondered for a moment—if this was truly the skull of the revered First K'Taran—why the Founders would not have graced him with Union. Did—

The silence in the hall was broken by the gasp Krptus gave when a voice tore through the quiet in his mind. Clerics and lay people alike watched with awed anticipation; their eyes filled with the expectation of a miracle.

It was with the same forbidden silence that had marked him all his life that Krptus opened his eyes, swiftly removed his hand from the skull, and turned toward Galadrin.

Suddenly, someone in the audience asked, "What did it say? What did it say?!"

Krptus gave Galadrin a helpless look. "I…I do not know the words; they used the Ancient Tongue, I think. But I…I understood."

Laypeople asked "They?"

Krptus continued, "Our Originator, she said, 'Have faith, Krptus,' then another one…it must be Him…He said, 'And if you act according to your faith, you will be saved. So, do all those who follow the faith.'"

The chamber was gripped by a growing, exploding murmur of awe and envy. Galadrin did not let the moment slip, and he said, "Welcome, son of Aiala! Brothers and sisters, let us welcome our new brother!"

Not knowing how to react, the Yerlayan stood there with a bewildered look on his face. He had never before been so excitedly welcomed anywhere, and especially not in the north where most people still looked at him with distrust and sneering frowns.

The clapping and cheering continued for a while. It ended when the First Cleric motioned for calm to return, then enjoined Krptus to take a seat in the front row.

Galadrin now invited everyone to stand and join him in prayer.

His priests started humming a fervent chant; their faces—all burnt to a greater or lesser degree—took on the peaceful look of the believers. Galadrin joined in the chanting, and his voice rang with a power not even the king could match. The laypeople, enraptured as they were, followed the First Cleric's example with frightening ardor. Krptus joined in.

This was a good night for the Church of Aiala and for Galadrin, and he thanked the gods for sending the young, lost soldier to him. That Sur'Elando had done the actual work made no difference; his Church's success was willed by the Founders, and everything followed from that.

V.   The Rain and the Hand

Ever since leaving the meeting in the Private Audience Chamber that evening, Aithen's thoughts had become more and more unsettled. In fact, he felt deeply troubled; not by the thought that he might soon be marching into Zebulonia with his soldiers, nor by the ongoing battles against that unnatural rokon—the Serpent—a creature which kept growing in strength with every encounter, and not even by thoughts of Elyana; no, what bothered him was the decline of his long-time mentor, friend, and former captain of his guard. The man, who deserved a glorious end, would now most likely die sitting behind a desk, betrayed by life's wretched turns, instead of at the head of the king's armies, defending the kingdom. It was also the thought of his *father's* weakening body, a weakening that had been all too visible during the past fourth and especially during their meeting earlier that day, despite Octavius's attempts to hide his condition. So, when he heard the sounds of the soft rain enter his chamber and cut through his troubled thoughts, Aithen put his cloak on and walked out of the palace.

The two guardians assigned to his protection this night asked where he was going as they began following him. Aithen turned his head slightly to his right and ordered them not to follow. When they grumbled, he sighed and told them he was going for a walk to clear his mind and wished to be left alone. Because no threats had ever been made against the prince's life, the soldiers acknowledged his orders, though they did so begrudgingly.

Suspecting that the men would probably stand there guarding empty apartments until his return, Aithen slowed his pace once more and told them they were welcome to join their comrades for a late evening meal. And with that, he exited the palace with renewed hurry.

When the first droplets fell on Aithen's shoulders, he paused for the briefest moment to sigh. Autumn nights were usually cool, but this night a warm spell had settled on the region, and the rain—which fell softly—felt good on his shoulders. He was annoyed again, however, when he spied Kil coming back from the stables. He saw the boy's mouth open, probably to ask where he was going. But the prince resumed his walk toward the gates with a determined motion he hoped would silence the boy, and he was glad when no one followed him.

The members of the Watch Guard, which had been doubled since the two attempts on the king, saluted their commander with quiet stomps as they saw him approach, having understood from his appearance and countenance that his mind was elsewhere.

Sergeant Telpornion, commanding the gate that night, saluted the prince and said with some concern, "My prince, do you intend to walk into *town*?"

"I do, Sergeant, please open the gate."

"My prince, a guardian should probably accompany you."

"No, Telpornion, I wish to walk alone."

"But, my prince, with the attempts against—"

"Sergeant! I will be fine."

But the portly officer insisted.

Not wishing to argue—and a part of him realizing that the man was probably right to be concerned—Aithen relented and said, "All right. Just have Piros called to accompany me. But I am walking out, so he will need to catch up. Now, please open the gate."

"Yes, my prince." And the sergeant nodded toward two guardians, who let the prince through at once, though their motions appeared to be irritatingly and intentionally slow, as if they, too, questioned his decision to leave the palace all alone. As soon as he had exited, the prince heard Telpornion bark orders at one of the guardians to go fetch Piros.

As promised, Aithen did not wait for his bodyguard and started down Triumph Lane. He put his hands in his cloak's pockets, and walked, eyes closed. He remembered often doing the same thing when he was younger, enjoying the sensation of the raindrops gently hitting his clothes, of their sound on the ground, on the plants, and on the buildings, walking with his eyes closed for as long as he could manage it. He wished he could return to those simpler times. He wished his father were younger, or that Octavius had not waited so long to—

A sound coming from behind interrupted his thoughts. He did not turn to see who was coming; he recognized the pace and the throat noises.

The soldier, who had heard about the prince's foul mood from Telpornion as well as from the two who had been guarding his chambers that night, set himself a short distance behind.

The prince thanked him silently.

Piros could sense his commander's trouble and need for space, so he followed from a few meters away, close enough that he could react in time if anyone tried to assault the prince in this wide lane, but far enough to not crowd him either.

As was typical at this hour, the restaurants were starting to fill with customers, calling them with their flickering lights to come and enjoy some food and drink, in company or alone. The more affluent shops and restaurants, such as those on Triumph Lane, lit their interiors with Living Lamps, giving them a soft and continually changing glow, whereas the rest of the facilities used blubber lamps to light their rooms with a yellowish glow. Aithen caught glimpses of the scene, absorbing the sensations that the moving silhouettes produced in him, telling stories without words behind the opaque windows of the establishments.

Presently, he increased the pressure on his eardrums, as he had also loved to do when he was a child. This dimmed the Human sounds, and it also made the sound of the rain, which continued to fall gently around him, take on a reverberating quality he loved. It soothed him, and he walked this way for a while, letting his mind wander to the calming memories of his youth. A quick, furtive movement on the left side of the street attracted his gaze, if only subconsciously, and he continued strolling this way until, a few blocks later, the shadow of an old man crossing the street pulled him out of his reverie. The man was using a stick, his old bones and muscles too weak to support him fully. This reminded Aithen of his father and Harlion, and he snorted sourly.

They say, 'May your bodies be worthy!' But do the gods and their priests even realize that most of us pass from this orb as old and weak creatures? Who is this paradise for?!

Aithen paused a moment and balled his fists in frustration. Piros arrested himself a few paces behind him and saw the prince nod to himself and then relax his fists and resume his walk, although he did so with a determined step that indicated he had decided to go somewhere.

After five more minutes of walking, Aithen turned into an alley and stopped in its shadow.

There, he put his hand into his pocket and pulled out a paint tube with which he masked the green of his eyebrows and facial hair under Piros's astonished gaze.

When he was done, Aithen said, "You need to change into some less conspicuous garb." Spying a clothing shop not far off, he nodded toward it and told Piros to go purchase a common long cloak.

That statement, however, did not appease the bodyguard, who was shaking his head furiously. Aithen stared at him a moment, his irritation growing—until he understood what was happening, calmed himself, and said, "Just do as I say, Piros, if you wish to accompany me. I promise I'm not planning anything foolish."

The man finally relented and without any more delay hurried to the clothing shop to find himself some more appropriate coverings.

Just before Piros returned, ready for whatever was afoot, another shadow crossed Aithen's gaze. This time, he looked but saw nothing. When Piros appeared next to him, he started, chuckled and chided himself.

"Did you see something, my prince?"

"No, no. It's just my mood and the rain."

Piros looked to the far end of the alley they were in, then into the street, seeing nothing except for a few couples walking hand in hand under the dim streetlamps, and a group of young men chatting and laughing at some joke one of them must have told.

After looking Piros up and down and finding his garb satisfactory, Aithen said, "All right, let's go."

And Piros followed as Aithen took several turns to enter the deeper parts of the city. His agitation increased when he saw him enter a slightly unsavory district of the capital. He hurried his step and approached Aithen. "My prince, pardon me. I do not wish to bother you, but where are we going?"

A sigh escaped the prince, but he paused long enough to answer his man's question.

"Uhh, are you sure that is a good idea, my prince?"

"I need to relax, and that is where I'm going. If you wish to protect me, I suggest you come too, though there shouldn't be anyone there you'll need to protect me from."

"But—"

"Piros! I've had a rough day and I need this. Moreover, it's not the first time I've gone there, and I can promise no one will recognize me."

Piros gave his begrudging assent then rushed to follow the prince who picked up his pace once more. As he did, Piros wondered about his commander's statement.

Aithen finally stopped in front of a dimly lit establishment with frosted windows. If he hesitated before entering The Muse, the prince did not show it, but Piros felt the hair on his back stiffen.

Aithen noticed his man's reaction and asked if he was coming. With a low growl, Piros followed his commander.

Despite the self-assurance he was trying to display to his bodyguard, Aithen opened the outside door cautiously. When a couple opened the inner door to exit, he paused despite himself. But the man and woman did not look at him or at Piros, and he continued. The unorthodox music enveloped them as soon as they crossed the third and last door. Aithen felt a soothing wave penetrate him, while it caused Piros's body to stiffen.

The place was nearly full. The door guard—a woman with a musculature that made Piros just as uneasy as the heretical music—scanned them, made a slight secretive nod toward the prince to which he responded with an even slighter nod, then demanded their blades. Piros, who had not noticed anything from his position behind the prince, was about to protest, but Aithen preempted him and handed his shortsword to the woman. Aithen then turned toward Piros with a silent stare. When the guardian surrendered his own blade, the door guard placed the weapons in a closet half-filled with other blades and let them through.

Tilting his head backward, Aithen whispered, "If you keep behaving this way, people will become suspicious. Just relax, Piros; I wish to enjoy this."

"Fine, my—fine, Sir."

With that, Aithen scanned the room for a table and chose one in the back of the establishment.

As soon as they had sat themselves, a waitress came to ask what they wished. The prince noticed Piros tensing up slightly. The guardian relaxed when the waitress called Aithen 'Master Rufius'. Aithen caught his guardian's questioning gaze but gave only a smile in return. Piros understood that he was being foolish and decided to let himself slump into the chair and to give the waitress his order after she took the prince's.

Leaning toward Piros, Aithen said, "Finally ready to enjoy the music?"

"I don't know I'd say that."

"Then the drinks and food?"

"I suppose."

"Good. But whether you like the music or not, you might be surprised to know that the singer is a former member of the Voces Creatoris."

"What? How can she—"

"She's not betraying anything…Anto." Piros stared at the prince. "That right, *Anto*. She's not betraying anything. She simply realized, as most everyone here has, that sometimes we need more than the prescribed daily chants to find some peace or to forget about the rubbish we endure every day."

Piros looked at the prince for a moment.

He's probably wondering what drove me away from the palace so late this night. Well, I don't feel like talking about it.

But Piros continued looking at him, studying him, and after they had thanked the waitress for the nectar and the food she had just brought them, he asked.

Aithen just shrugged his shoulders and said, "It's just…everything. Everything that's happened recently, in the kingdom, in Furan City, to my father and to Harlion. But I really don't want to talk about it; I just want to get it all off my mind for a while."

Piros bobbed his head slowly, picked up his mug and said, "May it warm your heart then…Master Rufius."

Piros then turned toward the stage, trying to keep an open mind as he listened. The fact was that the lyrics of this type of music, they were simply wrong; they made him feel rightly uncomfortable. And yet, as he listened, he felt his body start to sway. He stopped himself. But, after another mug of the powerful nectar and hearing the singer begin the next chant— was it even a chant, or something else?—, he started to move again, despite himself.

Presently, five men came to sit at a table near them. As unconcerned as he was this night, Aithen still stole a careful glance in their direction. That sufficed to recognize four of them as foreigners whereas one seemed to be a local, but the man had his back to them, which suited Aithen just fine as it minimized the risk he might be recognized. One of the foreigners—a large burly fellow—looked at him with a wide, brief smile before he returned his attention to his comrades who had just called the waitress. Aithen turned his head back toward the stage and let the music stretch his lips again, stretch them with a smile that one smiles when all other thoughts fade away.

Prince and guardian spent some time drinking, nibbling, listening to the more and more engrossing music, and exchanging thoughts about banal topics every so often.

Eventually, when the hour was quite late already and Aithen had totally forgotten about the glum thoughts that had brought him to The Muse that night, he yawned and told Piros he was ready to go.

Piros called the waitress over and asked for the total. He was about to pay when Aithen stopped him and gave the woman the one hundred secretes[6] they owed.

The waitress thanked them, and they left. Whispering, Piros said, "I should have suspected you'd have coins."

"I always do when I get out at night."

As they walked toward the entrance, the men who had sat at the table near them also made ready to leave, but neither the prince nor the guardian noticed, and they exited the establishment after retrieving their blades.

Aithen paused under the building's overhang to adjust his cape against the rain, which fell a little harder now.

Piros imitated him. As he fastened the last button on his cloak, Piros heard a noise coming from the side alley. He moved

---

[6] Secrete: A coin made from the colored secretions of a rare microbial species.

to go check what had caused the sound and lifted a finger when Aithen asked him what the matter was.

Looking carefully around the corner, Piros caught sight of two of the men that had sat near them. They seemed to be beating someone. He turned around urgently and hissed, "My prince, normally I would say, 'Let's call the senatorials,' but at this hour, it will take them some time to arrive and there appears to be someone taking a bad beating back there; I think we need to intervene."

"Let me see!" After peering around the corner, the prince said, 'Aren't those two—'

Piros nodded.

"Damned! I wasn't planning for this, but I am glad I only had a few drinks. Are you well enough to fight?"

Again, Piros nodded, firmly.

"Then let's go. But let's remove our cloaks; fortunately, the rain is warm tonight."

So, prince and soldier placed their cloaks on a cart, then went around the other side of the building.

Aithen whispered, "It's the same five as before. One of them is on the ground and grunting but no one's actually hitting him."

Piros gave a confused, worried look. "Perhaps we sh—"

"No, we are going."

And before Piros could object anymore, Aithen stepped into the back alley. "You there!"

The men turned toward him, though with less surprise than Aithen might have expected. But Aithen already suspected that the *beating* had been staged for the very purpose of getting him back there. The leader and his four toughs lined up across the alley while pulling their shortswords out.

Tipping his head backward, Aithen said, "I told Father a long time ago that visitors should be forced to drop off all their weapons at the Gate House. Anyway, you ready?"

"Ready or not, we're in it now, though I would have liked to have had your brother with us. No offense, my prince, but two of them could pass for Gorus and Rior."

An annoyed grunt was all Aithen gave in response. He was not a master in hand-to-hand combat, but he was nevertheless skilled, and with the training he had recently received from the Sisterhood, he was confident he could best any of these ruffians, outnumbered as they were, though he may not do it as easily as Toras would.

Aithen closed his eyes a moment, eliciting derisive laughs from their opponents. He smirked then took a deep breath, focused his mind, and waived Piros forward, his pupils fixed on their adversaries. The two stopped a few meters from the men. Aithen eyed the Furanite with unusually deep anger: How could a citizen of the capital turn on them? *The times are changing everyone.*

The lantern by the establishment's backdoor illumined Aithen's face, which the rain was smearing with the black he had used to cover his eyebrows and facial hair. Some of it was slowly flowing into the corners of his eyes and Aithen was forced to wipe them with his shirt lest the black blind him.

The leader pulled back his head derisively. "You should have thought twice before putting that on, on a night like this…Highness."

Piros hissed, "My prince, your black has come off!"

Without turning his head, Aithen said, "It's okay, Piros. I am sure these men are here for me, anyway. I noticed some movement in the shadows on our way here earlier from the palace, but my mind was elsewhere, and I dismissed it. I should not have, but as you said, we are here now."

While the thugs amused each other with all manner of vile, lude jokes about the pretty prince and his guardian, Aithen finished focusing his mind. The mounting jeers flowed over him without stirring him in any way. All emotion was locked away; only the reasoning part of himself remained, calculating, planning. He was a predator, assessing his adversaries, evaluating his options.

He said, "If you were planning to assassinate me, you will be disappointed; my friend and I will arrest those of you who remain alive after we are done here…Masters?"

"My companions and I disagree on both points, princeling; we are not your typical ruffians; we are members of the Originator's Hand and arresting any of us would mess with our plans. As for our names, they are not yours to know—with all due respect."

The men grunted in taunting agreement.

The Originator's Hand. Aithen felt a pinch in his guts. An old criminal organization that had not been heard of for decades, an organization that had threatened his father and the kingdom forty, fifty years earlier.

Not wishing to think about anything that might unsettle him ahead of a potentially deadly encounter, Aithen pushed all questions aside. He refocused just in time to see the leader's eyes narrow, and his muscles tense up for motion.

Aithen and Piros positioned themselves, placing their own shortswords forward, planting their feet as solidly as was possible on the soaked ground, and quickly surveying their surroundings to identify objects they or their opponents might use in their attacks. That done, prince and bodyguard turned their hips toward their attackers. Two against five; they should be okay. They *would* be okay.

The pack leader said to the men on his left, "You two take the guardian; I will take the green-browed princeling."

"What about us?" said the other two.

"You can join if you see me in trouble, but I don't expect I'll need you. I'll make short shrift of this foppet."

Aithen let the insult flow over him while a thin smile stretched his lips. He then took a deep breath and shot a glance at Piros who gave him a reassuring nod as he watched the colossus and the other, a quick-stabbing-looking fellow, approach him.

"Be careful," said Aithen.

"You too, my prince."

With jaws set and a rapacious gaze, Aithen advanced on his attacker.

The Furanite, excited as he was, charged the prince at once, a mad grin twisting his ruddy face.

Full of confidence, this traitor.

The prince did not change his stance, however, and limited himself to blocking the other man's opening attack to assess his strength and skills. When his arm reverberated from the man's strike, Aithen knew the ruffian had some strength in him and made the necessary adjustments to his movements.

The red-faced man pulled back, repositioned himself, then lunged forward. He quickly placed his foot behind the prince's, and was about to shove him back, to trip him. But Aithen moved first, pivoting on the man's blocking foot, and smacked him from the side.

The man growled and responded by quickening his attacks and lunging at Aithen from one side and then the other, head-on and then twirling and attacking from behind.

Where did this man learn to move like this?

Stepping back after the last attack, Aithen reconsidered his tactic while the man stretched his sword arm. Having made his decision, he rushed the man—with a feint. The man brought his blade down to block, but Aithen had already stepped sideways. He was now driving his sword toward the criminal's flank and was frustrated when his blade was caught in the man's cape. Aithen cursed.

Panting a little, the Furanite said, "Can't get through, my princeling?"

Aithen did not reply. *No, not yet, but the next time I catch your cape, you'll regret it.*

From behind Aithen, a grunt came which sounded like Piros's. Aithen stole a rapid glance toward the guardian and saw him holding his sword arm for a second then returning his attention to his attackers who lunged at him from both sides.

Worry creased Aithen's forehead. *Damn! I need to hurry.*

The pack leader took advantage of the prince's distraction to pounce on him anew. But, this time, Aithen *sensed* the movement. He spun before the man could plunge the shortsword in his back and, as he did, picked up the cape with his blade and wrapped it around the man's own weapon, making it momentarily impossible for him to attack or block. Aithen lunged forward and shoved his sword into the man's flank. The thug groaned, and Aithen shoved him back and down onto the ground.

Wasting no time, he moved to Piros's aid with a roar. The toughs turned their heads to look. One of them completed his movement to face the prince; he was the burly one. There ensued a frenetic back and forth between each pair, while the wounded leader urged his men on from afar.

Aithen was not as strong a fighter as his brother, who could bring a man down with the sheer ferocity and momentum of his strikes, but he had been trained by the best and *had* developed a level of skill and agility that surpassed most men's. Presently, facing a foe the size of a boulder, he decided to rely on his speed and stamina, and to avoid being in close contact with the man at all costs. So, he backed away, circled, and advanced to attack only when he found an opening.

The tactic was working, and Aithen was able to slash the man's right forearm twice, while avoiding all attacks and counterattacks. However, on the sixth bout, the burly thug parried Aithen's strike with such force that Aithen yelped and lost his sword. His arm, throbbing with pain, distracted him; he grabbed it and groaned a moment longer while trying to squeeze the pain out of it. He was forced to let go and scramble for his blade when his opponent advanced on him with a wild grin. Just before the goon pounced on him, Aithen dove left, grabbed his blade despite the throbbing ache, stood, and gave the man another cut with an angry yowl.

The colossus cried and Aithen felt he might finally get the upper hand when he sensed a presence behind himself. But with his opponent roaring and coming at him again, he ignored the feeling. Not a moment later, his spine shrilled with alarm, and he felt compelled to turn and look; he tried to side-step the colossus as he did so, but it was too late. The man punched him backward, and one of the fellows that had been standing aside—an ugly-looking one—slammed a post into his lower back. The blow sent Aithen forward and flat on his face.

Piros, himself, had succeeded in disabling his opponent—the fast and skinny one. When he heard the prince's groan, he looked around to find the large man right there behind him. The man struck him and Piros fell to the ground, exhaling hard.

The leader yelled to the colossus and to the howler-faced man who had struck Aithen, "You need to finish the princeling. Now!"

"Why? I thought we—"

"Finish him!"

The ugly-faced man picked up his post again and approached the prince to do as ordered.

The man had raised his arm as far as it could go and was preparing to bring it down to impale the prince. But, with a supreme effort, Aithen stretched for his sword, grabbed it, turned on his back, and drove the blade into the man's belly to rip it open. No scream left the thug—his mind, dulled by shock, did not register the pain—though the confused rictus on his face showed a measure of understanding.

As the man collapsed, blood and filth splattered the prince, who backed away—toward the giant. Fortunately for him, his senses were fully alert this time and he no longer ignored them. He sensed the enraged burly thug's decision to complete the job, himself, before the man even moved a leg. Aithen knew he needed to get up, but his lower back and chest still hurt like he had been rammed by a belwohr. Nevertheless, he found the strength to focus all his thoughts on his body, his arm, his hand, the sword in his hand, and from there onto the approaching assassin. The prince clenched his gut and got to his feet with a violent, powerful growl to help his body's motion, whirled around, and transpierced the man with a ferocious, frustrated, and vindictive yell.

Loud splashes caught Aithen's attention while the group's leader yelled at the last of his accomplices—a mouse of a man, the one who had pretended to be on the ground earlier—to join the battle. But it was obvious the man was no fighter.

The prince was upon the Furanite before the man could move, his weapon pressed on the man's neck. The Furanite stayed where he was, unwilling to test the prince's resolve.

Just then, the horn of the senatorials ripped through the alley as blinding cone lights illuminated the area; Aithen felt like laughing, especially when he heard the sergeant's shout: "Everyone! Drop your weapons."

It did not take too long for the sergeant to recognize the prince and utter a shocked curse. While the senatorials arrested the ruffians, Aithen asked that someone look in on his guardian and then proceeded to explain what had happened. As he did, a door opened on the side of the building. Aithen turned his head and saw the bar owner. The man had a look of confused relief on his face. Obviously, someone had told him there was a fight in the back alley, and he had sent for the senatorials. But he had not known who the poor wretches were that were being attacked. The prince gave him a thankful nod and returned his attention to the sergeant, who was still questioning him about his attackers while also cursing the gods for such mad business, right here in the capital, and asking why the prince was there in the first place.

Aithen did not answer the last question but swept the blood-soaked ground with an angry glare, which turned hateful when he came upon the thugs' leader and the mouse-faced man. He said, "You may take those two into custody. But deliver them to the Frumentariat; Prefect Harlion and his men will take care of the interrogation. The others can go to the morgue."

With a pinched face, the commander replied, "Certainly, my prince."

Aithen thanked the man, then raised his voice to ask a young senatorial, "How is my guardian?"

"He lives, my prince," replied the man as he helped Piros stand up.

Aithen ran to his bodyguard, elated.

The man looked embarrassed and slightly upset.

"Ha! You are a proud man, Piros, to make that face now. I realize you would have preferred to die for me, but I rather prefer you didn't."

When Piros shook his head and croaked a laugh, the others joined in. The laughter felt good to Aithen, and for a moment he forgot about the assassination attempt on him—the first. Would there be others? Would he survive them all, as his father had—to date?

Aithen asked if the senatorials had come with vorans or a transport, to which the sergeant replied they had their vorans on the street nearby. The prince requested one for himself and another for Piros after ascertaining his guardian could ride, and left the senatorials to clean up and take care of the prisoners and the bodies.

VI. Planning

Lusk was in trance in the middle of his Contemplation Room. His body was not as tense, today, as it had been when he met with Noctiferus, though his rigidity indicated he was not roaming the Bind for pleasure. He was meeting with the Umbra and the Serpent to update them on his encounter with the king. The two were in fact together: The Serpent was apparently flying the Umbra to the Yeltchek.

"Bene egisti, Vaedrin, et praemium huius tibi erit. Quomodo iam eum capiamus? An eum, si non ceperimus, quomodo amoveamus?"[7]

Lusk admitted that he had yet to devise a plan to eliminate the king.

The Serpent suggested that perhaps *he* could attack the king using his rokons, which the Umbra quickly dismissed.

"What about the young man you were supposed to have turned at court? Is he ready?"

"I am sorry, Umbra, I would not want to rely on him yet with such an important mission. But..."

"But...?!"

Lusk replied, *"Perhaps we can use a two-pronged approach to ensure the king does not escape us."*

The Umbra's form cocked a curious eye.

"We could lure the king into the Bind and attack him here, while my Convert springs a simultaneous trap on the king himself in the physical realm."

---

[7] You have done well, Vaedrin, and you will be rewarded for this. Now, how do we capture him, and if not capture him, eliminate him?

A smile seemed to begin to pull the Umbra's lips apart, but he did not respond and waited for more.

"I believe I can arrange another meeting with him; his Lux Baiula—a minder—is certain to accompany him, but the Alis Domini, myself, and two or three of the best from Kartak, along with my Convert acting in concert with us, will have no trouble overcoming them."

"Hmm, I like the plan. But I do not wish you to reveal yourself yet; you still have much work to do. The Alis Domini can have Marcus arrange the encounter."

The statement irritated Lusk, and he sighed before nodding.

"It is thanks to the Alis Domini that the other Luxor is now in our power."

Lusk looked perplexed.

The Umbra said with slight annoyance, *"Quid est, Vaedrin?"*[8]

"Please forgive me, Umbra, but why do you call them Luxori? From what I've learned since my arrival in Urbs Lucis, the last of them succumbed centuries ago to some epidemic. The king and the other may be Alterintrants, but they cannot be Luxori."

"You are mistaken, Vaedrin. These two are Luxori. I do not know how their ancestors escaped death, but they did, and these two are powerful, though they may not know it. With Marcus in our control, the other's capture is now more certain."

"My apologies, Umbra. Perhaps you are right." Lusk paused, then with unusual confidence and willingness to share in the presence of his tormentors, he added, *"In fact, you must be right. Near the end of our meeting earlier, I sensed a Sending between the king and his minder which was hidden in a manner too intricate to be performed by a simple Sensor."*

---

[8] What is it, Vaedrin?

The Umbra found the forthright statement curious and cocked an eye, but said, *"That is useful information, Vaedrin, as it adds to our convictions, and you are forgiven."*

A wind composed of a million tendrils of blue and yellow light blew past Lusk as the Umbra added, *"Please ensure that your Convert does not fail us; you would not enjoy reporting on another failure. And I urge you to accelerate the turning of other Humans within the Alvinorian court; your slow progress in this regard is disappointing. Do not force me to find you a replacement; the consequences for you and your birth mother would be most unpleasant."*

The words penetrated Lusk in a way no physical entity or object could; they invaded his mind then took hold of his body entirely and shook him violently. His form darkened and trembled even as the Umbra disappeared and the Serpent followed, grinning.

When he returned to his body, Lusk found himself looking at an image he hated in the mirror hanging on the wall of his Contemplation Room. He cursed and yelled at it and cursed more when his eyes fell upon the symbol which marked his forehead. All his life, he had been someone else's pawn, to do with as they pleased regardless of his skills or powers. The mark at the center of his forehead—the left part of it—was a sign that despite being a slave, he had achieved much: he had been called to serve the queen. And yet, it was also a reminder—with the addition of the right stroke—of his greatest humiliation, which had come when Zebula had found him enlaced with her lover; he had learned some time later that the Umbra had had his hand in the affair which entrapped him, but it was too late, and the Umbra had been his only means of escape from eternal humiliation. Remembering all this, he wished only to die. But he had to live and do what he must—to keep his mother safe, the only thing he had been able to keep safe and had some power to continue to keep safe.

VII. The Setup

"Mitsuko Lux Baiula, thank you for meeting with me."

Mitsuko's vaporous form watched the man's own projected shape with narrow slits. *"Why did you wish to meet with me, Master Vrol?"*

"I would like a private audience with the king. It is regarding the discussion we had today."

Mitsuko studied the man's features to try and determine the truth of his motives, but in the Bind, an insecure or nervous person could often appear quite the opposite, so she did not expect much from this examination. She probed for stray emotions and thoughts but sensed nothing. Still, she was not going to give him what he wanted so easily. She called upon her Other Sense and said, *"Master Vrol, what is this you wish to discuss with the high king?"*

Mitsuko was vexed when, after a brief moment during which he seemed to be about to answer, Marcus replied that he preferred to discuss things with the king directly. She insisted with all the cunning she could muster, cunning which pierced through any Nonsensor's resistance. But Marcus Vrol was an Alterintrant, and she gave up, thinking nothing of it. *"Very well, I will arrange this meeting...at Five after Highsun tomorrow."*

"Thank you, Lux Baiula."

Mitsuko did not make any verbal replies or gestures in response. Her mind seemed to be somehow...disconnected and she left the Bind with only the awareness of what she had just agreed to.

As for Marcus, he remained a while, and his form shifted between satisfaction and an urge to vomit, until he was called back to his body, in Kartak.

VIII.   Internalization

In her Urbs Lucis apartment, Kita Lux Baiula sat in silence on a plush green carpet. She found green calming, quieting; it helped her meditation.

Kita was performing the Memory Ritual to learn and organize all the memories she had gotten from Gina Lux Baiula.

The ritual was an essential component of Memory Transfer, key to retaining the memories in all their detail, in an organized and orderly state, and it was critical to maintaining the separation between the Receiver's memories and the transferred ones. The practice required fourthly meditations during which the Receiver called to her consciousness one memory after another and worked to tie together all its parts: visual, auditory, olfactory, tactile, factual, and emotional—as many components as existed for each remembrance. Those she had received from Gina's mind were incomplete and Kita found that the incompleteness led to fractured memories, with only the most intense bits remaining without any abatement.

Tonight, Kita had been at it for nearly three hours already, and her brain was feeling the strain of it. Non-receivers often made comments about how exciting it must be to receive all the facts another might record in their memories over the course of the years. But they did not realize that to the *rememberer*, even insipid events could be overwhelming given that they often carried with them intense feelings, emotions, and sensations, let alone when the memories were those of traumatic events. And the most vivid of Gina's memories were those of her final moments.

The last one Kita recalled was precisely one of them. She saw a…a woman approaching, a woman she knew…she should recognize…but she couldn't see her face…only her Red Sash, bright and vivid and violent. The woman put her hand on Gina's mouth, shutting it before a scream could escape. Kita's chest compressed and her heart seized as Gina's must have done. It was, to Kita, as if she were, herself, seeing her own murderer approaching and killing her.

Her internal voice, emanating from a deep, calm place she had forgotten existed, said, *"Kita, these are not your memories. Kita, let go of them."*

When Kita finally let go, she crumpled where she sat, drenched and limp.

PERMANERE USQUE AD FINEM

4. FRUSTRATIONS

I. Interrogation

In an infrequently occupied room of the Frumentariat, the high prince, the commander of the kingdom's Secret Police, and Frumentarius Elnon waited for another to arrive to begin the interrogation of the captured men. Aithen had considered retiring for the night, but only for a fraction of a second. He could not delay the questioning of the prisoners, and he had therefore sent Piros to rouse Harlion who had, in turn, sent for Frumentarius Elnon.

Elnon—a short, thin, middle-aged man with a wide mustache adorning a hard face—had replaced Parok, who had gone missing after the Serpent's attack on the capital, and despite all their efforts, he had still not been found, nor had any rumors about him been picked up by anyone. This still troubled and unsettled Harlion, but with everything else, he had stopped searching for his former first agent.

Of the two captives, one—the Furanite—was a trader known by the Frumentariat for his frequently suspicious dealings. The other, they did not recognize. But, however tempting it was to question the men, especially the local, Harlion had instructed his officers to refrain from doing so. The Frumentarii would normally have conducted the interrogation because the investigation of crimes on the person of patricians was one of their charges, as was the gathering of information on trouble-brewers across the kingdom. But, because they had failed to uncover anything useful from the leader of the group that had made an attempt on the king's life a few fourths earlier, Harlion had decided that their *special questioner* would handle the interrogation of all those apprehended for crimes against any member of the court in the future. This rankled his men, but only slightly; it appeared they were used to transferring certain cases to whomever it was Aithen and the others were now waiting for.

Aithen was having some difficulty standing still, now that the combat was over. He wanted to strike the assassins until they gave up the names of their leader and of the rest of their comrades; he wanted to ask them about *The Originator's Hand*. Harlion, upon hearing the name, became deeply worried. The organization was supposed to have been extinguished. Was this a new organization that had simply chosen to take the name of the former, an organization that had wreaked havoc across the kingdom?

Harlion, ignoring his own instructions, questioned the men about it. But fifteen minutes of interrogation brought nothing but mocking responses from the leader and gibberish from the other prisoner. He would have gone in and used more direct methods to get his answers, but it would not have helped his special questioner if she came and found them incapacitated, so he abandoned his attempts and decided to wait, as frustrating as it was.

A shadow of worry passed over the prince's face now. He had quarreled with Harlion over the use of Binding skills to obtain answers from the criminals for several long minutes. But in the end, Aithen understood the need for more extreme measures following the earlier failures, the continued attempts on the king's life and now on his, and he had relented. His agreement, however, had not quieted his mind, which continued to debate the righteousness of the procedure, not because he felt it was wrong to force an answer from a criminal's mind, but because if the practice were allowed and acknowledged, it would not be long before innocents were harmed by it. Aithen gave an exasperated sigh to dismiss the frustrating line of thought.

As for Elnon, a veteran frumentarius, he stood perfectly calm and blank-faced, except for the irritation revealed by the periodic twitching of his mouth for not being allowed to question the men himself. Well, if the woman failed, he would have his turn. And she might; he had seen it happen before.

At precisely Four Ahn, a hidden door in the corner of the room opened, letting through a Sister. The woman paused when she saw who waited there, then turned to close the door, behind which a long and narrow tunnel could be glimpsed. A small gasp escaped the prince's throat. Harlion turned to him with eyes that said: *"Please understand and accept this for what it is."* Frumentarius Elnon let his sentiments show in the disdainful setting of his expression.

The Lux Baiula did not let the prince's reaction escape her. But as hard as she tried and as skilled as she was at hiding her true emotions, she could not hide her own surprise as she acknowledged the prince's presence and shot a quick glance at the prefect to ask with her hard eyes why he had brought the prince here.

Aithen thought to himself: *Elyana is not going to believe this when I tell her. It seems that many more Lux Baiulae than she and the Magna Mater—or the disgraced Natalia—have the ability to forcibly enter the minds of humanoids. How will Urbs Lucis respond to this?* Knowing that he must address the Sister, Aithen smoothed his face and said, "Laranis Lux Baiula, you must excuse my surprise, but I was not aware of Sisters taking part in the questioning of prisoners. I had assumed some rogue Alterintrant would be doing the job."

The Yellow Sash, considered by most who knew her a frivolous madcap, pulled herself straighter though she was already standing straight like a stick, and said, "Indeed."

Aithen kept himself from shaking his head in response to the woman's reply which, though it was even more obscure than most answers Sisters gave, told the prince that these proceedings were nothing new to the woman. He said to her, just to have her speak the words, though he suspected the answer, "You intend to question these two today, but you have questioned others before?" *There! Try to slip out of this one.*

And indeed, Aithen's statement-question caused the Lux Baiula some trouble, seeing her delayed response.

Aithen observed her as she prepared to answer his question. It seemed she was conflicted or...or resentful, yes, resentful.

"I am here to question these men at the high captain's—" Laranis stopped herself when she noticed the looks of discomfort at the mention of the man's former title. She resumed, saying, "At Prefect Harlion's request. And yes, I have done this before, High Prince, though not so frequently as you might think."

Aithen crossed his hands and tapped his thumbs nervously as he decided whether he could or should allow this interrogation to be carried out. He continued tapping his fingers for a while, his head down but glancing at his mentor every so often, torn by the conflict in him. Mind violation was prohibited, it was against the law. And yet, his own mentor, the commander of the king's Secret Police had apparently permitted the use of the procedure on his prisoners for, for how long? For years? *How can I allow this? I embarrassed Father in front of his Guard about violating his would-be assassin's mind to protect himself, and now I am going to allow this???* The others watched him with clear apprehension—even the Lux Baiula. *I suppose I am.* When Aithen snorted, Harlion and Laranis let out silent sighs. Now, he nodded his head several times, slowly, then raised it to look at the others and said, "All right. How do we proceed, then?"

Laranis Lux Baiula wasted no time thanking the prince for his decision. Instead, she asked him what he had heard the prisoners say, if anything, as accurately as he could remember it. When she heard the name of the ancient criminal organization she blinked and swallowed. Then, looking at all three men, she asked, "What is it that you wish to know from the prisoners?"

Harlion was the first to respond. Pointing to the Furanite, he said with real venom in his voice, "I want to know who gives Hecrus Fioran his orders. Master Fioran is one we have often investigated for shady financial dealings and now we catch him trying to assassinate the prince."

Turning away from the local, who looked their way with a sneering smirk, he continued, "I want to know who the foreigner is; and I want to know if they planned to attack the king again after murdering the prince. And I don't want any *Noctiferus made us do it.*"

The prince and the frumentarius showed their agreement, the prince doing so reluctantly and the officer with the confidence of habit. They did not add any request.

Laranis moved to go to the other side of the thick, distorting glass from where captives and interrogator could see and hear each other clearly.

Aithen said urgently, "Lux Baiula, is it safe for you to show yourself?"

"I wish them to see me. But do not worry; they will not remember me."

The Sister entered the visiting section.

The Furanite turned an ugly grimace in her direction as she arranged the chair and sat herself. His accomplice, on the other hand, looked like he wanted to back away from her, but he was already standing against the wall.

Good, that one should be easy to break.

Laranis Lux Baiula now weighed both men equally, her expression unreadable. That seemed to unsettle the leader, who decided to spit in her direction. The other, unable to distance himself anymore, started clenching his fists.

She did not see the prince's apprehension, nor did she see the debate occurring in him about whether to stop the proceedings or not.

Seeing the Lux Baiula sit down and close her eyes, Hecrus Fioran shook his head, partly confused, partly worried. He had never seen one of the witches do what they did. Before long, he put his hand to his head, pressing his forehead, and started yelling at someone inside his mind. In a brief semi-lucid spell, he asked his accomplice what was going on, but the Breminese had fallen to his knees and lay slumped sideways, unconscious.

Aithen continued watching and turning uncomfortable glances toward Harlion, who gave no sign of discomfort.

Something unseen now caused the gang leader to stumble backward and stiffen, his eyes showing yellowed whites as they turned inward.

Laranis sent, *"I am here to get the answers to some questions; you may give them willingly and without trauma or resist and force me to drag the answers out of you."*

The man chose to resist, and he screamed, but no sound exited his throat; he was trapped in his own mind with only a fiery figure for audience.

The Sister exhaled in disappointment and began her search. She examined Hecrus Fioran's long-term memory centers as well as his recent memory, one cluster at a time, to find the answer to the captain's questions. The process did not cause the man any pain, but the releasing of memories into his consciousness against his will caused him tremendous confusion, fright, uncontrolled sadness, and even terror. Some memories were painful, others embarrassing, while others yet roused his anger. Few were the happy memories elicited by Laranis's probing, and even those did not improve the man's perception of the experience.

Every so often, the Yellow Sash paused to clear her mind of her target's emotions, lest they overwhelm her.

Presently, the prisoner began to shout out loud, like a mad man, asking what was happening to him.

Only the slightest flutter of her chest indicated that Laranis was disturbed by the man's vocalization; she was losing control of him. She hoped no one would notice the tension on her face. *I don't understand why I can't keep him paralyzed. He must have some malfunctioning neurotransmitters or some mutated receptors. I need to try something else...*

And though Hecrus Fioran's eyes were still rolled backward—indicating that he was still caught in some mental jail—he continued shouting, first asking his tormentor to desist, then asking for forgiveness, until he finally collapsed with the smallest murmur of a sob.

Aithen had watched all this with increasingly agitated hands, his eyes riveted on the unmoving Lux Baiula and the tormented thug. What had she done to him? If Hecrus Fioran had not tried to kill him—and who knew whom else he might have been commanded to attack next—his father for sure, since the first two attempts had failed—Aithen would have ordered the Lux Baiula to end her probing when the man first shook him with his cries.

Giving the others sidelong glances, he thought: *They've seen her do this before. That's why they're just standing here, blank-faced. Damn the Founders for forcing the worst on us!*

A confused, groggy voice grabbed the prince's attention; the mousy thug was speaking. It appeared the Lux Baiula had decided to let go of Fioran for a bit, to work on his accomplice instead.

"N…no…no, don't do that!"

The man went on for a bit, protesting whatever it was that he thought Laranis was doing to him, until his objections turned into acceptance and finally into welcoming demands for more. He then turned silent, sitting against the wall, his legs flat on the ground, his mid-section twitching—obscenely?—every so often, motions which were accompanied by crude, though—fortunately—barely audible whimpers.

Aithen could only imagine what was happening, and he gave Harlion a look of utter disgust. However, the old man simply shrugged his shoulders. Frumentarius Elnon, on the other hand, seemed to envy the criminal, if the little upturned corner of his lips was any indication. Aithen mumbled a curse, and—unwilling to continue watching the prisoner's reactions to whatever the Lux Baiula was doing to him—he went to sit along the back side of the room, where he waited, impatiently, for the interrogation to end. But he could not help himself from wondering just what the Lux Baiula might be doing and why.

Some time later, too long for Aithen, he heard Harlion speak: the Lux Baiula was done.

Aithen rose and rejoined the others. The Lux Baiula was leaning forward, with her elbows on her legs and her forehead against her hands; she looked exhausted. After a moment, she wiped her brow with the sleeve of her yellow robe, then peeked in his direction.

Aithen wanted to assault the woman with questions about the justification for such methods…until he saw the expression of deep revulsion and self-reproval on her face.

Understanding what the prince must be thinking, she said with a tight, exhausted voice, "Do not judge me, High Prince, for doing what you watched me do. And do not think I enjoy it any more than you do. In fact, I hate it because what I do in service to the stability of your father's kingdom—of our nation—means that my death—when it comes—will be the death of all that I am: the things I know, the things I've learned and experienced—all the things in my mind—will be lost forever as I cannot let anyone transfer my memories. I will only live on as a visual or auditory memory if anyone remembers me at all."

Aithen swallowed and could not speak a word until he forced himself to say, "I suppose you do it because of necessity, as we do the things we do, too. I understand."

"Necessity does not make a thing right, my prince. But neither does the thing's wrongfulness obviate the need to use it."

There followed an uncomfortable, silent minute which was broken by Frumentarius Elnon, who asked Laranis Lux Baiula what she had learned.

"I have your answers, and you will not like them."

II.   In the Lucian Atheneum

When she woke that morning, Elyana had felt a horrible knot in her stomach, and neither the wonderful breakfast Claren had brought to comfort her—the girl had probably heard the moans and groans her nightmares had caused her—nor the warm golden rays of the Red sun had loosened it. So, after swallowing the last of her bitter, she went to the Atheneum—the Lucian library—, which she had longed to visit anyway.

Entering the structure filled her at once with an overwhelming sense of comfort and peace; it was like magic. She sighed in silence—a slow, comfortable sigh—then nodded in response to the surprised but welcoming gestures she received from the staff.

For as long as she could remember, Elyana had never figured out why a library should have such a visceral effect on people, more than one's home even, and she wondered again about it just now.

As she gazed at the bookwalls that were up, the name of a book, suggested by Procta Lux Baiula, flashed in her mind. This time, Elyana's sigh was of a different sort; of course, she was glad she carried the memories of other Sisters, but it did get annoying when one didn't have full command of one's own thoughts, and the memories were becoming more and more insistent as the threat of a new Dark Battle coalesced into an ever more tangible reality. Still, Elyana nodded to herself and walked over to the fourth catalogue post, checked its entries to verify the accuracy of her Transferred Memory's *memory*, and—having confirmed it—pressed her hand on the call disk.

The floor in front of her opened quietly and a wall filled with old volumes rose quietly from the ground. The mechanism had been devised by ancient Sisters to keep the Order's written knowledge safe. After retrieving the book she was looking for, Elyana pushed the call disk again and the wall receded into the ground again, just as quietly as it had come up. She then looked around for an available reading table, and, having found it, walked over to it.

After sitting the book on the vertical[9], she tapped her lips for a while. She read the title: *De Permanentia cognitionis*[10]. *Why did you want me to read this, Procta?* Before the memory could answer, thoughts of the recent events in Urbs Lucis resurfaced in Elyana's mind as abruptly as unwelcome guests.

The Manu Dextra sat back and shook her head. Why did she think she could come here and find peace for any length of time? Gina Lux Baiula's murder still troubled her, as did the fact that they had not been able to identify the killer. Elyana even caught herself wondering whether she might have done it. *Why not*, she thought, if the turning of someone creates some sort of split

---

[9] Vertical: A stand used to hold books to prevent them from being damaged by ink or by the pointed hollows people used to take notes.

[10] Permanentiam cognitionis: The permanence of knowledge.

personality. She laughed it off, but not before berating herself for a fear which would surely paralyze the entire Sisterhood if it were to spread.

Her questioning by the Light's Assembly at the end of the long day implanting the Monitor into hundreds of Sisters for her use of Mind Violation to bring down a man—that was how Larca had worded the charge—had not helped her sleep either, and she felt mentally exhausted.

Fortunately for her, Elyana had avoided the worst, as had the king, and she had the quiet but honorable and rational Praefecta consuasores to thank for it. Ramela's arguments about the inadequacy of their rules in times of war had placated Bilena, Saara, and even Larca. Ramela had made one mistake, however, although she had made it with Krystiana's prior consent: Aware that Larca and Bilena still questioned Krystiana's decision to enter the Bind in search of the Serpent with intent to enter its mind a few months back, she had used the opportunity presented by the formal gathering of the Light's Assembly to make the same argument in favor of discharging the Magna Mater of any malfeasance in the matter. The questioning that had ensued had sickened Elyana, who could not believe her praefecta would find it wise to offer their leader to be interrogated, regardless of Krystiana's accord. And though the Assembly had formally accepted the Magna Mater's transgression after that horrid hour, Elyana wasn't sure whether to be relieved or not, because the mere fact that Krystiana's leadership had been questioned had weakened it as truly as if they had censured her; this now pained and frightened Elyana, who wondered when the first refusal of a command would arrive. She should have searched for the Serpent on her own. True, it had been Krystiana's idea, but Elyana should have argued to go alone...*and died at the hands of the Serpent, with the prince inside her mind?* No. They had done what needed to be done. And yet...

The Manu Dextra was shaken out of her grim thoughts by a woman she could not see and who cleared her throat in annoyance at the sound of the pointed hollow Elyana had grabbed from the table unawares and had been tapping on the reading table.

Elyana put the writing instrument back down and thought: *I really should try to enjoy the little time I have to visit the library. Otherwise, what's the point?* And she went to fetch another book—a tragicomedy she had always wanted to read—, placed it next to the other on the vertical, and immersed herself in it.

III. Back at the Mansion

When Harlion's mansion appeared through the right windowpane of the high prince's coach, the man—who had slouched on his seat the entire time, silent and brooding—sat up to look at his house, one of the most remarkable ones on Ministerial Road. It was not the most imposing house, but it was of a superb design with its curves combined skillfully with straight lines, the beautiful stone, the exquisite gardens surrounding it, and the wonderfully worked iron enclosing the entire property.

He wondered if it would all still be standing there at the end of this war against gods and beasts. Looking at it, he was reminded of his progress in the king's household, which he had joined thirty and more years before. He had climbed the ladder rather quickly given his background, surprising many. But he had always had a keen mind, able to see what wished to be hidden; it was this trait which had gained him his command of the Secret Police—the Frumentarii—and then the high captainship of the Royal Guard.

He had enjoyed heading the Guard, had enjoyed helping the king solidify his rule with wise determination and parsimony.

He had also loved training and educating the high prince, who certainly was a healthy, intelligent, and decent Human being who would someday be a good leader, too.

Harlion turned his head to look at the prince, but as if from a far-away place. He remembered now that there *had* been a time when he had hated the young prince, when the king had assigned him to command the Guard, which had demoted Harlion to act as the prince's first officer. However, those sentiments had quickly vanished, for, indeed, the prince had not only continued to rely on him and on his judgment just as the king had, but he had also retained a rare level-headedness despite his newfound authority. Would he remain so as the war approached the kingdom's doorstep and unfurled upon it to swallow everything? He hoped so, though he wondered if Aithen's equanimity was not beginning to fray in the face of all that was assailing him and his fam—

"High—Harlion, we have arrived. We've actually 'been' arrived for a minute already."

Harlion was not sure he had heard Aithen's tongue slip, but his lip did thin and stretch a little—perhaps his unconscious mind had heard—as he looked up at the prince to say, "My mind was elsewhere."

"You were thinking about the prisoners?"

"I was thinking about…family, the past, the future."

Aithen grimaced but did not press Harlion further on the topic. Instead, he said, "We will see you at the palace at Ten after Highnight? To discuss the situation with my father?"

"Yes."

"I will leave six of our best guardians here; you know them all. And remember, leave three here and take the others with you at all times from now on…at least, until we have uprooted the traitors and the threat has passed."

Harlion shook his head with an irritated expression, which he accompanied with a small growl. He then opened the coach's door, exited with a barely perceptible groan provoked by the pain in his chest, but a groan nevertheless, thanked the prince with a promise to see him and the king later, closed the door, and made his way up the steps.

Aithen sighed, slid the driver window open, and gave Mehan, one of his newest bodyguards, the order to return to the palace—slowly. Coris, a man who had unofficially acted as a personal guardian to him, like Piros, for a few years already, sat next to him. It had been decided that night that the high prince would finally have an official personal guard. The decision had jarred the prince, not because he disliked the idea, but because of what it meant.

When Aithen heard the vorans' toes resume their regular, soothing clip-clop, he pushed himself back into the cushioned seat and considered what had passed that night. As he did, the sound of the rain, resuming its slow, gentle fall, drew a long sigh from him. This was followed by a wince caused by the pain of the strike on his lower back.

My walk didn't turn out so good, and I don't feel any better than I did when I first left the palace. In fact, I feel worse, what with still making stupid mistakes, almost calling Harlion by his former title; discovering that a Sister is assisting our frumentarii in their interrogations; Laranis Lux Baiula scrutinizing me, wondering if I am going to report her to Urbs Lucis, and in every way possible except with words urging me not to do that; and finally finding out that there is at least one traitor in the palace, perhaps more.

Why does it seem like everything around me is weakening just when it needs to be the strongest? Kendor is a keen tactician, even a good strategist, and he is liked by the men, but he doesn't have the same judgment as Harlion. And yet, we did need to reduce Harlion's charge.

And then there's Father's sudden change. He used to hold himself so straight, always. Now, he often leans forward. But at least, he's finally accepted his Binding skills; perhaps they'll make up for his body's weakening. And his mind seems to be as sharp as it ever was. I hope it stays that way because…because!

At that moment, the skies above dropped a final, heavy curtain of rain. When the last drop pinged the top of the coach, a warm yellowish ray found its way into the carriage to announce the nascent morning just as the Dawn Chant broke.

Aithen had always had a split opinion about the Voces Creatoris. He knew the theory behind their organization: different vibrations produce different responses in the brain; some pleasant and others irksome, which in turn affect a person's mood. Singing voices, such as those of the Voces Creatoris, generate vibrations of the pleasant kind, and, depending on the song, could rouse, focus, or appease. The Dawn Chant was a rousing one, while the Evening Chant appeased people and readied them for the return home, to help ensure peace at their residence as well as a restorative night. Aithen wondered if the chant influenced him as it apparently did other people. But he did not wonder very long; in fact, he was certain he'd be just as he was, even without the chants. But he rarely had the occasion to experience the absence of the music, so he couldn't know for sure.

Regardless of what it was *supposed* to do, this morning's song irritated him; he was exhausted, in pain, and needed rest. So, when he arrived at the palace, he gave the shortest replies to all who greeted him, went to his chambers, told Kil to wake him before Ten, undressed, and dropped into his bed.

***

In the mansion on Ministerial Road, an aged, warm voice greeted the former captain of the Royal Guard. "Har, dear, I didn't know if you'd be back to break fast with us, but I'm glad you are, though you look troubled."

Harlion's wife was not the most beautiful woman, but she was the most kind and loving person he had ever known. She had an easy smile and a docile, even temperament, which had never ceased to surprise him with its ability to soothe him even when he didn't wish it.

"I will tell you at table, Kyla."

The woman nodded, took her husband's arm and the two walked to the small dining room where Harlion was greeted by their son.

"Good morning, Father. Will you break fast with us today?"

"I will, Octavian."

Trying to temper his sentiments, the boy said, "I am glad; we do not often get to eat with you in the morning."

Harlion and his wife had been honored by the high king who had agreed to give their son his name at the time of his birth. Harlion had hoped that the Giving would have helped open the gates of opportunity for his son and imbue him with qualities similar to the king's. And Octavian was certainly an intelligent boy, but he had developed a weak heart, and this had severely limited the opportunities for him, despite the White Sash's treatments.

Octavian had, nevertheless, made Harlion proud with his dedication to learning and with his decision to found a historical society at sixteen, with the help of Magister Setarcos and Lord Claudius; a society whose goal it was to record history devoid of any political bias, by collecting the letters and other writings of the young across the continent. Two years later, Octavian's collection was already considerable, and he had begun to pull it together into a first volume which he hoped to publish soon. Now, Harlion wondered if the book would ever see the light of day.

After accepting the hot beverage their servant had brought for her, Kyla took her husband's hand and said, "Har, why the guardians around the house?"

Harlion saw his son's reaction, and considered for the briefest moment whether to lie, but he was too tired for that and decided against it. He answered with much less rage than he felt, but the anger was still apparent in the way he pronounced the last words, avoiding his wife's and son's eyes, "There was an attack on the high prince last night, and it is likely one will be attempted against me unless we can stop these criminals first."

Kyla's and Octavian's eyes went wide. They knew Harlion's position meant he was often putting his life at risk, and they knew he had come close to death because of it, but the threat and the danger had always been physically remote; no one had ever invaded or even thought of invading their home to *assassinate* any of them.

Kyla made to speak, but Octavian spoke first, with the urgent, fear-filled voice of those not used to danger, "What do you mean assassins may try to murder you, Father? What does it mean?"

With a sigh and a pale smile, Harlion squeezed his wife's hand as he answered his son's question. "The war that is coming is unlike any other we've ever faced, Octavian. Its…actors are not just rebelling vassals or feuding or conquering neighbors; they are dark creatures, spurred not by their own wills but by the prodding of even darker things, and…leading them all is Noctiferus himself. Most of their tactics are foreign to us, though we do know about assassinations, and we can protect ourselves against them, but not so surely when they act in ways we have not faced before."

Kyla limited herself to grasping her husband's hand more firmly, while looking with eyes that asked the unanswerable. The young man became agitated, but Harlion raised a hand and said, "We will face the danger regardless of its instigator, son. And having guardians here is just one measure we must take to do that."

Octavian's face showed his fear and then the signs of acceptance of a reality which he had come to suspect. He said, "I've heard the rumors and the talk. I've even received reports from the kingdom of Jarah." Harlion tried hard not to roll his eyes at the term his son liked to use for the letters he received from other youths across the land. "They speak of things happening there which can only be the doings of Noctiferus, but I always believed them to be plain misguided. I guess they're not."

Harlion snorted and found himself forced to ask his son a question which should not be for him but for his own spies. "What do these reports say, Octavian? What are these things that must be the doings of Noctiferus?"

With great excitement, Octavian went on to explain that the Jarahni reports spoke of several very close friends and ministers of King Adid being recently arrested on suspicion of sedition but subsequently released upon recommendation by the king himself. The same reports said that perhaps the king was himself under the influence of the god. That drew an incredulous bark from Harlion, who could not believe that such information could be known by Octavian's teenage collaborators when his frumentarii had had to bribe people to learn the details of those arrests.

Harlion tipped his head to the side as he replied, "Your friends seem to be very well connected to know such things." His eyes suddenly showed alarm, and he asked urgently, "Is King Adid's daughter one of your contacts?!"

"I...I am sorry, Father. But I don't want to put anyone in...in danger. We are only recording these facts for scholarly purposes."

"I understand. But your friends, whomever they are, must understand that there are certain things that they should not be recording these days. In fact, I am of a mind to stop your project."

The mask of horror and guilt that covered Octavian's face just then shook both his parents, and Kyla said, "Octavian, dear. Your father's reaction is only natural; you must realize he is only thinking of your safety and that of your collaborators... especially if one of them is...a member of King Adid's court."

"Indeed, and given that your exchanges are not secret, there is a high likelihood that they will spell trouble for you if they should be intercepted. That is why I must—"

Kyla put her hand on her husband's arm to stop him and to ask if she might suggest a solution. The prefect, unable to resist his lifelong companion's way, nodded, and Kyla said, "I think your father will agree to let you continue your project if you instruct your contacts to only record what is publicly known, from here on."

Octavian looked from one to the other, unsure, until he saw his father nod in agreement.

A hopeful smile reemerged from the boy, which grew wider and brighter still when a servant came and set bowls containing a strange concoction on the table. Octavian thanked his parents warmly and then plunged his bread into the pale green stew with a voracious smile and nostrils widening with anticipation.

Relieved, Harlion sighed, then frowned suspiciously and said, "Is that—"

Octavian interrupted him to say, "It's coonay! Do you know it?"

"Where did our cook get that stuff?"

"I told Pemlo about it last fourth. I learned about coonay when I met with boys from Horn's Pass, to ask them if they would share some of *their* stories a couple of months ago, and I've become…quite acquainted with a few of them. Anyway, they invited me to dine with them last fourth. People think their food strange, but it's actually delicious! Have you tried it? You can eat coonay for breakfast or for dinner. You can eat it anytime actually, though Kilian says it's best for dinner, since that's when the bellowers—"

"Yes, yes, I know about how they collect the bellowers' sheddings. And no, I've never tried it, and I'm not sure I want to."

"Well, you should. I brought some raw coonay back and shared the recipe with Pemlo, who made it for us this morning. Mother tried some already, and she quite likes it."

"She does, does she? I suppose I will try some too, then."

And Harlion grabbed a piece of bread and dipped it into the thick casserole. When the stew covered his tongue, he could not hold back a "Well!"

Octavian gave a joyful "Ha!" in response, and the old captain felt a genuine smile, a smile accompanied by a sudden and unexpected sense of hope that filled him and took the place of the gloom he had brought into the house when he had arrived.

IV. Young Foreigner in Solinor

Looking at her son—a normally lively and highly intelligent young man she barely knew—with the deepest empathy, Darya said, "Ori, things *will* get better and you will see your father again as soon as the danger has passed in Alvinoria."

Ori, standing on the balcony of his mother's apartments, did not respond, and instead ground his teeth, unwilling to say to her that she was completely off the mark. Yes, the possibility that his father or his brothers might perish in this war, that everything he knew might vanish, frightened him. But that was not what had upset and troubled him since leaving Furan City and arriving in Kynaria.

Darya added, "If you do not wish to talk about it, I will not force you."

She watched as her son fisted his hands and turned his head away from her. Realizing that she had perhaps misjudged his sentiments, she said as much.

When Ori raised his eyes to look at her, her guts tied themselves into a horrible knot.

Ori exploded, "You want to know what troubles me? Do you know that everyone looks at me as if I were some kind of unholy thing?! Do you? An unnatural thing that may—"

Darya was struck mute and stared at her son for a long moment, battling a rush of guilty tears. She knew she should have warned Ori about the Kynarian attitude toward half-breed males, but she had—mistakenly—hoped that things would be different for her son, a prince, and in a time of war. And Aria had been well-received, after all. *But what did he mean by 'an unnatural thing that may…', may what?*

There was a look of fear mixed with anger on the prince's face, a mixture that gave his expression an unreadable twist. Her mind went chasing a hundred fruitless explanations. *Has someone done something to him?* Unable to find an answer that comforted her, she said his name with a pleading edge.

Darya watched Ori shake his head to himself, as if to reject some disturbing thoughts, then harden his jaw before blurting accusations she should have expected—hadn't Toras done the same when he was younger? Of course he had, and he had matured and learned to contain his outbursts to transform them into stinging shards rather lacerating ones.

"Why did you bring me here? Why did you bring me here if you knew this would happen? You should have refused when Father asked."

Darya was about to object but stopped herself, took a deep breath and said instead, "Because your body is safer here."

"My body. What about my mind? Isn't that just as important?! And who cares about my body? We are not Rhiians and I'm not planning to give it to the Founders who care only about conquering and enslaving their creations—if we even *are* their creations."

With a long sigh, and the tenderest gaze, Darya said, "Ori, of course your mind matters too. In fact, it is *more* important. Do you know how proud I feel each time I hear you speak? Each time you explain or describe the things you see as if they were all wonders? Everyone who knows you sees how special you are, what a wonderful mind you have."

"But people despise me because of my body, because I look *foreign,* because I'm not dark enough, and my lips and nose are wrong. How am I supposed to carry out the mission Father gave me, if people won't even *speak* with me?"

Several minutes of uncomfortable silence followed as Darya tried to find a satisfactory response to Ori's despair and an answer to this question, to restore his hope, let him know that things would get better. *But will they get better? And again, that conflict in his eyes. There must be more than simply feeling alienated.*

"Ori, I wish I were as wise as your father in the things that matter to you, or that I knew you better so that I could counsel you better. But I am not, and I do not know you as well as I should except for this: you are an extraordinary being, and you've remained so regardless of—and despite—the lies and cheating and conniving and prejudice you've seen displayed around you. That's because you pursue your goals no matter what, while remaining true to yourself and kind to others. I know these things because your father, your uncle Claudius, Harlion, Master Rackeli, and Magister Setarcos have *all* told me so. And I have seen your kindness and wisdom though I have spent so little time with you."

When Ori gazed at her briefly with a quivering lip, Darya said, "Believe me, son. When my compatriots finally see who and what you are, their guilt will shame them, and they will all vie for your company. You only need to persist a little longer, doing as you're doing, and they will come around. Most have accepted Aria; there is no reason it should be different for you."

Ori nodded, not with great conviction but willing to believe his mother, this woman whom he had known so little, and had never seen more than a few months every year until recently. He had often wondered whether it was because she did not love him. And though his father told him repeatedly that she did, he did not believe it until this year. Indeed, she had been different, and had expressed her desire to stay with them, to no longer go back to Kynaria. And she had spent most of the days with him, from her arrival in Alvinoria to when they both left for Kynaria. She had taken part in his lessons, strolled through the gardens with him studying the plants and creatures, taught him how the Bind could bring one closer to nature, and eaten every meal with him.

Ori turned his head toward her with a faint but comforting smile. It was suddenly replaced by that underlying fear…a fear he had first displayed on Master Brak's ship.

Carefully, she said, "Ori, is there something else you wish to tell me?"

Ori shook his head, looking away again.

Darya did not press him and instead approached him to touch his hand and say, "Your Day of Acquaintance is approaching. It will be the perfect time for you to consider your place here as well as to consider the things that have been troubling you since leaving Alvinoria."

The Day of Acquaintance. Ori had started observing it two years earlier, to mark his twelfth birthday. This would be his third and final one. Next year, to score the completion of his fifteenth year of life, he would celebrate his Day of Transition, a day which would mark the beginning of his manhood.

The Days of Acquaintance were meant to teach him to reflect on his growth, but starting with his fifteenth birthday, he would spend each subsequent one remembering what passed and preparing for the new year's challenges and wonders. The Days of Reflection, which were only formally celebrated every five years, would punctuate the rest of the long life he had a right to expect as a Halfling. He wondered morosely: *Will things even be here for me to celebrate anything next year? Will—*

Ori quashed the question, relaxed his jaw, which had just tightened again, forced himself to look at his mother, a woman he had come to love, a woman whose love he needed, indicated his understanding and thanked her with a feeble smile before excusing himself to go looking for his cousin.

Darya kept her worried gaze on him until he had closed the door behind him.

V.   Need for Evidence

Bilena leaned toward the Yellow Sash who sat in front of her and the Magna Mater. The Praefecta philosophas placed her hand on the woman's and said, "Kita, I can imagine the pain you've suffered retrieving Gina's memories so quickly. But what you are going through is normal and you *will* be able to find your mental balance again."

A brief detached nod was all that the woman gave for a response.

Krystiana said, "I must ask you not to share any of Gina's memories with anyone else until we can confirm who the killer is. But know that I will owe you—the entire Sisterhood will owe you—a great debt of gratitude for your service."

Kita shook her head, averting it from the other women to hide the angry revulsion which was creeping on her face.

Krystiana did not need to hide her emotions; her face was as plain as a polished pebble, and its softness revealed her care for her acolytes more than any expression or words might do. Presently, her face showed the conflict she felt with regards to the mnemonic transfer they had forced upon the young Sister.

Turning toward the Communication Rod by her office's entrance, Krystiana asked Lupa, her secretary, to let Sarrinia in.

The Healer of Bearers came in at once; she had been waiting—impatiently. She gave the required nod to the Magna Mater, though it was not a happily given one, then exchanged looks with her praefecta that said how wrong this entire affair was. Her expression was anything but stolid as she approached Kita. Whether Sarrinia's position required that she carry her emotions outwardly or not was an ongoing debate in Urbs Lucis. Whatever the case may be, Krystiana found the woman's unrestrained empathy as irritating as Larca's uncontrolled antagonism.

Krystiana said to Kita, "Sarrinia will work with you, to help you process the memories, and she will continue to do so until you have properly assimilated and compartmentalized them. One of her priorities will be to help you discover the identity of Gina's murderer. It must be in there, somewhere, as a visual memory, an auditory one, or a vibrational one."

Kita shook her head before briefly looking up at the Healer of Bearers, who smiled at her reassuringly.

After a brief hesitation, Krystiana added, "Aside from the few of us who were present when you accepted Gina's memories, no one else knows that you have received them. However, because the murderer may still be here, we have to take precautions to keep you safe. You will therefore stay with Sarrinia until the danger has passed."

The young Lux Baiula gave her assent.

"Sarrinia, please take Kita with you and keep me informed as to her condition and your progress in obtaining the rest of the information we need."

After the Healer of Bearers left with her charge, Bilena said, "Mater, what will we do? Knowing that it is a Red Sash Gina saw before being murdered?"

Krystiana stretched her lips as if to say *What do you think we can do?* But instead, she said, "There is nothing to do, Bilena, not until you finalize the method to detect Turned ones or until Kita uncovers the murderer's identity in Gina's memories. So, bring me results. I need this method. Not next month, but now."

Bilena repressed a shudder. Again, she felt the weight of her responsibilities crushing her, each time worse than the last. Was it going to end? Would she still recognize herself when it ended?

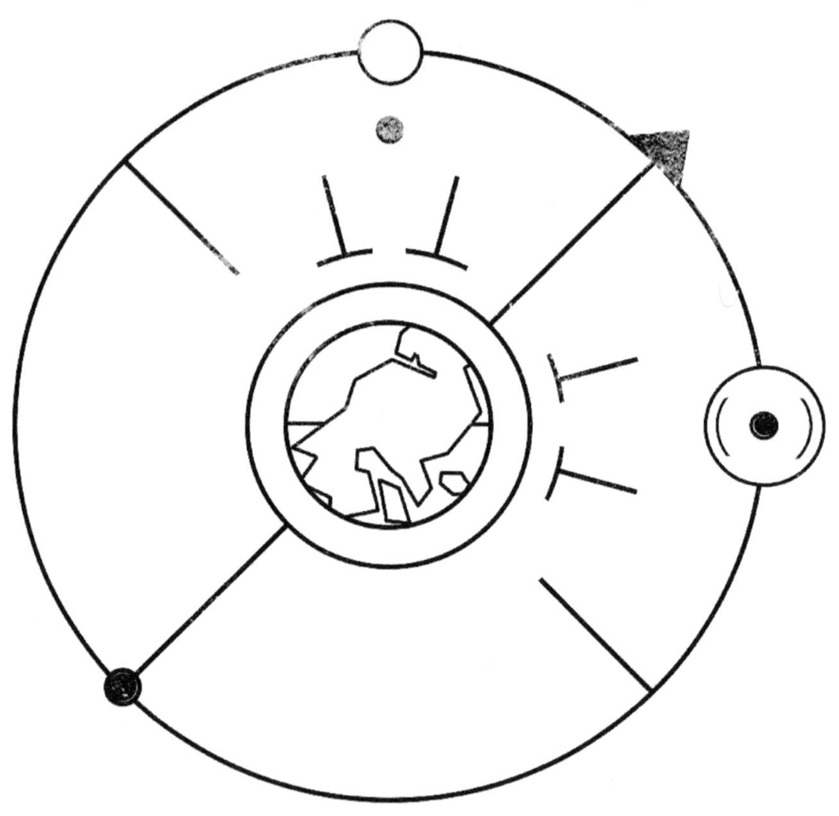

5. WHAT STUPEFIES

I.   At the Market

As the Manu Dextra made her way down the clean roads from the Inner Sanctum to the market sector, she came to a vast area of the town which enclosed both outdoor and indoor shops selling fruits and vegetables, and meats and seafood, as well as an incredible array of animal, plant, and microbial-derived products, including authentic bellower coonay and the more refined Crystalline coonay produced by a species of microbes evolved for the purpose. Other products peddled here included spices and herbs, and crushed bone, and the very expensive parasols made from the wings of the giant southern flyer, which vibrated under the suns and caused a welcome ventilation in addition to shielding people from the light.

Elyana loved the Lucian market as much as she did the Furanite market—or any other proper shopping square. The smells and sights were always a delight to her, unless the facilities were dirty. But the strong sanitary laws of the kingdom meant that only the poorest of villages in the remotest corners of the land might harbor nose-wrinkling marketplaces. Here, in Urbs Lucis, even the meats had attractive smells, seasoned as they were with the most fragrant spices.

The sounds of the plazas also pleased Elyana; they reminded her of...life. The life of sentient beings, talking, listening, moving or not, coughing or whistling, all to communicate *with* each other or *to* the others. Of course, the Alvinorian society was not perfect—though Lucians believed they were closer to the ideal—and there were, sometimes, unpleasant exchanges, such as when a foreigner was accidentally pushed by another rushing by. But Elyana loved it all because it meant the place was alive. And especially today, that feeling comforted her; it helped her shake the memory of the dangers they faced when it resurfaced.

At one point, as she made her way through the crowd, which did not part in Urbs Lucis as promptly as it did in other cities, the din receded into the background of Elyana's mind and passages from the *De Permanentia Cognitionis* resurfaced.

She had spent some time trying, unsuccessfully, to understand why Procta's memory had suggested the book to her. Was it for a particular decision she had made or needed to make? Was it to prepare her for the changes that were to come? She still did not know, and Procta would not respond to her direct questioning. The woman remained hidden in the recesses of Elyana's mind where she lived on as an intangible entity, and from whence she reemerged only at times of her own choosing, it seemed.

Nonetheless, the book did provide her with some interesting and presently useful perspectives on the nature of knowledge; its changing quantity, its changing value, its changing nature: *A thing known today is not necessarily true tomorrow. And a thing known to be true yesterday may be assessed to be wrong today, whether by the addition of new facts or by a changed perception of reality.*

Of course, she was familiar with such truths; only fools weren't. But sometimes, one benefitted from being reminded of the nature of knowledge. And her time at the library had done just that for her; it had reimmersed her in philosophical discourses so that she had emerged from the experience refreshed and prepared to see the world in a different way, a better way, a readier way.

So, what am I ready for? I've already accepted the coming of the war and its cause. Or perhaps you simply wanted to remind me of the impermanence of certain knowledge. But why?

Elyana shrugged her shoulders as she said to herself, not so quietly, "I have no idea," uncaring—this once—if passersby thought her odd.

As she passed a small craft shop, something caught her attention, and she snapped out of her musings. Sitting on a table dressed with a deep, vibrant blue cloth, there was an intriguing representation of the symbol of the Sisterhood made with the red dried fruit of the Bok tree, and its blue seed, which had been carefully extracted from it, symbolizing the Red and Blue suns respectively. What was most interesting about the object was the use of the fruit and the seed to symbolize renewal through emergence and shedding of the old. With contained excitement, Elyana thought: *I will give this to Krystiana!*

Having paid for her gift with ten worn-down, purple secretes, Elyana hired a pocket boy[11] standing nearby. She gave him the object, which he placed in his small cart, constructed with all shapes and sizes of pockets, each of which could be pulled out to carry the goods into his clients' homes.

Just then, the eclectic sounds of the market were muted by the Vox Publica, the Alvinorian news service. It was now Nine Ahn and Erona Lux Baiula—a member of the Cursus Publicus, the joint commission of the Crown and Urbs Lucis responsible for disseminating news across Alvinoria—greeted her audience. While Erona was responsible for the Lucian office, the operation was led by Elia Lux Baiula, from her office in Furan City. The news was transmitted across a network of permanent Sound Carriers distributed across the city. For the deaf, Sisters were located in known locations to render the news using sign language, projecting their motions onto the giant Living Screens behind them.

---

[11] Pocket boy: a young male who carried his clients' purchased goods using a small cart filled with pockets of all shapes and sizes, each containing a bag of similar shape and size.

Erona Lux Baiula proceeded to inform the citizens and visitors of Urbs Lucis of the day's events as well as about Lucian news of importance. The first topic included pleasant pieces about the upcoming holidays and cultural activities. But the final topic included only one piece, a piece about the recent murder of a Sister. And since only a very restricted circle of civilians knew of it, when Erona began the short, official account of what had happened, nearly the entire city froze, Elyana stiffened, and the Lucians standing next to her—all familiar with a Sister's typical stony face and noticing her unnatural reaction—stopped whatever they were doing, as if struck with a terrible fear that arrested even their breathing and their hearts; no one made a sound, and not a murmur took flight where normally gasps would sprout like weeds and rumors would take off like a flock of horned honkers.

When the dreadful announcement came to its end, Erona moved to the news about the kingdom, which were no better: news about rokons and gnarlers attacking villages across the kingdom and the mobilization of forces to prepare for the coming war. The more joyous news, though they were provided in greater detail, did nothing to brighten anyone's mood or to overturn the impression that things really were about to change drastically for everyone. The Lucians, who had found their voices again, began chattering about the meaning of it all, about the murder—in sotto voce[12], if a Lux Baiula was nearby.

Elyana tightened her lips, dismissed memories of the murder from her mind, and resumed her walk toward the Tarkoth Delicacies —Master Brak's shop in Urbs Lucis. This one was operated by an aunt of his, a pleasant, friendly woman. She hoped the woman would be able to brighten her mood.

---

[12] Sotto voce: under the breath: in an undertone, *also*: in a private manner.

But Tina Piscator did not welcome Elyana with her usual wide-faced expression. "Lux Baiula! It has been a time. It is good to see you. But—" With a hushed tone, the woman added, "I know Sisters are not supposed to show their emotions, unless they do it intentionally to misdirect someone, but you can't be trying to do that to me now, so I'm thinking—from the pinch in your lip—that you're troubled by the…by the events?"

Elyana did not know how to react; she liked the woman. Elyana stopped the frown that was appearing on her forehead and gave the shopkeeper a small sigh instead, and said, "I am, Mistress Brak, and I thank you for your concern. But let's not speak of such things."

"Of course." Then with her usual, happy voice, she asked, "What ink may I get for you, Lux Baiula? That is what you are here for, if I am not mistaken? And would you like to try this new, tart fruit we have just received? I know how much you like tangy fruits."

Elyana was about to respond when she sensed a vibration— a vibration like the one she had sensed so long ago it seemed now—and she saw the shopkeeper's pupils grow wide with surprise and fire.

Elyana turned away from the woman and toward the source of the vibration as an unexpected anxious feeling clinched her belly. Her heart skipped a beat, a single one, but skipped nevertheless, when she saw who had come. She instantly flooded her brain and body with a dose of dousing neurotransmitters. Her mind raced for a greeting that would not reveal what she had felt at the sight of the man.

Finally, she said with a voice a little breathier than she wished: "Master Methrim, what brings you here?"

"I came for you."

Elyana stood silent, unable to breathe and feeling an urgent need to flee from the place, from Lusk Methrim's presence, from the things she felt. But Tina Piscator's eyes, which had grown wide with desire and jealousy, gave her mind another thing to focus on, allowing the spell to be broken. Elyana let a deep line of displeasure and upset appear on her face.

"I am sorry, Lux Baiula. I misspoke. I meant to say that I came to the market to purchase something," and he showed her the bag he was carrying, "and then I saw you. So, I came to say hello."

The Lux Baiula wanted to respond with some sarcastic remark. Instead, she stood frozen another moment then replied with a statement that did not make any sense to her, even as she uttered it. "It is nice to find you, Master Methrim."

Lusk made a small, pleased smile rendered incredibly appealing by his foreign features. No, Zebulonians were not the brutes books spoke of.

The Zebulonian had been in the city-state for most of the last three months, being studied by one Lux Baiula after another, sharing what he could of the Janarae, and what he knew of Zebulonian sciences, culture, and politics. And, he had been permitted to treat Lucians, visiting them in their homes or seeing them in his apartment within the Inner Sanctum. That being so, Lucians had become used to seeing the foreigner—with his captivating ways, and remarkable, beguiling features—about the city.

Presently, Elyana's analytical mind reasserted itself as it began to take notice of the male members of the crowd, who seemed to be cursing under their breaths as their eyes shifted from their wives or daughters to Lusk. The women, on the other hand, either pretended to ignore him or—if they were unaccompanied by a partner—looked his way with undeniable desire; only a few were too caught up in their own thoughts, or too old to care, and ignored his presence entirely.

As she studied the crowd, Elyana reeled against herself. *I shouldn't be reacting this way! And my inability to prevent it is even more unnerving!* Lusk's mesmerizing smile caused Elyana's internal debate to dissipate like water under scorching suns.

When Elyana noticed Mistress Brak's jealous glances, she said somewhat curtly, "I am sorry, Mistress. Master Brak told me, the last time I was in Furan City, that he was working on some new inks. Has he sent any here?"

Tina drew her eyes away from the foreigner with the greatest difficulty, and said, "He has. My nephew created the most beautiful purple ink: rich, lustrous, and quick drying too. It is most striking on tan-colored paper. Would you like to try it?"

Still a little irritated, though none but another Lux Baiula would have noticed, Elyana said, "Yes."

The woman left to go fetch the ink, though her eyes seemed to want to look back rather than ahead as she made her way to the back of the shop. She waved distractedly at the wealthy patrons who had come to purchase fish and other exotic foods, directing her staff to serve one or another person with excited commands.

Elyana turned to look at the pocket boy who sat on the ground behind her, waiting patiently and wonderingly for her to finish her shopping so that he might take her things to her apartments. The boy seemed to be fascinated by the adult's and teenagers' reactions to the foreigner. Her eyes flitted toward the Zebulonian, and a thought unsettled her, a thought which felt like a betrayal of her sentiments for the high prince. She was about to reproach herself for it when Mistress Brak returned.

"Here it is, Lux Baiula. Try it, you will love it." And the woman gave Elyana a sheet of paper along with a left-handed quill, which she kept just for her. She then resumed her secret inspection of the Zebulonian.

After writing a few random words, which appeared to be not so random after all, assessing the effect on the tan-colored paper and making a few satisfied sounds, Elyana completed the purchase, thanked the shopkeeper, and handed the precious ink to the pocket boy. As she did, Lusk captured her gaze and gave her an approving nod, which heightened her growing need for flight, and she moved to take her prompt leave of him.

But Lusk asked with a voice that Elyana found irresistible, "Would you mind my company, Elyana? I am done with my purchases as well."

Elyana gasped silently. Why would he use her first name; she did not recall giving him permission. But it was so nice to hear it in his voice. She projected her response with a nervous breath, "Of course." Not a split moment later, conflicted thoughts manifested again, and again they disappeared without a trace.

After thanking Tina Piscator once more and nodding for the pocket boy to follow, Elyana departed with Lusk right by her side. As they made their way back up toward the Inner Sanctum, Elyana was surprised to notice that the crowds parted more easily for the two of them than they had earlier for her alone.

Elyana kept a hand's distance from Lusk, as was proper, but every so often, his right hand would accidentally brush her left, sending tremors through her body. *Why does he keep touching me?*

Another part of her replied: *He must be doing it on purpose because it cannot be accidental.*

And this vibration I get from him. I recognize it. It is the same one I felt that first time, on the way back from Horn's Pass. It had worried me back then, but now, it's...frustratingly inviting.

The cautious part said: *And you should be wary of it.*

The confused part of her was ready to brush the warning aside when she heard Lusk's voice.

"…whether you might come to the theater with me tonight. A play called *A God's Love* is being presented there. It is a tragicomedy about the effects of betrayal with the main characters being Aiala'Rhi and Aiala'Rho. Perhaps you would like to accompany me."

Elyana realized she had missed a portion of Lusk's comment and rewound her memory to recall the beginning of his statement. Having done so and relistened to his words, she felt her pulse quicken again. She knew she should refuse—she wanted to refuse. However, two impulses were urging her to accept: one, a powerful attraction to the man; two, a very rational calculation her reasoning part was making. As this tug of war went on in her mind, she remembered that she had been one of the women to vouch for Master Lusk Methrim, and she nearly faltered. That was when she heard a voice speak the title of the book she had read at the Atheneum, and those three words, *De Permanentia Cognitionis—About the Permanence of Knowledge*—recentered her mind and her thoughts, completely and without any lingering doubts about what she needed to do— whether it was totally voluntary or not. So, she turned to look at the Zebulonian and said, "I would enjoy that, Master Methrim. I have not seen a play in a long time, and I have heard the premiere was very well received."

Lusk nodded with a smile and eyes that threatened to overwhelm Elyana's senses once again. But she quickly turned away, and the two resumed their walk toward the Inner Sanctum. Every so often, Lusk found a way to touch Elyana's hand. She tried to distance herself from him without appearing to do so, but the touch of his smooth, nutmilk-colored hand was so very pleasant.

When they finally reached the residential building, Elyana and Lusk agreed to meet at the theater at Eight Ahs[13], and the man left to go to the guest house. She followed him with conflicted eyes for a while—the conflict greater now that she had decided to risk her life even as she realized what power he had over her—until curious looks from passing Sisters forced her to stop the gazing and start on the steps to the entrance of the residential building.

As she did, a high-pitched shout stopped her. "Lux Baiula! You're forgettin' your merchandise."

Almost cursing at herself for her distraction, Elyana apologized to the boy, gave him twenty yellow secretes, took her bags, and climbed to her chambers, her mind aswirl with an internal battle that was now being joined by the voices of Transferred Memories.

II. A Letter

Aithen, Kendor, Harlion, and Irania stood in the king's office as if struck by a trunk blown by the Bolingar Storm. Their faces ranged from baffled, to stupefied, to laughing in pure incredulity, to revolted. Even Irania had difficulty maintaining her composure. They had assembled expecting to discuss the attack on the prince last night by members of a revived Originator's Hand, but instead, the king—who was just as dumbstruck as they were—had requested their presence to hear the content of a letter that Kendor had delivered to him an hour earlier.

With a voice almost cracking, Irania asked, "High Captain, who delivered this? How do we know this is authentic?"

Kendor replied, "A Jarahni brought it to me."

"A Jarahni?! A messenger? Someone from King Adid?"

------

[13] Ahs: after Highsun.

"No. No. Just a man who was hired directly by Zebula. We have him in custody."

Relief—a very small dose of it—drew a sigh from Irania. But Aithen said, "Father, how can this be real? What ruler, what *person*—aside from a completely deranged individual—would demand such a thing?!"

Octavius shrugged his shoulders, feeling just as baffled as his son.

Kendor suggested, "My king, I am a soldier, and I would normally say to the Nethers with it. But if acceding to the demand will avoid us a confrontation with an army of Alterintrants, then I would say: Let's give her what she wants."

Octavius lashed out at his officer: "Give her the well-born among our prisoners?! We would have a patrician uprising even if those we jail *are* criminals. And our people, even when imprisoned, are still our citizens. I cannot, I will not *ever* agree to such a preposterous demand!"

Kendor stepped back, his lips tight and his face unreadable.

Mostly to himself, Octavius said, "At least, now we know her intent to invade was no mere rumor. I wish the girls had not been sent there just to verify this."

Irania said, "I will contact Urbs Lucis as soon as we are done here, Sire, to let them know of this development. But I would not ask that they be brought back; there is still much we might learn—need to learn. On the other hand, I agree with rejecting Zebula's demands; such an act would not only be beneath you, but also against everything the Sisterhood stands for. Your subjects are not bellowers or bleaters to give away to the enemy in exchange for peace."

"Father, perhaps we should ask…Lusk Methrim what he thinks of it."

"No! I do not trust him with sensitive information. I willingly accept him as an intermediary where he is in our hearing, but I will not share anything of consequence with him."

"I thought you *did* trust him; you accepted his offer of service after all."

"You still have much to learn, son. As you are aware, Urbs Lucis sent girls—*girls*—to infiltrate Zebula's court and confirm her intents…which we now know. But to succeed, they must be received and trusted, just as we are trusting one of theirs here. If we can deceive them, can they not deceive us?"

Aithen had no reply.

"We must keep entertaining the possibility that Master Methrim is a spy or at least under some external influence, regardless of the rigorous vetting he was put through. Ask Irania how their investigation of the murder of one of theirs is going. If a *Sister*—as is likely the case—can be turned and deceive her own people, Lusk Methrim can certainly betray us."

A cold air settled over the room as prince and captain realized that indeed, the Sisterhood itself had not yet uprooted the murderer who was, apparently, one of their own.

"Father, you know this means that any of us could also have been turned and still not raise any alarm until it is too late. That is not something I want to believe."

Octavius's features hardened, while Kendor seemed to wish the prince had not said that. Only Irania seemed unchanged and interjected to say, "Mitsuko Lux Baiula's minding of the king should protect him from any undue influence, my prince. As for the rest of us, we should be safe too. Turning someone, according to Praefecta Saara, is a long process; a Temptator must spend many hours and days with the person they wish to turn."

The prince bobbed his head with timid relief.

Kendor said, "To return to our previous topic, if I may, how will we verify the authenticity of the letter?"

Octavius rubbed his face, uncertain.

Aithen said, "Father, Lusk Methrim *is* the only person in the kingdom who might know the hand that penned the letter. He was, after all, in Zebula's service."

"I know, I know, Aithen." Turning to his advisor, he added, "Irania, please organize a Bound meeting with the man, for this evening. But we will *not* discuss our response in his presence. I only wish to hear his assessment of the origin of the letter."

Irania scratched her head, looking annoyed. The king asked why she hesitated, and she said, "Well, Sire, you already have a Bound meeting scheduled with Marcus Vrol, in a few hours. Having Bound meetings so frequently is…unsafe. Surely not as safe as in-person meetings. We should try to minimize them as much as possible."

The king considered his advisor's recommendation a moment, tapping his fingers on his desk. "In that case, I will keep my appointment with Marcus and leave the meeting with Lusk Methrim to you, Irania. You know what we need from him, and I am certain you can keep the discussion focused on the topic at hand without revealing anything else."

"I can, Sire. Thank you."

"It goes. Regardless of whether the letter will prove authentic or not, our strategy remains unchanged: we will attack Zeblinia, as I've promised Master Methor, at the start of Primus."

All nodded and the king concluded this part of the meeting with orders to Kendor: "High Captain, please question the man who brought us the letter, then let him go."

He then walked to his seat, put on a cynical smile, and said, "Now, what about my vassals? Have they all committed to support the war?"

As he sat himself, too, Kendor looked toward Irania to see whether she wished to respond and, seeing that she was letting him provide the answer, he shuffled uncomfortably for a moment before saying, "Juur no'Duur continues to insist that he will only support our offensive if his own land is attacked."

The prince shook his head, disgusted. "No'Duur—another fool. We need him firmly aligned; he *cannot* be neutral. If or when the Zebulonians invade us, he can't simply stand by and let our enemy restore themselves in Yerlah before marching toward the capital or Urbs Lucis."

Octavius agreed, saying, "A fool indeed, and you are right, Aithen. Perhaps we can help him commit, even if unwillingly. I intend to have all farmland in the south emptied before the end of the winter. All provisions, animals and plants alike, are to be sent to the regional capitals, and the populations relocated; they've already started doing it to protect against the Serpent, anyway, so it shouldn't be too difficult to move the rest."

Everyone stared at the king with wide, incredulous eyes. Kendor asked the king to repeat himself, fearing he had misheard.

Addressing his son but embracing everyone with his gaze, Octavius said, "You've read our ancient texts, Aithen—the ones whose origin we ignore but which are nevertheless priceless in their wisdom. One of them says that *the clever combatant imposes his will on the enemy,'* and that *'if the enemy is well supplied with food'*, the wise general *'can starve him out'*. That is what we must do. Ensure they find no food to be had on easy-to-conquer territory. If we concentrate it all in the capitals and other well-defended cities, Zebula's army will have to lay siege if they want any of it, or to demand food stores be released from the capitals in any case, and *that* is how we can force no'Duur's hand. If necessary, our furan-mounted force can intervene to stop any such traitorous release of provisions."

As Aithen nodded his head slowly in a sign of understanding, Kendor snorted and twisted his face this way and that, while Irania regarded the king with stoic appraisal of his suggestion.

"What is it, Captain? You disagree?"

Kendor sat back and crossed his hands nervously. "No, I do not disagree, Sire. But this means that our own forces will need to be supplemented with substantial trains of supplies or have ready access to those stored in the cities without being intercepted by the enemy." Kendor scratched his neck, then added, "This is not a strategy we have ever used before, and it will require significant planning and unprecedented measures to execute."

The king puffed his chest with a loud inhalation as he replied, "It will, High Captain. So it will. But that is what we must do if we wish to have any chance at surviving an invasion from Zebulonia."

Prince, captain, prefect, and advisor regarded each other with unequal conviction but with a belief, nevertheless, in this old king who had reigned over a thriving nation for more than a century.

Understanding from their silent gestures and facial expressions that all were ready to do their part to execute his commands, Octavius said hesitantly, testily, almost threateningly, as if warning them all against adding to the bad news, "Now, what about the rest of my vassals?"

Aithen watched Kendor and Irania with visible apprehension. Again, the Purple Sash let the captain reply but she turned a quieting gaze to the prince, and he relaxed, though the high captain rubbed his face a while before answering the king's question.

Finally, he said, "As you know, Arotek was still opposing our war preparations a few fourths ago. However, Fausta Lux

Baiula has been able to move him significantly closer to a decision of support. We should have positive news from Fausta in the next fourth or so."

Octavius tapped the tabletop a few moments then asked Irania whether she agreed with the captain's assessment of Arotek's likelihood of positively joining the war effort. The Lux Baiula's reply was slightly more tempered than Kendor would have liked but she did, nevertheless, agree that Fausta should succeed in obtaining Arotek's endorsement, and the king tipped his head, though he forced himself to do so.

Kendor continued, "But the rest of your vassals are, fortunately, all fully committed, Sire. Many, especially Lord Gaius's neighbors, are actually even offering to establish secure relay points for our forces to rest and to repair damaged ordnance."

The look of relief on Octavius's grizzled face could not have been more obvious and it comforted everyone.

"Thank you, Captain. It is reassuring to know that the majority still support me. So! Irania, please see to it that Mitsuko is ready for my Bound meeting with Marcus. Aithen, you and the captain can work with your officers and Lord Warbender to lay out our options and plans to concentrate the south's food stores as well as on the methods to ensure our own troops are supplied, should Zebula invade us. And remember, not a word of the letter to anyone. In fact, from hereon, not a word of the things we discuss here will be shared with anyone else without my express authorization."

Having said that, the king rose from his seat, which indicated an end to the meeting. The others did the same but did not all dismiss themselves.

Harlion, who had been silent all this time, cleared his throat, stopping everyone, and said, "Sire, shouldn't we talk about what we learned from the men who attacked the prince last night?"

The king's face took on a grim shade as he nodded. "Yes, yes we should, Prefect."

"Aithen, Irania, please stay, too. Kendor, you can go. I will call for you if there is anything you need to be aware of."

And so, the group spent another hour discussing the attack, trying to avoid questions about the appropriateness of the high prince's decision to go into the city as he did, and debating suggestions for handling the new threat. At the end of it, nothing had been decided, except that under no circumstances would the prince be allowed to leave the palace grounds without a full escort any longer, and without prior notification being given to the king, Kendor, and Harlion. Aithen, as indignant as he was, made no objection.

When all had gone, Octavius went to his desk, grabbed the letter, and almost ripped it. But he shoved it back down onto the desk, put his hand through his thinning hair, then walked to the balcony where three new members of his augmented guard greeted him with stiff bows. He paused, considered going back in, then continued forward with a small growl anyway, sat himself on the Lacora Leaf chair, turning himself away from the Lux Baiulae, and listened to the music for a while. The Voces Creatoris were now chanting a song called 'What the trees know', meant to help people focus. And so, the king focused.

III. In Melinor

A screechy, insistent voice said, "Ulvo, I tell you that if we remain aligned with the king, Zebula and her army will crush us just as surely as they'll crush him. But if we reject him and show that our land is ruled by both you and me, she will take us as allies."

Ulvo Arotek cast his eyes toward Fausta Lux Baiula, his new medic and advisor, to ask for her patience, while he tried to calm his wife.

"I don't know, Ursa. Zebula is not here yet, and may, in fact, not come at all."

With another screech, the woman said, "Whatever do you mean?"

"The king plans to strike first, to keep her in her own lands, and our own men may be sent there shortly."

Lady Aroteka's face took on a frightening aspect, and she yelled, "What?! Why did you not discuss this with me? You have doomed us! If you want to kill our men, kill them to fight this self-righteous king who worships logic as if it were a god, and whose stick-of-a-son humiliated you in front of your peers this summer. Nothing threatens our land anymore, now that the Serpent has come and gone. And we were left to our *own* devices to defend against it! Do you know how many men, women, and children perished when it attacked us?" Arotek looked back at his wife with an affronted visage and appeared to be ready to shake her out of her stupidity, but Aroteka continued, "Why would you now side with Octavius, to attack someone who will surely crush him and all those who follow him?"

Fausta was glad to see that the change in the landholder's attitude toward the high king was strong, and that the man was holding his own in the face of his wife's merciless tirade. Fausta had decided, when she was assigned to Lord Arotek, to work on him rather than on his wife, thinking that if *he* changed *and* maintained the respect of his peers, his wife would lose her hold on him and their supporters. But she suspected that unless Lady Aroteka relented soon, Lord Arotek would break, despite her best efforts. Moreover, she was tired of listening to the woman's rantings. So, she cleared her throat and, using all the skill she had, said, "Lady Aroteka, you must realize that stories of the threat to your lands having vanished are foolish at best. You should know that there exists a continued danger here, with hordes of gnarlers amassing and moving eastward as we speak, and with the Serpent having recently changed its habit to begin roaming the kingdom accompanied by an army of rokons. Moreover, stories of Zebula sparing your lands—when the best sources tell us she is ruthless and will not allow a single male to remain free—are just as silly. And I am confident that you too know the truth of this, and that it is only your dislike of the high king which causes you to lend any credence to those foolish stories."

Aroteka clenched her teeth, fought against something holding her back, then said, "Firstly, Lux Baiula, do not presume to know my mind. Secondly, why would we believe *you*? Where are those reports you speak of about the gnarlers, and the Serpent's changed habits, and about Zebula's real intents?"

"We have two independent witnesses testifying to Zebula's ways. And my own Sisters have been fighting the gnarlers to try and keep them from reaching the more densely populated coast. As for the Serpent, Prince Toras confronted it and two dozen rokons not three days ago."

Fausta watched Lady Aroteka for signs that she was ready to stand down. And though it appeared that way for a moment, when she pulled her head back and narrowed her eyes, Fausta knew the woman was still suspicious.

Aroteka asked, "You do not care what I said about Octavius or his son? You are not going to try and defend them?"

Fausta shook her head.

Ursa said, "Well, perhaps you know the truth of my words then. But, Lady Lux Baiula, you were sent here to heal our people, *not* to advise us."

Fausta knew she should not attempt to defend herself now, lest she appear to indeed have some ulterior motives. But neither should she cower in front of the woman, for Aroteka would surely read deception in that. Instead, she gave a stiff nod and kept quiet, waiting for the lord to harden his spine and make *his* will known.

To her great relief, Arotek did intervene and said, "Ursa, there is no reason for you to be so wary of Fausta Lux Baiula."

"Ulvo! You are a fool if you think this woman is here to defend our interests."

Now, Arotek reddened from anger and said, "Actually, Ursa, she already has. Just last—"

Lady Aroteka was overtaken by a sudden attack of vertigo, and she swayed, grabbing a pedestal near her to keep herself from falling.

Arotek rushed to his wife, asking what happened.

"Nothing, Ulvo. I…just feel dizzy. I…you and I need…"

Ursa shot a confused look at the Lux Baiula. Arotek yelled, "Ursa, you are frightening me. Lux Baiula, do something!"

But Lady Aroteka rejected the Lux Baiula's help even as she wobbled where she stood.

"Ursa, she needs to examine you. Please, sit down before you fall." And the man took his wife's arm just as a ferocious tremble shook her again, and he walked her to the divan.

Once she was seated, Lady Aroteka—holding her hands to her head and making jerky eye movements—made no more objections to Fausta's ministrations.

The Lux Baiula probed the lady, making small movements with her lips every so often. Each time, Lord Arotek quivered and asked what was the matter. Fausta did not reply, but after a few minutes, Lady Aroteka's eyes began refocusing, and her skin recovered some color. Arotek knelt by her and asked how she felt, asked for an explanation, receiving no response from his wife.

Arotek turned to the Lux Baiula with pleading eyes. Fausta said, "Your wife will be well, Lord Arotek, but she should rest a while."

With surprising urgency, the landholder said, "But what happened to her?"

"She had an access of vertigo, but she should be fine once she rests. If the symptoms return, I will need to probe her further and devise some treatment."

Lord Arotek bobbed his head cautiously, his face full of concern. He was relieved when, a moment later, Ursa finally spoke and asked him to take her to her chambers.

The man said to his wife, "These talks of politics are not good for you, Ursa."

The woman stared at him, confusedly, then turned an even more befuddled gaze at the Lux Baiula.

Fausta did not react in any way except to give the woman and her husband a soothing smile.

Arotek left with his wife. Fausta nodded to herself, sighed and took herself to her own apartments in the east wing of the small palace.

IV. Later that Day with Lusk

It was with a long sigh that Irania entered the Bind that afternoon to meet with Lusk Methrim. These meetings in the Bind were a fantastic thing, allowing distant people—so long as they had the capacity or were brought into the Bind by someone with the capacity to enter it—to connect and exchange information. Nevertheless, they had become so frequent now that they exhausted her and she knew, for a fact, that many other Sisters felt the same. *Hopefully, this is all over soon.*

Irania did not often need to show someone a document in the Bind, and she felt a little nervous about her ability to properly render it for Master Methrim, so she practiced conjuring the letter while she waited for the man. Upon the third trial, imagining the document in front of her and comparing it to what she remembered seeing with her open eyes, she succeeded in faithfully replicating it, and she sighed with relief just as Lusk appeared.

"Lux Baiula."

"Master Methrim. Thank you for joining me on such short notice."

Lusk gave his typical response, that he was there to serve, but Irania suspected, from the tension in his form, that he might not be so pleased. Still, all she needed from him was a yes or a no.

"Very well, I called you because we have received a letter."

"A letter?"

Irania's form expanded slightly and shrank again in place of nodding. She then projected the letter in front of her and turned it toward Lusk Methrim.

"Do you recognize the handwriting?"

When Lusk's form began to vibrate, Irania knew she had her answer. Still, she waited for him to speak his answer.

With unequivocal tightness in his thoughtvoice, Lusk said, *"I do."*

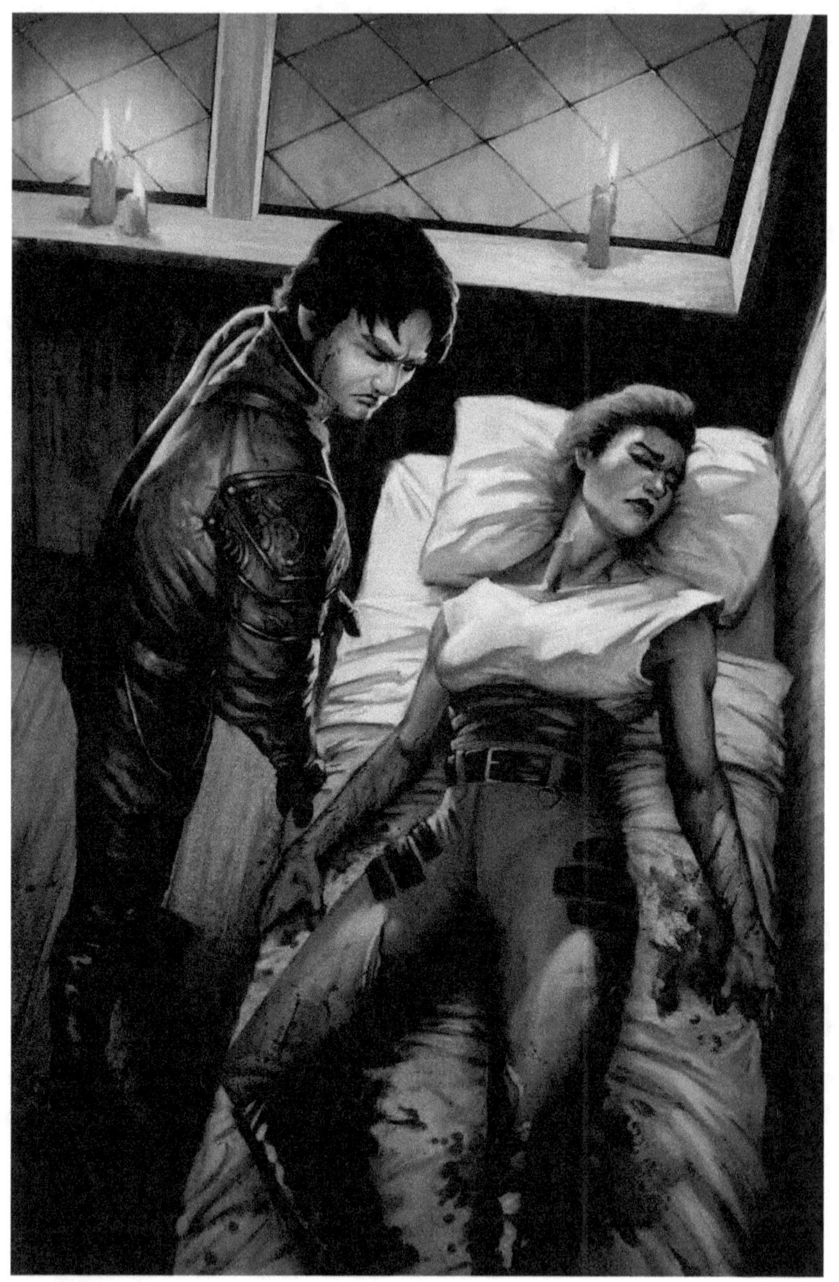

6. BATTLES IN THE BIND

I.   At the Theater

Elyana arrived at the theater, that night, under a heavy rain. Her coachman was coming to help her out and was ready to spread an umbrella over her when Lusk Methrim arrived and took his place, spreading his own umbrella open to cover the lady Lux Baiula.

Elyana looked at the man with a cautious smile but accepted his gallantry and stepped out of the coach.

She had spent the day ruminating about her condition, her sentiments for the Zebulonian, the net impression that her thoughts and perceptions were not her own, the madness of her plans, the risks and her chances, the ceaseless confusion. In that precise moment, however, she knew exactly what and who she was: a woman, a Lux Baiula, one in love with a man but with an unbreakable commitment to her Oath to serve others first and then, and only then, herself.

Standing under Lusk's umbrella, a hand span from him, Elyana said, "Why do I get these disquieting vibrations from you, Master Methrim?"

With false indignation twisting his face, Lusk replied, "Every so often, someone tells me they feel that way. I have learned by now, after researching the topic in the books I was allowed to read, that it must be because my vibrations resemble the signals you get from those of your kind you deem dangerous." Lusk paused to adjust the umbrella over Elyana as they climbed the steps to the theater, then continued, "I think you and your Sisters misjudge me like a predator misjudges a harmless prey species that mimics a toxic one. Except that I am obviously not trying to mimic what you call *Soiled Alterintrants*; I simply and accidentally resemble one—vibrationally, that is."

Elyana chucked. "The analogy could be better; we are not predators, and you are here of your own volition, not a prey. But I understand your point."

The smile that appeared on Lusk's lips, just then, was so captivating that Elyana could not prevent a sudden rush of desire. She struggled to quash the sensation and force the conversation back toward a more technical topic. "Why do we not get the same vibrations from Ooldrina and Raaviana?"

The man's expression darkened suddenly, his beguiling smile erased, if only for a brief moment. When he had recovered, he said, "I am sorry, Elyana, but one of those girls gave me only headaches. But yes, Zebulonian male and female Alterintrants do emit different vibrations."

Elyana nodded, but something in the way Lusk's eyes had narrowed and in the way his lips creased at the corners told her that there was more to it than the mention of Ooldrina's name. Perhaps—the thought disappeared, and Elyana blinked.

Lusk said, "Well, should we get in? The play will start soon."

Elyana blinked again and followed, though one part of herself railed against…against something she could not hold onto.

The Lucian Grand was not the Grand Hall of Furan City, or even of Antar, but it was still a beautiful building.

The stage, as in the best theaters, was set in the center of the hall and turned constantly so that the audience might experience the effect of the changing visual and auditory perspectives.

The seats were set all around on four levels. At her request, Elyana and Lusk were given seats in a two-place alcove of the second level. All alcoves were soundproofed so that people would not be disturbed by their neighbors' excitement and exclamations.

Presently, a loud, deep gong sounded. The actors walked onto the stage from the little staircase in its center as well as from the sides of the hall. Cheers erupted all around.

When the music started and the crowd grew quiet, the play's creator hopped onto the stage to give a brief outline of the story. The play was going to recount Aiala'Rho's abandoning of the Originator, his subsequent vow to destroy her creations, and finally his own destruction by Aiala'Rhi.

A story of betrayal. Pause. *A thought in my mind.* Pause. *What is it?* Pause. *My own thought or, or someone…Mattina's thought! Yes!* Elyana's muscles twitched. She looked sideways carefully, not to arouse Lusk. *Right. That's what I'm here for. To expose him and take care of him.* She wondered about the sanity of her plan. But she had committed to it in that moment of lucidity and Mattina Lux Baiula[14] had described a trick to shake herself out of the Zebulonian's hold. The trick did not work perfectly, and Elyana had to be more careful than ever if she hoped to get out of the theater alive.

The play started, and everyone turned their full attention to the stage, including Lusk—or so it seemed. Elyana continued to watch him from the corner of her eye, evaluating, assessing, fighting the lapses in her mind.

After a while, Lusk started to turn toward Elyana to make some impassioned statement, and each time the sound of his voice and the smell of his breath nearly caused her to give in to him. The fourth time, Elyana was so completely and wholly submerged by his charm that she only resurfaced with a supreme effort made even greater by the need to keep her efforts hidden from him. Her body smiled at his comments, with her typical small and cautious smile, and she gave automated replies, but her mind was reeling, screaming, gasping from the effort. Now,

---

[14] Mattina Lux Baiula: A woman who had been involved in rooting out the remnants of the Dark One's forces after the end of the Dark Battle.

she knew, as surely as she knew her name, that he was something else, and it frightened her. Having understood this, she committed to her plan. One little calculation encouraged her: it was that if she were wrong and penetrated Lusk's mind unjustly, he would not report her. But if she were right, whether she won or lost the coming battle, she would be in trouble. When the music picked up, Elyana resolved herself to her action and entered the Bind.

Lusk reacted swiftly, appearing in front of her, his form dark and—almost solid.

"Elyana, you are in my mind."

Elyana's figure stiffened.

"You should not have come here, Elyana." After a pause, he asked, *"Why* are *you here?"*

"Because you are not whom you say you are."

"I did not wish to turn *you as you call it, but simply to—"*

"You did not wish to turn me?! Should I be flattered?" And Elyana's unexpected laugh finally broke Lusk's calm. She felt a surge of distress and resentment whirl in Lusk's mind; distress in the face of the actions he would now be forced to take, and resentment toward her for forcing such actions on him.

When he resumed his Sending, it was with frightening detachment that he said, *"Now I have no choice."*

And the battle began, a great battle between two powerful Alterintrants fought in the Bind, while the gods' impersonators continued to play out their fatal love on the pivoting stage.

A foul sensation flooded Elyana's brain even while her opponent's nutmilk form wrapped itself around her own shape; his dark, coal-black eyes piercing her soul with all the evil they had done; the red mark on his forehead growing larger and blinding her with its intensity.

It seemed to Elyana that she was suffocating. Her mind was imagining the sensation, she knew it. But it could kill, regardless, and she focused all her vibrations to repel her adversary. However, Lusk's own vibrations remained coiled around her, and now, he insinuated himself into her form and, having succeeded, forced himself into her mind and, from there, into her body. Elyana experienced the rape as surely as if he had forced his member into her, and she split the vast expanse of the Bind with her shriek while her body lay stiffly on the seat in the soundproofed booth. She prayed to gods she did not believe in that the agony would end soon, and a small, contained part of her mind reeled from the realization that she had so overestimated herself—that everyone had wrongly believed in her. A thoughtvoice pulled her mind out of the quicksand she was digging herself into, if only to assure her of her nearing end.

"You should not have come here, Elyana. I cannot allow you to return as you were...I have no choice now. I...I am sorry."

Elyana panicked. She did not know if she could continue to resist Lusk. *He is so powerful...Aithen!* Her hesitation and distraction were disastrous, and Lusk engulfed her entirely, all parts of her bathed in his foulness. She yelled and then disconnected from the pain and the fear—from everything, and she escaped to her saferoom, that small part of herself where her thoughts were still safe. There, she began chanting *I control my mind; I control my body. I control my mind; I control my body. Others may touch, and prod, and goad, but I control my responses. Others may touch, and prod, and goad, but I control my responses...*

Lusk wished only to be done with it, to be done with this repulsive act and ensure that—*Ohh mother, what am I? How you will hate me if you should ever see me again. But what else can I do?!*

When he felt Elyana's form begin to dissolve in the way that forms did when Roamers left the Bind, Lusk Methrim's screams ripped the ethereal realm around him and, just when Aiala'Rhi learned of her lover's betrayal and, in anger, shattered planets and moons, which the theater company rendered with explosions of red and yellow and violet, Lusk said, *"I am sorry...Elyana,"* and the next moment, he sucked her mind right back into the Bind and pummeled her formless shape with all the vileness that remained in him.

When he exited the Bind, Lusk's eyes fell upon a catatonic Elyana. He locked his guilt away and racked his brain for a safe way out of the theater. He thought about leaving her there; no one would ever learn the truth from her. But the theater's staff and some of the spectators had seen the two of them come in together. In the end, he decided to scout the building and found a backdoor exit that was no longer guarded given that the play was nearing its end. He returned to the alcove, picked up Elyana, and made his way out of the theater as swiftly and inconspicuously as he could manage it.

II. Betrayal

When Octavius entered the Bind with Mitsuko and found Marcus, the man proffered his forearm with unusual intensity, ignoring the minder.

As soon as Octavius took it, he noticed a shift in the gaze of his old Head Frumentarius which made him extremely uncomfortable. He repressed a strong urge to withdraw his arm and instead prepared himself for he knew not what as he asked, *"What is happening, Marcus?"*

The Reader's eyes became hard and filled with an ugliness Octavius had never seen in him. With a tone that befit his words, he said, *"I am taking payment for the forty years of forced isolation."*

At once, every fiber in Octavius's body, sitting cross-legged in his antechamber, demanded flight. His mind reeled from a sense of disbelief and incomprehension and certain knowledge that he must exit the Bind lest he be trapped there—or worse. And so, the king tried to separate himself from Marcus, but he could not let go of the man's hand.

Mitsuko, who had been standing to Octavius's right, gasped and nearly panicked as she realized that this was a trap. She pushed all feelings of guilt aside and turned her mind to the only thing that mattered now: protecting the king. But what could she do? She was a Purple Sash, not a Red! After a moment that seemed all too long, an idea came, and she imagined a wall of light between the two men. As soon as the space lit up, she projected the wall toward Marcus with as much force as she could conjure—and prayed. The man's form was blown back.

Mitsuko closed her eyes in thanks to the Founders then told the king they needed to get out. She became alarmed when she saw that Marcus's hand was still holding the king's forearm, though the Reader was now separated from her and the king by the fabric of the Bind. She implored the king to let go, to imagine himself back in his body, but Octavius simply shook his head in dejected recognition that he was trapped.

Horror contorted Mitsuko's face when several new forms, including a gigantic, lizardine one, coalesced around them.

Having stilled itself, the Serpent's looming form hissed, *"The second Luxor. Or should I say: the coward who did not even deign address me when I came all those moons ago. If you had had more spine then, many would still live who died that day and since then. But perhaps you care not for your people as much as you wish them to believe."*

The king's eyes—filled with hatred, disheartening disappointment, and desire for vengeance—shifted from the Serpent to his treacherous friend and back to the Serpent. He said, *"What do you want, Serpent?"*

"I am the Ali—"

"I do not care what you call yourself. What do you want?"

With a mocking voice, the Serpent replied, *"What I want now, you will not willingly give, King of Humans."* A malicious grin appeared on his diaphanous form, now, and he added, *"Know that you will not leave this place unless you surrender to me. If you don't, you will die here, now or later—after eons of endless and senseless Roaming—depending on how things go if you should choose to resist."*

Mitsuko could hardly believe that vile thing's request. The king, himself, almost appeared to want to laugh. She sent, *"Sire, this is preposterous; but I do not know how we can fight or how to extricate you from that traitor's claws."*

"Can you read the Serpent's intent? Its state of mind?"

"I am sorry, Sire. I am a strong Sensor but not a Kynarian to be able to read beasts." The king sent a discouraged growl through the mind-tie, and Mitsuko added, *"But perhaps, if I am not mistaken...its wide pupils...it might be hoping that you will not resist. Perhaps it is something we can use to our advantage until help arrives."*

"You have called for help, then?"

"I have chimed Dana Lux Baiula and others, Sire. But sending a message when not directly connected is like sending a letter in a bottle. I do not know if or when it will be heard."

The king's long, disheartened groan hit Mitsuko like a sledgehammer. She sensed his desperation as he wondered whether they could hope to escape the Serpent and its accomplices. She also sensed his doubts…about her. The king wasn't used to mind-ties, of course, and it appeared he was forgetting that this Binding allowed his thoughts to be known by her. Mitsuko walled off the king's thoughts from hers as best she could lest they overwhelm her. She tried to ignore his insult when she sensed another thought in him, a thought of... uselessness, directed at her.

One of the Serpent's female companions crossed eyes with her at that moment. The woman looked from her to the king and back with weighing eyes. Had the assassin intercepted the king's complaints?

Mitsuko put it all aside then scrambled for an idea, for something she could do to get them out of the Serpent's grasp. But what *could* she do? And how could she sever the unnatural limb that bound the king to his former aide? She studied it, tried to understand the Binding, but such conjurations were beyond her capabilities.

She sighed dejectedly then turned toward the high king. He seemed to be elsewhere, calculating, studying; his face was now bereft of all emotions; she could tell from the intensity of his gaze, from the smallness of his pupils, that he was looking for ways to extract himself from the death trap.

The Serpent shook the king and Mitsuko out of their momentary *distraction* when he hissed in the king's direction, *"The only way for you to part from him is to kill him."*

Octavius snorted to himself, snorted with a disheartened shake of the head as his eyes lingered on his former, long-time friend. The king's appearance changed suddenly to let a hateful glare transfigure him and flood the Bind to penetrate the Reader.

Mitsuko paled when she heard—if only barely and only because of the intensity of his thoughts—the king wonder with self-loathing sentiments that frightened her, whether his former officer had already been a slave of the Dark One when he went to meet with him in his villa—scorning Urbs Lucis's edict in the doing—and whether Marcus was, in fact, a mind violator.

Octavius's self-loathing and his rage against his former friend were growing dangerously strong.

Realizing her mistake, Mitsuko dropped the wall; she could not—no matter what the king's thoughts were—separate her mind from his. It was urgent she pull him out of the hole he was digging himself into. Calling on all her Purple Sash training, she sent a powerful, *"Sire."*

But the king gave no response.

More powerfully, she tried again, *"Sire!"*

Octavius's blistering form turned toward his minder with the same deadly glare, while the Serpent and the others continued to watch, amused.

Disregarding the king's violent sentiments, Mitsuko sent, *"Sire, your mind is at risk of losing its grip of reason. Your emotions are too intense. You* must *calm yourself."* After a fraction of a second, she added something to appeal to the king's logical mind, *"You know that."*

And, to Mitsuko's relief, the king did begin to still his thoughts, and as he did an idea emerged, or rather sprang, out of the subsiding maelstrom. His eyes widened and she heard him think: *These women must be from Kartak. If Toras is reconnoitering the area and Mitsuko could send his prima the order to attack that wretched town, could that save us?*

The possibility to redeem herself and to save them excited the usually unassuming Mitsuko and she sent, *"Sire, that is a great idea! I will try to reach Laiella Lux Baiula; hopefully, she is listening for messages."*

Just as Mitsuko turned her thoughts inward to send a message to the prince's second in command, the Serpent—who had now grown impatient—hissed a question that shook the Bind with its power. *"Well? What is your decision, King of Humans? Do you choose life or death? I would prefer it be the former, but if it is the latter, we are ready to execute your wishes."*

Though Octavius felt hatred gain him again, he had enough presence of mind to let go of it and interact with his enemy with all the cunning he could muster. Indeed, he needed to stall the creature to give his minder time to reach her Sister in the Black Guard. However, he felt unexpectedly…sluggish, and he could not form any coherent thoughts anymore. All he managed to do was to turn panicked eyes toward his minder before his form wavered and nearly collapsed on itself.

The Purple Sash felt her heart sink. She could sense the king's confusion and…his muddled state of mind.

With a frightened whisper, Octavius sent, *"Mitsuko! I…I feel…I do not feel well."*

Mitsuko rushed to weigh her options. If she returned to her body, she'd be leaving the king to face their enemies, alone. But the king's body was possibly under attack now. Was this a coordinated attack on him? The Sisterhood might not have trained her in the defensive arts, but it had trained her in decision-making. So, she set her jaw and reached back into her body.

The Purple Sash found the king's body swaying and strangely swollen. Her mind rushed to understand what was happening. She gasped when she became aware of an acrid smell lining her own nostrils, throat, and lungs. Without any delay, she projected a fine mist toward the keeled-over Octavius. The king's inhalations, though they were slow and shallow, carried the microbes into his airways to coat every surface. At once, they created a protective barrier inside him, and their secretions began to neutralize the mind-bending compounds coursing through his veins and arteries.

The Serpent, who had been barking joyously, gave an angry snarl when the Lux Baiula suddenly spoke to say that they would not have the king.

Furious, the Serpent demanded again to know the king's decision. When the king formed defiant eyes on his figure, the Serpent released a frustrated growl for he could not kill the king. With a loud sigh, he commanded his accomplices to capture him and kill the witch.

One of the assassins, her red hair blowing violently around her black-skinned face, said she'd rather try to *turn* the oval-eyed Light Bearer.

The lizard responded with a hiss, *"No,* she *must be killed. He is our target and our prize."*

The fiery-haired Convert hid her resentment well and the Alis Domini did not see the defiance in her eyes.

While their enemies debated what to do with them, Mitsuko scoured her memories for some defensive Binding. Finding nothing useful, she cursed herself for having never trained in the defensive arts and never having volunteered for mnemonic transfers. Things being what they were, she forged the only Binding she knew which might provide some protection: an inhibition field around her brain and the king's. She then turned her mind toward their attackers and braced herself for the assault.

When the Serpent hissed his orders again, one of the assassins, a thin, dark-haired woman, sent a private thought to the redhead, *"Bracca, what are you waiting for?"*

"This Serpent's orders are not what the Leate commanded us to do. We need an alternative."

"But—"

"Lasra! We can do this, and we will. Send a Core knitter just after Alta hits the witch with a Borer. You must time it properly! I will alert our contact in the capital."

With that, the three attacked, just as the Serpent prepared to whip them.

The woman called Alta hit Mitsuko with a powerful Binding that started to twist her figure as it penetrated her. The strike drew a gasp from Mitsuko, and her body shuddered and swayed in the king's offices.

Amid the fog caused by the pain, Mitsuko heard the king scream, asking what was happening, before screaming again as if his mind were being ripped from his brain.

The Purple Sash drew on all her will, if not on her skill which she did not have, to concentrate and strengthen the inhibition field. But it was wasted effort: her attackers' Binding breached her shield, her brain was lit afire, and her body jolted with agony. In the fragments of clarity that interspersed the pain, she saw her final dissolution was upon her.

After a third attempt at snaring the king's mind, the assassin called Bracca took an unplanned pause. *He is strong. Much stronger than anyone suspected, and yet, he's never used the Bind in any active manner. Founders!*

Recovering briefly from his own agony, the king turned toward Mitsuko. Her figure was being pulled apart like gauze stretched in a twisting motion; he watched with horror in his gaze, powerless. His pulse quickened as the fear of the inevitable assailed him. He yelled his minder's name. His Sending got no response except a chance and bewildered glance in his direction, a glance shot by eyes that seemed to stretch across the Bind and fill the space with the fear of one who knows their end is at hand. Suddenly, Mitsuko's link to him was severed, and his mind now lay completely unprotected and…alone.

Bracca sent a thankful nod toward the others and prepared her final Binding to trap the king.

Octavius tried to remember defensive vibrations he had learned so long ago, but in vain, and without the connection with his minder, he felt naked, exposed. Nonetheless, when Mitsuko's final screams tore through the Bind, and despite the tightening grip on his mind, he still managed to reform his figure and address the Serpent to offer himself in exchange for the Lux Baiula's life.

But the only response he got from the Serpent was a joyous hiss, and his heart sank.

Just before Mitsuko's last threads dissolved, something sent his heart drumming. He perceived two thoughts: one was filled with a sense of...shame and...plea for forgiveness, while the other, leaving only an impression of urgency on him, crossed the Bind to go he knew not where. Octavius sent a desperate shout through the Bind, calling his minder's name—in vain. Ohh! The rage, the guilt, the sense of doom—they were like a great boulder split from a mountain, rolling down toward him, to crush him, a foolish, foolish man.

III. Toras

Following their failed attack on the Serpent a few days earlier, a catastrophe he attributed to his own misdirected impulses, and which had nearly cost his first officer her life, Toras tried to drown his guilt by leading grueling, repetitive training sessions for the entire Guard.

Laiella, fortunately, was recovering. A White Sash had come from Urbs Lucis to the Mountain Lake outpost, had stabilized her, and had followed them back to Horn's Pass to continue treating the Barrier there. The medic, who did her best to ignore the prince, had already done miracles with Laiella, and had only spoken to Toras to tell him that the prima, who now sat recovering in her own quarters, only needed a few more days to regain full use of her cognitive and motor functions.

For reasons Toras understood only too well, Laiella had remained somewhat cold toward him. But what worried him more was that she had started avoiding his gaze since the Bound meeting she had that morning, a meeting to which he had not been invited. He had asked her about it, but she had refused to give him any answers, refused to even tell him whom she had met with—her silence on the topic was 'Order prerogative' and not subject to Coriolan military law.

Disheveled and ragged-looking as he was after returning from his hours-long training session this day, the prince sat on a stool next to the Lux Baiula, who lay resting on her bed after a long therapy session. He was trying to start a conversation, but he could not find the words.

Feeling the uncomfortable tension as greatly as the prince did, Laiella took the initiative and said with a low, tired voice, "Lord Commander, there is no reason for you to be here so often; you smell like a belwohr and your presence won't speed up my recovery."

That broke the ice and Toras tried a hearty laugh, his left cheek scrunching the side of his face and giving him a goofy appearance. "I know I've already said it, Laiella, but I'm sorry. I acted brashly when I saw you in danger…and made things worse."

And Toras watched and waited for Laiella's response, while straining to show confidence in the result of his present action, straining to keep himself from lashing out at fate.

As for Prima First Barrier Laiella Lux Baiula of the Red Sash, she watched the prince with much more hesitation than was usual for her—for a Sister of the Order. At one point, her jaw tightened, as if she were angry with herself. Finally, she said, "I know why you did what you did, Commander. But I'm tired now and I just wish to rest…if you don't mind."

His prima's reply was not what Toras had hoped for. What did it mean? Her reply-not-an-answer stabbed him and sent his mind spinning. He felt torn between the need to convince this woman he…admired—his officer—that she should forgive him, the impulse to order her to accept what had happened as nothing more than the risks all soldiers accept when they join military service—including the possibility that a commander might make a mistake which might cost their lives—, and the fear that she might remove him from command—which is what his father had asked her to do if she felt the need.

And, for the first time, he stopped himself from acting on his fear though he felt the strain of the decision—was it also an impulsive choice or the result of some hidden rational part of him he did not yet know? He felt the strain of it on his innards even as he agreed that she should rest and that they could continue their conversation later.

He left, feeling confused and worried, worried that these battles within him might render him incapable of leading anymore. His fists were white as bone, but he finally let out a huge, great sigh and, setting his sight on the field outside the fortress, he moved himself there to take the next group of soldiers through the most demanding exercise yet.

IV. Helplessness

After witnessing Mitsuko's erasure, Octavius had cursed the Serpent and raged against the Founders. But his eruption had only caused the Alis Domini to lash him with a whip made of the most intense blue light. Strangely, and as terrible as the lash was, the pain did not reach his body. In fact, he could no longer feel any part of his physical self, even if he tried.

The realization reminded the king of his wife and sons, and a swell of panic surged and threatened to overtake him as he realized he might never see them again. However, Octavius was a disciplined man, and he reached inside to let the panic pass. But despite his discipline, achieving the calmness he sought was nigh impossible given the possibility he might never leave this place, alone as he was against an enemy he could not hope to overcome and with a mind still a little sluggish from the poison his body had inhaled, which realization led him to panic again and to wonder, for a moment, who the traitor was.

Fortunately for him, the pain diminished and the sinking spiral, which had nearly engulfed him, passed too. Octavius took a shaking breath and cursed at himself: *The hubris! The hubris that made me come here without a full guard, even after two assassination attempts! Coming with a woman who never had any chance against such foes. How did I live this long being such a fool?!*

When he finally calmed himself, he decided to assess the situation. He was glad to realize that Marcus no longer held him with his unnaturally stretched hand. But alas, the red-haired Rogue held him there as surely as if she had placed chains and shackles on him. How *could* he escape? How could he *fight back*? He had never been trained in the defensive or offensive arts by the Sisterhood, having refused their schooling—had his principles been misguided? All he knew, he had taught himself, which was mostly mind-reading along with a few sonactic Bindings, which he had let go wayside until he had needed them to save Toras and his guardians that summer. How could he extricate himself from his predicament? He had no idea; he felt trapped and angry, and he knew he would probably die there, whether then or later, roaming the Bind endlessly like some mad spirit.

Presently, what felt like a wind blew past him; it was neither warm nor cold, but it stirred new worries in him. The Serpent was looking at him with a vicious, victorious smile, while its companions mocked him with jocular screeches.

Having learned, by now, that the Serpent had no care for a Human's demands—be he a king or peasant—Octavius said,

"What is it that you wish from me, Serpent, which you believe I will not agree to?"

The Serpent enlarged its form to an incredible size before replying, *"You will address me properly if you wish any reply."*

Octavius tried to grow or reposition his form so as to be at eye level with the Serpent's head, but he couldn't; he was incapable of controlling his figure shape anymore and was forced to look up. The women laughed. He thought: *Very well. If I must.*

"What do you wish from me…Alis Domini?"

The Serpent rumbled satisfactorily, then replied, *"You may be of service to us…given your* perceived *authority on K'Tara, though you are no longer a threat to us or to our Great Lord's plan."*

"I will not help you subjugate my people, or anyone else on K'Tara. And you will not *turn me!"*

"Oh, but you will, and we will. And if not, it is never too late to end you or leave you stranded here for eternity so that you become irrelevant to us and a warning to all those who might otherwise choose to oppose us."

The Serpent went on, *"You have certainly not been an easy target, King of Humans."* Then, glancing at the shriveled Marcus, he added, *"But it was easy enough to lure you here once we understood your weakness."*

With a huff, the Serpent added, *"Frankly I do not know why the Dark One ever feared you or your friend here."*

Marcus recoiled further as Octavius turned a venomous glare toward him.

The king asked, *"How long has it been, Marcus? How long have you been in their service? Answer!"*

But the Serpent had finally grown weary of the spectacle and decided to bring their mission to a conclusion. He said,

"That does not matter, King of Humans. And he will not answer; you put yourself in this situation."

Then, turning his long neck toward his companions, he asked, *"How long will it take to completely bind him here?"*

The red-haired form answered, *"We should be done by the time the dreamers on the other face of K'Tara enter the Bind."*

"Very well. Get on with it, then. And let me know when it is done. In the meantime, I will go and report the news to the Umbra."

To the king, the Serpent said, *"When I return, you will answer my questions and help us make an ally of Alvinoria."*

Then, turning to Marcus, he added, *"You may leave if you wish it, or stay here and help your former friend accept his fate. I will need to thank the Leate when I see her next; she has done good work with you."*

And with that, the Serpent's form vanished from the Bind and Octavius watched the three Temptatori approach him—or should he say *Temptatorae*? But what silly thoughts were they? Of course he found himself in that predicament with such a stupid mind as his!

The women's cloaks and hair were buffeted by an invisible wind, and their eyes looked rapacious and hungry. Octavius prepared himself for he knew not what, but to resist in some way, however he might. At least, he still lived. He turned a pained face toward his former friend, hoping against hope that Marcus might choose to help now. But the Reader averted his eyes again and disappeared.

V. A Hostel

In the City of Light someone had awoken. She tried to look around but couldn't see anything. Confused, she tried unsuccessfully to recall what happened to her. Her mind ached and throbbed. She focused on her metabolism and with some effort increased blood flow through her brain and circulation in her lymphatics. It took a few minutes for her sight to be restored, but when it was, what she saw caused her to suspend at once all outward signs of life. Her pulse slowed near to stillness and her breathing to the shallowest she could manage while remaining conscious and retaining the functionality of her hearing and of her vibrational senses. Her sight, she could not use lest she announce that she was conscious.

She did not recognize the room they were in, but she did recognize her captor, and he was pacing, appearing to be debating what to do, if his motions and grunts were any indication.

The Purple Sash had a fierce internal debate, one part wondering how she lived and whether it wouldn't be better to be dead already, and the other part tormenting her and urging her to kill the damned man and then cursing her for not listening to her intuition months earlier.

Her debate might have continued for a while if she did not receive a thoughtcall, just then. Mitsuko's injunction sent her heart and mind galloping and her veins pulsing furiously. Someone was in mortal danger. Aware that her reactions might call Lusk's attention to her, she tamped them down with some effort.

But what could she do? She could not defeat a single Temptator; how could she be of any help against *who knew what*? Her mind began to spin with self-doubt and contempt. Had she fooled herself all these decades? Had her colleagues and superiors fooled her, praising her skills as they had done since she had gained her first Sash?

Nonetheless, she must respond to Mitsuko, and so she did. Her guts clenched and her heart surged through her throat when only silence met her Sending. She wanted to scream, cry. Had she just caused her Sister's death?

Realizing that she was being foolish, breaking her own rules by giving voice to her desperation, she took a moment to calm herself, and finally decided to question her Transferred Memories. But, given her condition and the urgency, she opened the gates somewhat carelessly, and the flood of clamoring thoughts stunned her. She was about to close the doors on them when Mattina Lux Baiula's iron-tempered voice rose above the others and quieted them all.

She said, *"Your Sister may still live, and it is unbecoming of you to let your doubts chain you as a mere red shoot!"*

"But—"

"There are no 'buts,' Elyana. I will do this for you."

"I don't—"

"I need control of your body, now!"

When Elyana hesitated again, Mattina said, *"People have not lied to you, Elyana; you have unparalleled skills, though some you owe to us. But you have rarely let yourself explore them for some reason unknown to me. If you wish to save your Sister, you need to let me help you. Will you let me show you?"*

Lusk Methrim staggered back in shock. Elyana had risen and stood before him with an unreadable, unrecognizable expression. "How—"

Before he had a chance to finish his question, he saw the woman raise her hands, palms forward. By the time he remembered the meaning of the motion, paralysis took him, and he fell backward, whacking the wooden floor with a loud thump. He groaned and tried to sit up, but the microbes had already immobilized all his muscles. He shrieked, but no sound exited his throat.

He watched with horror as the woman approached, then stopped, kneeled, and, with her still unrecognizable glare, triggered his brain's self-defense mechanisms. She was trying to invade his mind again! He tried to resist her, to establish a mind shield, but all in vain. She was in him, again, and this time, he was afraid.

While locked in their ethereal fight once more, Lusk clawed at Elyana's mind with all his might. It throbbed with pain and a thought escaped her. Lusk recoiled from it as if it were a miasma intent on swallowing him whole. She must be wrong; she must have intentionally let the thought through to deceive him!

"I did not. Ooldrina is Oolviana Methrim's birthdaughter—your sister."

"How?! That is not possible! You are lying!"

"She is not lying. And you are a vile man."

"She?"

"I am the mem—"

Elyana could no longer be the witness to the destruction of a man. If he must die through the actions of her person, then she must be the one to kill him. She spoke his name.

When Lusk heard his name, he knew it was Elyana speaking to him. He replied with her name, almost pleadingly. He asked if the thought he had intercepted was true.

The howling of self-hatred, the pleas and the revulsion, the disgust and resignation, the questioning of what he had agreed to do to save his mother intermixed and amplified each other and nearly caused Elyana to release Lusk. However, at the last moment, a new hatred surfaced and erupted from Lusk Methrim, a hatred directed at her, at the Sisterhood. It was a savage hatred, which would have overwhelmed her if she had not remembered Mattina's Bindings and proceeded to end the battle. She re-entered her body, put her palms forward again, and sprayed the Zebulonian with an even more toxic mixture that would soon stop his heart.

Her deed done, Elyana stood, her jaw tight with disbelief at what she had done. She took another moment to dampen her furious heart but did not stop the flow of adrenaline; she would need that to face whatever was threatening—and had hopefully not killed—her Sister.

After giving the dying Lusk one last glance, she moved to the far corner of the small room, sat on the floor, ingested a handful of sweet salt cubes, called the first three Red Sisters she could think of—praying that the Monitor would work—and after waiting anxiously a few seconds and receiving surprised acknowledgments from two of them, she entered the Bind following Mitsuko's directions.

VI. The Rescue

It did not take Elyana long to find the location Mitsuko had indicated via her fortunate, though desperate, thoughtcall; Elyana's senses stopped her in a space occupied by several Human forms, and there seemed to be after images of—*oh Founders! The Serpent!* But, no, though she could sense its lingering vibrational signature, the creature was not there.

As the forms came into focus, Elyana saw—High King Octavius! He was surrounded by three females she did not recognize. *Why is Octavius here—alone? What is happening? And where is Mitsuko?*

Elyana kept herself from coalescing immediately in front of the king's captors while she took in the scene and tried to make sense of it. *These forms, they are…Rogues. Founders!*

After verifying that her vibrations were shielded, she sent a thoughtcall to Sasha and Akula, ordering them to her. With the urgency of a fire siren, she added, *"Do not appear until I tell you to. Know that the high king is in danger. Three rogue Alterintrants surround him."*

Sasha and Akula fixed Elyana's location but remained as mere shielded thoughts as they approached. They watched with horror while, at some distance not so far and far away, the king's captors began to whip him with lashing scarves of light.

Elyana groaned as she prepared to send another command to her Sisters; her brain still throbbed with pain, piercing her focus every so often with zapping, snapping filaments within her form which risked revealing her. She forced her body to inhale deeply, counted down from three, and finally sent, *"Sasha, Akula. There is no time to discuss. Please keep your minds shielded as those may be Temptatorae. Mitsuko was here, but I cannot sense her anymore; please keep your senses open for her. Know, also, that I sensed the Serpent's after image. But let's pray it doesn't return."*

The two women sent resolute acknowledgments. Sasha asked, *"What is your plan, Elyana?"*

"We are three and they are three. We will take one each." The Sisters quickly agreed on their individual targets, after which Elyana added, *"But first...I need to shield the king."*

Akula asked, *"Without warning him?"*

Elyana sent the thought of her shaking her shoulders, which was rendered by a dull, short gong. The situation was urgent and dire, and she did not wish to alert the enemy until all was ready.

Presently, Octavius released another cry and jolted Elyana into action. Without another moment's delay, she descended into a Level 3 meditative state and reached out for the king's mind—and was kicked back out with such force that she coalesced, despite herself, in front of the enemy.

Seeing that, her colleagues moved to attack. Akula did so while pushing aside her uncertainty about facing these women of darkness in the ethereal space, for, indeed, the Order had not planned, and therefore not prepared its acolytes for this type of combat. On the other hand, Sasha felt no such doubts and welcomed the chance to test herself against these new foes whatever the setting.

The assassins put up their shields, which vibrated in the Bind with deafening intensity. The two confronted by the Red

Sashes took the fight to another location, leaving trails behind them so their opponents could follow them.

Akula and Sasha appeared in front of their adversaries with changed attire, uniforms even more striking than in the physical world. The women were covered with thin red plates so perfectly imagined that they looked nearly solid, especially Sasha's, who as a Barrier—the deadliest members of the Red Sash—took her appearance as an integral part of her identity. Both also had deep blue vambraces hugging their arms, while Sasha sported red rerebraces, just as finely shaped as the breastplate. But none of that was for mere show; their armor's tightness and compactness left no loose vibrational threads to be caught and pulled by an opponent, though Akula's lacked in some other respects.

Sasha, who was a stiff, stern and proud woman, said to the larger of the two Converts, *"You! Stand down. You have no right to wield the powers you use."*

The assassin gave her a baffled look, chuckled, then attacked.

It was all Sasha could do to prevent being speared by the narrowest weapon she had ever seen forged. Her opponent barked a mad laugh and attacked again.

Some distance away, Akula was facing her own opponent, the thinner of the two dark-haired assassins, the one named Alta, who launched a vortex of fire in her direction.

Meanwhile, Elyana watched with horror as the red-haired assassin blasted the king unconscious then shrouded him in some sort of dark and opaque cloud before slamming into her and ripping her from the place.

It took Elyana another moment to recover her senses and find herself in an arena of some sort with her red-haired opponent.

The woman studied her with excited eyes, then shook Elyana with a few simple words. She said, "You should surrender now, Elyana Lux Baiula."

Elyana wanted to ask how the woman knew her name, but she did not get the time to do so. Her attacker launched two quick firebolts which sent painful impulses all the way through and into her body.

The Purple Sash clenched her teeth and finally struck at the assassin's form with a blast of her own. The shape seized then warped and reformed itself just when Elyana's next attack came, only to disappear itself to the other end of the arena to avoid the blast.

But Elyana had played this game before, a long time ago, when she had been a Red Sash, a time when the Sisterhood regularly trained her members to fight in the Bind. Elyana had already possessed highly advanced mind-probing skills at the time, and these had enabled her to easily defeat her opponents, even when she could neither see nor hear them.

So, she called on those skills now and opened her sensitive mind to the faint vibrations coming from her adversary, looking for any sign of what she meant to do next.

It took Elyana a few tries and misses to remaster the skill, but each time she succeeded in anticipating the red-haired assassin's movements and strikes earlier and earlier, confounding and frustrating the woman more and more until, on the sixth round, Elyana not only anticipated the woman's action but also saw an opportunity to slip into her brain and send a powerful vibration to her amygdala, which interrupted the structure's chemical signaling.

The red-haired assassin became suddenly confused and stopped fighting. Elyana thought she had won, but the woman regained possession of her responses and sent tendrils across the expanse to wrap the neck of Elyana's form in a killing embrace.

The tendrils coiled themselves around her vibrations and were making their way into her brain, if not expertly.

Elyana's eyes went wide, nevertheless, as she gasped and struggled to free herself.

"I am Bracca, a servant of the One, and you can only dream of the abilities he gave me. Did you think you would kill me so easily...witch?!"

With more confidence than she felt, Elyana tried to taunt the woman, challenge her, distract her. She said, *"No, I imagine he taught you many things so you would accept to be enslaved by him!"*

The woman considered Elyana's insult a moment.

Elyana did not even waste a welcoming thought on the opening the woman was giving her. She immediately gathered her strength, amplified her vibrations until the noose around her neck dissolved, and launched a volley of fireneedles at her opponent. The Bound weapon crossed the infinite space in a flash—and found only the imagined wall of the arena; the woman had vanished again. Elyana cursed at herself, but at least she had succeeded in freeing herself.

When her probing returned nothing, Elyana began to worry that the Rogue had found a way to hide herself, but the structure the assassin had imagined suddenly disappeared, and Elyana knew the woman was gone. She roared with rage until she realized that the woman must have gone back to where the king was. Hurriedly, she recalled the signature of the location and transported herself there, ready to end the woman once and for all and be done with this unending day.

***

"Shakta!"[15]

---

[15] Shit!

Lusk pushed himself up onto his knees then lifted his head to look around. His eyes stopped when they fell on the Manu Dextra who was sitting, cross-legged, on the floor.

What…what is she—a terrible fit of anger and hatred—no, not hatred…yes, hatred, because he had not wished to make her one of his victims—seized him suddenly as he remembered Elyana's assault. He wondered for the briefest moment whether he could finish her while she roamed who knew where, but he derided himself, knowing that he was in no condition to take any risks.

So, nauseous and confused as he was, he stood, crossed the room as silently as he could, cursing again when he stumbled into a chair, and finally stepped out the door. As he released the handle, an unpleasant question popped into his mind: how would he explain to the Umbra that he did not finish the Sister when he had the opportunity? That he let someone live who now knew the truth about him? His muddled mind could not resolve the question, and he walked away, averting his eyes whenever he spied someone as he made for the hostel's exit and then for the wayfarers' stables.

***

A terrible scene greeted Elyana when she returned to the king's location. Sasha's form was zapping the way forms did when Roamers were exhausted. Her Sister's opponent was behind a distorting field and everything else looked to be on fire. She could not see Akula, but the king appeared to still be entrapped within the dark mound.

Elyana sent several thoughtcalls to Sasha, before the woman replied with a wearied Sending: *"I am okay. Please help Akula…the cloud."*

The nebula that Sasha pointed to was a morass of dark, violent colors which Elyana could not penetrate with any of her senses. It stood far above them, in the direction she imagined to be up in this virtual realm. She exhaled sharply—and went.

Vibrations which seemed to bore into her form, and from there into her very body's flesh, assailed Elyana. It was as if the vibrations were shaking every thoughtstring of hers. She switched off the visual signals a moment and stilled her mind. That done, she focused her senses until she finally spied Akula up ahead. The woman was struggling to resist a crushing wave of she knew not what.

The assassin, not too distant from the Red Sash, was weaving her Binding with joyful motions! When she noticed Elyana, she laughed and as she did, her Binding increased in intensity, causing furious spasms in Akula. Shortly thereafter, the Binding's effect reached Elyana, and, this time, it shook not only her mind but every cell of her body, as well.

A growl rose from deep inside Elyana. But before she let herself lash out at the enemy with a fruitless and likely ill-conceived vengeful strike, she took a fraction of a moment to decide on her response, then increased her form's density. The effect on her diminished and she was able to take another moment to think. A dozen different tactics scrolled through her mind to be evaluated and discarded within the space of the heartbeat that followed. When a solution finally presented itself—a complex one which would require several different Bindings acting in concert—Elyana let go of all rational thought and allowed her subconscious to take control.

The Purple Sash transformed herself into a howling, magnetic wind which began to encircle and envelop Akula's assailant. The woman turned flaming eyes toward her, but Elyana continued to weave her cocoon until she finally severed the Binding holding Akula.

She sent a thoughtcall to her colleague to ask her to distance herself then started blasting the Rogue with intense, low-frequency sonic vibrations. These started to drill into the assassin's form while high-intensity photonic vibrations began dissolving it.

The woman bellowed like a belwohr, which filled the Bind with a deafening and dizzying sound. She tried to burn Elyana out of the ether.

But Elyana continued as an automaton, adjusting her course and attacks with a perfection that no conscious, thinking mind can achieve.

The rogue Alterintrant fought to retain her form under Elyana's ceaseless pummeling.

However, Elyana soon began to create a Sound Shield around the woman, which was reinforced with each additional tear in the assassin's form. This continued until the shield was so very nearly solid that the woman was effectively trapped.

When the assassin tried to rip the capsule with a sonactic Binding of her own, she wobbled under the pain of the resulting self-amplifying reverberations.

Elyana reformed herself in an image of her own semblance which expanded and shrank as her body took a soothing breath.

Akula, having somewhat recovered from her injuries, raised her head in her Sister's direction and sent a grateful nod, which sounded like softly snapping fingers, and accompanied that with a motion of her head.

Elyana asked, *"Are you strong enough to pierce the sphere and create an explosion inside it?"*

Master firebinder Akula looked toward the embattled assassin with a wild, vengeful grin. She was preparing to do as Elyana requested when a singing, entangling thoughtvoice found its way through each Sister's mental shield and into their minds. The women became confused. Akula moaned.

Elyana shrieked then panicked when she sensed Akula's focus turn on her with unwilling but deadly intent. The reaction sufficed to weaken her focus and nearly collapse the Bindings that held the assassin. When she felt the air crackle with the sound of a firebolt emerging from Akula, Elyana sent her an urgent and powerful injunction. The command shook Akula out of the Rogue's grip, and the assassin was kicked out of her mind.

While screams of pain filled the Bind, Akula regained control of herself and retreated quickly into her body to release whatever sweet salts remained in her liver. She then returned to the Bind and—with a twist of violet vibrations which she formed into a furious, spiraling needle—she penetrated the shield around the Temptatora and followed it with purple vibrations to light it up.

The two Sisters did not hear the assassin's cry when the flame consumed her form and likely fried the brain in her body. But they did hear and feel the explosion which ripped the Sound Shield apart, leaving only an oddly shimmering space where the Bound cage had been.

But no sooner had the Sisters exchanged thoughts of thanks and relief, than the red-haired killer appeared.

Elyana let out an exhausted sigh then ordered Akula to take position on the woman's far side, while she vanished for a glimpse of a moment to reappear in her old Barrier uniform. The colors were crisp and blinding, her aspect unsettling.

The assassin's form warped backward a meter. Elyana grinned inwardly. The woman repositioned herself, her vaporous eyes taking on a murderous aspect.

Elyana sent a thought to her Sister. *"Akula, try to distract this wretched woman. I need to get into her—"*

"What fools you are! Do you think we cannot intercept your thoughtcalls?"

Elyana and Akula were taken aback by the interception of their exchange and froze momentarily. Their opponent, however, took advantage of the situation and wove a large web around each of them.

By the time the Lux Baiulae realized it, it was too late. They tried to escape, but they were stuck and looked at each other with hard, desperate eyes. They also wondered how they were going to communicate if their thoughtcalls were no longer private. But it did not take Elyana long to slap herself silly for not thinking of the solution earlier.

Wishing to test the security of the Monitor's connection, Elyana asked Akula to try and launch a fireneedle. When Akula did so without the assassin reacting in any way prior to the launch, Elyana had her answer: *It works!* She sent her colleague another thought: *"Akula, she cannot hear our Monitor-mediated communications. Please distract her while I will try to get inside her mind."*

"What?!"

"Please, just do as I say. Now!"

And Akula began striking at the web as hard as she could, making noise, and cursing, and threatening the red-haired Rogue with all manner of insults.

As soon as the woman turned her attention to Akula—initially regarding her with contempt then with worry—Elyana retreated into the deepest levels of her mind. There, no more thoughts, no more sensations at all—whether intra or extrasensory—clamored for attention; nothing to distract her, except for very faint vibrations originating from her Sister and from the assassin. She dismissed Akula's signals at once and focused on the others. Elyana had feared the web might interfere with her Binding, but it hadn't and she reached her target as easily as does the flame of a candle which follows the gases of a spent one until it reaches the wick and lights it. Elyana, however, did not light any fire. Instead, she sought the pituitary gland. When it seemed to Elyana that the woman had taken notice of an alien presence, she accelerated her search and finally found the little organ. There, she triggered a chemical cascade which would stop the assassin, if not kill her, and withdrew from the maelstrom before it engulfed her, leaving the sell-soul crying and shrieking.

The Rogue's web disintegrated, and Elyana reappeared next to Akula witnessing the frightening dissolution of the red-haired killer's form with cold, hard eyes until she was gone.

Akula sent, *"What did you do, Elyana?"*

Elyana responded from a place that still did not feel, and it was just as well, or an exasperated indignation might have accompanied her reply. *"I saved us. Please help Sasha, if you can. I need to see to the king."*

The Red Sash left, but not without giving the Manu Dextra a worried look.

Elyana thought: *I do not understand why they continue to think that one weapon is any less acceptable than another when the end result is our opponents' death—and don't they understand that in here, all our Bindings harm or kill by targeting our adversaries' brain in any case, whether they aim at their forms or...do what I did? Hopefully some sense can come to them or we will be defeated.*

And with that, Elyana took herself to the dark mound under which the king's vibrations were still trapped.

As she considered the situation, her emotions resurfaced unexpectedly and she shuddered, wondering if the king's vibrations were still connected to his body; if they weren't—she locked her emotions away once more, and turned a cold, rational gaze to the mound. She looked at its surface, studied it, scrutinized it with all her vibrational senses. She gasped when she saw it: a thin, weak bundle of vibrations leaving the mound and connected to a point outside the Bind.

Immediately, she started to hover and spin and hover again around the mound, again and again, trying to find a way in or a means to disrupt the string-formed cage. But she did not recognize the Bindings. Exasperation gained her and she growled.

Some distance away, Akula and Sasha were confronting the last of the assassins; she could feel the warping and the zapping, the heat. But it did not penetrate her; her priority was to get the king out of his prison.

What is *this shield?!*

As thoroughly as she raked her mind for an answer, she could not find any. But she did feel the king's vibrations trailing very faintly away from the opaque form. If *they* could cross the shield, then her vibrations must be able to do the same.

Before frustration could disrupt her focus, she decided to pause again—despite the dire situation—and called Mattina from the depths of her mnemonic centers where she had retreated again after Elyana's body, controlled by the ancient woman's memory, overcame Lusk Methrim.

The woman told Elyana how she had come across a shield like the one enclosing the king, long ago. She explained how she had broken it, then asked Elyana to be given control again.

"No! I will do it, this time."

Mattina agreed and Elyana let the memories infuse her active centers until she knew them as if she had executed them herself countless times already.

After running through the process described by Mattina a few more times and locking away the tiny doubtful part which still lingered, Elyana launched herself along the trail of the king's vibrations. She felt a smile—but whether it was Mattina's or hers, she did not know—when she found her way into Octavius's brain, easing herself into it as if she had done the procedure a hundred times before, calmly and quietly—confidently.

Once inside, she probed a moment, then poked Octavius's telesensory cortex to chime him, let him know that she was there. To her greatest relief, a response came, faint, weak, pleading: *"Elyana. I...I need help. Help."*

"Octavius, I am here to help. Please give me a moment." Elyana consulted Mattina's memory once more.

Mattina said, *"The reason he heard you and you heard him is because there remains a bi-directional link between his flesh and his mind, the latter of which is emprisoned in his form. Follow his vibrations outward this time, from his form in the cage toward his physical self."*

As Elyana followed the ancient Sister's instructions, she spoke to Octavius to calm him and urge him not to resist her when she joined him in his ethereal form and tried to amplify his vibrations. *"When I tell you to, think of yourself, of your body, and imagine yourself returning to it, whole and healthy."*

The king's response was weak, but he confirmed his understanding. After rehearsing the procedure one final time, Elyana moved into action.

The method was in fact quite similar to that which the king had used during the battle against the Serpent three months back, when he had enhanced Elia's firebolts. If the king could do it, so could she!

Another smile warmed her when she reached inside the dark mound holding his mind captive.

"My king, now. Think of returning to your body. As you do, I will combine my thoughts to yours to shatter this prison."

The king did as Elyana asked, and she started to synchronize her vibrations with his. This part was quite easy; she had known him for so long. The process led to an immediate increase in the intensity of the resulting force and to a painful crack, as their synchronized vibrational strings reached the shield and pushed against it. The king's and the Lux Baiula's combined form, an ameboid, whizzing shape, held together! But the crack was insufficient to let the king escape. So, Elyana prepared to significantly increase the amplitude of their vibrations as well as to modify the frequencies to shatter the shield—and do it all without harming the king's injured mind. A single and final thought rose from the part that was her before she proceeded with this final step: *Hic venimus.*[16]

In some other part of the Bind, both near and far, Sasha and Akula struggled to repel the hammering Bindings of the last of the assassins. The woman had not appeared to be so strong earlier, but now—perhaps because she was the only one left— she conjured one Binding after another in endless succession, varying them just as rapidly as an expert swordswoman varied the motions of each of two swords.

The assassin pummeled the Red Sashes with firebindings and sonactic Bindings and incredibly powerful distorting Bindings that almost dissolved their forms, several times. What made the fight even worse was that the woman moved like a needleflyer, appearing up and down and left and right and before and behind them, in a maddening sequence.

However, Akula, who was a teacher and therefore one who liked to study and understand things, had finally come to notice a pattern in the woman's tactics. During an unexpected pause, she sent to Sasha: *"Sister, watch our opponent's vibrations. Watch for a brief dip in the yellows and be ready to assault her with likewise yellow sonactics when that happens."*

Focusing on their opponent's changing vibrations caused them to weaken their defenses and they groaned in tandem as they were hit several times by the assassin. However, Akula

---

[16] Here we go.

urged Sasha to keep watching for the dip, and when the enemy's lashes darkened from the decrease in the bright, yellow vibrations, the Sisters blasted the woman with high intensity waves of yellow. The woman screamed, and to Akula's greatest delight, her form dissolved and finally winked out of the Bind.

They had done it.

Akula was surprised when Sasha turned to her and thanked her. *"We should do this more often, Akula. It helps to see a Sister fight alongside you, to see her in action and know—rather than assume—that she will not let you down."*

"Likewise, Sasha. Although I fear for our Order, for our Orb. Rogues should not be so powerful. How will we repel the Janarae when they come?"

"If all of us can work like this, we will defeat them too, no matter how powerful they are and who trained them."

Akula smiled doubtfully when an urgent thought popped into her mind and she asked, *"What about Elyana? Do you sense her?"*

It took the women a pace in the shapeless Bind to find their Sister. They called out to her and received an excited but exhausted response in return. At once, they moved themselves to Elyana's location and saw her with the king. His form was pale and blurry. But he lived.

When her Sisters appeared, Elyana introduced them to Octavius, and he thanked them as warmly as he could manage despite the deep embarrassment he felt.

The women tipped their heads briefly in recognition of his gratitude and quickly turned to their Sister to know her orders. Did they resent him for forcing them to risk their lives for him? Octavius wondered. But he let the thought go. He was in too much pain to keep holding the question.

Elyana turned to Octavius and said, *"Sire, you should exit now and let Tania take care of you. I will contact her later to find out how you are. But Sire, we need to revise your safety protocols.*"

The king did not argue and returned to his body at once after mumbling additional thanks to the Lux Baiulae.

The king gone, Elyana thanked her Sisters again.

The women placed the side of their fists on their forms' bellies with sonorous thumps before pulling them away with assured motions to acknowledge a truth that all Sisters held more dear than their own lives: that they were one body, serving together to safeguard humanity.

Knowing that there still remained things to do, Elyana said, *"I need to contact Tania and have her look in on Mitsuko because she is not responding, and I fear the worst. But I have a request for each of you."*

The women asked for the Manu Dextra's orders.

"Sasha, if there is any way you can locate the bodies of the two women we killed and bring them back to Urbs Lucis, please do so. If they are from Kartak, we will need to go carefully. But they may be from elsewhere, too."

Sasha sent, *"Perhaps a Roamer can find traces of them in the Bind, and from there locate their bodies. I will keep you informed."*

"Thank you. I will hear you later."

Sasha nodded and left the Bind.

"Akula, I need you to come join me at the Green Fureen Hostel. I am in a room there. Please bring a White Sash and two other Reds along. We need to bring Master Me—" Elyana screamed when, having gone back into her body momentarily, she saw that her captor was gone.

VII. Aftermath

A rancorous Dana forced herself to name the king to let Tania know that he was awake.

Aithen and Julian, who were in the next chamber, came running in as soon as they heard Dana.

Alba's soft purplish light shined through the windows and added to the too bright glow of the new Living Lamps, which had just been placed in the king's bedchamber.

Octavius's head still throbbed but the swirling was lessening. He looked at himself and saw he was still fully clothed though he was on his bed. He swiveled to sit, and his head swirled some more. He cursed. He looked up and saw Second Barrier Dana. The woman did not look pleased—she never did.

"Dana, what…what happened? I was…"

With a hiss, Dana said, "You roamed into a trap. We were informed by Elyana some forty minutes ago."

"A…trap." Then with sudden exploding anger, "Marcus! Marcus, that traitor! I…I was…How did I… Is Mitsuko…where is Mitsuko?"

Dana remained silent. She did not wish to tell the king about her colleague. Once again, she had failed in her duties and a Sister who never had any chance might die as a result. *Why did Mitsuko not call me? Why did she call Elyana?*

Tania approached the king and said, "Sire, Mitsuko lives. She is atte Domus Lucis's infirmary, under intensive care, and may not survive. As for you, you will recover, but you will notte live much longer if this keeps happeningge."

When Aithen and Julian looked like they wanted to ask the king questions, Tania gestured for them to be patient.

Aithen stood back and continued to look at his father, shocked by his appearance.

Octavius, himself, could barely recognize the person he saw in the mirror hanging on a side wall. He croaked, "This should never have happened!"

Dana, caring nothing for propriety, said, "Indeed, Sire. You should never have gone into the Bind without your Guard.

Mitsuko—may her body still be worthy—had no defensive or offensive skills to call upon, and now she lies on a cot, hanging to life by a thread."

Octavius's eyes narrowed reflexively, but he did not chastise the Barrier for her impudence. Aithen looked him in the eyes, to ask, to see if he was going to react to the officer's insolence. But Octavius simply shook his head.

Dana continued, "Despite all that, my Sister did manage to send a message to Elyana before she lost consciousness." The officer paused, then her features hardened before she finished her statement, "You owe Mitsuko your life, Sire."

Furious at the soldier's audacity, Aithen ordered her to stand down, but his words were buried by the loudest, angriest growl the king had ever uttered, a growl that breached the multiple rooms of the royal chambers, reached into the hallways, and rattled everyone and stiffened Dana, though it seemed impossible that her features could harden any more.

An uncomfortable silence followed the king's eruption, but those who knew him understood the cause of it, and it was not Dana's challenge.

Presently, Aithen cleared his throat and asked a question about Octavius's attackers.

The king thanked his eldest with a slight softening of his eyes and mouth for moving the discussion to something that would draw everyone's attention away from his person. But he wondered for a moment whether his experience ruling a nation, leading armies to subdue a revolt here and there; his experience thwarting all the enemies he had had in his long life—Unsensing enemies, normal humanoids those driven only by personal gain—were sufficient for him to survive the current threats and lead the nation to do battle against a god.

Finally returning to his son's question, Octavius replied, "We were attacked by the Serpent and its lackeys…while Marcus held me in place with some unnatural Binding."

Everyone turned alarmed gazes at each other; everyone except for Dana, who stood with an ardamantine face.

Julian said, "Elyana told us about the three rogue Alterintrants keeping you…caged. But she said nothing of the creature or of the Re—of the Reader."

"You will not upset me by calling him so, Primus. He is not what I thought he was…"

Octavius paused to palm his temples a moment, then said, "What worries me even more than Marcus's betrayal is the fact that someone, *here*, someone in my household tried to poison me while we were in the Bind! Do you *know* what this means?"

Julian said gravely, "That Noctiferus…that his Temptatori or Converts have infiltrated us."

Hopeless nods and involuntary gulps followed the primus's statement.

"My king, if this is true, we need to lock down the palace immediately until we have unmasked this traitor."

Tania Lux Baiula barked at the comment, and said, "Converts are notte necessarily traitors, Primus. From what we know, anyonne may be turned by a powerful Temptator."

"Are you suggesting clemency before we even know who tried to poison the king?"

Tania blinked, replied factually, "No, I am saying that we should notte go after this person with prejudice already in our minds."

"He tried to kill the king!"

Tania limited herself to shrugging her shoulders and looking at the king as if expecting him to agree despite the fact he was the victim.

The king stayed mute, scratching his head and shaking it, debating with himself the White Sash's statement, resenting her for it, and letting low growls escape him every so often.

Once more Aithen came to his father's rescue by moving the conversation to ask the White Sash a question. "Tania, you said you think you know how my father was poisoned."

Tania bobbed her head side to side before replying. "I think it was one of the Living Lamps; that's why I had them replaced."

Standing up with a wobble, with his ever-ruling self-consciousness causing him to close his eyes in frustration, Octavius asked, "The Living Lamps? How?"

"The one on the back wall was spentte, and it gave off a strange odor when I got here. I wentte to check it and smelled the remnants of a substance produced by the micro-organisms when they are fed natrium, which is used to feed some of the plants in your gardens. But when fed to the organisms lighting the lamps, it causes them to release pfernatrium—pfernatrium is toxic to Humans."

Calculations and suppositions of all sorts crossed Octavius's mind, just then, and at the end of it, he growled, "Where is Koricki?!"

Rackeli, the king's majordomo—as always standing in a corner—said with some confusion in his voice, "He should be in his quarters, my king."

"Bring him here! And if he is not in his quarters, alert the high captain to seal the city gates and send guardians out to scout the capital and its surroundings. I want him brought here at once!"

"Father, why?"

"Because *he* is the one responsible for the Living Lamps."

The stricken majordomo left with Primus Julian to do as ordered, his face dark and murderous, though he was a most peaceful man. How could that young man—a staff member he was partially responsible for—betray the king?

Aithen now considered something that had just come to his mind. *What was it that Neaj said about Lusk when investigating Luvius? That he likes to make apparently unimportant connections. And I've seen Luvius with Koricki a few times, though Koricki didn't seem to enjoy the other's company that much. Damned! I hope I did not miss something that could have prevented this.*

And Aithen rubbed his lips and chin reflexively as he tried to dispel the sudden feelings of guilt. To put his doubts out of his mind before they discombobulated him, he said, "Father, this is the third attempt on your life in less than two months. We are all exceedingly thankful to all the powers that be that you survived them all, but I would caution you against taking any more risk from here on, because it is obvious that our enemies wish you dead and will not stop until they succeed."

The pale and wan Octavius sat back on his bed. He shook his head, not because of this latest attack on him as much as for being seen in such a weak condition. Indeed, he had always been proud of his unfailing health and of his youthful vigor though he was nearly a century and a half old; not that he believed he needed to keep his body worthy for the gods. No, he needed to be strong for his sons. Now, he blamed himself for waiting so long to have his children…especially Ori.

A low growl escaped the king. *This self-pitying is not going to help.* He said, "I will not make this mistake again, son. I will tell Julian that from here on," and as if he were ingesting some foul-tasting substance, he added resignedly, "he may assign as many guardians and Sisters to my protection as he wishes …whenever and wherever he deems it necessary."

"Here in your bedchamber, too?"

Octavius gave no answer. He just shook his head and sighed.

It took Julian and Rackeli thirty minutes to return with Koricki, who was flanked by Julian on one side and Kendor on the other. Alturo Rackeli, normally a placid man, followed with a horrified and wrathful look on his face, whereas the officers looked ready to spend the night interrogating the young man, and not with gentle manners either.

Waiting impatiently on his Lacora Leaf chair, Octavius did not get up when his personal attendant was brought in, and he did not look at him. He acknowledged the captain of the Royal Guard with a grunt and, without any further ado, asked him where they had found the boy.

The captain of the Praetorian Guard replied promptly, "The high captain found him just a kilometer outside the gates, Sire."

Octavius clenched his jaw so tightly he almost broke a tooth. *Twice today, twice! I've been betrayed by someone close.*

He set wrathful, predatory eyes on Koricki and stared at him for a long, unsettling minute. The Kynarian, whom the king had known as a quiet, rational, intelligent, and even-tempered young man, started chuckling like a mad man until a sudden bout of terror took him. Shocked and dismayed, Octavius was about to order the boy silent when Irania irrupted into his bed chamber with unmistakable urgency.

"What is it, Irania?"

"Sire, you should let me handle this."

Octavius, who was visibly unsettled by the boy's behavior—and by the night's events—bobbed his head in consent.

"Thank you, Sire. It is best no one aside from a Lux Baiula interact with him until we know what he is." Turning to the officers, she added, "And I would request that Dana bring him to Domus Lucis."

If he weren't so disturbed by the boy's unnatural behavior, Octavius might have objected to Tania's request because he, too, wished to interrogate his now former attendant to understand why. But his attendant's madness frightened him, and he consented.

"It goes, Irania. Take him! But I cannot simply stay here to wear my floor pacing it while you determine if…this boy is sane. I will go see Mitsuko."

Tania, who had been listening quietly all this time, interjected, "Sire, I do notte adv—"

"Tania Lux Baiula, I am strong enough to walk, and if not, my guardians can support me. Do not argue with me."

Tania froze for a fraction of a second then tipped her head stiffly.

Dana looked at Irania with shocked surprise.

The Purple Sash made a quick motion of her hand, which she held close to her body, to say that she was not, herself, surprised by the king's attitude. Aloud, she ordered Dana to take the boy and follow her with another Red Sash to take him to the restraining chambers[17] at Domus Lucis.

Kendor and Julian appeared to want to protest; the boy had not done anything to them and had not presented any danger to them. Weren't the Lux Baiulae exaggerating the risk simply to take control of the situation? But the king gestured impatiently, and they let go of their charge, if with grinding teeth.

Presently, Octavius raised a finger. He said to his advisor, "Irania, the boy's arrest must not be spoken of, for now; remember that he is a relative of the Supreme Priestess and that

---

[17] Restraining chambers: Chambers where the Bind and the filaments produced by a particular microbe are used to subdue or paralyze dangerous people.

it would not do anyone any good for her to learn of this through unsanctioned channels. We will discuss how to share the information with her tomorrow."

"I understand, Sire."

And the Lux Baiulae left with their prisoner. His face was marred by alternating twitches of incomprehension and hate, which accompanied his mad laughs and groans.

Octavius fought very hard the desire to smash something—everything. But what would he smash? He had barely enough energy to walk to the royal coach despite his statement to Tania. So, when Julian called Jashan and Merr and instructed them to place themselves on either side of him in case he missed a step, Octavius did not object.

Tania snorted with surprise, "I expected you to make a fuss, Sire. Will you let me probe you before you go?"

The king motioned for the medic to do her thing. When she was done, his dizziness had lessened, though he still felt a dull pain in his head.

After exchanging a few words with his son, Octavius walked out of his rooms with Julian ahead and Jashan, Merr and two Lux Baiulae just a step behind him along with Tania, for appearances' sake; he looked like he was preparing to meet an enemy.

***

When Octavius stepped out of his coach in front of the Sisterhood's seat in Furan City, he caused a little stir in the plaza, where a small crowd of Sisters and patricians were sitting to enjoy a cream before retiring for the night, given that the earlier rain had ceased, and the sky was now clear.

Octavius straightened himself, and, as he pulled his jacket taut, felt a momentary spell of dizziness. He hissed to keep his guardians back when they became alarmed. He then lowered his head toward the back to ask the Red Sashes guarding him whether they could distort the air behind them, to obfuscate things in case he should feel dizzy again as they climbed the steps.

One of the Sisters, a short yellow-haired woman named Bela, grunted that she could, though it was not her expertise, and Octavius ascended the staircase to the main hall of Domus Lucis with as much confidence and energy as he could muster. Toward the middle of the climb, a shot of pain nearly caused him to trip. He paused, peered behind him to see if the onlookers had noticed, but his own view was also blurred by the Lux Baiula's Binding, and he resumed his climb, satisfied and thankful that at least *some* things could still be controlled.

Though it was not rare for the king to visit Domus Lucis, it was not a common thing either, so when he entered the building, especially at the late hour and surrounded as he was, the chatter stopped, and heads turned. Elia Lux Baiula, who was there speaking with a young acolyte, came to greet the king.

She welcomed the king first, then Tania, and gave Dana a nod.

The king responded with a brief, "Elia," while Tania responded with a gesture of the hand.

Elia said, "It is good to hear you, Sire. I heard what happened. Are you coming to see Mitsuko?"

Elia's sincere welcome soothed the king. *At least one who does not blame me for what happened.* "Yes, I am."

"She, too, will be happy to hear you, Sire. She might still be awake, though she *is* still very weak."

A small flutter of unwilling hope tied Octavius's bowels at hearing those words.

A White Sash he did not recognize now approached them and waited to be introduced.

Tania said, "Sire, this is Samrachi Lux Baiula; Dalima Lux Baiula's replacement. She has been tending to Mitsuko."

Samrachi, a stern-looking woman with ash-gray hair, said, "Sire. I must say that I am slightly disadvantaged in treating Furanites, not having the benefit of Dalima Lux Baiula's knowledge of your citizens' health since she died without a Memory Transfer." Everyone's face darkened momentarily at being reminded of Dalima's tragic end. Appearing to regret her choice of words, the White Sash hurried to add, "However, I did treat Mitsuko Lux Baiula when she was in Urbs Lucis, so her physiology is not foreign to me, and Laranis, who also treated her there and never forgets the impressions a mind leaves on her, is attempting to restore her cognitive functions. By all rights, Mitsuko should be dead; the damage that her brain and body have sustained is unparalleled. Certainly, it is nothing we, alive, have seen before. But, somehow, she lives."

That both relieved and vexed the king. He said, "Can't you call on your mnemonic transfers for a treatment? Surely, the medics who lived during the days of the Dark Battle must have had to treat such injuries."

Samrachi's face hardened with resentment. But Tania intervened and invited the woman to take them to their Sister's bed.

So, the gray-haired woman took the party to the infirmary.

As they walked, the king asked somewhat testily, "Doesn't the White Sashate keep notes about each patient that visits the medical facilities?"

Tania exchanged a guarded look with her Sister, then answered the king's question. "Of course, Sire, we do. However, the sensations we perceive when we probe a patient, we cannotte put those on paper. So, we mustte remember them. When a medic takes on someone else's patients, she usually receives a transfer of the sensory memories relating to those patients' psychosomatic health."

Octavius did not know whether he should be impressed or not. He felt tired. But he thanked Tania for her explanation.

Presently, Samrachi cleared her throat and said, "We are here, Sire. Mitsuko is in that room." The woman pointed to a dimly lit room three meters ahead. She then turned to the king's guard and asked that they remain behind, to avoid stressing the patient. Julian seemed to want to accompany the king into the room. But they were in a building of the Sisterhood. What danger could be lurking here? When the king's primus relented, Octavius nodded and Samrachi Lux Baiula went into the room to see if Mitsuko was awake.

The king watched anxiously as the medic went in, leant toward Mitsuko, murmured something, waited for her patient to stir, and finally returned after adjusting a lever on the left wall of the room.

"She is still very weak, Sire, in and out of consciousness. You may have five minutes with her. You may speak to her to let her know that you are there to wish her a speedy recovery. But no questions. I will observe her condition from the hallway and if I see your presence upsets her, I will need to ask you to leave." The king heaved a frustrated breath and turned his head to hide his expression. Samrachi added, "I have turned on the ventilator so that the moss wall does not become saturated with your emanations."

At that, Octavius entered Mitsuko's room with all the assurance he could muster. The bed, as all beds in hospitals managed by the Order, was right against the back wall, which was covered with a special moss. In addition to exchanging the air in the room, the moss also had indicator properties. Indeed, depending on the volatile molecules released by the patient, the plant's filaments took on varying colors, which the medics used as indicators of the patient's health and recovery—or worsening condition. About two-thirds of the moss's filaments in Mitsuko's room were a deep orange or violet color, while only a third were a dull red—their usual color; from the corridor and with a whisper that reached his ear as easily as if she had been next to him, Samrachi told him that this was indicative of a critical condition.

Octavius took a chair, moved it by the bed and sat, his face an unreadable mask. Uncharacteristically, he clasped and unclasped his hands then rearranged his position on the seat several times. It was the guilt, a deep sense of guilt, which threatened to overwhelm him at any moment, that was unsettling him. His past words to her haunted him; he had berated her for doing what she had been assigned to do: protect him from Temptatori; he had been annoyed by her mere presence; and then he had even thought her 'useless'. As wise as some said he was, he was actually still quite ignorant….and a callous man. He had practically been surrounded by Lux Baiulae all his life, first within his father's court, then in his own. And yet, he had never taken the time to *know* them, as a group and as individuals, except for Elyana and Krystiana. What sort of ruler was he that did not know those who served him, those whose support was so crucial to the stability of his kingdom?

Presently, he heard a weak groan. It startled him and he found himself wishing that Mitsuko did not wake; he did not know what he would say if she did. What silliness!

But Mitsuko did not wake; it appeared, from the sounds that escaped her and from the movements of her hands, that she was trying to flee some nightmare.

Reassured, he made a decision…and then hesitated. He turned his head halfway toward the door; hearing nothing from the medics, he turned back toward Mitsuko, took a deep breath, and said what he had come to say if he found her unconscious.

7. REVELATIONS

I.   While No one Watches

While everyone slept, relying on their devices to alert them if Mitsuko should awaken, a janitor entered Mitsuko's room. The chamber was suffused with a dim light that gave the patient a jarring profile.

The janitor approached the bed to remove the trash bag from the *spoiled* can. As she did, she placed her left hand on the bedframe, slightly touching the patient's listless arm.

For a few moments, Mitsuko's body stiffened, as if in prey to some horrible back pain. Her head jerked suddenly, several times, then went limp and fell on the pillow again.

An alarm started to ring in the distance. The janitor went about her task as if nothing out of the ordinary had happened, putting the trash in her collection bin and leaving at once.

II.   The Search for the Cadavers

Under the reddish glow of that autumnal morning, carried by a brisk, chilly air , three Red Sashes, two of whom were Barriers, hunted atop their furans. They looked exhausted; they had been at it for three hours already and they needed to complete their mission soon or risk finding themselves facing the Bolingars or having to find shelter in the region, which was infested with the Kartaki rabble.

So, it was with excitement that Second Barrier Sasha finally pointed to a copse near the foot of the Furan Peaks; the dark roof of a small house could be glimpsed between the trees' thick foliage. If the owners had intended to hide the structure, they had not done a great job of it.

"I sense the vibrations of the assassins' cadavers down there. They are faint, but they are the vibrations of the women we faced in the Bind during the king's rescue!"

Pointing toward another copse, some one hundred meters from their target, Sasha was about to order the descent when Ksarina shouted, "Second Barrier, I am picking up vibrations from a few others as well, and—whoever they are—they're alive and seem to be quite strong in the Bind. Perhaps we should rethink this."

Sasha shook her head and said too softly to be overheard by Ksarina Lux Baiula: "Terra Cottas[18]." Only Jima heard the insult and expressed a silent agreement. Loudly, Sasha said, "We are going down, Ksarina; we need to bring those corpses back by tonight if the Yellows are going to learn anything useful from them. And if we kill another few Rogues, we'll bring *their* bodies back instead since they'll be fresher, though it would be better to bring a prisoner back so we can practice against her. But we *do* want to be careful; I'll give you that much. So, let's make sure we have a quiet landing and then plan our assault in case you're right."

Speaking to Whip to instruct him to land softly, Sasha did not see the tension in Ksarina's jaw, nor the contraction of her pupils.

The furan purred his understanding then extended all his four wings as well as the secondary lamellae[19] and went down, followed by the other two.

The landing was as quiet as that of a snowflake. The women dismounted, hid their furans with an illusion, planned their

---

[18] Terra cotta: Terra cotta is a pale soft red type of clay. It is used by Barriers as an insult directed at their non-Barrier Red Sash Sisters.

[19] Secondary lamellae: Pennate structures located beneath the main lamellae of a furan's and some other flyers' wings. The secondary lamellae could be extended to increase the surface area of the flyer and afford it a more silent flight.

assault, checked their weapons, probed their bodies for proper functioning—in case they did find resistance—and approached the hidden house.

As Ksarina had suspected, there were indeed men and women in the structure. From the sound of them, they must be at least two or three men and two women. Sasha and Ksarina both picked up at least two different persons with Binding powers. Sasha felt her pulse quicken, partly from excitement and partly from the memory of the battle in the Bind, which had not been easily won. *That was in the Bind. Here, we will have the advantage!*

Sasha sent to the others using the Monitor. Her chime caused Ksarina to wince. *"There are at least four people in there, but we must assume there are five, and that at least two of them are rogue Alterintrants. We are slightly outnumbered, but fortunately for us, there doesn't appear to be anyone else in the area. The structure is not very large so when we crash in through the door, they might spread from one side to the other, but they will not be able to surround us."*

Jima and Ksarina waited for the rest of their leader's instructions, the latter doing so with narrow, worried eyes. Sasha thought to herself: *Why does she look like she doesn't want to confront these criminals? She's not a Barrier, but she* is *a Red! I hope she doesn't fail us, or I will have her hide when we are done.*

Refocusing on the task at hand, Sasha said, *"I will take the first two, and you will do the same with the next two, Jima. Ksarina, you will take the last one, if there is a fifth."*

The women nodded, Jima doing so a little too proudly and causing Ksarina to tighten her jaw again. Sasha noticed the reaction and promptly added, *"Ksarina, although we can rely on my and Jima's fighting skills to crush our opponents, we will need you to help shield us all against any Bound attack.*

Normally, we'd be fine on our own—as would you—but we have only fought these women once before and we don't know all the Bindings they may throw at us."

Sasha waited for a confirmation from Ksarina, a sign that she would have their backs. The woman blinked slowly, as if to say, "I see what you are trying to do, but yes, I will do my part." Sasha nodded, cautiously, ordered the warriors to conceal their vibrations, and finally motioned for them to follow.

They crawled, avoiding twigs and loose stones until they reached the door. Sasha listened carefully and—not hearing anything different from what they had heard earlier—stood up, posted Jima and Ksarina to the left and to the right, then reached for the Bind and with a powerful set of sonactic vibrations pulverized the door.

III. What Naming a Thing Can Do

Sitting on a cut log and watching Toras practicing a new Binding skill with a look on her face that was part deep curiosity and part worry, Laiella said to Lina, "What is happening? It seems…unnatural the way he is learning this Binding."

Lina had finally released Laiella from the infirmary that morning and permitted her to resume her duties, slowly, which meant that she could begin overseeing the activities at the fortress but not yet participate in any physical training. She still wasn't sure what to do about the prince, whether to tell him that she forgave him but that it didn't matter, or whether to do what she had been asked to do. If the Sisterhood knew of her doubts, they would surely replace her; in fact, she should replace herself.

Lina said, "Kelysia told Na'Riina that what the prince does, the way he learns things that normal people can't learn is something she's called alioception."

When Laiella frowned, Lina explained, "It's the ability to perceive another person's position and movement, the response

246

of their muscles and tendons and joints, as well as the firing within their nerve fibers. Sensing these things, he can replicate the most complex sonactic Bindings."

Laiella snorted and returned her gaze toward Toras, who was now practicing the sonactic strike. Again, her face twitched with unease. The thing was, she really liked him, especially when he was as he was now, showing excitement, laughing, laughing! Playing, even as he trained. But that same personality made him so unpredictable. How would she ensure that he was not going to put the entire unit at risk if she could not predict his reactions?

Just now, Toras looked her way with a boyish grin, thrilled that he had sensed—merely sensed—Na'Riina's Binding. She tried to smile back. She did not know whether she succeeded or not, but the prince was already preparing to replicate the skill her colleague had just shown him.

"I can't believe how amazing that was! I felt everything: your nerves, your blood flow, the pricking of your skin as you generated the Binding. Knowing that the things I've been feeling all these years are real, that there's even a name for it! I know how to do it."

The block-faced woman pulled her eyes and lips downward, in an expression that said, "Yeah, I'm glad you're enjoying it, but I'd rather you just got on with it."

And the Halfling did just that.

Toras imagined himself creating the Binding, making Na'Riina's motions and, as he did them, felt the pulsing of his nerves, felt the twitching of his muscle fibers, felt the blood flow through his veins to flush his intestinal tract—he felt like Na'Riina, felt as if he were her. It was the same as when he mimicked voices. When he sensed that he could not accumulate any more energy he unleashed it with a powerful—and elated—

cry. The sonactic strike hit the block of stone standing twenty meters from him and shattered it, sending shards across the field.

Scorch, who had been watching his master for an hour already with only a vague interest, stood and beat his wings to avoid an incoming missile. The guardians who had been observing their commander's exercises gasped and cursed.

But Na'Riina was not impressed, and it annoyed the prince.

"You are not taking this seriously enough…Lord Commander. You should show more respect for these skills you are developing. Mishandling a sword is one thing—you might hurt the person standing next to you. But Bindings are weapons of a completely different order; misuse them and you might harm dozens or hundreds."

Toras's reaction was like that of the dough that expands suddenly on a hot plate just to flatten again as the crust splits. He dared not look toward Laiella; he knew what she must be thinking. He did not look at anyone, except at Scorch with a sorry, frustrated and discouraged expression on his face; Scorch, too, looked unimpressed, aggravated even.

"Commander! I am here to train you, and that means not only helping you develop your skills, but also teaching you to control yourself so that when you use them you will not accidentally harm anyone."

Looking down while shaking his head and making frustrated hand gestures, Toras said, "Fine, fine. I understand." He then lifted his head and faced the Red Sash instructor to hear her advice. As he did, a sigh—he was sure it was a sigh— reached his ear. He turned the corner of his eyes in its direction and caught Laiella lowering her head, her shoulders slumping. He swallowed, then locked his jaw and returned his attention to Na'Riina, who called his name.

IV. Umbra's Doings

After landing on a high ridge near the foot of the forbidding Mountains of the Yeltchek, on the morning of the seventeenth of Undecimus, the Umbra descended from the scaly back of his reptilian mount.

For any other K'Taran, the ride would have been a difficult and painful one, sitting atop a creature whose skin was covered with sharp, cutting teeth. For the Umbra, however, it had been no bother at all. He could moderate his sensory inputs and his skin was impenetrable.

But as impenetrable as his skin was, the backflows from the Bindings that Lux Baiula had used against him and the Serpent, three months back—when she and her leader had surprised them in the Bind—had penetrated his brain and shorted the neurocircuit that controlled his eyes. Since then, an annoying twitch had developed. And the updates he had received recently did not contain any code to repair the damage, nor did they contain any to fix his speech process, which was something he needed urgently lest Zebula cast him out. How could a modern Lux Baiula inflict such damage on him when even the fierce Luxori he had faced during the Dark Battle could not have wounded him in this way? *I must find a way to repair the damage. Et debeo fidem Zebulae retinere, ne peream. Fundatoribus male sit! O utinam regulas quasdam circumscripsissem.*[20]

The Umbra walked to the Great Howler that had also landed nearby and checked the baskets the animal carried; all was in order.

---

[20] And I must not lose Zebula's trust, or it will be the end of me. Curse the Founders! I wish I had been able to circumvent certain rules.

Now, he said to the Serpent, "Remember, do not show yourself to the humanoids here. I do not want any distractions while I investigate these people."

A resentful growl was all the Serpent gave in response.

The Umbra began his descent, followed by the howler. Once he was out of sight of the Serpent, he stopped and retrieved travel garments from one of the baskets on the pack animal. These were clothes worn by high-ranking females in Zebulonia. Indeed, he had learned from his Yeltcheki contact that foreigners were more likely to be granted an audience—and to achieve better results—if they were of the female sex. He removed the clothes he was wearing and donned the feminine garments. As he did, his body transformed too, and when he was done he appeared to be the middle-aged, highborn Zebulonian female his contact knew as Misaya. The figure was reminiscent of Nihildrina, though slightly taller and with a beguiling gaze. A scowl, which had not been there earlier, marred his otherwise arresting face when he heard the Serpent take off with as much caution as its dim-witted reptilian cousins.

His transformation complete, he resumed his descent, following a narrow path on the side of the mountain until, thirty minutes later, he reached his first destination: a small town of conical stone hovels on the edge of which he found the home of the person he was looking for—a "fixer" is what they would have called the man in the place the Umbra had come from so long ago, a place where he had been known as Andrus3[21].

After the Umbra, or rather, Misaya, announced herself by reciting the required formula—three steps away from the house—a man with the highly wrinkled skin of full-blooded Yeltcheki and dressed in light flowing robes opened the old

---

[21] Andrus3: A META (or medical and tutoring android) of the third generation.

door, looked to see who had called, spread his arms wide, and said in his melodious native tongue, "Misaya! I did not expect you soon. But your call is received. By Horin it is!"

Looking at the impressive animal sitting behind his guest, the man said, "Let me first take care of your howler. It must be exhausted from carrying those large baskets."

Responding in nearly perfect Yeltcheki, the Umbra said, "Thank you. Would you secure the baskets in a safe place?"

"Of course. I will bring them inside after I take care of the howler."

When he returned from the barn at the side of his hovel, he said, "You are welcome to enter my home, Misaya." Then, with a motion of his arm and a bow, he added, "Please."

Misaya entered the strangely but comfortably decorated abode and waited, studying the contents of the room, while her host labored to bring the baskets in.

When he was done and closed the door behind him, the man said in an imperfect Zebulonian, "I not imagine what you bring with you for this trip, Misaya, but I am impressed by the endurance of your Great Howlers, because the baskets have to weigh a hundred kilograms each!" As he said that, some water accidentally spritzed from the wrinkles near the man's lips. He apologized quickly then stood back, obviously waiting for his client to respond to his unspoken question.

Seeing that the woman was not going to disclose the content of her baggage, he said suddenly, "I get us some refreshment."

Having returned and offered the woman a tall glass of a cold infusion, he invited her to sit at the table and said, "As I told you in my letter, Misaya, I am honored to introduce you to one of my compatriots who has the connection you seek."

Misaya gave the man a satisfied look and asked, "My thanks to you, Yushii. And who is this person? What is their role in this country's affairs?"

Yushii responded with glowing eyes but a hushed, conspiratorial voice, "It is Ooshia Vumiko.

"A female?"

"A male. But our names are not after the Ancient Tongue, so it is confusing to foreigners."

The Umbra shifted as he realized he made a mistake, one which troubled him deeply, then asked, "And what is Ooshia Vumiko's role in your people's government?"

"Administrator Vumiko is only best-connected official in the Yeltchek. He has eyes and ears in every place who report to him, and most importantly, he has the ears of our emperor."

Misaya tipped her head with satisfaction.

Yushii continued, "For you to be admitted into Administrator Vumiko's mansion, you require appropriate transportation and be ready to give the proper introductory formula."

"I understand. And I assume you can provide the first and instruct me on the second?"

"I can."

"Very well."

And Misaya pulled something out of a satchel tied underneath her robe: A Bound stone wrapped in a cloth woven from spun ardamantis. Before proffering it to the man, she said, "Be careful. Never touch it with naked skin. You must use the cloth to handle it."

The man took the gift with equally frightened and covetous eyes. He blinked and pulled his head back in surprise when he felt the weight of it.

"This stone must weigh a kilogram."

"Nine hundred grams."

"How does one use it, Misaya?"

"Its most accepted use is to regulate the temperature in Zebulonian habitations. After dropping it from the cloth into an ardamantis bowl, it will cool a fifty square meter room for several fourths during the hottest periods of summer."

Yushii's eyes widened until they could stretch no more. "And its other uses?"

"I will let you discover those."

"How does it release its energy?"

"You must let it release the captured heat either in the ground or in a large body of water. If you let it accumulate heat and then leave it wrapped in the cloth, you can use it to heat a room during the cold months, though I understand the temperature does not drop very low in this country."

"No, it does not. But this is for surely priceless, Misaya, and I thank you for it."

Misaya responded with a stretching of her lips.

Yushii asked, "You have more of these stones? For Administrator Vumiko?"

"I do; twelve more. And there will be more still for you if our affairs are concluded successfully."

"Excellent. With my help and your most exquisite capabilities, I am confident of a fruitful conclusion."

Misaya nodded again.

"Let us get ready then; it is about six hours to arrive. Firstly, I get you some more appropriate clothing." And Yushii passed into a side room, opened a door, went down some steps, spent some time there, probably hiding the Bound stone, then came back out with an article of outer clothing for his client, which was meant to indicate that she had been welcomed into the country by a native. Misaya deftly put the light scarf on at once, which the man adjusted under her unreactive face.

Stepping back to look at his client, Yushii's face flushed. He said, "Misaya, you could pass for one of our noblewomen! You be well received in Yeltchika, though your seriousness is frightening as well. But our northern women are so, too." And he laughed heartily.

Misaya did not react to the compliment, but said, "In that case, let us go. I need to be back here by tomorrow evening to return to Zebulonia."

"I fetch the coach and harness the vorans. In the meantime, you start learning this introductory formula, which you need to pronounce after I introduce you. I explain the rest while we drive to the capital."

And Yushii handed Misaya a piece of paper upon which was written an unusually formal and lengthy greeting.

The coach was an ornate black and green vehicle shaped like a flat cone and pulled by a team of four bay desert vorans. These were much smaller than the snowvoran, and slightly smaller than the Alvinorian breed. But they were lean and had some fatty pads on their haunches, which helped them cross the vast desert distances where grass was scarce. However, neither the vorans nor the shape of the coach were what struck the Umbra. Instead, it was the external surface of the coach, which was layered in narrow strips of a material unknown to him— *Mirabile.*[22] Larger strips of the material, which must cover the front of the vehicle, were presently pulled back and fastened to the roof. The interior had seats arranged in two semi-circles. A recessed section, obviously meant to protect the driver from the suns' rays, occupied the fore section.

Misaya asked Yushii about the material, and the function of the strange strips.

Yushii responded, "Ahh, I know you don't have them in Zebulonia, not also in Alvinoria. They be very useful when the suns reach the summit of their journey, and especially in the middle of the fourth, but perhaps you not be here then. Still, I

---

[22] Intriguing.

am surprised you choose this fourth to visit, because the midday hours burn, and they burn worser here than in your latitudes."

"Do you mean that you remain active during the Bolingars?"

Yushii did not respond right away but his face twisted this way and that in confusion. After a moment, he said, "Sorry, Misaya, I not remember the western name for Burning Hours. But yes; we stay active, all across the entire days, except during fourth and fifth day of the Burning Fourths."

The Umbra gave a snort, surprised to learn about useful technologies he had never heard of. But he asked, or rather Misaya asked, how the vorans remained active, what the material was composed of, and how it worked.

While securing Misaya's baggage in the back of the coach, Yushii explained that before Highsun, he would cover the vorans with a sheet composed of the same material as the coach, except for being see-through over the eyes. He said the material was made from spun cocoon sheets from native bellowers, and that the strips of this material, layered in this manner—Yushii swung of his arm widely—created a cooling wind.

Once everything was in place, the Yeltcheki invited him to climb aboard the vehicle, then sat himself in the front cabin, and whipped the vorans forward.

The Umbra took five minutes to learn the long and complex introductory statement, rehearsing it in his mind. He then spent another half hour admiring the forbidding landscape as a way to let time pass before *Misaya* announced that she was done learning the introduction.

Yushii showed his surprise once more, squeezing some humidity from his forehead but without the embarrassing squirt, this time. Speaking in Yeltcheki, he said, "Our neighbors from Mo'Rokoth take several hours to learn the formula, and several days to pronounce it properly, Misaya. You are truly an exceptionally skilled person."

Misaya made no response to that.

The fixer spent some time explaining to his client what she needed to know about the rites surrounding political or favor-seeking introductions.

At precisely thirteen hours and four minutes after Highnight, fifty-six minutes before midday, Yushii stopped to cover the vorans with a sheet that completely surrounded them and molded itself around their head, belly, and legs though it left a space of about a centimeter between its surface and the voran's skin. That done, he pulled down the outer sheets, darkening the inside of the coach quite significantly, and returned to his seat to resume the ride.

"I see how you protect the vorans from the suns, but how do you protect them from the Storm?"

"The Storm is not as strong here as it is in Alvinoria. And, as in Zebulonia, there is little for the winds to blow here. Only sand here and snow in your country. The covers around the vorans protect them, and we are protected inside the coach."

The Umbra nodded to himself as the coach lurched forward and the vorans released a loud, excited trumpet.

Some thirty minutes into the last leg of the trip, the Umbra noticed a sudden, almost imperceptible, clicking sound coming from the outside of the vehicle. A moment later, Yushii shouted in Zebulonian, "It begins. But no worry!"

The Umbra was not worried, but he *was* captivated by the cooling technology. Despite their organic failings, the creativity and problem-solving capabilities of humanoids had always fascinated him. Presently, he watched the strips of cooling material on the outside of the cabin begin to lift and close, from top to bottom and over again, in a controlled and increasingly rapid sequence as the suns reached their apex. The movement produced a refreshing circulation of the air. The noise, however, was quite irritating, and remained so until his auditory pathways became habituated to it.

The vorans' sheets now attracted the Umbra's attention. They were inflating and deflating around the animals, as the strips steadily lifted and closed. In the distance, where a few shielding trees stood, warning shrieks and growls added to the ceaseless noise and told the Umbra that the animals without sunshields—predators, competitors, and preys alike—were gathering under the trees to protect themselves from the killing rays. The sounds elicited a thought in the Umbra's mind: *Hopefully, I can keep the Zebulonians, Alvinorians, Kynarians and others from uniting against us.*

The trip to the coastal city of Yeltchika continued this way, with the Umbra taking notice of one thing or another and the Introducer making a comment when he believed his client might benefit from it, until the last hour when Yushii decided to instruct Misaya on the ways and mores of the Yeltcheki, and of the powerful in particular.

To the Umbra, all humanoids were strange, what with all the unproductive interactions. He had never understood why they were necessary, and he had tried to prevent their establishment in his charges, long ago. But, despite his best efforts, they had all developed the same idiosyncrasies and had espoused the same illogical and unnecessary behaviors that he had come to detest in his creators. He would have been more forceful—if he could have—in weeding out these imperfections, but alas.

As Yushii continued chattering, the Umbra's mind leapt to something else. He wondered why these people had never changed the name of their land—Mo'Tarkoth was the name given it by the Locari, when it had belonged to them. On the other hand, he marveled at the changes that evolution—the disruptive natural process that affected living beings—had imparted on the desert people. But the Humans sent across the galaxy had been endowed with HAAP complexes, or Highly Advanced Adaptation Promoter complexes, so their high adaptability made sense. For example, the Yeltcheki did not sweat nor urinate much, and their highly wrinkled skin allowed them to capture moisture from the soil—thus their preference for walking barefoot—or anything they touched, hold it there, and funnel it to the corners of their mouths as needed. The adaptation evolved in a mere two thousand four hundred and fifty years. It was impressive, and yet, most humanoids were still just humanoids and animals of all kinds were still just animals; only directed evolution could create something truly superior in all respects, such as he had done with the Janarae. But even so, no biological species matched him…and he served.

Some thirty minutes before they arrived at their destination, the sheets slowed their flapping, and the Umbra was able to see that the shimmering over the sands had diminished in intensity. But a low, powerful vibration now rose from the west; the Bolingar Storm was coming.

As the Umbra had come to expect by now, Yushii leaned his head backward slightly and shouted, "The Storm. It is awakening. But do not be concerned, Misaya. As I said, it is really only sand, and we will be fine in here." The man then leaned forward and turned a lever to lock the ventilating strips in a closed position. The cabin darkened but a Living Lamp lit it up soon thereafter.

The Umbra thanked the Introducer for his reassuring words. And yet, for the first time since his arrival in the Yeltchek, he felt nervous. Indeed, though he could withstand heat and cold and powerful physical impacts, and though he could withstand the penetrating force of sharp objects such as the Serpent's tooth covering, abrasion from the fierce Bolingar winds could do serious damage to him. To take his mind off the possibility that Yushii might be wrong and the Storm might wreck the coach and leave him in the open to be disintegrated, he decided to investigate how the vorans' covers resisted the winds. He could not very well see the material from where he was, but he did begin to hear clicking sounds which gained in intensity over the next minute, and he deduced from it that the strips must be lined with tiny articulated clasps, which aligned with hooks on the opposing face. *Subtilissimum.*[23]

And the winds *were* ferocious. They rattled the coach and caused the sheets on it to stiffen with horrible noises. But the car did not topple over and the winds did not shred everything in their path, and the Umbra eventually relaxed.

Presently, Yushii turned his head slightly back to shout, "Yeltchika! We will be at Administrator Vumiko's palace in fifteen minutes. If you wish to rehearse again, now is the time."

The Umbra said, "I have no need," then, thinking it was time that he finish adjusting his behavior and replies, as annoying as this was to him, he added, "Thank you, Yushii. Your reminder is well received, and I can promise that my interview with the administrator will not bring you dishonor."

The fixer made a dismissive sound and the Umbra set his mind to the coming encounter, letting go of every other thought.

V. Under the Water

In a mesmerizing submarine hall, with stalagmites cut to serve as benches and luminous organisms covering the stalactites to light up the cavernous place, thoughts were being

---

[23] Ingenious.

exchanged in a strange silence broken only by the sound of the underground river flowing past at the back of the cave.

Sitting awkwardly on one of the benches, which formed a semi-circle in the center of the grotto, Torrent sent, *"Unveiled himself, the enemy's lieutenant has. The storms he prepares for the Hrackmol!, destructive hurricanes will be."* His glowing, wet, gel-like skin gave him—as it did the other eight Locari in attendance—a remarkable appearance as he spoke in the great hall.

He continued, *"These waters, familiar to a few of us they are. Suffer we did when the winds against us the Umbra raised, and into the seas forced us."*

Mental nods were exchanged for a while between the Locari's ruling members as they processed the thought and the memory of the battles, the suffering, and their final exodus from the surface.

Presently, the skin of a wide, brightly colored Locara who stood on her stiffened, tubular hind fins, shimmered to request the right to send a thought. When their leader sent a mental nod that sounded like a gulp in her mind, she said, *"Torrent, with the kin of the Walking One who Eight and Ten is called, the Locari should align."*

A soft, amused sound escaped from another Locar, the junior member of the Ruling Mind.

Alga, the Locara who had just spoken, sent, *"My rendering of the Alvinorian name mock you, Current? Perhaps a better teacher we need."*

Current shrank a little on his stalagmitic seat, and Torrent intervened to prevent the development of a distance between Alga and his protégé. *"To disrespect you, Current did not intend, Alga. Young he is, and still much to learn he has. But agree on a plan to enter the coming storm we must, so that learn and thrive under new suns, we may."*

A large, bulky, and dark Locarus sitting to Torrent's left presently spoke aloud, "Too long as limpfish we have lived, and extinguished we may be, if in a new battle we engage."

The omen shook all members of the Mind, some reacting with watery rumbles, while others did so with dull squeals.

Torrent sent, *"Perhaps more like the sleeping volcano we are, Kelp, which after repeated blows erupts."*

The solid but old Kelp, who had always enjoyed irritating others, replied aloud again, *"'Perhaps', you say, because uncertain everything is until to the test we are put. Will this our test be?"*

A dark, elongated Locara named Shoot requested the right to send. Receiving it, she said, *"If this battle we join, Torrent, then demand the return to our ancestral land we must. Many among us there are, who under the suns wish to…stroll again, and residence take."*

Loud externalized barks of revulsion accompanied by images of tails whipping Shoot's statement rose from five Locari, while a quiet rumble of agreement accompanied by an image of Locari walking side by side atop the land emerged from the other three. When the former received the treasonous image, they responded with skin-stripping rip currents to bring the others back in line. The arguing continued for a moment, with images of freedom and return to the land battling images of disaster.

When the fighting had gone on long enough for all to be exhausted and have reached a point of readiness for resolution, Torrent sent a gulping sound to acknowledge the propositions and counter arguments equally. The barks quieted as did the rumble, and all waited—as if in suspended animation—for Torrent to ask the question.

It came to them crisp and clear, almost painful in its sharpness, as the image of a river fork. The left branch showed their species rising out of the water to face death—and hope; the right one showed them remaining still underwater to be extinguished by the Founder when He came. Four replies came choosing the left branch, while four still dissented. Torrent sent an image of himself taking the left branch too. It was decided.

After a long, quiet moment spent unifying all thoughts and emotions with the decision made, Torrent dismissed everyone except Current.

Current sent, *"To do your bidding is my wish, Torrent."*

"A message you must carry when next with the Walking One you connect."

Current listened, then bent his triangular head in assent and exited the Minding Chamber, leaving Torrent to mull over what had been decided.

VI. What Old Memories Contain

A woman with a modest, unassuming way gasped too quietly to be heard when she completed her review of five transcriptions—all recorded by different Sisters over the past month but all providing the first compelling account of the Temptatori's capabilities. The scholar was an expert in all things related to the Temptatori, having studied all that had been written about them, and having now studied the transcriptions being made by those who carried memories of the Dark Battle. The only thing she had not had available to study was a living Temptator.

When Praefecta Bilena had put her in charge of the effort, she had been clear about the goal: 'We must get all those memories transcribed within two months and only you and Molara may study them all to uncover our enemy's weaknesses. You will provide me with fourthly summaries and when you think you've identified what we are looking for, you will tell me and only me.'

Now, Pilara eyed the other Yellow Sash assisting her this day—Molara Lux Baiula, a spymaster and Ooldrina and Raaviana's handler. The woman could not have heard her gasp, and yet she made a motion that indicated awareness.

The contrast between Pilara's dark skin and yellow robe was feebler than the contrast between her position as leader of the Transcription effort and her lack of confidence, so much so that when Molara was assigned to her team, she had fretted an entire fourth about being embarrassed by the spymaster's skills.

But when Pilara knew a thing, her insecurity transformed into dogged certainty and self-assurance that persuaded even the most tenacious doubters. And at this moment—having absorbed all that had been recorded on paper by the twenty-three Sisters with memories from the Dark Battle—Pilara felt tremendous confidence, and she turned to Molara to say, "I need you to confirm the meaning of this phrase here." Pilara placed a revealer on the only passage she wished Molara to study. It was from the transcript by Tera Lux Baiula, the Keeper of the Baths.

Molara kept her eyes averted as she wondered about the meaning of Pilara's sudden assurance. She approached the woman and took the notebook from her; it was a heavy one, probably counting some two hundred pages of detailed memories, the transcription of which must have caused Tera great turmoil. She looked at the neatly scribbled sentence visible at the bottom of the right page. She tapped the thick paper hiding the rest of the page a few times. On its own, the passage could mean one of two things.

Molara asked, "Does Tera indicate if this woman was a Sister? From the pronouns used it would seem so, but then they are not consistently used in this transcript. Knowing this would help me ascertain the meaning of the phrase."

"I prefer you not be influenced by the context. Please give me your opinion of the meaning of what you *can* see."

Perennially even-tempered, even when she was vexed, Molara replied, "Well, then, I have to assume this passage is about a woman that the memory's originator had difficulty categorizing and, thus, difficulty speaking about consistently."

Molara paused for dramatic effect, which had always irritated Pilara. The scholar made an impatient gesture now, and Molara said, "My best guess is that the woman in our ancient Sister's memory was a Rogue, and this Rogue was releasing sexual pheromones when questioned by our Sister."

Pilara blinked. "Are you sure? How do you know?"

"I am sure; Yellows used to alternate between synonyms of the words fragrance when speaking of pheromones. As you might know, the Sisterhood was quite prude back then. This behavior is consistent with the pieces of information we have gathered from the other transcripts, and I have observed the behavior in Kartak."

Despite her excitement, Pilara raised a brow.

But Molara did not share any more information about her experiences in the rogue city. Instead, she said, "We could ask Tera to show us her memories to know for sure what this passage meant."

"The procedure is not safe."

"Well, I've given you my opinion." Molara held Pilara's gaze for a moment, as if to say more.

Pilara sighed. "What is it, Molara?"

"We have what we were looking for, Pilara. This, along with the other pieces of evidence we have, clearly points to a pattern that we can use to recognize a Turned individual."

"You mean a Turned woman."

The spymaster gave a suffering smile in response.

Impatient to bring the news to the praefecta, Pilara dismissed her Sister with instructions for her to return on the morrow to finish verifying the meanings of the remaining passages in the transcript she had been working on.

Molara left with a stiff nod, obviously still upset that this charge had not been given to her. Deciphering information was her expertise; Bilena should have assigned her to lead the task.

A few minutes later, after she had collected the various pieces of evidence pointing to a peculiarity of the individuals turned by the Temptatori, a peculiarity which appeared to be testable, Pilara left the Schola Luciana, taking a circuitous route to Praefecta Bilena's offices, repeatedly slowing her step and then balling her fists with quiet excitement.

VII. What Should Have Been about Lusk Only

Elyana had called a Bound meeting with Irania, to warn her and—through her—the king and prince about Lusk. The king's advisor had arrived late, and Elyana's legs had begun to ache. Sitting cross-legged was nothing unusual to her, and the Contemplation Room in her Lucian apartment was comfortably appointed, but she was unusually tense that morning, and she was still drained and recovering from the injuries she had sustained during her recent battles in the Bind. She missed the signs on her colleague's own form, which spoke of unpleasant news. After the conventional but brief greetings, and without any preamble, Elyana sent, *"Lusk can no longer be trusted."*

Irania exclaimed, *"What are you saying, Elyana?"*

The question rattled Elyana—though she had expected it—since she had been one of those to release the Zebulonian, in Sextus, to serve the king and the high prince. But, given that she was speaking to one of her Order, she said it as it was, *"Lusk is a servant of Noctiferus."*

Irania's momentary silence, accompanied by the zapping and twitching of her figure while she processed the statement, unnerved Elyana.

"I am sorry, Elyana, but I still do not understand what you are saying. What happened?"

Elyana sighed, then told her colleague of her recent, growing doubts about Lusk, their meeting at the theater, the ensuing battle between the two of them, and finally about his escape during the king's rescue.

Irania remained silent for quite a while after that revelation, her figure shifting fitfully.

"I do not know what to say, Elyana. You must be feeling awful, but the decision to release him to practice was not yours alone."

Elyana's form made an ugly, insulted frown.

"Well, I know how you enjoy taking accountability for decisions you take part in. Still. Anyway, I am surprised that he did not take the opportunity to kill you; it would have been very easy for him to do so while you were locked in battle against those women."

The vibrations forming the Manu Dextra's figure twitched this way and that, but she remained silent.

Irania sent, *"I suppose you wish me to inform the king?"*

Elyana nodded.

Irania's profile shifted for a while longer, crossing her arms, placing her hand underneath her vaporous chin, shaking her head, casting away some thought that kept creasing her face with unusual sadness and finally, looking up, having apparently come to some realization.

Despite her unease and self-reproach, Elyana was able to discern her colleague's sentiments, this time. She said, *"What is it, Irania? Something else than my news seems to be bothering you."*

Irania started to speak, stopped, then spoke again, *"I will tell you after. Let's finish with Master Methrim. I was thinking that we do have one saving grace, and it is the king's aversion to sharing anything of importance with anyone until he has no choice but to reveal his strategy, and then, only to the members of his Privy Council. I am quite certain, then, that Lusk Methrim has not learned anything from the king's court that could endanger the Crown's or the Order's position."*

Elyana sighed with some relief and bobbed her head a few times but then said, *"You are probably right, Irania, but the fact that I agreed to his release still troubles me deeply, especially because I can now see the clues which were right in front of me, plain and evident. But I simply could not act on them. It was as if he had numbed my mind."*

Softening her form's visage, Irania said, *"He probably did dull all of our minds and you won't be the only one heading for the Thermals for a flogging when this is all over."* A very small, thankful smile stretched Elyana's lips. *"But tell me, has he been part of any sensitive discussions of the Societas? I ask because our self-confidence often makes us quite careless."*

Elyana did not respond, but not because the question disturbed her. She was simply staring into the void, as if her mind had been suddenly commandeered by some other thought.

"Elyana."

"Aghr! I am sorry, Irania. It was that annoying Locara…or rather, Locarus. He is trying to contact me. But, to answer your question, Lusk has helped train the two young spies we sent to Zebulonia, and he has provided us with the contacts in the queen's palace. He could—"

Irania's form stiffened when she understood what Elyana meant: the girls were in danger.

Elyana could not keep her guilt and worry from marring her figure, and Irania said, *"Elyana, if I may. I understand you feel responsible. But do not 'go down that hole', as they say."*

Elyana scoffed at that, and she nearly challenged her colleague for suggesting that one should not be fully accountable for one's decisions, whether shared with others or not.

"I will inform the king this afternoon and let you know what he says. But, Elyana, you asked me what's bothering me. Well, Mitsuko..."

Elyana did not need to hear the rest. In fact, she did not wish to. So, she steered the conversation toward a more topical one. *"Have you informed the king already?"*

Irania shook her head before nodding. Elyana could appear to be a very cold woman, at times.

"How is he?"

"He...is not well. He blamed himself for Mitsuko's coma and won't do any better once I tell him she has passed. But he also blames himself for something else—something more personal, perhaps for sending the young prince away. It appears prince Ori does not feel welcome in Kynaria." Irania paused before continuing. *"Laranis told me the king almost kicked her out of the palace when she visited him, this morning, to check on his mental health."*

Despite her own uncertainties and concerns, and notwithstanding Octavius's foolish decision to enter the Bind with only Mitsuko at his side—a decision which many in Urbs Lucis would consider to be the direct cause of Mitsuko's death—Elyana kept the exchange focused on more objective matters. She said, *"The king knows how to segregate his feelings from the facts, and he will get through this."*

Irania's arched eyebrow told Elyana that her colleague was not convinced by the statement, and she chided herself for it. Wasn't she finding it hard to put her own sense of guilt aside?

How many times had Irania reminded her that she was not…*solely* responsible for welcoming the Temptator?

Elyana continued, *"What I would like to know is who received Mitsuko's memories."*

The Manu Dextra's abrupt bifurcation obviously annoyed Irania. However, the woman did not try to argue and replied, *"Krpta."*

"Krpta?!"

"None of the others here were ready and it was felt that, because Krpta easily integrated Juliana's memories, she could receive Mitsuko's too."

"Tania and Elia agreed to this?"

Irania's form vibrated as she nodded; it seemed *she* did not agree with the decision.

"Well, it is what it is. At least, she is not so close to the king." Elyana paused, troubled by a fleeting thought, then asked, *"When will we know how the transfer went?"*

"By the end of the fourth. But she will be staying in the clinic at Domus Lucis, this time, so that our medics may keep a closer eye on her."

Elyana nodded, asked Irania to keep her informed of Krpta's condition, then made ready to depart when she noticed a question in the administrator's eyes. Elyana took a deep breath and asked her Sister to speak her question.

"Are the girls aware of the potential danger they will face in Zeblinia?"

Elyana shook her head dejectedly, then rushed to add, *"But they have not yet arrived."* More slowly and with audible uncertainty, she said, *"Molara is trying to contact them."*

"It is a shame they left before they could have the Monitor implanted in them. Well, as you love saying, Elyana, letting oneself be troubled by worry does nothing to solve a problem."

Elyana snorted and sighed but did not reply. *"I will leave you now so you may take care of what needs be taken care of, Irania."* And almost as an afterthought, she added, *"Please let me know how the king does."*

This softened her Sister's features and the two separated with a promise to hear each other again as soon as either had new information to share.

***

When Elyana left the Bind, she spent some time in a gloomy disposition. Her mind raced with feelings of inadequacy and frustration, as well as struggled with a sense of deep sadness and worry. Refusing to let herself wallow in misery any longer than she already had, she remembered the Locarus's chime. The creature had not yet learned that Elyana could not always be available. *I suppose I understand Aithen now. Well, let's see what he wants.*

Elyana accessed that field in her brain's telesensory cortex where the Monitor was located and thought of her contact. As if by magic—it still felt that way, even to her—the Locarus responded.

"Elyana."

"Fins touch. You wished to speak with me?"

"Fins touch, Lux Baiula. The Ruling Mind obtained a decision."

"The Ruling Mind?"

"The leaders of the Locari."

Elyana sent a nod using the Locari's signal for it.

Upon hearing the clopping sound, Current explained, *"The Ruling Mind has decided to join the battle."*

A wave of hope flooded Elyana. She let herself feel it for a long moment, as if to wash away all the recent bad news, before her ever-rational mind called her back to practical matters. As a Purple Sash, she knew that important declarations should always be ascertained. She asked the Locarus what he meant.

Current spent the next few minutes detailing his leaders' decision. It appeared Elyana was right to request the clarification. The Locari would not, in fact, get immediately involved, at least not directly. But they *would* begin providing what knowledge they could about the true nature of the enemy and reassess the extent of their involvement at a later time.

Someone else might have been unimpressed and disappointed. However, Elyana understood the Locari's desire for caution, and she sent Current an image of herself lying down in front of him, which earned Elyana a laugh and a lengthy correction: a Receiver presents themself prostrate in front of the giver while a defeated combatant shows themself actively lying down in front of the victorious party.

Elyana blinked, felt like laughing. But she sent the thought of herself already prostrate in front of the Locarus. To her surprise and frustration, the creature stopped her to tell her that given that she had been corrected, she should now respond with the active motion of lying down. Annoyed, despite her training, Elyana decided to send her thanks in Alvinorian, instead. Wasn't the Locarus trying to learn their language, after all?

Current looked amused. Elyana gave her interlocutor the customary Locaran parting formula, which Current replied to with a smug hint to his thought, and the two disconnected from each other.

Once the connection was dropped, Elyana stood and began pacing around the Contemplation Room, quickly forgetting the irritating Locarus and thinking, instead, about his people's decision to support them in the coming battle. But her rational mind did not linger long on the possibility of something good that was yet to prove itself true and returned to the realities of the present: their failures—*No, my failures*— with respect to Lusk, which had perhaps endangered Ooldrina and Raaviana. She needed to speak with Molara, the girls' handler, to make certain they were not compromised by the man's treachery. Still, the hopeful part of her brain peeked through once more to tell her that though things were bad, all was not necessarily doomed, and that was a good thing to hang on to even as her rational part—more pessimistic in nature—foresaw the tragedy that might befall the girls.

VIII.   In Yeltchika

Misaya's introduction into the house of Administrator Vumiko was as maddeningly tedious as the Umbra had expected from the fixer's unending descriptions. But he was received and now sat in the man's simple office which, though plainly decorated, was adorned with objects of obvious quality—a sign of the man's position in the kingdom. The only disturbing aspects of the office were the noise from the flapping sheets outside the windows, and the heat; it appeared the cooling contraption had a limit to its capacity. The Umbra adjusted the properties of his skin to account for the heat.

Administrator Vumiko, at first sight a bubbly and welcoming man, had in fact the eyes of a calculating predator, which the Umbra was able to discern quite easily. This meant the negotiations would likely be needlessly long and tortuous, but only the result counted now.

After smoothing the tips of his thick mustache, Vumiko said, "Misaya-rava, the great queen's representative is received in my abode, and I am most pleased to do so, especially for one who honors us with such a command of our language."

Misaya bowed her head, with a grace that Andrus3 had learned over the course of centuries, bowing to one queen after another. And what he learned could never be unlearned but only perfected. Or was it so? His language centers continued to suffer from intermittent errors, which he had not yet been able to fix despite the recent update from Terra. Hopefully, he would be able to make the necessary repairs soon, before Zebula forced him to go see her medic.

Without further preamble, Misaya said, "My queen wishes to hire the services of the Yeltcheki fleet in the coming war."

"We have heard about Aquinos's woes. But they do not concern us; your gods are not ours and the beasts pose no danger to us."

The Umbra could not help a mocking expression starting to form; the Serpent had brought him here and could easily be dispatched to wreak havoc across this desert land. But he did not wish to antagonize his host, and he wiped the forming grin from his lips.

The man smoothed his mustache, then said, "Ours is nation at peace, and it must remain so because without it none of us would survive on this scorched continent. To engage in a war that is not ours and risk bringing the threat here is not in our interest."

"I understand, Administrator Vumiko. My apologies for not explaining myself better and for insisting, but if Zebulonia does not survive the war, it will no longer be able to provide you with the goods you've come to...rely on—things which only our people can create. This means that the Yeltchek *will* be impacted, regardless."

An Alvinorian would have reacted with indignation at Misaya's comment, but Vumiko stared at his guest for a moment then said, "Yes, your technology does allow us a level of comfort we would rather not do without, Misaya-rava. But it is all a matter of balancing cost and benefit."

The Umbra considered sneering at the administrator's statement, but only for the briefest moment. He decided that it was time to reveal his chips. Retrieving a cloth-wrapped object from his pocket, he said, "Would this change the equation?"

Vumiko withheld a gasp, though he let an expression of cautious interest stretch his almond-shaped eyes. He leaned forward to view the stone that Misaya unwrapped on his desk. It glittered with a blackness he had never seen before. Not even the night sky was as dark. And what was that cooling feeling, just then? The sheets covering the windows were not flapping any faster than they had been.

"Please, Administrator Vumiko, do not touch it with your hand. It must be handled with the cloth lest you burn yourself."

Vumiko pulled back his arm, but his face now showed a wet curiosity and puzzlement. Was the Zebulonian offering to buy Yeltcheki ships with some unknown *precious* stone? "What is this? How would it alter our calculations?"

"If I am not mistaken, you have already noticed one of its properties: heat exchange. One of these could cool this entire room for…three fourths and without the noisy sheets flapping out there."

"Three fourths?! What other properties does it have?"

"It can, of course, do the opposite and release heat in colder weather. But a dozen of these can heat up the air inside what we call a flying bag, which—when connected to a basket—can carry three or four people across vast distances."

This time, the administrator's eyes opened wide with shock. "You mean you have a contraption that allows you to fly?"

"We do."

"Then why do you need our ships?"

"These flying bags can only carry a few people at a time. And they are slow, but faster than travel by voran or any other land animal."

Caught in the excitement of the technological possibilities of the stone yet still uncertain about its true value, the administrator asked, "Do you mean that you cannot add more stones to lift as large a flying bag as you need and increase its speed?"

Misaya took a moment to respond, "I understand why you are a trusted man of Emperor Shinoa's. You are insightful and perhaps a scientist too. But no, adding more stones will not help."

The administrator made a small dismissive smile in response to Misaya's compliment and waited for a more detailed response. But, seeing that the Zebulonian would provide no further details, yet appreciating the extraordinary value of the technology she spoke of—if it truly worked as she described it—the administrator moved on and said, "Did you, perhaps, bring the equipment to do a demonstration? If these stones can do what you say, then your queen shall get what she desires."

"I did."

"Then let us see this magic, Misaya-rava!"

In the florid and noisy courtyard, with staff standing along the edges holding the palace's captive animals under leash and the administrator sitting on a bench, Misaya directed three burly men to unfold the bag, assemble the basket, and tie the former to the latter. All watched with curious frowns and grunts, wondering what this foreigner was preparing.

The watchers' curiosity grew when Misaya climbed aboard the basket, waved one servant to bring over a head-sized container—which the man carried with huffs and puffs filled with astonishment—and place it in a shallow ardamantis concavity at the center of the basket. The administrator's eyes were riveted on the contraption and on the container, which he suspected held similar stones to the one he had seen earlier.

Once all was in place and secure, Misaya began to crank a small lever on the container. Superheated air emerged from it and distorted the view. Some of the staff said that it looked like the haze over the sands during the Burning Hours. As soon as the shimmering air reached the entrance to the bag, magic started to happen: the fabric began flapping, first near its opening, then toward the closed end, and the entire bag started lifting from the ground, moving from its horizontal position to a vertical one, little by little and with the grandest sound the administrator had ever heard—the sound of life being given to the otherworldly contraption. The administrator's staff backed away partly from fear and partly from awe, while Administrator Vumiko rose from his seat, took a step forward and stretched his hand out, as if to touch the wondrous machine.

Screams rang through the courtyard when the flying bag gave one final clack as it started to rise. The Yeltcheki gaped at their employer, and the shine on his face and the exuberance of his movements told them that *he* had made possible—thanks to his remarkable negotiation skills—the viewing of this wonder—of this marvel. Administrator Vumiko dreamed of what he could accomplish with this technology in his hands.

When the flying bag had reached just above the small palace's tallest tower, Misaya closed the heating container again. The bag slowly deflated, and as it did, the basket returned to its position on the ground. Misaya ordered the servants to pull the bag to the side so that they might rewrap it afterward.

Gasps and wows and curses were heard all around, and the administrator himself let out an expletive as he responded to his staff's astonished gazes. When Misaya stepped out of the basket, Administrator Vumiko approached her with wet lips despite the heat and said with a voice filled with the lust of opportunity, "I will speak to the emperor's secretary in favor of your request and get you an audience tonight, Misaya. Your offer will be most welcome…assuming," he added without taking his eyes from the fantastical contraption, "that the cost to the Yeltchek will be limited to the provision of ships with small non-warring crews."

"That will be our agreement."

His eyes still on the flying bag, Vumiko added almost dreamily, "Good, because our people have no wish to do battle in the tree-infested lands of Alvinoria and Kynaria, or in your snow deserts. But with this machine, we will be able to roam our deserts as never before, and to finally get the upper hand on those damned Mo'Rokothians."

The Umbra nodded to himself and sent a thoughtcall to the Serpent to let him know he would be at the meeting point as planned.

8. WHEN IT BEGINS TO CRUMBLE

I.   Preparations

Sitting at his desk, with his Small Council across from him, Octavius opened the spore dish and brushed the surface of the letters he was sending to each landholder with the brusque, interrupted movements of a man who has other preoccupations on his mind. The powder bound itself to the ink and disappeared everything, including his signature. The recipients would brush the letters with the correct counter chemical to reveal the text.

The letters confirmed the orders he had had Administrator Irania Lux Baiula communicate to the landholders' advisors earlier that day, orders for the nobles to dispatch the conscripts from their respective lands to the regional garrison within a day of receiving the missive. Jarah, Pargah and Yerlah were to send their men to the Yerlayan garrison, while Arotek and his dependents, as well as the king's brothers and their dependents, were to send their own men to the garrison in Spiritii. The letter also contained orders for his southern vassals to harvest everything that could be harvested and ship the goods to their own fortresses and other, select fortresses; nothing was to be left in the fields. The inhabitants of the depleted regions were to relocate to the major centers, if they had not already done so to seek protection from the Serpent over the past three months.

Having placed the letter in its packet, Octavius lifted his head, looked at the prince, and grunted, "Please have these orders delivered to their recipients without delay."

Aithen took the packet from him without any comment, but Octavius could still detect a measure of anxious energy in his son's gestures. Aithen called Kil and handed him the letters with instructions to take them to Master Pombo, the palace's porter, for immediate dispatch.

As Kil exited, Octavius raised his voice to call Primus Julian who sat at his own desk in the Guard Chamber. He told him that there might be someone waiting in the hallway and to let him in if that were so.

Kil's surprised voice reached the king upon exiting the Guard Chamber. *Ah, he must have arrived. Good.*

A moment later, Julian stepped into the king's office with the 'someone' following behind.

The surprise on everyone's face, except Irania's, was clear as day as they twisted in their chairs to look toward the door. Aithen stood up and went to his uncle, who walked in with only the slightest hesitation in his step.

"Uncle! What brings you here?"

"Your father's request, of course. He sent a message two days ago, letting me know that he wished to have my advice in the matters which you would be discussing today. *Ergo, hic sum.*"

Just now, Octavius walked over to welcome his brother. He saw the veiled, sudden concern in Claudius's eyes. He forced his back to straighten more, clearly overcompensating for the Lacora Leaf corset, causing his brother to snort gently then smile.

"Claudius, it is good to see you. Please take a seat; we were just about to discuss one of the first matters on which your advice will be welcome."

Once all had greeted each other and Claudius had taken his place next to Aithen, the king crossed his hands and turned toward the tall and small-mustached overseer of the armory with a worried edge to his voice. "So, Lord Warbender, how goes the requisitioning of the vorans?"

Warbender straightened his back more and said in his business-like voice, "All your vassals have accepted to send their quota, Sire…except for Lord Arotek. But I suppose it was expected given his…worsened disposition toward the Crown, of late."

The king felt his pressure rise. How to respond to that imbecile's—or traitor's—affront? Obviously, Fausta Lux Baiula had not yet succeeded in her mission. He would need to take care of things himself and respond to the landholder's challenge. *If I seize his vorans, it will cement his opposition and turn him into a declared enemy. But, if I let things be, it could very well embolden others who might be on the fence, despite their promises. Damned be stupidity!*

Octavius suddenly realized he had been squeezing and rubbing his hands together angrily during his internal monologue. He moved them to rest on his chair as he lowered his head with a smirk and a huff, then reaching inside, taking a few deep breaths, and…nothing; he could not calm himself. The fact was that Mitsuko's death troubled him greatly; it troubled him and distracted him. His fingers gripped the armrests, causing the Lacora's branches to swell. The plant's haptic responses seemed to have a greater effect on him, and he let go.

He tried once more to calm himself and finally succeeded enough to sit back and to reach a conclusion with respect to his vassal's refusal. He now leveled a warning look toward his son and the captain of the Guard, and said, "We will send men to requisition the vorans."

Octavius watched Aithen and Kendor bob their heads, though Aithen's lips twitched anxiously. He followed his son's gaze move furtively toward his old mentor. He also scanned the other faces, studied their gestures and postures. *They are not all comfortable with the decision. Aithen is looking for Harlion's opinion; Harlion seems to be unwilling to get involved in military matters anymore, though—if he spoke—he would probably disagree too; and I suppose that Irania is feeling the sting of her Sister's failure but does not otherwise object. Only Kendor seems satisfied. And Claudius seems to be debating the matter with himself. Well, let's find out what he thinks.*

"Lord Claudius, if I trust what I am seeing, my advisors are not all in agreement, and those who disagree are looking for the words to object to my decision. Do you have an opinion on the matter? I did ask you to take this long and tiring trip from Bremin so I could avail myself of your knowledge and wisdom."

"Thank you, Sire. I do indeed."

"Please proceed, then."

"Well, the right of requisition was established by the Coriolan Carta, as you know, and it is probably your understanding of it that led you to decide as you did." Octavius nodded, and then twisted his lips slightly downward when Claudius added, "However, the right in question does have several conditional clauses attached to it, one of which…I believe…would invalidate your decision."

A sigh escaped the king's throat as his mind began imagining various outcomes of his inability to act. But he soon realized he was being foolish and decided to hear the rest of his brother's statement before worrying more. He gestured for him to continue.

"There must be a declaration of war before the right of requisition may be claimed."

The high king rubbed his face anxiously as he considered matters. He only perceived rather than heard Kendor's fury when he spat, "My Lord Claudius, are you seriously going to tie the high king's hands on the basis of…your interpretation of the law?!"

Claudius, used as he was to the reactions of the 'injured parties', did not take offense. Calmly but confidently, he clarified things for the officer. "High Captain, the Carta's interpretation is something I have studied for over eighty years and my understanding of it comes from the full knowledge of the entire thousand-page text. The passage in question says verbatim: 'The right of requisition, needed for the defense of the kingdom, being immediately necessary, shall be enforceable by the sovereign without any forewarning.' You will agree, High Captain, that for there to be an urgent need to defend the kingdom, the enemy must be advancing against its shores and borders or else there must have been a declaration of war."

"Actually, no. What it *does* say is that the right of requisition is granted a priori for the purpose of defending the kingdom."

"I am sorry, High Captain, but that is not the meaning."

The high captain's grimaces and aborted profanities told everyone what he thought of Lord Claudius's interpretation of the law. He turned toward the king to ask whether he was going to let semantics dictate their actions. Getting no response from him, he added, "Sire, we *need* Arotek's vorans; without them, we will be hobbled!"

Octavius raised a hand to quiet his officer and asked his brother whether he was absolutely certain of his interpretation.

"I am, Sire. Even if it is a clause which many like to debate so that they may use it for their own purposes, the majority— including your most important allies—interpret it as I do."

"So, I need to declare war. But the fact is that I do not wish to do it just yet. It would alert the enemy that we are preparing for offensive as well as for defensive action, and I cannot alert them before we—before we make our first move." Octavius had been about to say, 'before we attack Zeblinia.' However, and though he trusted his brother implicitly, he did not wish for certain elements of their strategy to be known by anyone outside the few who were directly concerned by it.

He turned away from his brother, whose pupils narrowed with a question. Frustrated, Octavius rose from his chair and placed himself behind it, leaning on it and then gripping it as a shot of pain flared through his back. When his expression relaxed, he said, "Does anyone have any ideas how we might overcome the legal obstacle? Irania?"

The Lux Baiula only responded with a curving of her mouth, and for a long, unpleasant moment, no one made any suggestion. Frustrated, Octavius finally said, "Claudius, aren't there any precedents that would allow us to…circumvent that clause?"

The Lord of Bremin shook his head, "Not any legal precedents, Sire."

Octavius snorted in disbelief, cursing the absurdity of the situation. Speaking to himself, but loud enough to be heard by the others, he said, "These chains that the rule of law puts on those who are well-intentioned just as tightly as on those who would abuse their powers for personal gain." He snorted again, and the action caused his back to seize anew. The pain lasted a while and dissipated only when he heard Harlion clear his throat. A hopeful, cautious smile bloomed.

"Sire, my Lord Claudius. If I recall correctly, there is a political precedent to the situation we find ourselves in, one which may offer a solution."

Octavius beckoned his old friend to speak, but before Harlion could answer Claudius said, "If it is some obscure machination of the past, it will not help, Prefect."

If Harlion was insulted, he did not show it, but he did pause before saying with a calm and confident tone, "It is not a well-remembered fact, but neither is it obscure, my Lord."

With Claudius's nod and Octavius's repeated gesture for him to speak his idea, Harlion began.

He explained that during the great plague that wiped out the Luxori in the years 1566 to 1567, High King Tarkian II had sequestered the medics of half the landholders of the kingdom, despite the opposition of many, to try and save the Luxori as well as the commoners who had been afflicted by the deadly virus. He explained, too, how this had led several landholders to file a Recrimination, which had forced the king to go and explain his actions at a special meeting of the Union, but that, in the end, the majority had ruled that the high king's actions had been necessary and intended for the greater benefit of all, and what came to be known as *force majeure*, had been used again by Tarkian without repercussions, at a later time.

When Aithen, Kendor and others turned to Octavius and Claudius to ask whether they recalled those events, the two eyed each other with some measure of embarrassment. Octavius pivoted toward Irania.

The Lux Baiula did not immediately reply, and Octavius understood, from the shifting of her eyes, that she was sifting through her Transferred Memories.

Having ascertained the facts, Irania said, "Prefect Harlion is correct, Sire." A hum, a murmur of relief, now grew in the king's office. "Your ancestor did indeed use what came to be known as force majeure, and it was ruled by the majority of landholders that the monarch should be allowed to use it, when necessary, for the greater good of the kingdom. And yet, it was never written into law; if my memories serve me well, it was due to the Union Council's inability to agree on the proper wording of the exclusions which would prohibit the monarch from using the noted declaration when its exercise might significantly harm the Council's members."

Frowns and grunts of irritation now shot toward the Lux Baiula. The king, himself, wondered whether she meant he could or could not requisition Arotek's herd.

Irania smiled patiently then added, "I believe that you, Sire, should be able to use the force majeure in the present situation."

Another sigh, louder and deeper, filled the room as Octavius returned to his seat and plumped into it with a twinge of pain.

"All right, then. Thank you, Lux Baiula. And thank you, Harlion." Leveling a surprised gaze at his friend, he said, "You will need to tell me, when we have the time, how you knew of such a not-so-well-known episode of the kingdom's history."

Harlion nodded respectfully. The sudden surge of pride and relief did not escape the king. *You still have much to contribute, my friend, and we are all glad to have you still by our side.*

After acknowledging his prefect's unspoken sentiment, the king flattened his hands on the desk with a thud and said, "Claudius, how do we ensure the Union Council will remember the existence of this precedent in case Lord Arotek should not and decide to resist us when we go to seize his herd?"

"I can call a meeting of the Council's leadership when I return to Bremin. If you give me until the end of the month before sending the Royal Guard to Arotek, I can ensure his cooperation."

Shifting his gaze toward Irania, Octavius asked whether the plan could be achieved even if Fausta Lux Baiula failed in her mission. Irania responded that her Sister would be successful but that even if she were not, his plan would succeed, so long as Lord Claudius could deliver.

Octavius nodded and looked at Aithen and Kendor to get their agreement. That done, he gave a satisfied grunt and moved the discussion to the next agenda item. "How are we on food stores, Lord Warbender?"

Shifting somewhat nervously on his seat, which fortunately was a leather seat and not a Lacora Leaf chair—this would have made clicking sounds as he moved—Warbender said, "The army's food stores will suffice for five or six months. But those for the civilians vary across the kingdom. It is worst right here, in the capital, since they were almost depleted to feed the Horn's Passers. Nonetheless, this fall's harvest is expected to be a good one, and we should be able to secure it all in each region's capital, so long as the war doesn't break out in the south before the end of the month."

Octavius's eyes turned left and right as he considered the situation. Sitting back and accompanying his words with worried yet defiant gestures, he said, "It is unlikely any foreign army will reach us for a long time, what with winter and snow coming in the south, and with extreme dryness in the north. I expect we will have another five or six months before the Zebulonian army reaches us."

The prince shook his head and a wrinkle appeared on Octavius's forehead. "You disagree, Aithen?"

When all Aithen did was shrug his shoulders, Octavius tensed his fingers and pressed him again.

"I am just not certain that the Zebulonian army is the only one we will have to face, Father. With Noctiferus doing everything to weaken our allies, and to bring our enemies here— and I am convinced he is the one behind Zebula's decision to invade us—it does not make sense to believe that they will be the only force set against us."

Kendor frowned, said, "Pardon, my prince, but you forget the gnarlers, and the Serpent with its army of rokons."

Aithen shook his head dismissively, "Those are distractions, Captain. Sure, they are sowing fear and destruction, but they will not stand against our organized forces. Not even the Serpent can withstand an army's assault. No, I'm—"

Putting aside his injured pride, Kendor said, "You are thinking of the Rokothians?"

The prince bobbed his head side-to-side then shook it negatively.

"The Yeltchek? Beltania?"

"Them and…internal enemies."

The prince's suggestion that the Crown might need to be worried about internal threats raised the hairs on the king's back while it twisted the high captain's face into an ugly frown, elicited a nervous laugh in the ministers, and got approving, but worried nods from Harlion and Irania.

"You two agree with my son? His suggestion that one of my vassals might not only protest or resist me, as Arotek is doing, but might actually take overt action against the Crown?"

Responding for both, the king's special advisor replied, "We do, Sire."

The king would have normally reacted to such unexpected and undesired notions with pause and consideration. But he was not totally himself this day and he threw his arms up as he growled before sweeping his Prefect Praetorian, his advisor, and his son with a hard glare, demanding to know what evidence they had of such threats.

With Aithen's consent, Harlion replied, "My Frumentarii have picked up voices—nothing definite, mind you, but voices nevertheless—about Zebulonian agents visiting some southern *courts*."

It was with a numb voice that Octavius repeated to himself what Harlion had just said. Rubbing his head to stem a nascent headache, he asked, "What courts? Do these voices say?!"

"I am sorry, Sire. I have attempted to gather additional details about this claim, but our sources know no more than this. It may be nothing, and it may be—"

"Something! Very well. I assume you are continuing to investigate these reports?"

Harlion nodded.

"Then please bring me confirmation or refutation of these rumors within the next two fourths."

"I will, Sire."

Octavius rubbed his head with the palm of his hand, this time, and said, "Regarding these other forces we haven't yet considered, I will remind you all that Toras expressed similar concerns at the Ball, and that we agreed at the time that we should find a way to keep an ear out for the Beltanians—which we have—and have established that there is no concern to be had there. As for the other nations, the only one which could even *hope* to try and breach our borders or shores is the Yeltchek. But they have never been a warring people. Everything we know agrees that Zebulonia is the only external threat we have to contend with."

"As for the possibility of a serious internal threat, we will need to factor this into our plans, especially if Harlion's Frumentarii should confirm the reports. But until we know more, let us not waste time hypothesizing."

Octavius now put his chin in his cupped hand as another concern surfaced in his mind. He looked toward his son and said, "How has the relocation of the smaller populations gone? Are things still tense?"

Aithen replied, "They are…more or less tense everywhere, Father. As you might suspect, in too many centers the natives are resenting the refugees, the refugees are complaining that they cannot find employment in their chosen fields and are forced to work for the state, and the local administrations are having difficulty managing the increased demands on their resources."

"Yes, I suppose that was to be expected: Our imperfections and those of our laws and decisions, combined with the vagaries of nature lead to mediocre outcomes for the majority; it is a natural law, which we can only escape in times of peace."

Annoyed at getting only shrugs in response, Octavius directed another question at Aithen: "Is there any risk of starvation or of a revolt anywhere?"

The king watched the nearly imperceptible changes in his son's features. Aithen's pupils narrowed, and he replied with a flat "Not yet."

"Then keep monitoring the situation and alert me before any crisis develops so we may reallocate our resources as need be."

The members of the Council acknowledged their orders.

"Anything else?"

All shook their heads, except for Kendor, who asked whether they could discuss Lusk Methrim.

The king did not immediately answer but looked at the time disk on his wall: it indicated ten hours thirty minutes Ahn. He stood up hurriedly, thumping the chair's arms in the process and causing the Lacora plant to distort itself as it tried to readjust both the seat and the armrests. *I'd rather not go there now. Talking about Temptatori and their turned victims and—*

Straightening himself, he responded, "We will discuss our fugitive later as I have no wish to ruin my mood. We will reconvene at Two Ahs, when we will be joined by a…special guest."

"A special guest, Father?"

"Yes."

II.   The Church of Aiala

Standing atop a large dais placed in front of the Church of Aiala, First Cleric Galadrin welcomed the faithful to the ceremony. The Bolingars were an hour away, on this Fourth day of the Second Bolingar fourth, with the Red sun and its blue twin already heating the air, though this late in the fall season one could stay out in the open at noontime without risking death.

Without preamble, and without hesitation, Galadrin's words boomed across Furan City, thanks to the services of a retired Sister. His words were accompanied by a lifting song of the

Voces Creatoris, who stood behind him. Galadrin had hired the Voces for the event.

Inside the palace, an unwelcome sound jolted Octavius from his lunch. He stood with a quiet, angry rumble, momentarily alarming the guardians posted in his chambers.

Despite himself, he walked to the balcony of his office chamber to witness what he knew must be happening. As soon as he stepped out, his eyes fell upon the large sacred structure that symbolized the Day of Union: an alpha connected by means of the most delicate projections to the representation of a humanoid within an omega, the two dancing around each other in a mesmerizing motion, high above the Church's dome. Octavius growled again, causing the Red Sashes on his balcony to roll their eyes.

The event taking place in front of the Church was a yearly one, where new members were officially welcomed. Octavius had completely forgotten about it, and no one had reminded him; not that he cared much about it anyway.

However, if Octavius had been told the details of this year's celebration, he would have fumed. Indeed, today, a few important Furanites as well as a few important others from across the kingdom were being inducted into the Church along with hundreds of commoners. But he would be fuming soon enough since he could not block out Galadrin's voice, which would be announcing the inductees, unless he asked a Lux Baiula to create a Sound Shield.

Looking both grand and awe-inspiring—at least to those who believe in connection with the Founders—Galadrin held up his hands and began his speech, addressing his members first.

"Faithful, Rhiians, because you are Rhiians you are faithful, and because you are faithful you are Rhiians! And because I serve you and serve the Originator, I am, here, addressing you today. For Aiala and the other Founders we live, and for them we, today, welcome our new members."

Hands clapped legs loudly, fervently.

With a simple motion of the hand, Galadrin silenced the crowd.

"This year's welcoming is even more important than past ones because war is upon us, and the gods are angry with our king. He has repeatedly denigrated our beliefs and done so not only by completely separating himself from our Church and denying it any voice in the affairs of the kingdom, but also by defiling its sanctity when he imprisoned my clerics and myself during the Serpent's attack. And now, he plans to defile the bodies of our brothers and sisters by sending them to Zebulonia where they may be enslaved by its queen and her kind to be made unworthy. What will the gods say about us when they come and find not the faithful that they expect to receive their spirits?"

The first angry roar rose from the crowd and swept across the capital, like a wave of the great Sea of Tarkoth, until it reached the king's ears. The roar and the questions caused a furious ripple to spread through Octavius's body, cramping his still-weak muscles.

He growled to the Barriers on the balcony, "Why does the Order allow your Sisters to sell their services to broadcast this manure? Doesn't Krystiana understand that this can hurt us?"

Letta Lux Baiula, a tall but stocky, dark-haired warrior said, "I am sorry, Sire. It's—"

"What?"

"Well, retired Sisters are free to sell their services, so long as they do not infringe our laws."

"I was told tha—"

Octavius was interrupted by his eldest who came running into his office: "Father!"

"Aithen. Did you hear that exalted mad man?"

"I did, and I imagined you wouldn't be happy, especially given the number of people, including a significant number of patricians, being inducted this year."

"No. No, not in the least! But if those rogue Binders did not project Galadrin's voice across the city, it wouldn't be as bad."

"I hear what you are saying. But they are not really rogues; they're retired and it's often been this way with them. They did the same thing during the Storm City revolt."

"Yes, and I told Krystiana *then* that she needed to keep all Alterintrants in the Sisterhood's fold, one way or another."

"I supp—"

Just now, Galadrin's voice boomed again, and interrupted the conversation.

Galadrin said, "But regardless of our king's and his family's ill-deeds, there is reason to rejoice today because we will now welcome an impressive number of new members, members who will add their voices to ours to shake those who would keep us from reclaiming the Founders' favor."

The First Cleric of the Church of Aiala swept a bejeweled arm toward the first candidate to invite him on the dais.

Krptus's heart skipped suddenly, and his eyes blinked a few times while he snuffed away the momentary indignation he had felt owing to the way the First Cleric had characterized the high king and his family. All hesitation vanished the moment Senator Sur'Elando, who had decided to sponsor him, encouraged him forward with a hand on his shoulder. An unexpected and overwhelming sense of pride took Krptus as the vast audience, composed of Furanites and neighboring plebeians and patricians, clapped hands on legs to welcome him—a Yerlayan.

The clamor increased as others approached the First Cleric to be welcomed. A total of one hundred and sixty new Rhiians were going to be received as acolytes of the Church on this grand day of the eleventh month of the year 1800.

A paroxysm of joy overtook the crowd when First Cleric Galadrin motioned with his hand and two acolytes brought forward a luminous cylindrical case inside which stood the First's Skull.

The cleric called the supplicants to kneel in front of him then placed his hands around the skull, bowed his head, and spoke his prayer. The congregants and inductees watched with a rapt attention so silent that it seemed the capital had just died.

When his prayers were completed, Galadrin passed in front of each supplicant and struck them at the base of their necks with the Union Scepter, which was carved with the representation of the Founders entering the bodies of the Worthy. All one hundred and sixty supplicants fell forward, unconscious for several seconds during which an eerie murmur shook the audience. When the newly inducted men and women finally rose, the Voces Creatoris erupted in a sublime song, and the entire congregation joined in. Some, among the newly anointed Rhiians, followed suit, chanting along as if they had been raised within the Church. A few—such as Krptus—focused on the refrain until they learned it well enough to sing that part while Galadrin read the names of each new member.

The high king's and high prince's faces darkened thunderously when they heard a few of the names of those who had just joined the Church: a guardian and six landholders, including Lady Aroteka. Octavius spat some words, walked indoors with his son, slammed the doors shut, and asked the Red Sashes to create a Sound Shield to block whatever remained of the ceremony.

III. Foreign Strategies

With a nervous step, Master Brak walked into the high king's office, following Alturo Rackeli, that afternoon. The majordomo halted two meters from the others then bade Master Brak next to him.

Confusion painted the faces of the king's aides, except for Lord Kaffin's. Thinking of the announcement he was about to make, Octavius let his worries about Galadrin's growing influence, an influence which now extended to the patriciate, retreat to the back of his mind; he would deal with this new problem later. As for his lingering feelings of guilt for what happened to Mitsuko, they had retreated on their own with everything else preoccupying and occupying the king's mind in that moment.

The fisher bowed with a smile that swayed between pride and timidity, as he tried to not be overwhelmed by the austere splendor of the king's office or by the presence of so many high and powerful individuals in the same room. Sure, he had been in the presence of one or the other when he served them his culinary specialties, but those situations were not the same, and his worries in those instances were not the same either. Here, they were discussing matters of great importance, and who was he to take part?

After dismissing his majordomo, the king welcomed the merchant with as bright and pleased a voice as he could muster.

The king's tone relaxed Brak, and the man bowed again with the most honest, ready-to-serve smile on his face.

Aithen gave the fisher a quick glance then said to Octavius, "Sire, why is Master Brak here?"

"Because, my son, I need him to execute a part of our strategy."

Yet greater incredulity flooded the chamber.

The merchant, seeing the others' reactions, stiffened a little.

The king continued, with all the seriousness he was known for, though he was unable to keep a little uncertainty from betraying him to those who could read him. But he went on, nevertheless.

"Master Brak, as Lord Kaffin informed you, I have a very important mission for you, one which will make use of your culinary skills and foreign contacts."

Octavius saw the way everyone, except for Lord Kaffin, stared at him now, as if he had suddenly lost his wits. Master Brak was just as confused, but—being the confident, jovial person he was known to be—he decided to go along with his king's game—if it was a game—and said, "I am at your service, my king, and all my resources, whether they be spices or ships or inks are yours to use, however you see fit."

When Aithen shook his head in continued disbelief and incomprehension Octavius decided to stop the foolishness and tell his son and the others what this was all about.

He said, "Good, good, Master Brak. Thank you."

He then turned toward his advisors and explained how he intended to use Master Brak's skills and connections. Of course, the disclosure caused more consternation still, except perhaps in Irania, whose lips seemed to stretch a little, as if in appreciation of what she understood.

The first to question the king's request was not one of his advisors, however, but the fisher himself who almost fell over and paled, despite the financial opportunity the king's request presented.

Brak Piscator squeezed and turned nervously the tricorn he held in his hands until he had recovered sufficiently to speak. He said, "Pardon, Sire…smuggle a million and a half fish pastries? Into Zebulonia? I must admit that the number is, well…and the destination is…When do you need this order by, Sire? And what for, if I may ask?"

Octavius made a calming gesture toward the stocky man then said, "Lord Kaffin has informed me that you sell some of your products to Zebulonia—there is no need to hide it, because it does not harm the kingdom, as illicit as it may be. But now, it so happens that it will prove useful to my purposes. I have heard that only the commoners of Zebulonia, and more specifically, the males, purchase this pastry. Is that correct?"

Master Brak replied in the affirmative with a slow, suspicious bob. A cold sweat began wetting his fine shirt. *I suppose he is afraid that I am going to ask him to deliver poisoned product to the enemy, and afraid of the consequence when he refuses.*

"Good, I need you to stuff the pastries with a message for them."

A great sigh of relief mixed incredulous looks and stares, met Octavius's words.

Octavius thought to himself: *I am sure none of them can imagine how I came up with such a scheme, though I am surprised even Irania seems confused.*

An exasperated Aithen pulled the king from his inner thoughts, almost demanding to know what was that business of pastries and messages.

The king exhaled loudly and said, "This business is the business of cunning strategy and subterfuge, to put the odds in our favor when we attack Zebulonia. The messages, to be delivered at regular frequency over the next few months, will inform the males of the kingdom that they have a friend outside of their borders, one who understands their struggle and desire for freedom and who will be at their side, on a day to be announced, to end Zebula's tyranny. It will instruct them to ready themselves to support us on the appointed day and to seek guidance from their male leaders until then."

Kendor exclaimed, "Sire, this is unprecedented. I have never heard or read of such a…foreign strategy before. And you believe this will have the effect you seek?"

"Indeed. With the help of the OLZM, it will."

Kendor, Harlion, Irania and Aithen nodded, hesitantly at first, then looked at each other and nodded with greater and greater conviction as they recalled the reason for the king's visits to Marcus the Reader.

"I am glad to see you are ready to get behind this plan."

Kendor said, "We are, Sire, though it will be interesting to learn—when the opportunity presents—where such a strategy came from."

"I will be happy to explain it all, High Captain, when the opportunity presents."

The king continued after a short pause. "Now, Irania Lux Baiula, I wish you to write these messages. I believe you will know better than any of us how to word things, though I wish—"

Octavius suddenly lowered his head, feeling utterly frustrated, cornered.

"What is it, Father?"

"Irania could have had Master Methrim's help with the messages, but no longer! And I need to find new means to connect with Lub Methor given that Marcus has also proven to be a traitor. Will you be able to ensure that the messages are properly understood by their target, Irania?"

"On my own, no, Sire. However, I believe Molara Lux Baiula—she's the handler of the two girls we sent to Zeblinia— has learned our enemy's language quite well and will be able to help me."

Octavius closed his eyes and took a long, slow, breath.

"Thank you, Lux Baiula. Thank you. Please make arrangements with Master Brak so he can retrieve a copy of the first message from you by this fourth's end."

Turning to the merchant, the king added, "Master Brak, you will print the message on resistant paper and stuff one and a half million of your buns with it, which you will deliver to Zebulonia. You will make three such shipments over the next three months, taking them to the Port of Worm."

Brak Piscator made a soft, unsure grunt. Octavius invited him to voice his concern.

"Sire, my shipments are always inspected by the Zebulonian customs before my clients are allowed to take possession. I worry—"

Octavius stopped the man and said, "You will not need to worry about that, Master Brak; our contacts will have their own man at the post on each occasion—one named Lak Rikor. He will perform the inspections, though, given our changed circumstances, I will need to confirm this before your departure."

The fisher merchant and soon-to-be royal smuggler nodded cautiously.

"I will make certain we establish a new route of communication between the rebels and us, do not be concerned about that, Master Brak."

Brak Piscator blushed and said, "I would never doubt you, Sire."

"Of course." Octavius did not remark on what he thought about his royal infallibility.

Brak continued timidly, "But—"

"You are concerned about the possibility that the substitution will fail?"

Master Brak nodded then said, "I am, as there are often auditors who drop in unannounced after the initial inspection."

Methor had not told me of this. A low growl was beginning to rise from the king as he grappled with the sudden thought that the universe was conspiring against him. But the fisher interrupted his growing anger.

"I am sorry, Sire, I did not mean to worry you needlessly; I may have a solution. I would recommend adding another quarter million unadulterated cakes to the shipment. I will dispose them among the rest such that they will be more likely to be picked during any secondary inspection." Brak hurried to add, "Naturally, I will bear the cost of this addition, my king."

Octavius gave a genuine, contented smile. It felt good to know—and to have the proof—that there still existed honest, loyal, and disinterested people in the nation. However, his expression quickly regained its serious aspect—though something in it projected… guilt. He said, "Now, my real concern is this, Master Brak: We cannot let the content of your pastries be known—or even rumored—because if that were to happen, the word would surely reach our enemy, as surely as the suns rise every day, though we may not see them through the clouds." Octavius watched Brak Piscator stiffen his back to signify his readiness for whatever condition might be forced upon him then said, "I will need two things from you: Firstly, I will need you to agree to having your and your aides' short-term memories erased after each production. Secondly, you must only employ people you can trust implicitly to not ask questions about the content of the messages nor to tell anyone anything about this mission while production is ongoing. This must be so, or I would be forced to have you and your aides sequestered for the next three months, should you still wish to take on the contract."

It was obvious, from Master Brak's reaction, that he had not expected such conditions. Even the king's advisors turned stunned looks in his direction. *Irania looks properly infuriated. I hope she understands we have no other choice here.*

"You may not be aware of all the types of creatures we are fighting in this war, Master Brak, but I can assure you that there are some who can steal a person's thoughts without them even knowing it, and these servants of the Dark One are now everywhere. These measures are therefore necessary as otherwise we would also need to assign you a permanent guard of Sisters, which would actually make it impossible for you to carry out the mission, which must remain secret."

For several long, tense moments, Brak Piscator rubbed his face and passed his hand on his neck.

Octavius watched him with a calm, patient gaze. Out of the corner of his eye, he spied Aithen approaching him with an urgent step. Octavius listened to his whispers but did not look away from the merchant and gave only short, terse responses to his son. When the fisher cleared his throat, Octavius raised a hand toward Aithen and whispered something back to quiet him.

"Have you made a decision, Master Brak, and can you guarantee the trustworthiness of whoever will help you with this task?"

"I have, Sire. I will assign these productions to my son and my niece as well as to one of my assistants. As to your first condition, I understand your arguments, and though I have no idea who these creatures might be that might come steal our thoughts," and Brak shivered as he said that, "I have always had the greatest respect for you and for your rule. Therefore, I accept your condition—as unsettling as the thought of having our memories erased is."

"Don't you want to ask your son, niece, and assistant whether they agree, too?"

Brak Piscator bobbed his head this way and that for a moment, made a few grunts, and finally shook his head firmly. "They will agree too."

The sighs of relief that quietly lifted from the throats of Octavius's aides were almost physical; in fact, they did manifest themselves in the way Aithen's eyes closed, in the way Kendor's and Harlion's figures relaxed, and in the manner Lords Warbender and Kaffin let their shoulders sag. As for Claudius, his face showed he was having some internal debate about all the things he had heard this day; it even showed some discomfort. Octavius thought: *He's probably wondering whether he should be here to hear these plans. You have never given me reasons not to trust you, brother, though having heard what you have will surely weigh on you. But such are the burdens of our positions.* Octavius turned his eyes to look at Irania. The woman sat stolidly unreadable. *I know what that rigid expression means, Irania. But you, too, are bound by your role and by your oaths, and you will need to convince the Sisterhood of the necessity of using Confusion repeatedly on so many individuals.*

Returning his attention to the fisher and soon-to-be agent of the court, he said, "Excellent, I am glad to hear it, because I do not know how else we might have carried out this mission, if you had refused."

Now, the merchant said somewhat nervously, "I do have a question, Sire, if I may."

The king motioned and Brak said, "Has the debt erasure policy[24] been put in place yet?"

The king smiled and turned to Lord Kaffin who was glad to reply that it would become effective as soon as the war was declared, likely in the next few months, but that this particular

---

[24] Debt erasure policy: A policy which cancelled accumulation of debt and made all new transactions cost-free nation-wide for the duration of the war.

contract would be payable upon delivery, even if the declaration came into force before the job's completion.

At that, Octavius dismissed the merchant, who left with a mixture of feelings transfiguring him as he walked out of the king's office. He went with emotions ranging from worry to eagerness to pride.

Once the king and his advisors were alone again, he answered all their questions and explained his rationale for such an irregular plan, revealing only very broadly what had inspired him. When all were ready to support his strategy, the king dismissed Lords Warbender and Kaffin and asked the others to remain so that they might talk about Methrim.

The king's mood changed markedly as the discussion began, though Kendor, himself, had nothing concerning to report except the usual troubles expected in any army where conscripts are thrown in with regulars—this, despite Octavius's repeated prompts and challenges to think hard of anything that might indicate some foul play by Lusk Methrim.

All the while, Aithen remained tense and anxious. Finally, the king asked him what the matter was.

As he prepared to answer, the prince bit and licked his lips as if he were getting ready to reveal something highly unpleasant, and his eyes darted about as his mind settled on the way in which he would make his revelation.

Octavius's guts knotted themselves with distasteful anticipation. Everyone eyed Aithen for hints, but the prince would not give any, and Irania—studying his changing expressions, the tensing of his muscles or the depth of his breathing—could not guess.

After another moment's hesitation, Aithen finally spoke his piece. "Earlier this month, Kil came to me with a request to intercede for one of his acquaintances to have him admitted as an apprentice to Master Vorak."

Octavius's face took on a befuddled look.

Aithen said, "I had Master Trebloc look into his background and he discovered that this Luvius Arco is connected to Lusk Methrim."

A cloud thunderous and dark began covering Octavius's face, while alarm disks marred the others' expressions.

"At the time, I thought the matter a mere coincidence," Aithen paused and forced himself to remain calm and project as much assurance as possible, "but I don't think so anymore. I think Lusk Methrim sent Master Luvius here to get to Koricki, and through him, to you."

Octavius inhaled loudly then snorted several times, just as loudly. He noticed Aithen's averted gaze; his son seemed to feel guilty for the last assassination attempt.

Octavius raised his hand and said, "We have *all* been fools, all of us! We've let a stranger—a—" Octavius stopped himself before he let anger get the better of him and make it sound like their mistake had been to trust a foreigner. And yet, if the news of Methrim's betrayal spread through the populace, many would see it just that way, and they would blame their king as well as the prince for trusting a Zebulonian because anyone should know 'Zebulonians are brutes and untrustworthy'.

"We've let a *stranger* dupe us all, and now he's on the run, after nearly killing Elyana herself, and if not for her greater strength or for her good luck, I might be dead or imprisoned in the Bind forever."

Taken by a sudden access of rage, the king knocked a vase from his desk, and just as suddenly as a furious spring gust dissipates, his anger evaporated and left him tired and exhausted, exhausted from dealing with emotions that he was not built to deal with except to ignore them. But the recent months' events and his part in Mitsuko's death had truly shaken him.

Turning back toward his son and the others with a measure of sarcasm to dispel his other feelings, he said, "When we find him, he will regret having ever come this way and *offered* us his services."

Octavius's words did not appear to please Aithen, who said, "Father, you trusted Lusk Methrim because of me, because of my own recommendation that he be trusted. The fault is… mine."

Octavius sighed and Harlion rolled his eyes. Such was the prince, holding ever strongly to his principles, but in the present situation, it seemed uncalled for. After all, Urbs Lucis had also trusted the man.

The king snorted quietly as a prideful smile appeared on his face. "My son, these impulses that motivate you, that move you, they provoke great joy in me and dissipate the fears I have about the future of the kingdom—so long as it still exists after this war. But, in this instance, your guilt is misplaced, if not quite narcissistic."

Aithen pulled his head back with a mixture of indignation and embarrassment.

"The fact is—and everyone else here will tell you the same—that misjudging another person's character is not a rare thing—it can even happen to Lux Baiulae." Octavius shot a glance at Irania, who kept a blank, impassive face, except for a slight pull of her nostrils, which Octavius noted. "But once one's true character is recognized, it must either be accepted as it is, or the person be removed from one's circle. Unfortunately for us, the realization came too late, and the action has been taken out of our hands…but not for long, if I can help it."

Aithen nodded, hesitantly, unwilling to completely dismiss responsibility, though he knew his father was right.

Octavius recognized his son's reaction for what it was and, acceding to another bout of pride, said to Kendor, "This—this sense of responsibility and accountability, High Captain, is what the throne must expect from all who serve it. It will be a crucial trait to cultivate in our troops in the coming times. Along with the fortitude to accept its consequences."

The officer regarded the prince with weighing eyes then bobbed his head and acknowledged the king's injunction.

He now asked the king whether he should have members of the Royal Guard's security arrest Luvius Arco.

"Yes, but please release him into the Frumentariat's hands. I wish the Prefect's questioners to interrogate him." When Harlion nodded, Octavius continued, "But, we need to make sure that he did not turn anyone else against me. Irania, can you and your Sisters trace everyone he may have been in contact with and probe them?"

"We can, Sire, though that could be a large number of people, and may take some time."

"It is what it is, Lux Baiula."

Noticing Aithen's twitches and gestures, the king urged him to speak up.

Aithen eyed Irania before saying, "Father, I do not think the task will be so great; from what Elyana told me, the turning of someone requires that the Temptator be in frequent, extended contact with them, which reduces the number of potential victims."

"Victims...I suppose that is what they are, aren't they?... even Koricki Dar'Muntake."

As badly as he had initially wished to punish his attendant, he understood, too, that those who were turned were not necessarily criminals or evil persons. And in any case, he could not—as much as he might have wanted to—punish the Supreme Priestess's distant cousin, a young man who was also a member of the Sisterhood, and the punishment—if there were going to be any—would probably need to be formally decided by the Magna Mater.

As expected, not everyone agreed with his statement. Kendor, and even Harlion, seemed to believe that a 'turned' individual bore as much responsibility for their own actions as anyone else did; responsibility was one of the Rhiian religion's precepts.

Feeling suddenly tired, Octavius thanked his son for his suggestion, asked Irania to focus her Sisters' efforts accordingly, and finally dismissed everyone.

Once he was left alone, except for the permanent Guard, which Octavius had slowly come to learn to ignore to his own surprise, he went to sit—or rather, plump down—on the couch. He tried to relax and forget about his royal duties, but it *was* difficult. The memory of Mitsuko's death was returning to torment him. Still, he was glad he had been able to forget, if only for a while, partway through the meeting, or who knew how things would have turned out; his Council would have started questioning his ability to lead.

So, he sat there, groaning and growling quietly, for a long time, only every so often looking suspiciously toward the guardians and Sisters. When he had tired himself thinking of what he should or should not have done, whether he should have ever trusted Marcus again, why he had gone into the Bind with only Mitsuko to protect him and what sort of a man he was who would curse a person for annoying him when that person had given her life for him—when he had tired himself thinking of his stupidity, then, he released his mind from its captivity and sat up suddenly, with a gasp, that alerted the Lux Baiula standing by the door between his office and the bedchamber; he had just remembered that on the morrow Ori would be acknowledging his final Day of Acquaintance.

Fourteen years old! Will I be here for him, to mark his fifteenth and twentieth birthdays?

Octavius shot up, though his back still ached, and ran to Irania to ask her to send a note to his son through her colleague in Kynaria.

IV. The Night of Endings

While undoing her braid to ready herself for bed after the long, exhausting day, a dark figure appeared in the Supreme Priestess's mirror, a figure made even more frightening by the descended Red sun, which projected its last rays into her room. The sight seized Ylana's heart. Her mouth opened to call for help, but a dart stuck her in the neck, and she dropped to the floor without ever uttering a sound, not even a gasp. Only the soft sound of her body hitting the soft carpet disturbed the quiet. The assassin carefully and expertly slid over and down the balcony of the former leader of the Kynarian Order.

On Second Seat Hill, the nation's administrative center, other shadows had infiltrated the private chambers of the powerful: one visited Priest Trainer Morek while another entered Priestess Financier Narana's apartments, and another still penetrated the home of Administrator Loren, the civilian official responsible for civic works—one of two civilian offices in the Kynarian government.

The Kynarian nation lost two of her officials without any alarm: Morek dropped to the ground while reviewing Aria's proposal for a new technique to track wild animals, and Narana slumped forward on her desk while endorsing a check to release funds for Octavius's war effort, which the Supreme Priestess had finally agreed to support more openly. Only Administrator

Loren, who could not sleep and prowled around his house like a restless howler, had the time to cry and alert his household when an assassin appeared in his bedchamber. The killer spat her dart anyway and fled.

Another assassin had just entered the queen consort's bedchamber and cursed himself when the floor creaked.

Ori, who was still awake in this last hour of his Day of Acquaintance, heard the noise and walked to his mother's chamber, wishing to let her know he still had not figured out what he was though he knew *who* he was.

When he parted the heavy curtains in front of her chamber his eyes fell upon the back of a dark-clothed man looming over his sleeping mother with his knife ready to plunge into her chest. Ori could not tell whether time had stopped or was rushing to bring about his mother's death, but something moved him out of the physical realm and all thoughts and questions ceased in his mind when he saw the assassin's arm start to descend toward its target.

A scream he had not called forth now rose from Ori and exploded through the Lady Darya's apartments in a reverberation that shattered glass and ceramic…and—

The assassin shrieked and collapsed while Darya woke from her sleep only to buckle and spasm from a wound unseen.

Ori howled and ran to his mother, calling her name, afraid to touch her and recoiling when blood seeped between her lips. Tears poured from his bloodshot eyes.

Just then, Aria entered her aunt's bedroom, and yelled, "Ori! What happened? What, what happened?! Aunt Darya!"

Ori did not respond, did not become aware of his cousin until she appeared next to him.

Unable to utter a single word, he simply pointed toward the assassin, who lay on the ground on the other side of the bed.

Aria gasped and struggled to ask if his mother still lived.

"I…I don't know…I don't know what happened to either of them."

"What do you mean? And why is your face yellow?"

"I don't know! I don't know anything. Mother! Please wake up! Aria, please help! Mother, Mother…Mother…"

It took some effort for the guardians, who had finally arrived following all the commotion, to remove the catatonic Ori from his unmoving mother and to bring him and Aria into the parlor. Shock and disbelief and incomprehension marred Aria's face. Her expression seemed to ask, 'How can our world be upended so abruptly?'

A tall and thin guardian came presently to try and question the boy, but it was obvious he was in shock and would not respond. The man questioned Aria next, who was herself greatly distraught and only repeated, "This is not possible," on and on.

When finally Sergeant Yluno arrived with Priestess Medica Salina, both panting from running up the steps—the cleric more so than the soldier—he ordered everyone down to the safe rooms of the complex. A mid-sized, muscular guardian carried the barely breathing and bloody Lady Darya, while another two took the assassin's body to the morgue.

The guardian who picked up Darya stopped unexpectedly, soon after crossing the door to the hallway. The sergeant and priestess turned around to ask what he was waiting for. The man looked down at the queen consort then looked up with a pale face. He started to speak, but the priestess silenced him with an urgent gesture. The guardian nodded and followed them with Lady Darya's body hanging more limply than it had just a moment earlier.

Once in the basement, Salina asked the son and the niece to remain in the larger room and ordered the guardian to take

'Lady' Darya to the smaller chamber on the left so that she might probe her privately. Only the princess protested but relented when Salina assured her that she would appraise them soon of the result of her examination. The boy did not say a word and simply sat where Sergeant Yluno had placed him.

The moment the guardian had carried the body into the room, placed it on a couch there, and closed the door behind him, Salina exhaled, knelt, and began her slow and deliberate examination. It did not take her long to confirm that Lady Darya was dead; her lips tightened as the political consequences of the tragedy manifested themselves in her mind.

She probed the body further to try to determine the cause of death. One thing she was able to ascertain after several minutes of careful probing and auscultation was that Darya's immediate cause of death must have been the seizing of her heart. Her lungs were also bleeding. She shook her head; she had no idea what might have caused those injuries—at least, not the bleeding lungs; if it had been a toxic gas, the boy would have suffered too. And an assassin would not *deliver* toxic gas, anyway. Darya had been a healthy woman; her heart would not suddenly seize, not even from fear. Nothing made sense.

Musing to herself, she said, "What could have caused this? I haven't seen anything like it before...except."

Salina stood, walked to the door, opened it partially and called Sergeant Yluno.

Before the sergeant moved Aria demanded urgently, loudly: "Priestess Medica, how is my aunt?"

"I am sorry, Senior neo Aria; I have not completed my examination, yet. I need you to be a little more patient."

"But—"

Aria did not notice, from her position, that the woman was pinching her thumb as she replied, "Please be patient. I will let you know your aunt's condition as soon as I have completed my examination."

Not getting any support from Ori, Aria sat back, dejected, and Salina waved the sergeant closer.

The soldier, who had fruitlessly questioned the prince and his cousin, as well as the first of his guardians to arrive on scene, answered the priestess's call gladly but with silent curses.

"Priestess Medica?"

Whispering, Salina said, "What weapon or weapons did the assassin carry?"

"He had a dagger, but I don't think he used it as there are no traces of blood on it."

"Thank you, Sergeant."

Salina returned to examine the body one last time, and—finding nothing more—came back out, shut the door and walked over to the dark corner of the room where Ori sat.

Standing herself a meter from the princeling, she tried long and hard to coax him to talk, but to no avail. With every new question, the boy simply tensed up and closed in on himself further. Getting nowhere, Salina decided to sit on the chair next to the prince and bent forward to try and catch his gaze.

When her eyes fell on the Halfling's face and hands, she immediately pulled back with a gasp: "Sergeant Yluno, please find a Lux Baiula—any Lux Baiula that might be in the city—and bring her here at once!"

Startled and confused, Yluno still said, "At once, Priestess Medica," and left to do as ordered.

Twenty minutes later, an irritated and frustrated sergeant returned with the only Lux Baiula in Kynaria. The woman had demanded to know what was happening, as if she had a right to, and no one had told the sergeant what he could or could not tell the Lux Baiula.

The moment Salina spied the Lux Baiula, she rushed out of the small room, leaving the door open, thanked Yluno and with a whispered hiss, demanded that she examine the boy.

"I need you to tell me what you see, to confirm what *I* saw on the Halfling."

With a thin, slightly croaky voice, Kenya Lux Baiula said, "That is the young prince, Priestess Medica, not just a boy. Moreover, I am not a medic but a seeker."

Salina stiffened at that and said, "There is no need for you to be a medic. Being a mere Lux Baiula should allow you to verify what I saw."

The Yellow Sash's lip turned up slightly at the off-hand insult, but she said, "What you think you saw."

"I do not *think* I saw, Lux Baiula, I *know* what I saw. But I need you to verify it."

If the Lux Baiula resented the woman's attitude, she did not make a big show of it and instead asked what happened to the young prince.

In the moment it took for the other woman to reply, the Sister scanned the room. She noticed Aria, but she did not know her and paid no more attention to her except to give her a noncommittal smile. When her gaze fell upon the queen consort's body in the other room, she exhaled sharply. Her head moved from one person to the next, in search for a reaction that would confirm what *she* was seeing, which must be worse than whatever might have happened to the young prince: the queen consort was dead. She reached for the Bind to see if she could sense any activity in her brain, but the priestess medica's ringing voice interrupted her.

"The boy has been this way since his cousin found him, sitting next to his mother, who was lying unresponsive on her bed. She was attacked; we found the assassin in her bedchamber—dead." Lowering her voice, she added, "Now, I am not certain her attacker was the cause of her d—of her condition."

Aria, who had heard the truncated word, screamed, "What are you saying, Priestess Medica, is she…is she dead?"

Not getting an answer, Aria ran to the other room, shaking off the priestess's arm when the woman tried to stop her. She grabbed her aunt's hand and did not sense any resistance whatsoever. When she did not hear her breathing either she screamed again and called her cousin with pleading cries.

Ori seemed to curl in on himself even further and did not go to see his now dead mother.

Salina finally decided to acknowledge that Darya was dead. Aria ran to Ori and shook him, then started screaming angrily when he did not respond. Salina ordered Sergeant Yluno to take the girl into the corridor and to keep her there until she calmed herself.

Kenya Lux Baiula said, "Someone needs to inform the high king."

"That is our responsibility, Lux Baiula. Now, please do as I asked."

Kenya, whose specialty was the study of toxic plants, and who was there to investigate the properties of a particular Kynarian plant for possible use in combatting the poison used by the assassins who killed her Sisters a short while back, wasn't sure what the other woman expected her to see. Still, she went to Ori; at the very least, she could try and pull him out of the abyss he seemed to have sunk into.

As soon as she reached the boy, however, Kenya Lux Baiula saw what Salina had seen: the boy's skin had the color of oki pollen, a darkish, yellowish pastel color—the sign of certain microbial toxins being expelled from the skin, something that only certain lizards and her Sisters of the Red Sash could do.

The wide-faced, thin-lipped woman—her traits giving her a strange but almost comical appearance—moaned quietly, whispered to herself, "Oh, young prince, what did you do? How *could* you have done this?" She put her hand on the boy, caressed him, then went to Salina to ask the woman that she join her in the other room.

Before the priestess medica could respond, Yluno cleared his throat to tell the priestess that he needed to alert his commander.

When the priestess gave him permission to go, she turned to the Yellow Sash and said, "Well, what is your conclusion?"

But Kenya would not speak until they were in the other room, so Salina followed, though she did so somewhat indignantly.

Salina's eyes flicked between the body, the Lux Baiula, and the boy whom she could still see with the door standing ajar. In something that was a little less than a whisper and made Kenya cringe, she said, "Well, he's an Alterintrant, isn't he?"

Kenya Lux Baiula bobbed her head glumly.

"Then he was the one to—"

Kenya's deadly glare stopped the woman.

Still, the Medica could not resist adding with a hushed, hissing voice, "It *was* the boy."

Kenya felt her blood boil. The woman's disrespect was unbearable. True, it did look like Prince Ori caused his mother's death. But if he did, then it was an accident, a horrible accident, one which would have grave consequences for him, both self-inflicted and external ones. Before Kenya could make any reply, the outside door opened again to let in an officer with a confident yet good-natured aspect, followed by Aria, who had finally calmed herself.

As she walked in, Aria began to sob again, though more quietly, and she ran to her cousin. The captain followed her with his eyes and saw the prince. He continued toward the cleric and Kenya, who waited in the adjoining room.

Pulling the door shut behind him, the officer rushed his greeting to the priestess, only tipping his head in her direction, when he noticed Lady Darya's body on the bed. He stood there by the bed a moment then swallowed and shook his head desolately.

When he turned back toward the women, he spread his arms, palms forward, and said, "Priestess Medica," with a sigh.

"Captain Illaro."

"And you are Kenya Lux Baiula."

"I am, Captain."

The leader of the Rhiian Guard lowered his gloomy, softly rumbling voice to say, "I heard what happened. That is—how things are. But you should know that a band of assassins came to decapitate us tonight. This will be a night remembered and etched in our history."

Salina gasped, put her hand to her throat, and asked who else was murdered.

The officer hesitated for a long moment, then named the dead, pausing between each, "Priest Trainer Morek. Priestess Financier Narana, and…" after a long sigh, which sent shivers through Salina, he added, "…our Supreme Priestess."

Salina stumbled into the captain's arms. The man was surprised but let the priestess rest there a moment. When she pulled back, Salina said, "Good Aiala, what have we done? How is this possible, Captain? Why? Who attacked us?"

"We do not yet know why or who, Priestess Medica, but if Aiala wills it, we will find out."

Kenya said, "One of my Sisters was also murdered recently; the last time such a thing happened none of us were born. And I heard there have been several attacks on the high king too. This is most likely the doing of Noctiferus—or of his servants, in any case."

Salina barked in response, "We've heard about your Order's suppositions, Lux Baiula, and they are not opinions we appreciate here."

Kenya pinched her brows and shook her head, showing very clearly what she thought of the cleric's beliefs.

Feeling the uncomfortable tension, the captain scratched his neck then pointed with his chin toward the main room to ask about the prince.

Salina did not immediately give a verbal response but shook her head with a pained and angry glare that included the Yellow Sash. She said, "The boy…he is not well. He is an—"

Against all accepted customs, Kenya cut off the cleric to object to the statement she had been about to make. "We have not confirmed anything yet, Priestess Medica. All we have are a few facts, and they do not tell the story. And please give the prince the respect he deserves, not only as the son of two well-respected people, but as a boy who has just lost his mother."

The captain was shocked by the Lux Baiula's nerve, but he knew the leader of the Kynarian medical college and was not surprised to find the Lux Baiula irritated and exasperated. Still, he tried to soothe things before they escalated by making calming gestures toward the cleric, whose face was growing dark.

After a moment, Salina calmed herself—she knew she had to tolerate the woman given that she would still need her assistance to fully unravel what happened there that night—but did not do so without making a deprecating snort to make certain that the foreigner knew where she stood, regardless.

Presently, she said, "We will need to autopsy the bodies to understand what happened. But," and Salina looked at the Lux Baiula with tight jaw, hoping the woman would not object again,

"I *believe* the Lux Baiula will agree that we should keep the…prince under surveillance until we complete the autopsies."

The officer looked at the Lux Baiula for her reaction, and was comforted to see her assent, though she did so reluctantly. Continuing in a whisper filled with sadness, he said, "I would like to hear what part you think the young prince had in what happened here, Priestess Medica. But first things first. I—"

Aria's voice now rang through the door, cutting short what else the officer had been about to say, demanding to know what was happening.

The cleric and the captain of the Rhiian Guard looked at each other. When the captain nodded, the priestess gave a thankful smile and they returned to the main chamber, the captain letting the priestess as well as the Lux Baiula pass before him. Another hysterical shout assaulted them as they exited.

"Who was that assassin? Why would anyone want to kill my aunt?"

The captain replied, "We do not know yet, Princess."

Aria turned toward Ori and put her hands on her mouth to retain another sob. Without turning her head back, she said, "Priestess Medica, someone needs to tell my uncle about…about my aunt."

Salina said, "Yes," and continued, "Captain Illaro, please have someone escort the neo to her friend's home and the b— the prince to the medical building…so my colleagues may take care of him. And have someone else take the…bodies to the morgue."

Kenya snorted under her breath. The priestess medica was obviously not a fan of Halfbloods to refer to them as she did, be they of royal blood or not. She looked at the princess and prince with sorry eyes.

Illaro called the guardians and gave them their orders. That done, he told the priestess medica that he needed to escort her to

Aiala's Chamber where the surviving members of the Kynarian Council would be meeting shortly.

The woman nodded, still feeling discombobulated and, forcing herself to turn toward the other woman, said, "Lux Baiula, would you mind going to the medical building? It would be good if you stayed with him, in case he…"

"Yes, I will stay with the young prince."

Illaro said, "Very well, let's go."

Salina muttered, "Hopefully, we find some answers before all of Solinor wakes and demands to know what we did to Aiala to be punished in this manner."

The captain gave a grunt in reply, then he and the priestess medica walked out. They did not hear what Kenya Lux Baiula and Aria heard the young prince murmur as he rose to follow a guardian: "I was Ori, and I am a killer. I was Ori, and I am a killer. I was Ori…"

EPILOGUE

*H*ow go the preparations, Andrus? We will arrive soon, and I
am eager to hear that you have succeeded in weakening the
factions."

Andrus3, or the Umbra, or Nihildrina—sometimes, it
seemed the neural networks for his different personalities were
losing their integrity and were becoming confused—hesitated an
infinitesimally small fraction of a second. Presently, he needed
to be Andrus3, one of *very* few third-generation medical and
tutoring androids—or METAs—that had been sent with the
insemination pods two-thousand four-hundred and fifty years
earlier to care for the Terran embryos and help the grown
Humans establish new colonies for the continued survival of
their kind, but his devotion to Zebula seemed to percolate
through the firewalls that separated his personalities and, for a
moment, he resented the mission that the general had tasked him
with some time after the establishment of the colony on K'Tara.
During the instant of self-doubt and reflection, an instant too
brief for the general to perceive, Andrus3 decided on a reply that
would not conflict with any extant rules.

"Things go well, Master. The attack on Kynaria has
succeeded, and my sources tell me that the assassination of the
High King's wife will surely des—destroy him."

Before Genghis had a chance to comment on Andrus3's
incomplete news, the android sent an urgent question. *"Master,*
it is imperative I receive an update to repair my speech
processes as even my thoughts are being affected by the failure,
and this may well cost me my life."

General Genghis, Proconsul of Earth Force, looked annoyed
by the interruption but let it slip. *"Andrus, I have all the*
necessary parts on ship. If the updates cannot be encoded onto

a long-distance carrier and reach you before I arrive, you will receive them when I get there. Until then, find a way to circumvent your issues."

Andrus3 gave a small nod, which hid the anger that would have shown on his form if he had not decided to nod instead.

The general, not forgetting the scope of his question, demanded an update on the situation in Zebulonia.

Andrus3's reply did not wholly satisfy the man—or founder, as he styled himself in his interactions with the K'Tarans. But *was* he a god? Andrus3 no longer knew the truth of certain things; time seemed to have affected more than his speech centers.

Now frankly irritated, Genghis urged him to soften the Zebulonians before he arrived lest there be trouble for him. Trouble! Perhaps he should welcome the possibility of his termination instead of fearing it. At least, it would bring an end to his continued degeneration and to the destructive contradictions he had had to live with the last seven hundred years, since before the Dark Battle.

APPENDIX I – MAPS

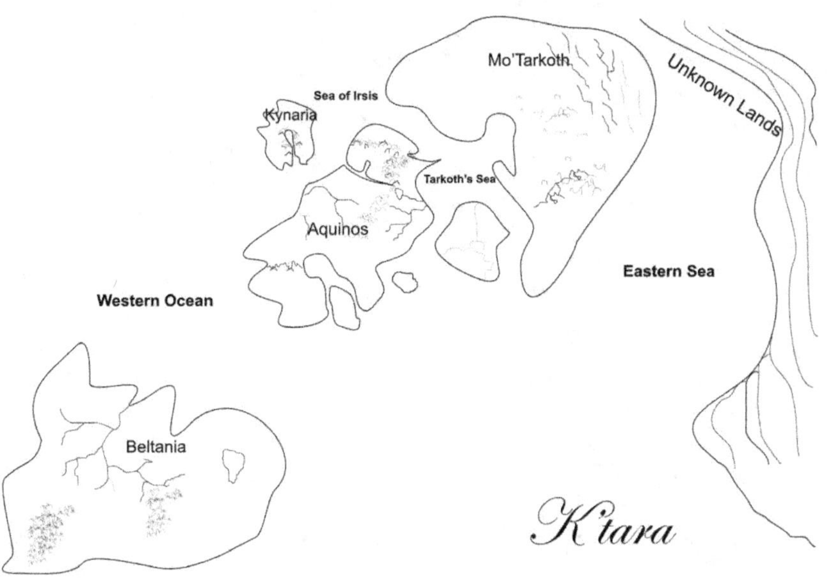

Kynaria
Sea of Irsis
Lake of the Light
Solinor
Rokoth
Furan City
West Amalor
Upper Alvinor
Tarkoth's Sea
Jarah
Pargah
Lower Alvinor
City of Unumia
Alvinoria
Unumia
Yerlah
Coral Lake
Great Lake of Shadows
Zeblinia
Zebulonia
Terrae Regis

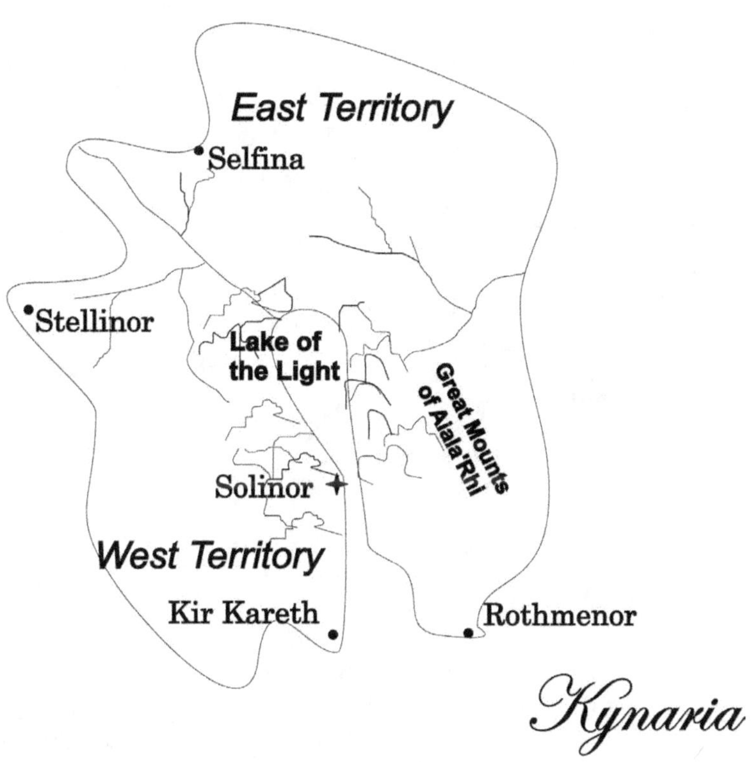

East Territory
Selfina
Stellinor
Lake of the Light
Great Mounts of Alala'Rhi
Solinor
West Territory
Kir Kareth
Rothmenor
Kynaria

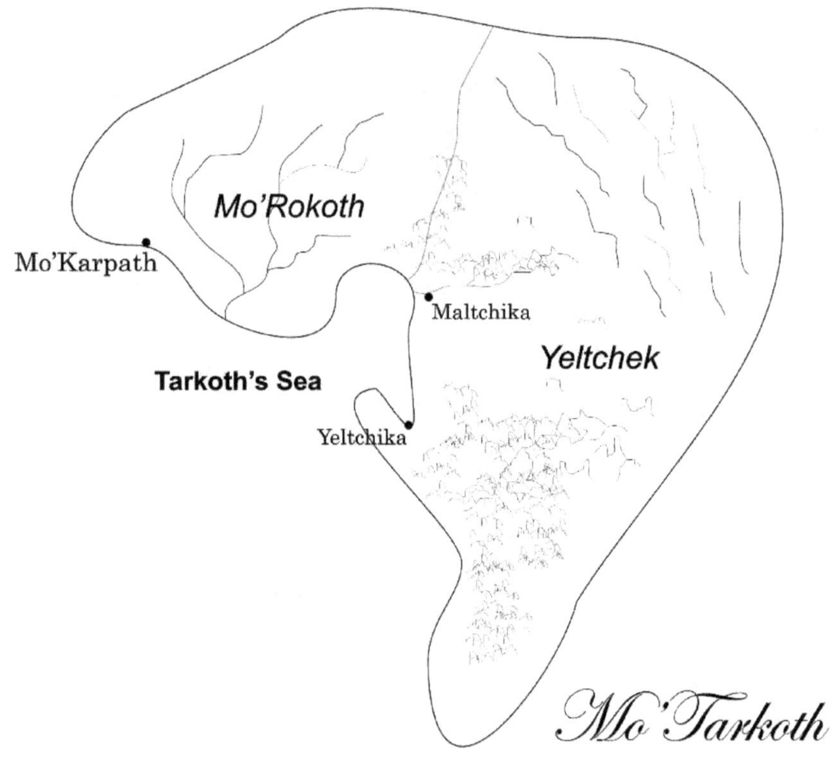

Mo'Rokoth
Mo'Karpath
Maltchika
Tarkoth's Sea
Yeltchek
Yeltchika
Mo'Tarkoth

Furan City
Domus
Lucis
Imperial Lane
Ministerial Road
Triumph   Lane
House Royal
Senate
House

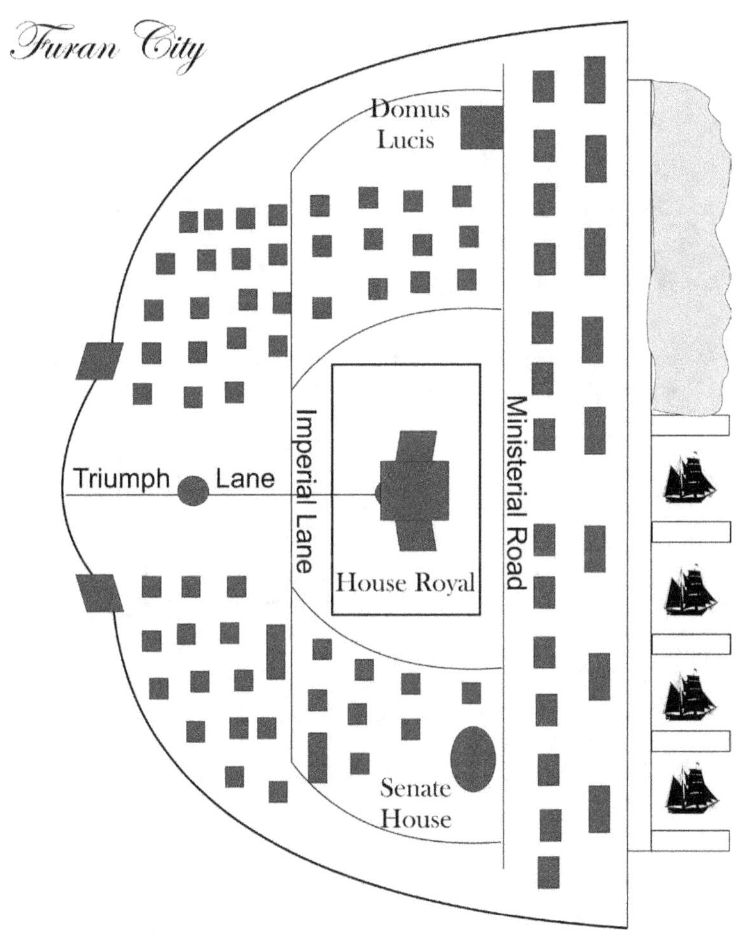

Urbs Lucis

Apartments
Inner Sanctum
Library
Palace of the Light
Schola Luciana
Elevation Chapel
Domus medici
Market
River Argon

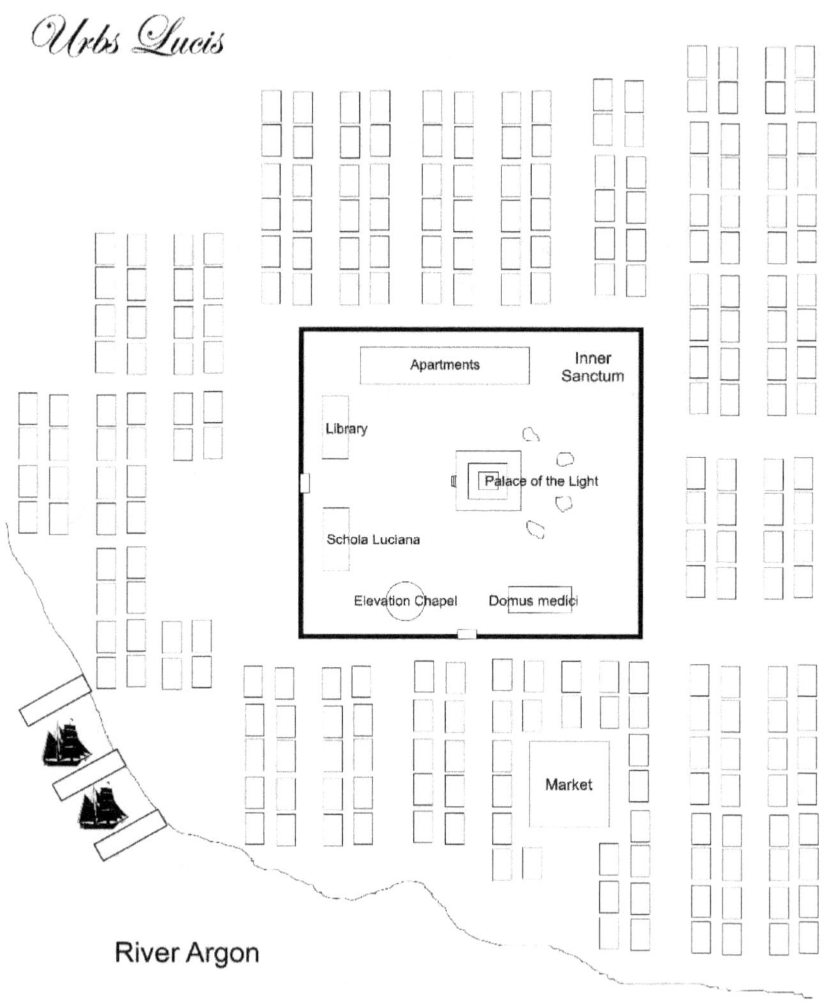

APPENDIX II – NEW CHARACTERS OR CHARACTERS WHOSE ROLES HAVE CHANGED

Black Guard

1. **Areto:** Young recruit.
2. **Lento**: Medic apprentice.
3. **Marius:** Lucian-trained medic assigned to the Black Guard. He was distinguished by a white flame on his arm.

Royal Guard

4. **Mehan**: Aithen's new bodyguard, replacing Almiar who was killed during an assassination attempt on the king.

Others

5. **Alga**: A member of the Locari's ruling body.
6. **Alta**: Assassin in the Bind.
7. **Bracca**: Assassin in the Bind; black-skinned, red haired.
8. **Elnon**: A veteran Frumentarius, commander of the Frumentarii.
9. **Hecrus Fioran**: Furanite merchant who tried to assassinate Aithen.
10. **Kelp**: A member of the Locari's ruling body.
11. **Lasra**: Assassin; thin, dark-haired woman.
12. **Octavian**: The son of Harlion Stormbreaker; received his name from Octavius; seventeen years old.
13. **Ooshia Vumiko**: A Yeltcheki; administrator of the capital, Yeltchika.
14. **Pemlo**: Cook in Harlion's household.
15. **Pombo**: Porter of the royal palace.
16. **Tina Piscator**: Master Brak's aunt and manager of the merchant's Lucian shop.

17. **Shinoa**: Emperor of the Yeltchek.
18. **Shoot**: A member of the Locari's ruling body.
19. **Yushii:** A Yeltcheki; the Umbra's contact.

Sisterhood

20. **Akula**: A dark-eyed, fair-skinned Jarahni of the Red Sash, with short brown hair tied in a bun; a master firebinder often called 'scarhead' by juniors.
21. **Bela**: A short, yellow-haired Red Sash with harsh teaching methods.
22. **Bietta**: An old but sturdy Barrier.
23. **Erona**: A member of the Cursus Publicus responsible for the Lucian news office.
24. **Iyawa**: A dark-skinned Yellow Sash from Pargah; deeply religious.
25. **Kenya**: Yellow Sash stationed in Kynaria; thin, wide-faced and thin-lipped; specialized in the study of microbial toxins.
26. **Letta**: A tall but stocky, dark-haired warrior assigned to the king's protection.
27. **Lina Lux Baiula**: A Yellow Sash assigned to Horn's Pass as a member of the Beacon team.
28. **Mattina**: A Lux Baiula of the Yellow Sash who had been involved in rooting out the remnants of the Dark One's forces after the end of the Dark Battle.
29. **Procta**: A Lux Baiula who lived during the Trionian War; was involved in what became known as the 'Days of Necessary Expiry'
30. **Samrachi**; A White Sash in Furan City, Dalima Lux Baiula's replacement; in charge of the juniors.

Kynarians

31. **Illaro**: Captain of the Rhiian Guard.

32. Morek: Priest Trainer; assassinated.
33. Narana: Priestess Financier; assassinated.
34. **Salina**: Priestess Medica.
35. **Yluno**: Sargent of the Rhiian Guard.

Furans
36. **Switch**: Xena's furan.
37. **Whip**: Sasha's furan.

APPENDIX III - GLOSSARY

Alioception: The ability to perceive another person's position and movement, the response of their muscles, tendons and joints, as well as the firing within their nerve fibers.

Borer: A powerful Binding that penetrated and twisted other people's forms in the Bind; in the physical world, a Borer entered the brain where it elicited pain and confusion.

Celebrated personal days:

- **Day of Acquaintance**: Was observed from the 12th through the 14th birthday. The occasion was meant to give the child time to reflect on their present and future place in their family and in society.
- **Day of Transition**: Was celebrated at the completion of the 15th year of life to mark the beginning of a child's adulthood.
- **Day of Reflection**: Was formally celebrated every five years for the rest of a person's life starting with the 20th year of life.

Core knitter: A Binding that hit the vagal nerve and caused the innervated muscles to twist and contract as if in response to an epileptic attack.

Cursus Publicus: Joint commission of the Crown and Urbs Lucis responsible for disseminating news across Alvinoria.

Days of Necessary Expiry: Refers to an ancient practice of the Sisterhood to quash laws that have become maladapted to new social or political circumstances rather than to force society or organizations to remain true to them.

Giving: An Alvinorian ritual by which parents give their newborns another person's name in the hope that their children will grow to have similar qualities.

Lacora Leaf corset: A medical corset made from the Lacora leaf plant. The corset could be adjusted by rubbing or tapping the leaves or stems.

Mind – The: Ruling body of the Locari.

Minding Chamber: Sea cave where the Locari's ruling body met.

Pansoma: A religious belief holding that the spirit lives not only in our brains but in every particle of the body and must therefore be inhabited by a worthy spirit in order for a god to assume the body on the Day of Union.

Pointed hollow: A writing device built from the tubes sustaining the membranous vanes of a flyer's wings.

Recrimination: An official reproach addressed to the king by Alvinoria's patriciate.

Tunnelers: Sisters skilled in the tunneling technique.

Tunneling: A technique used by instructors of the Sisterhood to contain Bindings within a safe area.

Una memoria: The condition of Lux Baiulae who hold only their own memories.

Voces Lucianis: Urbs Lucis's choir, similar to Furan City's Voces Creatoris. The choir sang from morning till night, all year long six days a fourth, with singers alternating throughout the day. Their voices were carried across the city by the Bindings of retired Lux Baiulae.

Vox Publica: News service of Alvinoria operated by the Sisterhood.

THE AUTHOR

L.A. Di Paolo is a tri-lingual, Canadian-born Italian American who lives in Milton, Vermont. By day, because of his background in science and business, he manages drug development projects. By night, he writes and the constant questions trotting in his mind are those about evolution, nature, and the human condition. He has been writing to explore them and their answers, first in student newspapers, then in a magazine he authored and published, and now in this novel.

If you are interested in learning more about L.A. Di Paolo or about this novel, you can visit his author web site at https://ladipaolo.net, or scan the QR Code below.